THE Rebel WEARS PLAID

ELIZA KNIGHT

sourcebooks
casablanca

Published by Sourcebooks Casablanca, an imprint of Sourcebooks
P.O. Box 4410, Naperville, Illinois 60567-4410
(630) 961-3900
sourcebooks.com

Printed and bound in Canada.
MBP 10 9 8 7 6 5 4 3 2 1

With much love to my own warrior for believing in me, and to my tenacious daughters, who are a constant inspiration.

Dear Reader,

When I first imagined the concept behind this series, I knew I wanted to create a cast of incredibly brave female heroines who would have to risk nearly everything for the good of their country and their future king. The Jacobite era of Great Britain's history is the last civil war fought on the united soils of Scotland and England, ultimately coming to rest in a rather tragic ending for many. Throughout the tumultuous years were born many heroes—dozens of which were women.

I wanted to incorporate their bravery, tenacity, and enthusiasm for their cause and their loyalty to a prince they wanted to be king, so I used many of their stories when creating those within this series. In *The Rebel Wears Plaid*, you will find Jenny's story to have a flavor of the lives of Lady Anne (Farquharson) Mackintosh, Jenny Cameron, and Lady Margaret Ogilvy, mixed in with a generous helping of my imagination.

There is also a fun rumor that the Christmas carol "O Come, All Ye Faithful" was in fact a Jacobite call to arms, and that the line "come and behold Him, born the king of angels" was code for "come and behold him, born the king of the English"—who just so happened to be Bonnie Prince Charlie. Allegedly the Latin verse was actually a celebration of the prince's birth rather than of Jesus's, all connotation of which was lost when it was translated in the nineteenth century. Learning that his people were nicknamed angels, it seemed a fun theme to incorporate into the series: Prince Charlie's Angels.

I do hope you enjoy reading this book and the rest of the series as much as I have enjoyed writing it!

Best wishes,

Eliza

One

WIND WHIPPED AT JENNY MACKINTOSH'S HAIR AS SHE raced for her life to escape from the English. She and her small band of men pushed their mounts to the limit, flying across the moors, the crack of pistols cutting the night air behind them. At any moment, she'd feel the sting of a bullet in her back.

What else should a rebel recruiting an army expect?

Sweat beaded on her brow and dripped down her back, and her hands trembled against the leather straps of the reins.

"To the forest," she called to her five partners in rebellion following behind her, but her words were lost in the noisy thrum of pounding hooves against the earth. Leaning to the right, she urged her horse down a slope, over a boulder, and onto an unmarked path that led toward the forest, hoping they'd lose the redcoats.

The shouts of the dragoons behind them were fainter now, but that didn't mean they were out of danger.

She burst through the trees, and a twig caught in her hair, the wrench stinging her scalp. Still, she didn't cry out.

Once she knew they were out of sight, she reined in her horse, her heart racing. Jenny tugged the twig from her hair and threw it on the ground, wishing it were the bloody English so she could stomp them into dust as easily. She stroked her mount's mane, patting his neck in thanks for the hard gallop, then reached up to rub at the tightness in her own.

They waited in silence, their breaths growing slower as the minutes ticked by. The shots had ceased the moment she and her soldiers had been able to break away from their enemies' sight, but the pounding of the horses' advance still thundered in her ears—or was that her heart?

Jenny focused her gaze through the foliage and waited for the dragoons to catch up. They'd only been caught once, a few months ago. Jenny had escaped with her life that time, but there were several others who hadn't been as lucky. King George, the usurper, had sent his dragoons to apprehend anyone with sympathies to Prince Charles Stuart, the rightful heir to the Kingdom of Great Britain. King George had given Charles the moniker the Young Pretender, and his father, the Old Pretender.

Prince Charlie's father, King James, had named him Regent of Great Britain, and regent was the name under which she and other Jacobite supporters were bent on returning the prince to the throne. King George would be tossed back to Germany where he had been born and raised and should have remained.

Despite the brightness of tonight's moon that allowed them a good view of the road, the brambles and pines were thick, veiling her and her men's massive horses from their enemies. When the first half dozen redcoats rode past, they did not see the Scots hidden just a few feet away. They barely slowed, too busy chasing phantoms.

As soon as they passed, Jenny and her men let out a collective sigh, only to freeze as several more dragoons rounded the bend and headed right for them. Eyes wide as the moon above, she watched them advance. The gold buttons on their muted red coats glinted in the moonlight, as did the muzzles of their muskets, their pistols, and the hilts of the thin swords at their hips.

Their dress was so different from that of the Scots. They wore starched white breeches, where her men were allowed freedom of movement in their plaids. Stiff tricorns covered their heads, while the Scots wore soft woolen caps that were broad and flat on the top. When Scots were feeling particularly rebellious, they pinned white rosette cockades on them in support of the Stuart line.

The redcoat leader issued an unintelligible order, and for a second, she thought the dragoon was staring right at her. Would he order his men into the forest? Her lungs burned for air, but she couldn't risk even the tiniest sound be heard by these bloodthirsty monsters.

She touched her pistol, prepared to shoot if needed, but then he was pointing and shouting for his men to continue down the road. Jenny watched them kick their horses into a gallop, clouds of dust following in their wake.

Only once the dust settled did Jenny allow herself a

moment to exhale. Despite the risk she was taking every time she came out here, there was no way she'd stop her nightly missions. The fate of the entire Mackintosh clan was now Jenny's responsibility. She would not let her brother's betrayal destroy her clan.

Which was exactly why, on this night—while her brother was busy with his nose up an Englishman's arse—she found herself a few miles from an English garrison and several hours from home.

For three generations, her people had been trying to reclaim their country. Jenny, along with all the other Jacobites, had a restless need to do *something* to aid in bringing the rightful heir home to Scotland. Soon there would be a war, and she knew on which side she'd stand— with Bonnie Prince Charlie, the regent of Scotland. She'd made a vow a lifetime ago, it seemed, to support the Stuart line, and she planned to keep it—to follow in her father's and grandfather's footsteps and honor the warriors who had died for the Jacobite cause. Even if it meant going sword to sword with her brother in battle, a notion that made her stomach sour. At least she was faster and more agile than he was and had bested him more than once in the past because of that.

"We should turn back, my lady."

Jenny glowered at the shadowy figure on the mount beside her. Her cousin Dirk was always with her on these nightly raids. "What did I tell ye about calling me *my lady* when we're out?" She glanced back at the road, her hand on her pistol, ready to strike should a redcoat suddenly leap out in front of her.

"Apologies, *Mistress J.*"

Jenny couldn't help but smile at the affectionate moniker her people had given her. It took away her title of lady and also didn't give away her given name, keeping her identity shrouded in secrecy. It'd only been a few months since she'd taken up her most sacred duty, and in that time, she'd gained a reputation as a leader.

"We canna go back now," Jenny said. "My brother will return any day now, and there is every chance Hamish will allow the English to billet at Cnàmhan Broch. That'll be a death sentence for me, for ye, and for all loyal to the true and rightful Scottish king." Jenny shuddered at the thought of dozens of redcoats flooding her family's castle.

The bastards had already done enough damage.

Dirk shifted uneasily in his seat. "Aye, but—"

"Cousin, ye grew up with me," Jenny interrupted, running her fingertips over the initials carved into the hilt of her broadsword: JM—*Jon Mackintosh*. Her voice grew hoarse with emotion. "Ye were beside me listening to all the tales of our clansmen fighting for the Jacobites." Both her father and her uncle had joined the rebellion some thirty years before. Labeled traitors, they had been hunted down and eventually executed by English loyalists and their Scottish supporters when she was still a young lass. "We have to honor them."

Dirk sighed, his shoulders slumping slightly. It was the same conversation they'd had many times. "But not by getting yourself killed. Ye ken the danger of being so near the *Sassenach* garrison." Dirk grumbled something that sounded a lot like he was warding off the devil, a sentiment echoed by the four men grumbling behind him.

Jenny couldn't blame them. The English dragoons were known for their brutality. Raping, pillaging, and destroying anything on a whim. That was precisely why she *had* to stand against her brother. How could she wait idly by and let him consign his people to a lifetime of terror? He might have pledged his loyalty to the King George loyalists, but that didn't mean the bloody devils would ever treat them as equals.

"If we're caught, Mistress, they'll not hesitate to shoot us."

Jenny inhaled deeply through her nose. The dragoons had been searching for her for going on two years now, and what Dirk said was true. Even still, she put on a confident front. "We'll just pretend we're looking for a wee one gone missing. They canna fault us for being out late in search of a bairn." They'd used that tactic before.

Dirk nodded, but the air was thick with unspoken words. She knew he wanted tonight's recruitment to come to an end, but she was the leader of these warriors, and she would make that call when she was ready. And something in her gut told her it was not yet the right moment.

"One more village." Dirk rubbed his fingers over his jaw. "But if there is any danger…"

"We'll turn back, I promise."

"We trust ye, Jenny. And we believe in the cause as much as ye do," Dirk reassured her.

If her brother had any idea what she was doing, at

best she'd be locked in a dungeon, and at worst she'd be hanging from the ramparts for the crows to eat. The soldiers would suffer certain death, and her mother would be devastated. Already her son's betrayal was enough to have her mother take to her bed and rarely come out.

"I'll never be able to thank ye enough." She reached over and patted Dirk on the shoulder and then eyed the men behind them. "And when the regent is on the throne, we'll see that every risk was worth it."

"Ye needna thank us for being loyal Scots," Dirk said.

"Aye," the four men murmured in unison.

Jenny straightened in her saddle, the creak of the leather mingling with the sounds of insects and the distant birds of prey. "All the same, I'm grateful to have ye by my side. The prince regent will land in Scotland in less than a month. The more soldiers we can gather, the more coin and weapons we present him, the better."

She glanced at Dirk and then the men behind him. In addition to the other two Mackintosh warriors, tonight they'd only gathered two new recruits—the lowest number of any night since she'd started a few months before. And the coin they'd gathered was barely enough to buy a meat pie and ale at the local tavern.

The last village she wanted to visit tonight happened to be closest to the English garrison. Most of the men and women who lived there had been treated cruelly by the soldiers. There had to be at least half a dozen men she could sway to the cause, if for no other reason than the fresh rounds of arrests that had taken place just that morning.

Jenny returned her attention to the road. Not a single redcoat had passed in at least a half hour. "Are ye ready?"

"Lead the way, Mistress."

Jenny grinned, excitement thrumming in her veins. She had no doubt she was doing the right thing. Soon she'd be bowing before the regent, a leader who could oust the English from Scotland for good. And then she'd look into her brother's eyes, and instead of executing him for his betrayal, she'd sway him back to the cause. Wishful thinking, aye.

For now, she needed to focus on what lay ahead. The risks she took could get her killed, and yet she seized them boldly. Fear had no place in a rebellion. Well, perhaps that wasn't entirely true. But one had to *master* their fear. And if there was one thing she'd been good at since she was a bairn, it was taking control over anything that scared her.

"We ride." Jenny took the reins in both hands as she nudged her heel into her mount's flank.

———

"Bloody hell," Toran Fraser muttered under his breath.

It was nearing midnight as he stood in the center of the English garrison's courtyard, working hard to hide his alarm. His cousin Archie stood among the condemned. The men had been dragged behind horses, hands shackled in front of them, and in the torchlight it was clear they'd been viciously beaten. Each of them was still dressed in his traditional Highland attire—kilts, shirts, waistcoats, boots. But they'd been stripped of their weapons.

And in mere moments, they'd be stripped of their lives. This was not what was supposed to happen. Aye, he'd intended for the rebels to be caught…but executed? He'd been naive to believe Boyd when he'd said he'd use the men to extort information. Served him right for trusting a bloody Englishman.

Of course Archie recognized Toran. The surprise and hope in his gaze quickly turned to outright disgust when he realized that Toran was standing beside the very *English* Captain Thomas Boyd.

Toran shifted uneasily. He, too, wore a kilt in Fraser colors. Boyd believed him a loyal deserter, taking up the position his father had vacated upon death, but understood Toran had to play the part of a Scotsman to gather information to hand over. Even so, if Archie let slip that he'd just spoken with Toran about Boyd's plan to trap the rebels, then he'd have a lot of explaining to do to the English captain. It was a careful line to walk—having betrayed one allegiance meant that his new one would always be suspicious, and with good reason.

But family was family despite allegiances. Toran followed in his father's footsteps, solidly on the side of King George's government, while some of his family had chosen to support the Young Pretender, Prince Charles.

Toran had cautioned Archie to stay out of the rebels' planned break-in, refusing to relay how he knew of Boyd's plan. His cousin had obviously ignored his warnings. Maybe Archie had not believed him, or maybe he'd warned the men that it was a trap, and they'd devised a new foolish plan. It didn't matter. The English had won this fight.

Bloody hell!

The only reason that his cousin was imprisoned at all was due to the information Toran had seeded for the rebels, who believed him to be one of them, about the garrison's weaknesses.

Archie was knocked to his knees by a boot to the back of the leg. His gaze never left Toran, silently declaring him a traitor to his country and his own family. Could Toran really stand there and watch his cousin be hanged?

Disgust at himself made Toran's insides burn. He cleared his throat. The knot of his neckerchief grew tighter and tighter, cutting off his air supply. Never once since he'd made his choice had Toran regretted dancing on this double-edged sword. His mother had been sacrificed by Jacobite rebels she'd trusted. How could Toran *not* try to seek vengeance in her name?

But now, watching Archie face death at English hands, his choice looked more and more like a foolish one.

Captain Boyd paced in front of the condemned. "You have all been charged with treason for betraying King George, your rightful monarch. Do you confess?"

Not one man opened his mouth, and a prickle of pride slid along Toran's spine.

Boyd appeared surprised at the silence. "Then you are all sentenced to hang by the neck until dead. The sentence shall be exacted…" He checked his pocket watch as if trying to determine a time and then said, "Why wait? Let's do it right now."

Toran grimaced. Archie's gaze never left his, and if one could be killed by a glower, then Toran would be lying in a bloody heap. Hell, he would deserve it.

Captain Boyd turned his gaze toward Toran and the other men standing beside him—some Scots, some English, but all known supporters of the English throne.

Toran cleared his throat. "Captain, if I may?"

Boyd narrowed his eyes, probably never having been interrupted during one of his sentencings before. Depending on the man's mood, Toran could very well end up on his knees beside his cousin.

"What is it?" Obvious irritation dripped from Boyd's words.

"I recognize that one." He pointed at Archie. "Might I take him inside for questioning?"

Boyd raised a brow. "You think he knows something?"

"Aye." This was a lie, and Toran was acting as fast as he could to save Archie from death. While he wished he could save them all, that was impossible. Even this hasty plan could fall awry. There was a very high probability that they were *both* going to die tonight, but at least he'd go to his maker knowing he'd done the right thing.

"Fine. But as soon as you get what you need, bring him back out here to be dealt with."

Dealt with, like rubbish in need of disposal. The sour taste in Toran's mouth grew stronger. After what he was about to do, he'd not be safe anywhere near the English. He'd be labeled a traitor, and the bounty on his head would likely be enough for even his own mother to turn him in, God rest her soul. Hell, he'd not be safe near the Scots either.

Boyd flicked his hand, dismissing Toran, who walked over to Archie and yanked him up by his shackled arms.

"Dinna say a word," Toran warned quietly against Archie's ear.

"Where are ye taking me?" Archie shouted, ignoring Toran's request.

"If ye want to live, ye'll shut your trap," Toran warned once more, then nodded to Boyd. He half-dragged, half-carried his cousin back into the garrison, once a well-fortified Scots castle, the tenants long since evicted. Archie had been badly beaten, both lips split, one eye swollen shut, and a cut above his forehead that dripped down his face. An odd bump on his arm hinted at the broken bone beneath. He didn't know if Archie wasn't walking properly because of an injury, obstinacy, or exhaustion. And there was no time to figure it out.

Toran dragged Archie through a musty corridor dimly lit by a few torches. He nodded to the guards they passed, praying that no one asked questions.

"What are ye doing?" Archie asked. "Ye want to kill me yourself?"

"Keep quiet," Toran ordered.

"I'll not."

Toran pushed his cousin against the wall beneath a torch so Archie could see his eyes. Manhandling his cousin appeared to be the only way to get his attention. He gripped the front of Archie's shirt and leaned in close to whisper. "I'm getting ye out of here. A task that will cost us both our lives if ye dinna shut your mouth and listen."

Archie's one working eye widened, and then he nodded in understanding.

Toran dragged him up a set of dark stairs, pausing to listen every half dozen or so, and then hurrying his cousin as much as possible considering the shackles. At the top of the stairs, he tossed his cousin over his shoulder—not an easy feat since Archie was nearly as tall and easily just as full of muscle. He whispered prayers up to a God he wasn't certain would listen, given his many sins.

But at last he found the door he was looking for, one that led to nowhere.

"This will hurt," Toran cautioned. "We're at least fifteen feet in the air, and once we land, they'll be able to smell us for miles."

"What?" Archie didn't sound convinced by his plan.

"There's no time. 'Tis the only way. Are ye ready?"

"Aye."

Toran didn't hesitate but leapt, arms around his cousin, into the rubbish pile below. They landed with a thud and a disturbing squish.

Archie groaned. Toran ignored the jolt of pain in his back from the landing. "Come on, we've not much time before Boyd tries to find out where we've gone. He'll send out every man with a pistol he's got to shoot us on sight."

Archie rose to his knees, gagging at the scent.

"There's no time to retch. We've got to run." His hands under his cousin's arms, Toran hauled him to standing, thanking the heavens the men had not been shackled at the ankles.

"Have ye a key for these?" Archie asked, holding out his hands.

"Nay, and I've had to leave my horse behind. Damned fine horse, too." Thankfully anything incriminating he always kept on his person, sewn into the lining of his waistcoat—close to his heart, rather than with his mount.

"Thank ye, Cousin."

"Thank me later. Now run."

Grabbing hold of Archie's elbow, he dragged him out of the muck. They ran without looking back, keeping to the woods and hiding behind boulders to catch their breath. Toran had learned over his years of espionage that looking back only got a man killed. They ran for a mile or two following a familiar path, one Toran often took from the garrison to Fraser lands. Any other night he would have been glad for the fullness of the moon to light the way. But tonight he knew it gave them away, two hunched figures running for their lives.

Archie stumbled over pebbles, roots, his own feet, often falling to his knees, and Toran continued to lift him up.

"I canna, Cousin. Go on without me." Archie sank to the ground, defeated.

"I didna save ye from the English only to let ye die on the road." Toran scanned the moors, waiting for the shadows of their pursuers to make themselves known. "We've got to get this muck off us. Boyd's dogs will be following the scent."

Archie lifted his head. "Ye're no' going to leave me?"

"Of course no'. Where're your Fraser ballocks? Come on."

Archie mustered the strength to stand, but they weren't going to be moving very fast. Thankfully, the sound of rushing water filtered from ahead. "Hurry, we're close to the river."

Less than five minutes later, they were at the river's edge. The glossy black depths reflected the moon and a sprinkle of stars. Holding onto Archie's arm, Toran pulled him into the chilly water.

"Ye didna drag me all this way just to see me drown, did ye?" Archie asked.

Toran chuckled, feeling the weight of his kilt increase as water soaked into the wool. The river bottom sucked at his boots, but he waded in until they were waist deep. That was where the river bottom went out beneath them, and he had to swim the rest of the way across with his cousin in his grasp. "I'd not have risked my own arse only to drown ye in a river."

Once on the other side, Toran wrung out their kilts and shirts, dumped the water from their boots, and used the sharp tip of his *sgian dubh* to fiddle with the locks on the shackles, but the small dagger wasn't narrow enough to fit.

He pulled the pin from his neckerchief and despite the dark was able to use it to free his cousin from the chains, which he tossed into the water.

Archie's teeth chattered. "I dinna know how much further I can go."

"Only a little more," Toran said.

He had no idea where to take his cousin, but he did know staying this close to Boyd was a death sentence.

Dressed again, they continued on their way. Though it was summer, the night air was cool, chilling their sodden clothes and shoes. Another thirty minutes or so passed while Archie's gait continued to slow. Toran led his cousin to a good hiding spot behind a thick boulder that shielded them from view.

"We'll rest here a mo—" But he cut himself off at the sound of a stick breaking.

Toran jerked around. Suddenly, figures melted out from the shadows. Scots, but in the dark and dressed as they were, he couldn't make out what clan they hailed from. At the center of the five men stood a lass. Aye, she wore trews and had her hair up under a cap, wisps of golden strands peeking through, but there was no hiding the curves beneath her shirt and waistcoat. In the moonlight filtering through the trees, she looked bonnie—high, arching cheekbones, a mouth that puckered into a frown. But what struck him most was the spark of fire in her gaze. Her eyes reflected the light of the moon, almost making her look like she was glowing.

And the muzzle of her pistol was pointed right at him. Outlaws… Of all the bloody luck. He reached for his own pistol tucked into his belt.

"Dinna move," the lass said. Her voice was throaty, sensual. "Else I put a bullet through your heart."

A slow grin formed on Toran's face. "What's to say I won't put a bullet in yours first?"

The lass looked down at Archie and then flicked her

gaze back to his. "Ye're outnumbered. Let's say ye were willing to pull your weapon before I took my shot, and then ye were to waste your bullet, there'd be five more cutting through ye before ye were able to see the result." Again, she looked at Archie. "And your friend doesna seem like he will be much help."

"We're verra close to the English garrison, lass. Any shot ye make will be a beacon to the dragoons lurking about. And trust me, there are hundreds of them headed this way as we speak."

"Is that so?" She glanced at Archie once more. "A prison break? So ye two are rebels, aye?"

Toran didn't answer. Let her come to her own conclusions.

"We have horses." She kept her gaze on his, and he had the intense urge to draw closer. "Ye and your friend can have one when we return to my camp—for a price. Why not donate your coin to the cause and join us? We've a need for more rebels."

Toran did not want to join her. Now, if she'd asked him to join her for some mutual warmth under a plaid, that would be another story. Then again, she had a point about the bullets. And he truly did not want to die.

"I'm guessing from your current circumstances ye are in need of a helping hand, sir." Her voice was smooth, even melodic, but still filled with authority. And considering that she was the one speaking, she certainly gave the impression that she was the one in charge. Fascinating.

A group of men led by a woman? Not a common thing, and intensely intriguing. Whoever she was, she had ballocks as full of steel as his own. And if he weren't trapped in the woods with her, a hundred redcoats on his tail, he might have asked her to join him for a dram.

"Who are ye?" Toran asked.

A soft laugh escaped her, and her hand waved dismissively. "Not yet, sir. Ye'll have to prove yourself first."

Prove himself? He gritted his teeth. "All right, we'll join ye." There really was no other choice. He and Archie needed a quick escape, and her horse would provide that. Just because he was taking her up on the offer now didn't mean he had to stick it out. In fact, as soon as he could, he'd steal the horse and somehow get Archie back to Fraser lands where he could make certain the rest of his family was safe from Boyd.

"Good." She nodded to Dirk. "Search them for weapons, and then help the wounded man onto your horse."

Toran stood still for the inspection, gritting his teeth as his weapons were removed. "I've said we'd join ye. Why then are ye treating me like a prisoner?"

The lass cocked her head to the side, a slight grin curling her upper lip. "We must first see that ye are trustworthy." With an added challenge echoing in her words, she said, "Ye can ride with me. And dinna try any tricks, else ye find yourself verra dead."

The lass didn't beat around the bush, and there was no hint of humor in her tone at all. She meant what she said.

Toran climbed onto the back of her horse, his cold, wet body flush to her warmer, dry back. Beneath the icy exterior was a lass full of lush curves. *Mo chreach...* Good heavens, but she felt good. Hesitantly, he placed an arm around her waist.

She shuddered. "Blast, but ye're soaked," she hissed. "Ye should have warned me. And ye smell like the devil's own chamber pot."

Toran chuckled. "A hazard of escape, lass."

Her back straightened, and she leaned forward, away from him. "Ye can call me Mistress J."

Mistress J? Why did that sound familiar?

"And ye are?" she urged.

"I'm called Toran," he said slowly as realization struck him. The night had taken a very interesting turn. For he was holding onto the woman he suspected might be responsible for his mother's death.

Two

THE RIDE BACK TO THE ABANDONED CROFT ON Mackintosh lands seemed interminable. Behind Jenny, the strange warrior—who smelled as though he'd swum through hell before she'd found him—kept a firm grip around her waist.

Despite his stench, his grasp was warm and powerful. Was it because he was a complete stranger that his touch, as simple as it should be, felt…different? Plenty of other men had touched her when they were training, and she'd never felt so…warm. There really was no other way to describe the sensation that toyed with her than that. Warmth. Desire.

"Ye ride astride, like a man," he pointed out, interrupting her disconcerting line of thought.

Jenny wanted to ignore him, but it was too hard. Besides, she took offense to him saying only a man could sit a horse in this fashion. "I ride as I please."

He only grunted by way of answer, leaving her bristling. Maybe if she tossed him off the horse and put her boot to his throat, his grunt would turn to praise. Devil take it, what did she care about his approval?

Why exactly had she forced him to join her? Absconding with men in the night, strong-arming them into her company was not her normal style of recruitment. So far the men she'd raised for the prince's army had volunteered, all willing to fight for the cause. But she'd heard wind of a group of rebels planning a break-in at the garrison, and he and his companion had clearly escaped, which meant they knew the lay of the fortress, valuable information she could use.

More than half of her senses were stuck on Toran, distracting her from the ride. His touch at her waist, the breadth of his body behind her, the low scrape of his brogue against her ear. If the situation—and his current unwashed state—were different, she might think he had a mind for seduction. If so, she might just have taken him up on it, if only to escape for but a moment from the world and thoughts of death.

Dirk was giving her side glances from where he rode next to her, clearly questioning her motives. He thought her addled. But what other choice had there been? If she'd not taken them, the two strangers might have given her and her men up to the dragoons, even if it was unintentional. The one was badly injured, and they weren't going to be able to outrun the bloody English bastards for long. If they'd been caught, there was no telling what they'd say to get out of it. She just couldn't risk it.

So here they were, with two recruits who may or may not be loyal, one of whose hard chest was pressed so flush against her back their breathing could have been from one body. Jenny purposefully changed the rhythm of her breathing, but he continued to match hers. She didn't know whether to be irritated or find humor in it. She decided irritation was the safest emotion and forced herself to focus on the road. She urged her mount to go faster. The sooner they arrived at the croft, the sooner she could have the blasted man off her back. Literally.

The hours did not fly by as she'd hoped, but eventually the familiar trees and rising crags came into view, and not a single dragoon had been sighted along the way. As they passed key lookout points, Dirk mimicked a bird of prey. The calls he sent into the air were answered by someone in the distance—announcing their presence so they would not be shot by the scouts she had strategically placed to guard the croft they'd commandeered as the rebellion's headquarters.

When they eventually reached the croft doors, another signal would be given to those within by a certain knock at the door. A signal that they'd have to change if Toran and his companion chose to flee. Maybe she should change it anyway once he was returned to wherever his clan was, even if he did commit to the cause. And with that notion she paused, realizing she didn't know what clan he was from as his plaid was plain and covered in muck.

A cold knot formed in her belly. Every other recruit she'd picked up had been known to her, from conversation before the request or personal referrals. But Toran was a mystery.

She would find out before this night was through.

The farm's main yard had a low stone fence surrounding it to keep in the animals, though the sheep often hopped over the enclosure without effort, as did the horses if the keepers weren't careful. This particular croft held about ten acres of land, with a forest along the left side that curved around the back and acted as a natural barrier. The rest of the acres were covered in lush green grass for the few cattle and sheep they had to graze.

The thatched-roof house was just a main room with a cot, a table and cooking area, and a back chamber whose walls were lined with more cots. Above was a loft where the men who worked the croft lived.

There were two outbuildings, a barn and a stable. A small chicken coop pressed up to the side of the barn. On the right side of their yard was a vast vegetable garden surrounded by a wooden fence to keep the sheep from eating the crops.

From the outside looking in, this was an ordinary croft, complete with animals and people working the land. *Nothing to see here, keep it moving.*

Hidden beneath the seemingly benign wattle-and-daub house was a hoard of weapons, coin, and supplies, with new recruits sleeping above in the loft if they'd no place else to go.

The other men—all two hundred and forty-seven of them, if these two were to be included—lived their everyday lives as though nothing was amiss. They pretended to live in accordance with the rule of their laird— Jenny's brother—doing what they must to survive until the day she called them to arms in the name of the prince regent.

Jenny frowned at the thought of her brother as they slowed their approach, coming just up to the stable. With the death of their father, Hamish had become chief of clan Mackintosh—and then promptly rejected the sacrifices of the generations before him who'd protected their Scottish heritage. When he'd ridden away from them, he'd left their mother sobbing on the castle steps. There'd be no turning back for him.

"After we get the wounded one inside, fetch Annie, will ye?" she asked Dirk.

"'Tis the middle of the night."

"Aye." Jenny left it up to her cousin to figure that part out. "We've a wounded man who needs tending." She was grateful her childhood friend was visiting Cnàmhan Broch from MacPherson lands. Her expert hand would aid in healing the wounded man. And by doing so, the two new recruits would be more endeared to her, seeing that she was willing to take care of her own.

"I dinna trust that one." Dirk nodded toward Toran as though he wasn't sitting right behind her. The way her cousin was glaring at their new recruit, he would likely insist the men be locked away or executed in case they should decide to run off and expose the rebels to the English.

"Have faith, Cousin."

"Aye, Mistress," Dirk grumbled as he peeled away from their caravan to head toward the castle, the peaks of its roof showing just above the forest that separated them from the road.

A rumble shook against her back, and Jenny stiffened. "What are ye laughing at?"

"I'm hurt he doesna trust me." The way he spoke soft and low in a teasing lilt, as though it were a secret shared between them, sent an unbidden shiver of pleasure down her spine.

Jenny rolled her eyes, though he couldn't see it. "Dinna pretend to be offended, wee *messan*." She didn't even care what he was laughing about anymore. It would probably only irritate her further.

"Och, I'm no lap dog, Mistress, but if I were, I'd let ye pet me."

Jenny clenched her jaw, refusing to play into his insults, but the image he created in her mind—him curled up at her feet while she stroked his head—did make her want to laugh.

Jenny swung her right leg over the front of her horse and then slid down the side of her mount instead of waiting for Toran, who didn't seem to be in a hurry to follow.

When she glanced back up at him, she could see a hint of surprise in his face despite the darkness and then a smirk as he carefully studied his surroundings. Too carefully. That cold knot of dread grew icy.

"Get off the horse, afore I have him buck ye off," she ordered.

"Aye, Mistress, will do, Mistress." Coming from anyone else the words might have been taken as respect, but she knew very well he was mocking her.

Her gaze roved over to the other man, whom her guard, Mac, was carefully taking down off the horse. "He's unconscious, Mistress."

Toran moved then, leaping off the horse in much the same way she'd just done, only his kilt rose when he did, showing a fair amount of his muscled upper thighs with just a hint of his arse.

Jenny swallowed hard and jerked her gaze away,

pretending she'd not just seen so much of his flesh and refusing to be impressed by the blatant show of strength.

Toran rushed over to Mac, and she hurried after him in case he was about to attack her man. He only took his companion into his arms, giving a little shake. "Archie, wake, man."

Archie did not stir.

The look of anguish on Toran's face was palpable. But Jenny forced her emotions aside. How could she show sympathy for a man who'd only teased her since their first moments of acquaintance, a man she had no reason to trust? Well, she didn't have to. But she could help his friend.

"Bring him inside." She shoved open the double wood-slatted door, heavier than most croft doors for extra protection and privacy.

A single small candle lit the inside of the house, its dim light casting shadows on the walls, revealing the familiar furniture as black lumps.

They cleared off a long trestle table where countless men in the same predicament had lain and placed him on it.

When more candles were lit, she could see how badly wounded Archie was. The man was swollen, his entire body covered in dark bruises, and if she wasn't mistaken, one of his arms was definitely broken—beneath the surface of his skin, bumps protruded that shouldn't. There were cuts about his face that likely needed stitching.

What she hadn't expected to see were the similarities between Toran and Archie. They could have been brothers. Both sported dark hair, though only Toran's seemed to glow auburn in the candlelight. Their bone structure was similar, with a wide square jaw and cheekbones sharp enough to cut. They shared the same wide brows, though one of Archie's was split open.

Toran held a candle over his cousin, examining his injuries as well, and when he glanced up at her, the light from the flame brightened his eyes, eyes the color of the sky where it met ice-capped mountaintops.

"Ye'll help him?" he asked, a desperation in his voice that slugged her in the chest.

"Aye. We will."

"We will be forever in your debt." He looked disappointed about that, his mouth a grim line.

"I didna bring ye here to be in my debt." Jenny jutted her chin out. "I brought ye here to fight for your country."

Without missing a beat, he replied, "Ye ken Archie was imprisoned for doing just that."

Jenny gazed down at the wounded warrior, taking in the extent of his injuries. When she looked back up at Toran, anguish had crippled his features once more before he visibly exhaled and his face was calm again.

Guilt ate at him, that much was obvious. Did he blame himself for this man's condition? Judging from the quick look she'd given him, Toran's injuries were slight, just a few scratches and the awful stench. But Archie had taken a brutal beating.

Archie was imprisoned... Was Toran not?

"Were ye with him when he was captured? Beaten?" she asked.

Toran grimaced. "Nay."

"But ye helped him escape."

"Aye."

"Were ye from the party staging a break-in? Or were ye arrested before him?"

Toran stared hard at her, and she wondered if he would answer the question at all. His eyes gave nothing away. He unnerved her.

"I was already there, aye."

His cautious answer sent a warning prickle along her spine. But before she could question him further, the door burst open, and Jenny's childhood friend and confidante, Annie MacPherson, rushed into the croft, Dirk right behind her. Her long dark hair flew around her face in wisps that had pulled free of her braid.

She scanned the room, her amber eyes wide, settling on Archie's still body lying on the table behind Jenny.

"Oh," she gasped. "What happened? Were ye set upon?" She looked Jenny up and down, even as Jenny pushed her dear friend away.

"Nay, nay, not us. We happened upon them on the road." She nodded her head toward Toran and Archie.

"Who did this to him?" Annie asked as she examined his wounds. "Dragoons?"

"Aye. The English are responsible," Jenny said, but her own gaze had settled on Toran.

He refused to look up, eyes on Archie. Was he afraid of giving something away? What wasn't he telling her?

Annie ordered everyone away from her patient and

directed the men to bring her boiled water and clean linens. She'd brought a satchel full of medical supplies and the box of herbal medicines she'd created. In truth, she never went anywhere without them.

Jenny was used to seeing Annie work, but Toran wasn't. He started to hover, and it was only Jenny's hand on his arm tugging him back that had him finally giving Annie some space.

"She'll take good care of him." Jenny watched as her friend cut away the fabric of Archie's torn *léine* and frock coat. Annie motioned for Dirk to help her, which had Toran twitching at her side. "We've taken care of many such as him, and in worse shape. Beaten bloody and left for dead by the English. Ye need have no fear."

She stared at Toran's profile, the strength of his jaw and the line of his rather noble nose. Aye, there was a slight bump on it from having been broken. It was rare to see a warrior who didn't have that. Faint scars on his cheeks and forehead spoke of years of training as a soldier, even participation in battles. Jenny had grown accustomed to searching out such marks. They helped her determine the level of training a recruit would need before being paired with an experienced rebel.

Toran ran a battle-scarred hand through his shoulder-length hair and then swiped it down his face, pinching the bridge of his nose.

"How many?" he asked.

"Pardon?" She eyed his profile, mesmerized by his striking features and fighting herself to ignore the strong urge to run her fingers through his dark locks.

"How many have ye treated?"

Jenny cleared her throat. "Hard to say. These are bloody times."

Toran opened his mouth as though he were going to say something and then pressed his lips back into that firm, grim line, putting a stop to whatever he was going to share. He might want to go quiet, but she wasn't going to allow it. "How many were in prison with ye?"

"Too many." He offered no more.

"Even one is too many, aye?" she asked.

He grunted and ran his hand through his hair again. A nervous habit? He flicked his blue eyes at her briefly, and she found herself momentarily stunned. "So ye've recruited us. Now what?"

Jenny had never been one to go into a tizzy over a man, even when she was younger. She was pragmatic, knew her role in this world and hadn't let anything get in the way of it. So why the bloody hell was this man unsettling the strategic foundation she'd built?

"We need to get Archie well first, and I suspect ye'll want to remain with him."

"I'm no' a nursemaid, lass."

"Mistress," she corrected him. "And no one suggested ye were. But even if I had, if that's where ye're needed, that's where ye'll be."

He turned to face her, those startling blue eyes locking onto her own. There was a danger that lurked in their depths that sent a shiver racing through her.

"Are ye related?" she asked.

"He is my cousin."

"Ah. How many more of your clan were there? How did ye get arrested?"

He shook his head. "'Tis my turn to ask a question."

She narrowed her eyes. "I invited ye to join our army. I am providing healing for your cousin, your blood. I saved ye from the redcoats. I'll be the one to ask the questions."

He ignored her. "What is your real name, J?"

"That is my real name. Again, how many more of your clan were there? How did ye get arrested?" He crossed his arms over his broad chest and eyed her through slanted lids.

"Let me ask ye this, Mistress J. Are the men within your company dispensable?" The way he said her title was nearly a sneer.

She wasn't so certain she'd enjoy keeping him on, and she certainly didn't like what he was insinuating. "Every man is important. No one is dispensable. What kind of question is that?"

"I want to know what kind of leader ye are."

"So ye'd insult me to find out?" The gall of this man. But she supposed she shouldn't be so surprised. He'd done nothing but prickle her nerves since they'd met.

"What are ye willing to risk? How many men?"

Jenny scowled, refusing to answer.

"'Tis a valid question. How many men are ye willing to risk?"

She shook her head in irritation and disbelief. "I want no one to perish."

"But ye see, they will."

They will. Not *we* will. He didn't consider himself one of them.

"If that's your stance, then I'm happy to have ye and Archie taken back out to the woods where we found ye. For ye see, Toran, my men are no' dispensable. But from what I'm hearing, ye dinna consider yourself to be one of them. And my enemies, well, I have no concern over whether they live or die, just as long as we win."

"Who are ye fighting for?"

"The prince regent, Charles Stuart, ye ken that."

"Who recruited ye?"

She narrowed her eyes, again not liking what he was insinuating. "Ye think that because I'm a woman I must be working for someone else. That I canna be in charge of this uprising."

He arched an eyebrow. "Aye."

She laughed, but there was no humor in the sound. The men in the room fell silent, recognizing the shift in mood. Toran noticed it too, glancing around. When his eyes alighted on hers, there was an understanding there that hadn't been present before.

"Who is your clan, Toran?"

"I'd rather not say."

"A man who hides behind a veil is not one I'm certain I can trust."

There was a flicker of some unidentified emotion on his face. He cleared his throat, shifting his gaze back to the patient as Annie cleaned the blood from Archie's wounds.

"Archie and I are both…MacGillivrays."

That made sense. The garrison was close to MacGillivray lands, which edged her own. Many of the

men in her own regiment were from the MacGillivrays.
"And Chief MacGillivray?"

"Distant relative. We are nothing."

"I see. Then why were ye arrested?"

"We're both rebel soldiers." His chosen words were
clipped, and Jenny's gut told her he was definitely hiding
something. "Dragoons are always rounding up fighting
men." His gaze slid slowly back to hers, and she suddenly
felt exposed. "And what about ye, Mistress, have ye a
laird?"

Jenny was keen to avoid any of Toran's prying
questions—especially this one. She'd *had* a laird. But the
moment her brother had betrayed them all, she'd decided
he was no longer hers. That was also when she'd decided
to take up this mission.

"I follow no man but Prince Charlie."

"Ah, but I see ye're a lass of many faces. We may be
more alike than ye'd care to think." And then he winked
at her, flashing a conspiratorial grin.

For the first time in her life, Jenny was struck speechless. So casual a gesture, that dip of a single lid and the
flash of teeth. As though they were comrades or companions…or more. Why did that wink and smile have
her belly doing flips and her mind swirling with all sorts
of thoughts she'd never meant to entertain? Thoughts
about desire and…kissing.

Ballocks! That's what this was. A big wagonful of
ballocks.

He was trying to make her uneasy. Trying to disarm
her, to *seduce* her even. Why else would he bring out the

charm while questioning her? The man was full of tricks, she could see, and now he would attempt to add seduction to the list to try to break her down. She wouldn't allow that.

She needed some air, to put distance between them.

Dragging her gaze from Toran in a way that indicated her annoyance with him, she searched out her cousin. "Dirk, I've some things to attend to before I leave. Will ye please take over?"

"Aye, Mistress." Her cousin eyed Toran with obvious dislike.

Toran raised a brow at her, as if he knew exactly why she was leaving, but she just glowered at him. "Dinna give my men cause to put that promised bullet in your heart."

"Aye, Mistress," he said with a mocking bow. The smile on his face was anything but confirmation he would behave.

———

Doctor Annie, as the men within the croft referred to her, had finally stopped working on Archie just before dawn. One of the men had seen her back to wherever she'd come from, all of them very careful not to give away any information in front of Toran. However, he'd snuck a peek out the small window and seen the direction they'd gone.

The men didn't trust him, with good cause as he'd refused to answer most of their questions, though in truth they'd refused to answer his as well. Their distrust was fine because he didn't trust them either. Jacobites were the reason his mother was dead. Every person in this room, save his cousin, was his enemy.

He was quite certain that Dirk wanted to rip his head off and feed it to the wild boars lurking in the forest. The feeling was almost mutual.

As the sun began to rise, men filtered upstairs to sleep, while others dispersed. Except for Dirk, who pulled up a chair in front of the door and sat in it, arms crossed, his gaze fixed on Toran.

Toran smirked at the man's obvious intent to keep him inside. If Toran wanted to leave, he was damned well going to leave. But damnation, he needed to question Jenny, and he was furious that she'd not returned. Getting to the bottom of his mother's murder was one priority. His other was getting back to his great-uncle's castle and making certain his siblings weren't ambushed by Boyd's men. They were still too young to care for themselves, the guardianship having fallen to him on his mother's death.

Trying to ignore the man set on intimidating him, Toran laid on the floor beside the table where Archie slept, arms behind his head. He stared at the ceiling, at the ancient beams that looked to have been put into place in the Dark Ages. He tried to get some rest himself, but every scrape of a bootheel on the floor, every creak of a board overhead had him waking and ready to fight.

Every question, whether prying or casually disguised, went unanswered. The men were more tightly sealed than Boyd's treasure. Giving up his interrogation, Toran had concentrated on sleep, but that hadn't worked either.

By midafternoon, he gave up on rest and checked on Archie, pressing a damp cloth to his cousin's forehead and giving him sips of a bowl of broth that had been pressed into his hands by a small woman who had come by to serve the men.

Archie did not push the broth away but didn't finish it either.

Toran wanted to warn the woman away, to tell her that to remain at the rebel croft would only mean her death. The men jested with her, thanked her for the food, seemed to actually care about this woman. But Toran knew better.

There was no sign of Mistress J, and when the sun started to set again, Dirk, who had not slept at all, was replaced by two Highlanders standing in front of the door, arms crossed over their chests as they stared at him.

Was he a prisoner, as she had suggested? Because it damn well felt like it.

Toran wanted to ask where Jenny was. To demand she return and give him some answers. But he already knew his words would fall on deaf ears. He also understood there would be no escape. They'd not let him past the doors, and if he tried to climb out the window, they'd stop him from doing that too.

What was completely obvious to him and anyone else who might be looking in was that these men were loyal to her and to their cause. They would not betray her and would definitely not do him any favors.

It was all rather fascinating—and damned confounding. He was fairly certain he knew who she was, what she was doing, and the crimes she'd committed. Mistress J was a moniker well known on both sides of the war. Loyalists whispered of her misdeeds in dread or with a vow of vengeance; rebels would sing her praises, as though she were a modern-day female Robin Hood. The latter, he couldn't understand. How was it that the rebels could all follow her when it would mean certain death?

As the evening turned into night, still he waited for her to return. By day, she no doubt had to pretend to be someone she wasn't. Was she married? Did she have children? For she couldn't be Mistress J all the time. He wasn't lying when he'd said they all wore many faces.

Toran prayed Mistress J never saw any more than what he was willing to show. Giving his mother's name, MacGillivray, he'd hoped to see some sort of reaction, recognition, worry—but there had been none. Well, soon enough, he'd be free and able to tell Mistress J exactly what he knew of the crimes she'd committed and how he was going to punish her for them.

"Toran." Archie's hoarse voice called from across the croft.

He approached his cousin with caution, the guards at the entrance watching him with suspicion.

"I'm here, Cousin."

Archie beckoned him to lean down. "What are ye still doing here?" he growled. "Dinna think I've forgiven ye for what ye did."

"Saving ye?"

"Nay. Killing them all."

The muscle in Toran's jaw flexed. "Whether or not ye believe me, that was not supposed to happen."

"What in bloody hell did ye think was going to happen? That they'd all be asked to tea?"

"I expected they'd be imprisoned, and I didna expect ye to be a part of them. That I'd get to question them about…my mother."

Archie quieted then, the fight going out of his face. "Is that what it was about?"

"Uncle has done nothing to find her murderers."

Archie shook his head. "Uncle plays both sides, ye know that. But he's already told us what happened."

Toran and Archie were both great-nephews of the chief of clan Fraser, who once was the most illustrious spy in Scotland—the Fox. The man had gone back and forth between the highest bidder for decades and right now claimed to be back on the side of the Jacobites, though the English had yet to receive that missive.

Toran didn't respond, not wanting to confess that he too had played the Jacobites in order to gain information. "I want justice."

"This is not the place ye're going to find it."

"'Tis a start."

"Have caution, Toran. For they will find out why ye were at the garrison, though not from me, ye have my word on that."

Toran straightened, a pounding headache starting at the base of his skull. He nodded curtly and turned to one of the guards. "My cousin is in need of whisky." Then he turned back to Archie. "Drink and sleep. Ye're going to need your rest."

It didn't do yet to tell Archie that after he gained the

information he needed, Toran was going to plan their escape.

―――――――

"Why are ye sitting here in the dark?" Annie slipped into Jenny's chamber at Cnàmhan Broch as easily as they'd done as children and sat down beside her on the floor before the hearth.

Jenny avoided the question, mostly because she didn't want to put voice to her thoughts. "Why are ye not asleep?"

Annie shrugged. "I was working on a new salve. Your turn." She bumped her shoulder against Jenny's, which brought a smile to her face.

"Ye always did know when something was on my mind."

"Aye, what kind of friend would I be if I couldna tell?"

"Not such a nosy one?" Jenny laughed despite the subtle insult, and Annie joined her, comfortable in their friendship.

"Now tell me, else I'll be forced to guess, and ye know how vivid my imagination is."

"How is your patient?" Jenny asked.

"Avoiding the topic, I see." Annie sighed with dramatic flair. "All right, I'll play along. Archie was awake and eating. The swelling in his face has gone down, and he claims the pain has as well."

Jenny cleared her throat, pretending to pick at

something on her nail, but given it was dark, the move was silly. "And his cousin?"

"His cousin?" Annie asked with nonchalance.

"Toran."

"Ah, that cousin. I had no idea who ye referred to." The sarcasm in her dear friend's tone was not lost on Jenny. "Only minor scratches."

"I meant his mood?"

"Oh." Annie cocked her head, studying Jenny in a way that made her want to squirm. "He didna talk much. But he did ask when ye'd be by. How often ye came by. And how long ye'd leave them there."

Jenny pressed her hands to the floor to steady herself. Why did the man have so many questions? "And what did ye tell him?"

Annie snorted. "That I wasna your keeper."

Jenny grinned.

"He's different, aye?" Annie scrutinized Jenny's face, and she worked to keep her feelings inside. She still hadn't fully figured out how she felt about the man.

"He's dangerous." That was the truth.

"Dangerously handsome." Annie giggled.

"I had not noticed."

Annie laughed. "One day, ye'll not be so immune to a handsome face, mark my words."

Jenny shook her head. "Impossible. No man, no matter how bonnie, will get in the way of my mission for the prince." She let out a frustrated groan. "He's avoided all questions and acted on edge, according to Dirk. How can I trust him?"

"Ye'll get nowhere sitting here in the dark. Go and talk to him."

She wished she could use the excuse that it was late, but, quite honestly, that wasn't excuse enough given she did most of her work in the dead of night.

"Why is this man causing such a stir? How many recruits do ye have now—hundreds?"

"Aye. I dinna know. 'Tis driving me mad." A flash of ice-blue eyes came across her mind as she thought of Toran MacGillivray. She wondered if he would recognize any of their MacGillivray recruits.

Annie hopped to her feet and held her hands down to Jenny. "Come on. I'll go with ye. Like old times."

Jenny smiled, picturing how in their youth whenever their clans had met to discuss plans for the rebels the two of them and Fiona, the third link in their trio, had raced through the woods, pretending to fight off enemy dragoons.

MacPherson lands bordered Mackintosh lands to the south. Annie, Jenny, and Fiona MacBean, from another neighboring clan, had been inseparable since they had been barely tall enough to see over the table. When their clans suffered extensively at the hands of the English, they'd made a childhood pact to honor their fathers' devotion to the Scottish king—even if it meant an early grave. The three of them had kept to that promise, each sacrificing pieces of themselves in an effort to put Prince Charlie where he belonged. On the throne.

"All right," Jenny agreed.

They sneaked into the secret passageway built into

the stone wall of Jenny's father's study. Light from their candles illuminated the passage. Jenny stripped out of her gown and into her trews, *léine*, and waistcoat. She twisted her hair up into a knot and topped her head with the cap.

"Ye make a pretty man," Annie teased.

Jenny snorted. Despite her attempts, she knew she didn't resemble a man, but it was enough to make people look twice before deciding. She blew out the little flame and took Annie's hand in hers as they made their way through the tunnel in the dark.

Stealing out of the castle was necessary in order to avoid anyone asking where they were going. Most of her brother's men—who she considered to be *hers*, thank you—were Jacobites, but there were a few who were still staunch supporters of her brother, and some she suspected might even be spies. Her mother could not know about what she was doing, of course, or she'd suffer a heart affliction. Her mother had not been the same since Hamish had left them to fend for themselves, spending most of her time alone in her room.

Hamish's hasty departure and subsequent drain on the clan—with his endless demands for supplies for the government armies—and Lady Mackintosh's withdrawal had left their problems in Jenny's hands. To pick up the pieces. To take care of the people, her clan. It was a responsibility she did not take lightly.

At least Jenny had no worries that her mother would betray her to Hamish. The woman was heartbroken that her only son would go to such lengths, when every one of their kin had fought so hard to keep Scottish roots Scottish.

The first time Jenny had gone out in search of Jacobite help, she'd been alone. Though terrifying, it had also been informative. She'd walked to a local tavern that night, just after her mother went to bed. Disguised as a wayward traveler, she'd only listened, getting a feel for what the people were saying about her brother and where their loyalties lay. She was surprised and delighted that there appeared to be significant resistance against his allegiance to King George.

Dirk had caught her returning in the wee hours. But instead of ratting her out to her brother, her cousin had said he'd join her—though she still suspected he had only taken the position to make certain she didn't get herself killed. Jenny could handle herself in any skirmish, any raid, even in battle. She'd been training with her brother since she was a wee lass, as her father had thought it important for her to learn the basics to protect herself. Still, Dirk insisted on going with her, and he always brought at least two other Mackintosh warriors who could be trusted to guard her.

Traversing the path to the croft a few miles away without Dirk with them was probably dangerous given the redcoats swarming the Highlands, but Jenny didn't dwell on the concern. She had a *sgian dubh* in each boot, another dagger strapped to her thigh, and yet another strapped to her left arm beneath her sleeve. Annie was equally armed. Tucked into the waistband of her trews and beneath her waistcoat, Jenny had hidden a pistol. Aye, there was only a single shot, but she had deadly aim.

Jenny could make this journey with her eyes closed. She

knew that for a fact, because she'd done it more than once with her eyes bound by a strip of cloth to practice the walk for nights when the moon would be covered by clouds. She made note each day of where newly fallen trees had been downed and where weather might have otherwise changed the vegetation. She was nothing if not prepared.

Their journey was short, and she gave the bird of prey signal as the shadows of the croft drew into view. Moments later, they were inside.

A tall figure stood at the rear of the croft, arms crossed over his chest as he stared right at her.

"Toran," she said by way of greeting. "How is Archie?"

"Awake. Moving around." His voice was low, laced with irritation.

"He is doing much better, then."

"Aye. He's a Highlander, trained as a soldier."

Jenny knew what this answer meant. Men, warriors, did not complain about ailments. They could be dying and still try to force themselves out of bed.

"Impressive all the same."

"Perhaps to a woman." His tone was combative, and the energy in the room seemed to match his mood.

Jenny narrowed her eyes but grinned instead of lashing out. He was trying to rile her up, that much was evident. "It bothers ye that I am in charge, does it not?"

He studied her a long moment before answering. "Nay."

She didn't believe him. But before she could drill him some more, Archie limped inside, his arm bound in a sling and a guard behind him.

"Ah, my lady." A lock of dark hair fell over his striking face, only slightly less hard than that of his cousin.

"Mistress J," Toran corrected his cousin but eyed her mockingly. "She's in charge."

Jenny forced herself not to roll her head toward him and skewer him with a glower. If he wanted to challenge her, why not just say so? She wouldn't back down.

Archie ignored his cousin and stepped forward, holding out his hand to her. Jenny paused a moment, worried that he would try to kiss her hand, a show of chivalry she wasn't interested in. But when she grasped his hand, he only squeezed it in a show of mutual respect.

"My gratitude for taking us into your fold, Mistress. Would ye happen to be *the* Mistress J?" Archie smiled, the expression giving him a somewhat boyish look.

She found herself smiling back. "The one and only."

Toran snorted so low it was barely audible, but she caught it. She was too aware of everything he did, every sound he made. *Arse.*

"Glad I am that ye found us upon the road, not only because ye saved our lives"—Archie passed Toran a look she found quite curious—"but because if there's any way I can get involved with kicking English arse, I'm more than happy to do my part."

"Well, then I only await your cousin's refusal."

Toran let out a great sigh. "I think we've gotten off on the wrong foot, Mistress."

It was the first time he'd said it without sounding like he was mocking her.

Toran shouldn't have been surprised that it was the dead of night when Mistress J returned. Jenny was her true name; he'd overheard her high-handed henchman Dirk use it when he spoke with another of the Highlanders, Mac. The two of them thought he was asleep. Toran would sleep when he was dead.

Whenever he'd closed his eyes, the faces of the Frasers he'd condemned to die flashed before his eyes, haunting him. They weren't supposed to die. Their deaths were on his hands, as though he'd been the one to tie the nooses around their necks.

At least now he could be distracted from his guilt by the lass. He had to find out the extent of her involvement in his mother's death. She'd always been on the side of the English government, so it had been a surprise to Toran to learn that she had defected to the Jacobite cause and a bitter draught to swallow to find out they'd killed her.

Despite the hour, Jenny looked bright and fresh, and her eyes found his quickly. She was there with her healing friend, Annie, who whispered something to Jenny before trotting to the other side of the croft.

Toran resolved to pretend to get into her good graces, for the best way to gain information was to ingratiate oneself.

"Let us start over," he drawled. "Mistress J." After having spoken his words of a truce, he bowed low before her.

"Toran." His name lingered in the air between them, said with a mixture of suspicion and curiosity.

"Might I have a word?" He glanced at his cousin, who took the hint and got up. "In private?"

"Aye." Her gaze roved slowly over him, as though she didn't quite recognize him. And he supposed she wouldn't, since the last time they'd spoken he'd not been so accommodating.

He flashed her a grin in hopes of disarming her a bit more and then spoke the words he'd been practicing for when they met next. "We're eager, Archie and I, to rejoin the cause. I beg your apology for my hesitation previously." He ran a hand through his hair, having learned along the way that to incorporate various banal gestures while talking could distract an enemy from any hint of subterfuge. He slowly locked his eyes back on hers. "We were tense from our escape, from near death, and I was finding it hard to…manage. But given the care of my cousin and the safety we've felt here…" He let the words fade, taking in her expression, which did not give away much.

"I understand." Her voice was softer than it had been before, a sign of a weakening resolve. "My invitation to join us still stands. We're well represented by MacGillivrays. Perhaps ye might even know some already."

"Aye, I'm certain to. Thank ye. We'll not let ye down, Mistress." He dropped his gaze and then peered up at her, keeping his expression soft, imploring. Lord, but he was almost disgusted with himself for the tactic he was using. He pressed his hand to his heart. "As a sign of my fealty, I've drawn something for ye. A map of the garrison."

Jenny's expression brightened with interest, and she leaned just ever so slightly forward. "Show me."

Toran pulled from his frock coat the scrap of paper that he'd drawn on the day before using supplies he'd pilfered from the men in the croft, and he handed her the folded bit.

As Jenny unfurled the scrap, taking in the etchings, her shoulders relaxed, and he felt himself sliding effortlessly into her good graces. Excellent.

"This will be of much help to us," she said, smiling up at him. "Thank ye for entrusting this to me."

"Aye. And I can help ye get inside when the time comes."

"That will be most helpful."

Mission accomplished.

Three

JENNY SAT ACROSS FROM ANNIE AT THE SMALL DINING table in her solar where she preferred to take meals. The sun had barely risen, and the two of them had only just returned from their midnight visit to the croft.

The room was small and cozy, the wood floors softened by a rich woven carpet, the stone walls covered in rose-and-gold silken wallpaper. It had been this way for as long as she could remember. A few landscape paintings hung among the portraits of the Mackintosh ladies—her mother, grandmother, aunts. All elegant and beautiful. Sitting in her day gown, her hair in a simple plait, purple smudges of exhaustion beneath her eyes, Jenny did not feel as elegant. Annie, too, was dressed more casually this morning, in her riding habit since she planned to leave shortly for home. Jenny was going to miss not having her for company.

"Will ye go to the croft today or wait until tonight?"

"I ought to rest, but if I do, Mama will think I'm ill," Jenny said with a short laugh. "'Tis probably best I go back. I need to speak with Dirk now that I have the map."

"He is not as bad as ye thought, this Toran MacGillivray."

"Nay, it would seem not. He is proving himself to be an asset. I'm sure I would have been able to come across a map of the garrison at some point, but now I dinna have to guess at when."

"Still, be cautious."

"As I always am."

Annie smiled. "The brave and rebellious Mistress J."

"The fearless and iron-stomached Doctor Annie." They shared a laugh, and then Jenny pushed up from the table to embrace her friend. "Write to me."

"I will."

"And I'll see ye soon. I'm due for a visit."

"Aye. My brothers will be glad to see ye. Especially Graham."

"I'm no' marrying Graham."

Annie laughed. "I ken, but I dinna think he does yet."

Jenny smiled and hugged her friend again.

"Go on, now, back to your croft, back to the dangerously handsome soldier," Annie teased. "I'll send word when I reach home."

Jenny rolled her eyes. "I dinna think he is handsome."

"Perhaps ye're not feeling well?" Annie held a hand to her forehead and tsked.

Jenny batted her hand away. "I'm perfectly fine. Go on with ye. And thank ye for all of your help."

"I'd do anything to help the cause. I only wish I could help more."

"Someday I fear ye will."

"We must all do our part."

When Annie had gone, Jenny pulled the map from her bodice, running her fingers over the ink-etched lines, memorizing the way in, the corridors, the Xs that marked where the guards were most likely to stand on watch. The map was detailed, much more so than she would have expected from a prisoner. Then again, she was grateful Toran seemed to have memorized the entire fortress.

If she was going to go to the croft, now was the best time to make her escape, before her mother woke. Jenny hurried through the tunnel, running through the motions of changing her clothes and exiting through the tunnel. As she crossed into the forest that stood between the castle and the croft, she paused at the sight of fresh ax marks in a tree.

What in the world? She reached for the marks, running her hands along the newly cut bark, feeling the freshness of the grooves. Instantly, Jenny was on high alert. No one was supposed to be cutting trees here—which it didn't appear anyone had. Only great gashes in the trunk.

She listened for unusual sounds that would signal the intruder's whereabouts. The rush of birds from branches. A squirrel scurrying up a tree and out of sight. The slight whistle of the wind rustling tree limbs. She sniffed, taking in all the scents around her. Pine, oak, grass, scents of animals, and the freshly chopped bark.

No flames. No cooking. None of the foul stenches of outlaws that seemed to permeate for miles.

So why would one chop wood, if not to fell a tree or light a fire?

She didn't like that someone had been on this route. Nothing else gave a hint of passersby, outlaws, or—worse still—dragoons. Even so, she pulled one of her daggers from her boot, clutching it in her hand as she continued silently, stopping every so often to listen.

With her instincts on high alert, every little sound had her jerking toward it. If not for her tight control, several forest animals might have been skewered, along with several branches and even the occasional gust of wind.

The trek to the croft took nearly twice as long as normal as she doubled back a few times, just to be certain she wasn't being followed.

She spied the front of the croft in the distance and two shadowed figures moving about the outside. Jenny edged closer, keeping her steps silent. At all times she had two men on duty to guard the dwelling. To remain inconspicuous, the men on guard acted as crofters going about their normal daily chores and duties.

However, at night this was a little more difficult. Her men were instructed to sit or hide in their watch posts, not walk around.

The closer she drew, however, the less fearful she was, for she recognized the guards. Jenny quickened her pace, no longer worried about stumbling on dragoons.

At her approach, one of the men looked up from chopping wood and nodded. John, she recognized, touched the tip of his cap. "Mistress J."

Jenny nodded in turn. "Any news?"

"All quiet."

"There was an ax mark in a tree about halfway between here and Cnàmhan Broch. Were any of the men chopping any of the trees beyond the croft border?"

John wrinkled his brow and shook his head. "Nay."

Jenny didn't grimace on the outside, but she most certainly did on the inside. This was not good. "Keep your eye out. I saw nothing else, but 'tis a warning all the same."

"Aye, Mistress."

Jenny left him to go inside, her eyes adjusting to the darkness of the crofting house. The two small windows had the curtains pulled back to let in light, but that didn't help much. She stood for a moment, making out the shapes of the ladder leading upstairs, the table and chairs, the long trestle table where Archie had lain previously.

The men stood near the hearth with cups of ale in their hands.

"Mistress. Would ye care for some ale?" Toran asked from where he stood near the hearth.

The drink was likely to make her sleepy, but she didn't want to refuse and come off rude now that they'd formed somewhat of a truce the night before. "Aye, thank ye."

Toran pushed away from the hearth, limber muscles fluid as he poured her a drink.

She raised her cup, taking a small sip.

Archie gulped down the liquid and wiped his mouth on the back of his hand. "Your servant, the healer, she was bonnie."

Jenny didn't reply. What a laugh Annie would get if she heard herself—a noble-born lass—being called a servant. Jenny decided she would be more flattered about being called bonnie.

"Will she be back?" Toran asked.

A spike of jealousy, very unlike her, gave Jenny an unpleasant feeling in her chest. "Not likely."

Archie drained his cup and then bit into a piece of

jerky Toran passed him, a wrinkle of disappointment on his brow. "I'll be back. Need to attend a private matter." And then he was gone, leaving her alone with Toran.

"Did ye have a chance to study the map?" he asked, sitting down at the table.

Jenny took the seat opposite him. "Aye. It is well laid out. Ye've an incredible memory."

He smiled. "Aye. My mind seems to paint a portrait with my memories."

"That is verra lucky." Jenny admired those with the ability, and she'd not met many.

Toran leaned back in his chair, studying her through hooded lashes. "I'm lucky ye found us when ye did."

"Ye seem clever enough to have found an escape once. I'm sure ye could have done so again."

He shrugged and took a leisurely sip of his ale. "All the same. A question, Mistress."

"Aye?"

"Ye know of our clan. When do we get to know of yours?"

Jenny mulled over his inquiry for a beat. "In due time."

"Come now, I've given ye the map. Having done so is certain to get me killed should King George supporters find out."

"Ye're no stranger to putting your life in danger."

"And neither are ye."

"Are ye suggesting that with ye, I am?"

He chuckled and leaned forward, his blue eyes mesmerizing as he locked them on hers. "Quite the opposite. Listen, ye clearly need more from me. So I'll share something else."

She waited, barely blinking.

"The Fox is double-dealing."

Jenny frowned. "Everyone knows that."

"Aye. But not everyone knows he's got a spy within his own clan."

"And how do ye know?" She crossed her legs beneath the table, finding it hard not to fidget with the excitement of such new information.

Toran leaned even closer across the table until she could make out the flecks of darker blue near his pupils. "Because I met the bastard at the garrison."

"Who was he?" Her voice was barely above a whisper.

"Another Fraser. I didna catch his name, but I'd know him as well as I know my own reflection."

Jenny uncrossed her legs. "Because of your ability to paint a portrait from memory."

"Exactly." He refilled her mug of ale. "Where do we go from here, Mistress? A raid? Straight to sacking the garrison?"

"We're not quite ready yet."

"What have we left to do?"

"Gather more men, more weapons."

"What about more women? Are ye the only soldier?" While his face remained passive with only a slight hint of interest, his body was tense.

"There are other female recruits."

"Any MacGillivrays?"

"Nay."

His gaze sharpened, and she felt a prickle of warning racing over her spine.

"None at all?"

"Have ye one in mind?"

He shrugged. "I'm surprised. I'd heard there was."

"Ah." Toran had heard right, but she wasn't ready to share that bit of the rebels' painful history just yet. "I'm sorry to disappoint ye."

Toran took a long sip of his ale. "Perhaps we can rectify that."

"The women in my forces will fight, Toran. They are not to be used as typical army camp women."

Toran pressed a mocking hand to his chest. "Och, ye wound me. Have I proven myself to be such a rogue?"

Jenny rolled her eyes. "That has yet to be seen."

Archie returned then, breaking the intense spell, and Toran sat back in his chair, winking at her conspiratorially.

"What did I miss?" Archie asked, a great smile on his face. He was clearly the less intense of the two cousins and generally seemed like a cheerful person.

"Mistress J was just expressing her interest in gaining access to the garrison."

Archie stiffened, narrowing his eyes at Toran and then flashing them back at her. "Mistress, pardon my forwardness, but I think 'tis best to avoid that."

"Why's that?" Jenny asked.

"Because it's full of the bloody English and traitor Scots."

"And prisoners."

"Aye, prisoners too," Archie reluctantly agreed.

"Tell me, Archie, how did ye end up in English captivity?" Jenny twirled her cup slowly on the table, taking note of the way Toran stiffened across from her.

Archie grunted. "Bastards caught us when we were trying to break into the garrison."

Jenny's heart leapt. That was one thing she'd wanted to do but had not yet planned for, and now that she had the map it would be possible. The garrison was full of rebels she could recruit to her army.

Archie glanced at Toran, more unspoken words passed between them, and Jenny wanted to demand that they tell her exactly what the two men were hiding.

"We'd been given information on how to break in undetected," Archie said, "in order to rescue some of our men. But the damned redcoats were waiting for us as soon as we'd breached the walls."

Toran must have been one of the men they'd been trying to rescue, since he'd told her that he'd already been at the prison when his cousin arrived.

"We tried to fight. Some of the Fraser men didna make it. The rest were taken before Captain Boyd for execution. That's when Toran... That's when I first saw Toran."

Jenny's pulse leapt at the name Fraser. As surreptitiously as she could, she studied their plaid *feileadh-beags*. Because the kilts were covered in muck, it was hard to discern the woven plaid colors, not that they were likely to identify their clans anyway. Half of the Fraser men were firm Jacobite supporters, but the other half were traitors, including their chief, a notorious spy whose throat she'd like to loop a rope around.

"Frasers?" She spoke slowly and, with her hands beneath the table, pulled one dagger from her sleeve, prepared to strike now that there was a chance the enemy was indeed within her midst, for Toran had said nothing of Frasers and Archie had said nothing of MacGillivrays.

All the blood in her body felt like it was draining down into her ankles as her mind raced. Was Toran an English supporter? If so, why had he offered her the map? Why had he told her about the double-dealing Fox and his traitorous clansman? Good God, was *he* the *traitor* and only toying with her? Why wait so long to launch an attack if he was? They'd been here within her men's midst for two days.

Their entire mission could be compromised. She gripped the hilt of the dagger until her fingers tingled.

Toran interrupted Archie's response, as she suspected might happen. "Aye, the MacGillivrays were working with the Frasers."

She narrowed her eyes but did not look toward Toran, her gaze concentrated on Archie. He did not seem as adept at hiding his emotions. "Is that so?"

Archie nodded, seeming to have regained his composure, but he flicked his gaze toward Toran, and she didn't miss that spark of anger flaring in his eyes. They were lying.

Quick as her reflexes allowed, Jenny leapt back from the table, arms whipping out to the sides. She pulled her pistol from her belt, pointing it at Toran, and held her dagger at Archie's throat.

The bastard had tried to confuse her with talk of their similarities, with his allegiance and the map, sharing secrets, but it was just a trick. How could she have been so foolish? Why hadn't she trusted her gut when it came to him? He couldn't be trusted. But which parts were a ruse? Did it matter?

"Who are ye?" she demanded through gritted teeth, eyes now on Toran. "The truth this time."

Toran had barely moved since she'd pulled her weapons, but Archie held up his hands in surrender.

"We are Jacobites, Mistress," Archie pleaded, but Toran only bristled. Gone was the conspiratorial comradery, replaced with that dark and dangerous energy she'd recognized in him the night they'd first met.

Within the next second Toran had leapt over the table, shoving Archie to the floor and out of her way and wrenching Jenny's pistol from her grasp. She swung her blade, but he caught the edge with the butt of her pistol, sending a jarring buzz up her arm. Then he flattened her to the floor, pinning her in place.

The weight of him pressed her into the floorboards, her spine pushing painfully on a knot in the wood.

"Get the hell off me," she said through clenched teeth. "Ye think ye'll not be shot the moment one of my men steps through the door?"

Archie was pulling himself up from the floor, confusion and pain in his face.

"Not before I kill ye," Toran ground out.

"Then we'd both be dead."

"What the bloody hell are ye doing?" Archie growled. "Ye broke my rib, ye bloody bastard."

"Saving your life! The wench had a knife at your throat."

What Toran didn't realize was that he was about to have a knife at his. She slowly reached for the blade in her boot. But Toran felt her move and slapped his hand over hers, his touch branding her calf. Before she could make another attempt or even protest, three *thunks* sounded on the side wall followed by two more.

"'Tis a warning," she whispered.

All three of them silenced, listening, and then she could hear it. The sounds of horses, the chinks of the bridles. Men marching.

"Dragoons," she hissed. "Ye've brought them to our verra door. I'm going to kill ye."

"We didna, I swear it." She actually believed Archie when he said the words, but Toran... He only looked like he wanted to kill her too.

"If ye dinna get off me, I will no' be able to be rid of them, and as much as I'd like to toss your arse out there, I'd never willingly give up anyone to the redcoats, even if they are my enemy."

Toran's face contorted, a look of accusation on his face, but all he said was "How can ye get rid of them?"

"Ye'll have to trust me."

Toran still hesitated until, with his good arm, Archie tugged at the back of his shirt. "Let her up. She's no' the enemy."

Toran did slowly pull himself off her then, and she rose, resisting the urge to punch him in the mouth.

"Dinna move," she warned.

Her guards would have continued about their duties outside as if nothing was happening, as they had been trained. But the closer the sounds of marching men drew, the harder her heart pounded.

Jenny shoved the dagger back into her sleeve, eyeing Toran suspiciously, but he stood cautiously to the side. "Ye'd better not get us all killed," she muttered, lifting an easily donned gown from a hook. She tossed it over her head and tied the belt into place. The gown was a simple and plain working dress, not at all the fashion, all the better to help her remain unnoticed. She picked up a basket, tucking the pistol underneath a layer of cloth.

"What do ye expect to do with that?" Toran waved his hand toward the basket.

"Save your wastrel life. Stay here." Why was she even bothering? Toran would have slit her throat if the bloody dragoons hadn't happened upon them.

It wasn't just his miserable life she was saving but all of their lives.

Heart pounding, Jenny stepped outside and called to John about a chicken for the stew. As practiced, he called back that he'd get one ready for her, and she headed to the garden to pick a few herbs. Mac would be hidden somewhere from view but readying a crossbow to silently take out any attackers, should she give the signal.

The dragoons were well within sight now, and though she felt like running, she remained where she was. Archie and Toran weren't the only men recovering or hiding inside the croft, and she wouldn't leave her men to suffer at the hands of the English. Down on her knees, she snatched at herbs and carrots and anything else she could grab and shove into her basket until the cloth was covered, concealing any lumps her weapon left behind.

"Ho, there, wench."

Jenny bristled, leaning back on her heels. She held her hands to her eyes to shield them from a sun that was not at all impairing her vision.

She acted startled, as if she'd not seen them coming or expected them to stop, then stood slowly with her basket in hand.

"Good morn, sirs, can I help ye?" She tried to keep her voice as cordial as possible but not so friendly as to raise suspicions.

"What are ye doing?"

"Picking herbs." She cocked her head as if that were obvious. "For stew."

"We're looking for two men. They've escaped the garrison. Very dangerous."

"Oh," she gasped. Feigning fear, she allowed her hands to shake slightly as she raised one of them to her chest.

The leader of this pack of wolves shifted his horse forward several steps. The horse's nostrils flared, his dark eye scanning over her as though even the animals had been trained to despise Scots. Jenny took a step back, partly as an act and partly because she genuinely wondered if the redcoat would order his horse to trample her for the fun of it. She'd heard a tale of this happening only the month before, near Perth.

"Allow us entry into your home," he demanded.

"What? Why? Ye dinna think they are inside, do ye?"

She laughed, stalling for time. "I assure ye, 'tis small enough I'd have noticed."

They did not laugh back. The one who seemed to be in charge made a grunting sound and pointed at the entrance to the croft. Two dragoons dismounted, peeled off from the group, and started for the door.

"Please," Jenny said, her face feeling like it might crack from her smile. "My house is not suitable for guests."

They ignored her, which she'd guessed they would, slogging through the damp earth toward the croft. She hurried forward, reaching the dragoons before they reached the building. As she'd done countless times before, she pretended to trip in their path, effortlessly maintaining the balance of her basket so as not to spill its contents. Her fingers itched to grab the pistol, but she was outnumbered by many, and doing so would not aid in their cause.

Jenny let out an "oof" as her body slammed against the earth, blocking their way.

"Foolish wench, get up," shouted the man in charge of the dragoons.

Jenny reached her hand up, keeping her face from showing any revulsion at the touch of a *Sassenach*, but it was hardly necessary. Neither of them offered to help her up in the first place. *Bastards.*

When she made a great show of trying to stand, her feet getting caught in her skirts, the captain shouted again, this time dismounting as he did so. "Get out of their way. I'll not hesitate to have you whipped."

Jenny bristled, keeping her head tucked down, and

managed to get to her feet. The dragoons shoved past her, and all she could do was pray that she'd bought the men inside enough time to get into their hiding spots in the trenches beneath the floorboards. If not, this moment could be their last.

Four

WHEN JENNY HAD ORDERED TORAN TO STAY PUT, HER pistol pointed at him as she donned her costume and exited the croft, he'd been quite truly speechless. The lass thought to protect *them*? Shouldn't she be tossing him to the wolves as she'd surely done to his mother? Or dispatching him, as she'd promised when he'd tackled her to the ground?

Her words came back to haunt him… *As much as I'd like to toss your arse out there, I'd never willingly give up anyone to the redcoats, even if they are my enemy.* They'd been spoken with a truthful vehemence, and he couldn't help but question his own belief in her involvement. Was it possible that his uncle, that Boyd, had fed him the wrong information about his mother's death?

Now was not the time for questioning.

He was still in shock that she'd actually had the ballocks to aim her pistol at him and press her knife to Archie's neck. It was damned impressive, the kind of strength he'd rarely seen in a man, let alone in a woman. In fact, today was the first.

It was a day for firsts too. Because never before in his life had he disarmed a woman and pinned her to the ground. Guilt riddled him at having further injured his cousin in the process, but the edge of her dagger had been pressed too closely to Archie's neck.

He'd not saved his cousin only to have someone else

kill him. Every muscle in his body was still taut, his chest pulsing with anger, and Archie was eyeing him from across the room as though he'd gone mad.

Why the hell had he let her leave? The answer to that was twofold. One, he didn't have a choice; that lass was going to do whatever the hell she wanted. And two, if she had a plan, it was the only thing that might not get them all killed.

When she'd pulled on the ridiculous and unflattering gown, tucking her bloody weapon into her basket as though she were going bullet picking instead of berry picking, his first instinct had been to tell her she was addled, take her pistol as he'd already done once, and go out to face the bastards himself.

But it made more sense for her to do it, dressed as a crofter, and doubtless whoever stood on the other side of the door would recognize him instantly.

And so he'd watched through the slim opening in the window shutter as she carefully rushed toward the garden to pretend that she was working. It struck him how very practiced the movements were. Not unlike his own actions, having to work with both the English and Scots.

As the dragoons grew closer, he expected her to run. To tremble, at least, but she did none of that, save for what he now could see was a show she put on. He might not have known her long, but he could read the fierceness in her shoulders, the anger in her eyes. He hoped she didn't look at any one of them directly, or they'd see it too.

Toran's chest constricted when he recognized Captain Boyd at the head of the red-coated caravan. *An Diabhal fhéin!* The bloody devil himself looked so smug.

The men in the loft above him scrambled into action, sliding down the ladder. They pulled back a carpet covering the wood-planked floor. One yanked open a hatch showing a shallowly dug pit, which looked unnervingly like a grave. None of them spoke, but they gestured for him and Archie to get inside.

Toran shook his head and pointed toward the window. They were leaving. This was the first opportunity they'd had without a pistol or a dagger threatening to end their life or a guard riding their backs.

Archie frowned and shook his head in turn, jamming his finger toward the hole. There wasn't time to argue. The bastards would shove open the door to the croft any moment and would find them both there. They'd recognize Toran right away and would run him through—not without a fight, of course, but either way, today would be his last. And it would be a bloody painful end, if Boyd had anything to do with it. Toran would be labeled a traitor and die a horrendous traitor's death.

Toran gripped his cousin by the front of his shirt and hauled him forward. Barely audible, he said, "I saved ye once. I'll no' be coming back for ye."

"I owe ye a debt of gratitude, Cousin. And I'll best serve that here by not telling them who ye really are."

Toran gritted his teeth with irritation but let go of Archie's shirt. His cousin might think he could serve their country better buried beneath a croft, but Toran didn't. He had to get back to his people, his younger siblings. Though they shared the same parents, Camdyn and Isla were significantly younger than Toran, who'd just entered his twenty-ninth year. His wee brother was seventeen years old and Isla but thirteen. Between the three of them had been two others—a wee bairn sister who'd died just a month after birth and another lad who'd made it to ten before falling ill with measles. Now they were all that was left, and they counted on Toran.

Captain Boyd was certain to take his anger out on anyone with the name Fraser, if he hadn't already. Enough time had been wasted.

"I need to save my brother and sister," Toran whispered.

"Go then, afore 'tis too late. If ye dinna make it, I vow to keep them safe," Archie said, as he made his way into the pit.

"I'll haunt ye if ye dinna."

Archie smirked but said nothing, pulling the false floor into place.

Toran made quick work of removing any evidence that either he or his cousin had been there and then peered once more out the front window to see Jenny arguing with the dragoons. The lass had ballocks of steel. In two quick steps, Toran was at the back of the croft and squinting through the window, seeing no evidence of the English in that direction. He hauled himself up and out but stopped cold on the other side, feet just hitting the ground, when Jenny let out a cry of pain.

Mo chreach! What the bloody hell was Boyd doing to her?

Toran edged around the side of the building, catching only a slight glimpse of the crowd in the courtyard. Boyd had his hands in Jenny's hair, her head wrenched back.

Toran gritted his teeth, and some tiny part of him that wasn't entirely certain she was responsible for his mother's death cut a ding into his conscience. She'd willingly gone out there to save their arses, knowing the risks. Boyd was leaning close, whispering something in her ear, and rather than her skin going pale as any damsel's might, her face flushed red with anger. Boyd saw it too, his hands roaming over the front of her dress. He gripped her breasts, squeezing hard enough to elicit a hiss from her.

Anger boiled inside Toran, as he imagined that this was the same situation his own mother had been through, tossed to the bloody English wolves by her own rebel pack. A pack run by Mistress J. How could she claim to have never tossed anyone into the enemy's hands? A very small part of him thought that perhaps this was Jenny's just punishment, for she had to have borne witness to his mother's demise. The better part of him knew that no woman should have to endure the unwanted touch of any man.

Toran pulled his pistol from his belt, where he'd tucked it after stealing it back from Dirk when he wasn't paying attention. He only had one shot, and then he'd have to run like bloody hell. He cocked his pistol, aimed, ready to shoot Boyd in the center of his forehead, when someone touched him on the shoulder. Toran jerked around, coming face to face with Mac, who shook his head.

Glowering, Toran shook his head back.

Mac mouthed, "Let her be. She can handle herself."

"Bugger off."

But a second later, Boyd was laughing and Jenny was on the ground. The captain of the dragoons was climbing back onto his horse and shooing his men into the croft.

"Go," Mac whispered. "I ken what ye were about."

Toran hesitated, looking around the front of the croft at Jenny, still lying on the ground. A smart move on her part. Her hands were planted on the grass, her eyes cast down, but he could feel the hatred coming off her in waves. He had no ties to her, no reason to stay, and every reason to leave. Why did he feel guilty about turning his back now? She didn't mean more to him than his own sister and brother, who would certainly suffer more than Jenny at Boyd's hands.

Still, he wanted to knock every bastard off his feet and lift her back up to hers. To see the strong woman he knew she was—the one who'd just nearly killed him and his cousin—brought so low... It made him angrier than when he'd seen her knife at his cousin's throat.

Mac shoved him in the back. "Get the hell out of here," he muttered. "Else I push ye out front to meet your maker. And if ye so much as tell a soul about this croft, not only will ye have the rebel army to deal with but the Mackintosh clan too."

The Mackintosh clan... Was that some kind of jest? Everyone knew them to be in favor of King George's government. Toran only hesitated a fraction of a second before tucking his pistol back into place and running toward the woods as though the English had already seen him. As soon as he'd broken through the cover of trees, he jerked to a halt. He couldn't push himself to leave just yet.

Something was pulling him back. Guilt.

But what did he have to feel guilty over? Archie? Jenny? Aye, maybe them both. But what was he to do? Camdyn and Isla needed him. They'd already lost both parents to the war with the English. He couldn't risk losing them or them losing him. Remaining at the croft meant certain death not only for him or for his siblings but likely for everyone in that building as well.

Jenny couldn't have gotten this far if she didn't know how to handle the bloody English, and he had to trust that she knew perfectly well how to get out of this situation. The woman was strong, her conviction as formidable as any stone wall. He'd not deny being drawn to those qualities, to her. Wasn't that what he'd wanted for himself all along? To be able to believe firmly in one thing? The notion that he might admire something about her unnerved him all the more, especially since he wanted to hate her.

She would not waver in her beliefs. But she'd not lost her mother to the war, either. Aye, she'd lost her da, but so had most of them.

He had to get to Dùnaidh Castle. He had to make sure that Boyd had not already gotten to his family. The lives of his younger siblings could be in peril.

Rebels be damned, along with the bloody English.

He picked up his pace once more, running at a full sprint. He'd have to steal a horse, or he'd never make it home in time.

———

She wanted to close her eyes, not to watch, but to look away was tantamount to turning her back on her men. So Jenny pushed to her feet and watched the redcoats walk into the croft, prayers on her mind but not her lips. She waited a beat, counting in her head.

Silence.

"Who is your laird?" the dragoon who'd just assaulted her said from behind. She could still feel his breath on her neck, his hands gripping her body, smell the fetid stink of his mouth. Oh, how she wanted to cut those hands from his limbs.

The hair on the back of her neck prickled as she realized that he could pull a weapon and put a bullet in her skull right now if he so chose. She'd not be the first rebel to have that punishment exacted on her. She clutched her basket closer, wishing she could pull out the pistol, that she had enough shot to silence them all. When she didn't answer right away, he shoved her to the ground. She was desperately glad she'd had the forethought to keep the basket from tumbling away. Unfortunately at the expense of her chin, which smarted from colliding with the ground.

The answer to his question was easy and true and might very well gain her some favor. "Mackintosh," she said. "He's no' a Jacobite. He's loyal to King George."

The man was silent behind her, but neither did he shoot her nor assault her once more. Ironic that the name of the brother by whom she felt so betrayed would be what saved her from rape and murder.

Anger prickled just beneath her skin, begging to be let out. She dragged in a deep breath, blew it out. Again. And again. It didn't help. Jenny itched to unleash her rage on this man. She made a promise to herself that if she ever faced him on a dark road, just the two of them, she'd put a bullet in his head.

Thankfully the two dragoons who'd entered her croft came back out, arms loaded with the food she and her men had stored for the week.

"You've a lot of provisions," the man behind her said.

"I've a hearty appetite. As does my husband." She turned slowly to face the dragoon, keeping the anger shielded from her gaze.

"Where is your husband?"

"He was getting me a chicken. Then took some of our cattle out to graze, I suppose."

"Are you often left alone?" Boyd hungrily let his gaze rake over her body, causing her skin to crawl all the more.

Jenny bristled. "I can take care of myself just fine. And he's never gone long."

Hard lines etched the man's face around his eyes and mouth. He was cold, his eyes like those of a dead fish out of the loch. She knew that he wouldn't hesitate to rape her if she only gave him an excuse.

"May I ask your name?" Jenny wanted to know exactly who it was who'd assaulted her. She'd etch his name into the hilt of her sword as well and wait for the day she could claim his life in the name of every innocent he'd violated.

"I am Captain Thomas Boyd. And you are?"

This too she'd practiced. "Mary Mackintosh."

Behind him, redcoats were putting her provisions into their saddlebags.

"We thank you, Mrs. Mackintosh, for your hospitality," Captain Boyd said, his eyes glittering with malice.

Go away, she wanted to shout. *Go back to England, or suffer the end of my sword!* But she remained silent, managing a bob of her head, and bit the tip of her tongue.

"You have not happened to see two prisoners run by, have you?"

Jenny shook her head, not commenting on the fact that he'd already asked her if she'd seen them. "Nay, I assure ye, I'd not have been tending my gardening all alone if I'd known there were fugitives running around." *Ye bloody bastard.*

Captain Boyd narrowed his eyes. "But you must realize the fugitives are everywhere. Jacobites swarm the Highlands like rats."

He was trying to get a rise out of her. "Aye, we're infested, 'tis true. But no' so on Mackintosh lands. Our laird doesna tolerate it."

"Good. If you should notice anything, be certain to report it to us."

"I will, of course, Captain." She did her best to sound obliging and not like she wanted to shove her dagger in his eyeball.

"I'm certain we'll cross paths again, Mrs. Mackintosh."

"Why's that?" She couldn't help but ask, with an innocent cock of her head.

"My men like your bannocks." But the way he leered,

his eyes roving over her breasts, Jenny knew that the oat-cakes were not what he was referring to.

She pasted a smile on her lips. "I shall bake extra next time."

He raised a brow in challenge, and she feared for a moment he might demonstrate exactly what he'd meant by touching her again. Her breasts still ached from when he'd squeezed. There would be bruises.

Thankfully, he ordered his men to move out.

Dinna collapse. Dinna fall. Dinna move. Jenny remained in place until the last of their shadows had disappeared in the distance before she rushed back inside the croft. The dragoons had tossed a cot against the far wall, perhaps looking for someone underneath.

"They've gone," she said to the air.

Several loud sighs could be heard from beneath her feet. Thanks be to the heavens, for if even one of the dragoons had decided to stick his sword through the floorboards to see how far the ground beneath went, they would have all been murdered.

"We'll give it a half hour and then ye can come out," she said. And then she could take off this awful gown. In the meantime, she prepared a soup for the men when they emerged. They'd be starving, no doubt, but not her. She still felt like vomiting.

Some months back, Jenny had lain in that same hole beneath the floorboards so she would know exactly what it felt like as the floor was put in place and the rushes spread over. Very little light crept in, and every foot-step was loud, creaking on the wood, the dust from the walker's boots falling into one's eyes, and every sound echoed. If one were to sneeze, belch, or pass wind, it would be heard. That was perhaps the hardest part, holding in every bodily function when one's instinct was to let it out.

Every man was made to endure pit training when brought to the croft. She certainly hoped that Archie had been able to endure it without the practice, and Toran, she hoped he had been tormented a bit by it. This was not the first time they'd been visited by dragoons, but it was the first time they'd been so unprepared. There was only one reason for that—Toran MacGillivray or Fraser, whoever he was. He'd distracted her, else she would have sent out scouts to search the area after having found that ax mark.

Still, she wasn't so certain that the tree had been marked by dragoons. Why would they?

Blast it all, but Jenny could beat herself up with that question all day if she allowed herself the indulgence.

The scent of the cooking soup, normally pleasant, started to make her queasy, and she was glad for the need to step outside for fresh air. She paused a moment to inhale before heading to the coop to see if John had managed to snare a chicken to add to dinner. The sun overhead was shadowed by clouds rolling in, as if mirroring her mood. Jenny paused for a moment, staring up at the sky and watching as small white puffs of clouds blew with the gentle breeze. They'd come so close to being caught. Too close. She wrapped her arms around herself, letting out a ragged breath.

Not until that moment did she realize her heart was still pounding right out of her chest. How had Captain Boyd and his dragoons not heard it? How had he not felt it, with his hands on her? Or had he taken pleasure in her fear?

Away from the men, she sank to her knees, pressed her hands flat to the earth, and retched until there was nothing left in her stomach. She wiped her mouth on her sleeve and sat back on her heels. Her throat burned, head pounded. She closed her eyes briefly, dragging in clean air, before they popped back open in fear of the return of the English.

"We're safe," she whispered to no one. But she knew that whatever safety they might have at the moment, it would be fleeting.

In the coop, she found John holding a prepared chicken in one hand and his sword in the other.

"They're gone," she said and took the plucked chicken. "Thank ye."

"I hate that ye make me hide."

"I know."

"Dirk will be furious."

She rounded on him, snapping before she could stop herself. "Dirk is not in charge here, I am, and ye'll do well to remember it."

Immediately she felt contrite. Her skin still tingled with anger and pent-up nerves from her encounter with the dragoons, with Boyd. And she was glad that John had been out of sight and hadn't seen what was happening. He would have been waiting for her signal, a whistle, and she was glad he'd stayed put even when she'd screamed.

"Aye, Mistress," John said. "We all respect ye as our leader. Ye're braver than anyone I know. I just—"

"Dinna say it, John," Jenny warned. The men so often felt the need to tell her they wanted to protect her. She understood their chivalrous need but wished her sex never came into play. "We protect each other."

"Aye."

"Now let's go tell the men they can come out."

As they crossed the muddy yard, made worse by the horses' hooves, Jenny scanned the woods and road for any sign of dragoons. All was quiet. She shivered all the same. Mac appeared from around the corner of the croft, and one look from him said that while John hadn't seen, Mac had observed all. He nodded in respect and held open the door for her.

Inside the croft, the herbs and vegetables were boiling, and she dropped the cleaned, plucked chicken into the pot to cook.

With enough time having passed that it seemed safe for the men to come out of hiding, she nodded to John, who pulled back the rush floor covering.

"Ye can come out now," she said while he pulled up the floorboards, revealing the men below.

One by one they crawled out of the space, stretching the kinks from their bodies. Five. The three men who'd been in the loft, one of her other guards, and Archie MacGillivray-Fraser.

There was one person notably missing.

"Where is Toran?" she demanded of Archie.

The man hung his head for just a moment, before looking her in the eyes. "He left, Mistress."

She narrowed her eyes. "And left ye to spy like any good Fraser?"

Archie's face turned red at that, and his jaw muscle ticked. He clearly didn't like being called a traitor.

"With all due respect, Mistress, I'm no' one of *those* Frasers."

"And Toran?"

Archie straightened. "His family is in danger. He saw an opportunity to go to them and took it." She didn't miss that Archie had not answered the question.

"Who and how?" she demanded. If he was really one of her men now, then he would answer the question.

"His wee brother and sister. Their mother was…" He paused, his throat bobbing, and his eyes narrowing. "She passed. And so has their father. With our escape from prison, the dragoons will retaliate."

"They know he has a family?"

"Aye. They know a great deal about many."

"They do seem to keep a good measure on all the people in the Highlands, do they no'?"

"Toran told me once they've had pictures drawn so they might recognize rebel leaders and arrest them should they ever be found."

Jenny gritted her teeth. Did that mean they had pictures of her? Was that why Captain Boyd had so…boldly taunted her?

"Will he be returning?" Jenny had to ask, for whether Toran returned would determine his future.

"Not likely, Mistress."

"Perhaps ye'd like to go with your cousin."

"Nay, Mistress."

"I canna trust ye."

"I will endeavor to prove I'm loyal to the Jacobite cause."

Jenny frowned. The man appeared sincere, but so had Toran. "I'll allow ye to stay with us, but ye're not to be alone. Any sign that ye've betrayed us and I will put a bullet in your head myself."

Archie nodded. "Ye have my word."

The dragoons had already forced her to make the choice to abandon their safe house come nightfall, but Toran's departure solidified the need to move quickly. Dirk would want to send a search party after him, to bury Toran and all he knew before he could reach his destination. But if there truly were two young ones who needed him…she wasn't so certain she could allow that. Damn the man for confounding her.

To one of the men who'd come from the hole, she gave orders to rush to the castle, unseen, and tell Dirk that poachers had been seen in the forest—their code for needing to vacate the croft.

"Prepare the wagons. We canna stay here."

"Where will we go?" John asked.

Jenny studied each and every one of the men, thought of all those across the moors who were hiding in plain sight, eager to fight for Bonnie Prince Charlie, eager to get the bloody English off their lands.

"We're going home."

Five

CROUCHED BEHIND A TREE, TORAN WATCHED TWO dragoons who'd dismounted from their horses to take a piss. One shouted a jest over his shoulder to the other, who laughed as he gave the punch line. Something about a Scottish woman and three dragoons. Toran itched to grab for his dirk, to take aim and land the point in the center of the bastard's head. For though he told a jest, the way they both laughed at the brutality of it, Toran was certain they'd have participated.

Alas, he needed a horse.

It was now or never. Steal the horse and make away at neck-breaking speed. Or steal both horses and let one go far enough away that they couldn't catch up with him. Or kill or otherwise detain both of them, which he could easily do.

Two dead dragoons couldn't tell tales.

Decision made, he pulled his dirk from inside his sleeve and another from his boot and took aim. He tossed first to the right, the thunk and cry startling the other man. But he didn't move fast enough before Toran had sunk another one in him.

He removed his blades from the bodies, dragged them beneath some gorse bushes, and then searched their belongings for any clues as to Boyd's plans or information he could use to barter for his siblings' lives should the need arise. Sewn into the lining of one dragoon's coat was a coded message, which Toran stuffed into his sporran. Once he'd made it Dùnaidh, he would try to decipher it.

Finished with his search, Toran took both of the dragoons' horses and rode away at a clip that was only slightly slower than breakneck speed. He'd already wasted enough time on foot.

He was at least another hour's ride from his great-uncle's castle at Dùnaidh, and every second was agony until he finally spotted the turrets over the trees. But even the turrets weren't as much of a relief as seeing the gray chimney smoke that signaled someone was in residence. He'd been fearful of arriving back to a pile of rubble. It wouldn't be the first time the English had razed a house when they deemed the inhabitants to be traitors to King George. The Duke of Cumberland, youngest son of King George, had been given full authority over the king's army and allowed his dragoons to run rampant in Scotland doing as they pleased.

Was Boyd waiting for him inside? Had he left the croft and headed straight for Dùnaidh? He'd have had enough time, considering how long Toran had been on foot. Had Boyd convinced his great-uncle to turn his nephew over to the English?

At one time, Toran would have said nay, but he knew his relation better than that. The man had been double-dealing for more than thirty years.

Ballocks…

Whether Boyd was there or not, had turned his great-uncle against him or not, it didn't matter. Toran had no choice but to push forward. Camdyn and Isla were counting on him. And as soon as his chief found out that Toran had been the one responsible for the deaths of so many Frasers, to have betrayed Boyd while he was at it, he would do everything in his power to bury Toran—even if that meant using Camdyn and Isla as bait.

Toran urged the horses faster toward Dùnaidh, his uncle and Boyd be damned.

Just before he broke through the trees to ride across the heather-covered moor, he paused, searching the area for clues that the dragoons had already arrived. The grasses did not look more trampled than usual, the earth not turned into a hundred divots created by hooves.

When he was certain there were no English in sight, he slowly exited the forest, not wanting to alert the men on the wall with the rapid pace his pounding heart demanded.

Dùnaidh was not an overly large castle. The tower keep was only five stories high. It boasted seven chambers on the upper floors and a great hall above the kitchens. A wall surrounded the property, and within the wall were the stables and other outbuildings. A small village surrounded the wall, of which nothing seemed out of sorts.

As he drew closer, the guard on the wall shouted down, recognizing Toran even with the setting sun. The gates were opened, and Toran was welcomed into the bailey by men he'd known since he was a lad. He searched the faces for his uncle, but he wasn't there—and neither were Camdyn and Isla, who normally shoved their way through the throng to greet him.

"Where is his lordship?" Toran asked.

"I expect he's inside, sir."

Toran nodded. "And Camdyn? Isla?"

"Same."

Toran handed off the two horses. The men looked at the animals suspiciously. Though he'd gotten rid of the dragoons' personal effects, there was no mistaking the English saddles with King George's crest carved into the leather.

"Destroy everything but the horses. Change their shoes to be rid of the King George crest and repurpose the iron for shot."

"Aye, sir." The men were used to such requests, given his uncle's way of life. And his own.

Toran didn't waste another minute before rushing inside. The doors to the great hall were open, and voices could be heard inside, but before he reached it, a hand snaked out of the dark, wrapping firmly around his forearm.

"Toran." He whipped his head to the side, recognizing the grizzled, shadowed face of his cousin Simon. "We need to talk."

"Not now."

Simon gripped him harder. "Aye. Right now. I know what ye did. And my da knows too."

Toran felt his blood running cold. Was he too late already? But instead of reacting, he yanked his arm from his cousin's grasp. "Ye know nothing."

Simon laughed, the sound always reminding Toran of a dagger scraping against stone. "Ye're just like your mother."

Toran was swift to react, wrapping his fist in Simon's shirt and slamming him back against the wall. "Dinna speak of my mother."

Simon's lips peeled away from his teeth in an ugly smile. "Traitor," he whispered.

But to even suggest that Toran was a traitor when Simon and his own father had made a life from doing such was absolutely ridiculous. His cousin always had been one to shoot off at the mouth when he shouldn't. Which could only mean one thing—he did know something.

Toran shoved his cousin back, letting go of his shirt and raking him with a look of disgust. "Watch your back, Simon."

"Is that a threat, Cousin?"

Toran didn't bother to respond. He backed away slowly to the great hall, where he found his uncle at the head of the table, Camdyn and Isla flanking him along with several other Frasers. Slowly his uncle raised his glittering gaze, the threats Simon had issued in the corridor clear in his uncle's eyes. Toran braced for an attack, or men to rush him from the dark corners, but none came—yet that didn't mean they wouldn't.

"So, ye've returned." His uncle sounded surprised, but the satisfied grin on his face only set Toran's nerves on edge.

"Toran!" his sister called as she and their brother pushed out of their chairs. Isla bounded for him, and Camdyn walked as stoically as any adolescent on the verge of manhood might.

Toran tugged Isla into his arms, the impact of her body

making him waver. He held her tight and pressed a kiss to the top of her head. She resembled their mother so much it made him ache—auburn hair threaded with gold and eyes the color of the sea. She was taller than their mother had been by several inches, taking her height from their father.

"I see ye've suffered greatly in my absence," he teased, tugging lightly on her braided hair.

"Aye, ye were gone too long, Brother. Another week and we'd have forgotten ye existed," she taunted right back, giving him a tug of his locks in turn.

Toran grinned, proud of the backbone his sister had—another trait she'd inherited from their mother.

Camdyn stopped a couple of feet away, nodding to his brother, though Toran saw a yearning for an embrace in his eyes as well. Staring at his brother was like glancing into a looking glass, the same dark hair falling around their shoulders and eyes that were blue as an afternoon sky. With a year or two more to grow, Camdyn might end up being as tall as Toran himself, but for now he came just about up to his chin. His body was lanky, not yet filled in with a man's muscles, and his face was smooth of any of the hardness war would soon give him.

"Ye look well," Toran said.

"Ye look alive," Camdyn replied with a quirk to his lip. "We thought ye were dead."

Toran clapped his brother on the back, squeezed his shoulder, and then rubbed his hand over the lad's hair.

"Why are ye not dead?" their uncle said from across the room.

Simon slinked into the great hall then, leaning against the wall by the door, a grin of evil satisfaction on his face.

Toran faced the man who'd raised him after the death of his father. "Uncle."

"Leave us," his uncle demanded, and those at the table leapt up. "Ye too," he instructed Camdyn and Isla. "Go with Simon."

Toran offered his siblings an encouraging smile, not willing to let them know how much the escalating situation worried him. Nor did he want to let on his feelings to his uncle and cousin.

No matter how careful Toran had been, with his uncle's constant spying, the chief of clan Fraser would have figured out at least some parts of Toran's dealings. The problem was, though the old Fox had made his declarations to the Jacobites, it wouldn't have been the first time he'd done so and then swung round to the usurper's side. It always came down to whomever was willing to give him a better deal. Aye, Toran had lied when he'd agreed to join the Jacobite cause with his cousin Archie, but how was that any different than what his uncle was doing?

Revenge was a seed Toran had kept hidden in the shadows, along with his irritation at the old Fox for doing nothing about Toran's mother's death. She'd been his niece, daughter to his own sister, and married to one of the Fraser men, Toran's father. Her naked, battered body, covered in bloody gashes, swollen and bruised, hair torn from her head, had been delivered to the castle doors in a pine box carved with the name *Mistress J* and with a note pinned to her bare breast that simply read *Traitor.*

The morning of Toran's mother's death, the old chief had aligned himself once more with the Jacobites and wasn't willing to question them about her death. For it was they who had killed her, his uncle and Boyd had confirmed that. His uncle's lack of interest in avenging his niece's brutal murder felt like a stab in the back, and Toran had decided to take matters into his own hands.

When Toran kept silent, the tension in the room became palpable. By now his uncle would have heard what had happened at the prison, though not necessarily which side Toran had been on. Clearly he'd presumed Toran dead as well, along with the others.

The Fox drummed his fingers on the table, gaze boring into Toran. But he didn't squirm. Instead, he sauntered toward the table and sat down casually at the other end. He'd subsisted on dried meat and bannocks for days, and the scent of the stew made his mouth water. But the first bite tasted bitter as he remembered those he'd left behind and the threat of his presence here became more than clear.

"Do ye know what a traitor's death is?" the Fox asked, swirling his spoon slowly in his stew.

Mo chreach, so this was how it was going to be. How easily his uncle had given him up. "I dinna know a man who doesna." Tied around the ankles, a traitor would be dragged to the hangman's noose by a horse, where he'd be hanged until he was only mostly dead. Then cut down, still gasping, body filled with pain, he'd have his twig and berries chopped off and his guts pulled from his body to be burned before his still-breathing body. Only then would he have his head chopped off and his body quartered. For certes, it was not a good way to go.

"So ye understand, then, what ye're risking. That it is not just your life in danger."

Isla and Camdyn. Toran's heart kicked against his ribs. "When will Boyd be here?" He was done playing this game. He'd not let the man intimidate him. It was clear from Simon's warning and from his uncle's cryptic talk that he planned to give Toran over.

"Soon."

Toran slowly stood, keeping his face a mask of disinterest. The Fox stared up at him but didn't move or signal anyone to apprehend him.

"I believe we've overstayed our welcome," Toran said.

"We?" his uncle challenged.

"Aye. I'm taking Isla and Camdyn to the MacGillivrays. We've not visited with my mother's clan for some time." That was of course a lie, but he wasn't about to give his uncle any further information.

Toran expected the man to argue, to demand more information. But he only nodded slowly, eyes studying him with the practiced ease of a man used to lies. His silence was more terrifying than if he'd ranted. Fortunately for Toran, he'd been thwarting that gaze for more than two decades.

"Simon will go with ye."

Toran ground his teeth. "Nay."

"He'll go with ye or ye'll not go at all."

It was a trap. A guard and spy for his uncle. So though

he was going to let Toran out of here, to let him live a little longer, he wasn't letting him go completely.

Sly bastard.

He was lucky that Boyd had not yet come for him. It would only be a matter of time, which meant he had to leave as soon as possible, and with his siblings. They would be punished in his place if he were to go. He knew how Boyd worked. The man was an evil bastard. He also knew very well how cold his great-uncle's heart was, and Simon wasn't any better. His cousin would twist a dagger in Toran's chest the first chance he got.

Toran would not go down without a fight, and neither would his siblings. Though he was young, Camdyn was skilled with a sword. Hell, Isla could gut a man if given the chance.

Toran grinned, though it wasn't truly a smile. "Fine."

And where the hell was he even going to go? A flash in his mind of beautiful and angry emerald eyes nearly stopped his heart. *Jenny*. The way she'd blasted him with that heated look when she'd believed him to have betrayed her. He didn't blame her—she'd been right. That was clearly not an option.

Then again she might be the perfect option. Archie had sworn he'd keep Camdyn and Isla safe and at the very least would offer to take them in. And Simon might prove to be useful. As the son of the Fox and newly on the side of the rebels, he'd be the perfect peace offering for Jenny, at least on the outside, in order to gain her trust. There was always the chance that she would see Simon as a potential threat, and in that case, he'd be imprisoned, and Toran could brush his hands of his wretched cousin.

Despite what had happened, Toran still had a personal mission to figure out who was responsible for his mother's death. The loss of her left a gaping wound in his chest that would continue to bleed until he got to the bottom of it. He needed to make one last attempt to infiltrate the rebels. He'd offer his apologies, even accept her tossing him into her version of a prison, if he had to prove to her that he was true.

If there was one thing Toran had learned over the years, it was how to play each side just right.

———

Jenny's muscles screamed from exertion, midnight long since come and gone.

They'd managed to move all of their stores from the compromised croft and grounds to Cnàmhan Broch and done so without encountering any redcoats, which might have been more effort than the actual manual labor.

They'd had to do it one wagonload at a time and with satchels packed to the brim strapped to their backs. They'd sent a few things on horseback but with only a limited number of riders so as not to draw attention. Every step had been an effort, but Jenny had borne it without complaint, taking fully loaded sacks just like any of her men.

She'd made it a point since she'd first begun never to let herself falter in any task simply because she was a woman. Aye, there were some things she physically couldn't do, such as take two satchels at a time like Dirk, but she damned well wasn't going to go empty-handed. Her men respected her all the more for the efforts she put into pulling her own weight ten times over.

Sneaking the items into the castle had been something else she'd worried over. Despite their use of the hidden tunnels, they'd still had to do a lot of carrying through the castle stairs and corridors. The few men who still supported her brother couldn't be made aware of their presence. In fact, it had been Mac's job to find them, ply them with whisky laced with a sleeping agent, and put them to bed so they'd be none the wiser. But secondly, where could they hide the coins and weapons so that Hamish wouldn't happen across them if he made a surprise visit?

At first, she'd thought of the dungeon, but while she didn't plan to have to toss anyone into its dark depths, she didn't want to cut it off from use completely should they have need to confine someone.

Someone like *Toran*. She had a vision of him standing in the croft, arms crossed and the muscles of his corded shoulders and biceps stretching the fabric of his shirt, his ice-blue eyes watching her every move. Blast it all, but he was a handsome, dangerous devil—and it still rankled her something fierce that he'd been able to trick her. If she ever got her hands on him… Nay, *when* she got her hands on him, she was going to make him pay.

Was Toran going to be that one problem she envisioned?

At least with Hamish off kissing *Sassenach* arse they were safe for now. As long as he stayed away. She could never really be too sure about his movements since he rarely wrote home, save for when he was demanding supplies for his men. It had been two years since she'd last seen him, luckily, but the threat of his return was always hanging over her head.

They'd decided on the chamber in the highest part of the tower in case the tunnels were breached by the enemy, one that had been used as storage for old gowns, weapons, supplies, pieces of furniture. A place to keep things no one wanted and subsequently a place where no one went.

With the last of her satchels stored behind the slats of an ancient bed upstairs, Jenny collapsed into an old oak chair in the great hall, the same chair her grandfather used to sit in and hold her on his knee as he regaled her with stories of the first Jacobite uprising, when he'd been a young man.

"Ye shouldna have sneaked off like ye did," Dirk said.

Jenny blinked at her cousin, so exhausted she'd not even noticed he'd entered. She was too tired to even roll her eyes at him.

"What are ye talking about?"

"This morning. Mac told me what happened. Are ye all right?"

Jenny tapped nervously on the arm of the chair. She'd hoped that he'd not have found out about Captain Boyd, but there was nothing for it now. "I'm fine. Besides, I'm glad I went out there, or our men and our hidden stores would have been depleted."

Dirk grunted. "Ye know what I'm going to say."

"Aye, and I'll tell ye again that the cause is worth more than my life."

"A point we will always disagree on."

Jenny leaned forward and held out a folded piece of paper. "I need ye to get this to Fiona."

Their dearest friend Fiona's role in the rebellion was as a courier, delivering secret messages and packages between the clans. No one would ever suspect a lass of such a task, and so far she'd been able to get away with it. Of the three of them, Jenny often thought, Fiona's choice of position was the most dangerous.

"She'll pass on the message that we've…moved."

Dirk took the piece of paper. "What does Lady Mackintosh say about all this?"

Jenny glanced up toward the rafters, imagining what her mother might be up to at that moment. "She's asleep. Has no' come down. But given she was devastated when Hamish left us, I dinna think she will object."

Dirk raised a brow. "About which part?"

Jenny bristled at the implied threat of exposure to her mother of her position within the Jacobite army. "Leave off it, Cousin."

"She will worry."

"As would any mother, but what I'm doing is the right thing. The prince needs all the support he can get so future mothers dinna have to worry over their daughters."

"I did no' say otherwise."

"Ye implied."

Dirk held up his hands in resignation, the folded

missive pressed to his palm by his thumb. "I imply nothing other than my admiration for ye."

"Och, I dinna have time for your games, Dirk." Jenny pushed out of her chair, prepared to stalk away from him, irritated more so than usual by her exhaustion.

He stopped her, his voice softening. "Answer me one more thing before I'm on my way."

She waved her hand in permission, too tired to speak.

"We rounded up two new recruits the other day, but alas, there seems only to be one left."

Jenny regarded Dirk, waiting for him to say more. When he didn't, she found the energy to reply, "Is there a question in your comment?" She knew exactly what he was after, but at least she didn't have to answer right away.

Dirk crossed his arms over his chest. "Where is he? Will he be a problem?"

Jenny stiffened, narrowing her gaze on her cousin. She loved the man dearly, but he was in a combative mood, and she needed to stand her ground. "I questioned Archie. He says Toran went to their uncle's holding to get his siblings. That they'd be in danger after what happened at the garrison. The man is not safe on either side. He'll not bring us trouble, especially when he could have already. Besides, he left his cousin with us, and we have to trust that after saving him from the garrison, he'd not want to bring harm to Archie."

"What do ye mean 'could have already'?"

"When the dragoons were at our door, he didna call them in."

"He was a fugitive."

"We knew that."

"So ye trust him."

Jenny rolled her eyes. "I didna say that."

"What makes ye think we can trust Archie?"

"I didna say that either, but so far he's given no cause not to trust him."

"Other than being the relation of a blasted liar."

Jenny sighed. "The fact that he stayed when he could have run."

"As a spy. The Frasers are all spies."

"He's got a guard on him at all times, Dirk. I'm not going to toss him out and risk him running to the other side. He already knows too much. Instead of labeling him an enemy, why not embrace him into the fold? He may end up being one of our best soldiers."

Dirk's frown gave away everything he wasn't saying. "When did Toran run? Before or after the captain touched ye?"

Jenny's face heated with both anger and embarrassment from the memory. "Ye're a prig, Dirk."

Dirk's arms fell to his sides, and his shoulders slumped. "I'm sorry, lass. I shouldna have brought it up. I'm just… There's no excuse for it." He took two wide steps, closing the distance between them, and pulled her into his arms.

She was stiff at first, angry and hurt, but then softened. She couldn't stay angry at Dirk for long, even if he did let his mouth fly more often than he should.

"Forgive me," he said, his voice full of emotion. "I just wish I could have been there to protect ye. I am angrier with myself than anyone else."

"Ye'd have gotten yourself killed, and then I'd never forgive ye. But for your angry words, aye, all is pardoned." Jenny pulled away from Dirk, patted his chest. "I dinna know what I'd do without ye, Cousin. But for now, let us keep our eyes and ears peeled for Toran—though I dinna expect to see him ever again. We've no way of knowing if he made it to his uncle. In the meantime, we'll pray for the Green Lady of Cnàmhan Broch to protect our treasures."

All their precious supplies were waiting, piled almost in plain sight, high in the tower. Jenny prayed that the stories of the Green Lady's ghost would help her keep the room as deserted as it should be. But more than that—a dozen of her recruits had been smuggled in as well, now dressed in local fashions and hiding in plain sight. When her brother's men, who'd been drugged to keep them from finding out what they were up to, woke tomorrow, she feared the questions they'd be asking.

———

Wisps of silver clouds danced across the beams of moonlight overhead.

"It's an abandoned croft," Simon said accusingly. "What the bloody hell are we doing here?"

Toran narrowed his eyes. Indeed the croft did appear to be abandoned. But that didn't mean it was. It could also mean that Jenny and her men had signaled one another of their approach.

Without answering Simon, Toran dismounted from his horse and told Isla and Camdyn to stay put.

Cautiously, he approached the dark and quiet croft, keeping his footsteps light. His sword weighed heavy at his side, but he didn't pull it out for fear whoever was watching might take that as a sign of attack, which this wasn't.

Recalling the signal Jenny and Dirk had used, the bird of prey, he pursed his lips and made the same call.

But there was no answer. Reaching the croft door, he pressed his fingers to the wood and pushed. The hinges were silent as the door creaked open to reveal that the croft was indeed empty—even the furniture was gone.

What the devil... Toran ran a hand through his hair. This was the right croft. He'd have known it anywhere.

But the rebels had clearly abandoned it after Boyd's visit. This did not bode well for him. How was he going to find them?

The slightest whisper of a running figure caught Toran's attention, and he whirled around, half expecting to find Simon charging him, but his three companions still sat on their horses. Behind them, however, he caught sight of a darting figure.

"Ho, there! Stop!" Toran called, racing after the rascal in hopes they'd be able to give him answers.

Whoever it was sprinted toward the woods, their speed increasing with every step, but Toran too could run like the devil. The kilt-wearing devil was a man, or at least appeared to be one, from the back. Tall and lithe, his hair covered by a cap, and a sword whacking against his thigh as he ran.

Toran caught up to the fugitive, tackling them to the ground, with both of them grunting at the impact.

"I'm not going to hurt ye," Toran growled. Slowly letting up his weight on the fellow, he rolled him over, recognizing him instantly. "Mac."

"I told ye not to come back." Mac shoved away from Toran.

"And yet here I am."

"Go back to where ye came from."

"That is impossible. Besides, I only left to bring more recruits back." He nodded toward his family.

Mac studied the three of them with narrowed eyes. "How do I know 'tis not a trap?"

"Come see for yourself. If it'll make ye feel better, ye can hold a blade against me."

Mac grunted and pushed himself up. "Maybe I will."

Toran walked in front of Mac to make the man feel a little more at ease, though he was surprised to find that Mac didn't take him up on the offer to hold a blade against him.

At the horses, Mac glanced up and demanded, "Who are ye?"

"Simon Fraser."

"Isla Fraser."

"Camdyn Fraser."

Mac groaned. "Ye brought me a bunch of bloody Frasers?"

"Frasers'll—" Toran cut off whatever threat Simon was about to spit out.

"My cousin, Simon, is son of the Fraser chief. Mistress J could use someone like that on her side. And these two are my brother and sister. Young, impressionable, and with a great interest in seeing their country restored for future generations."

Mac hesitated, his body still tense. "I'm not the one to make the call. I'll bring ye to Mistress J and let her decide whether to toss your arse into the dungeon. Pardon my language, Miss," he said with a doff of his cap in Isla's direction.

Toran nodded. "Good. I think she'll see reason."

"I doubt it. Ye forget I know what happened inside the croft. I'm hoping she puts your arse in the dungeon."

"If she wishes to see me rot, I will do her bidding if only to prove my loyalty."

"Brother," Isla said with a gasp, but one stern look from Toran had her quieting.

"If it pleases ye, Mac, take us to Mistress J. We beg an audience." Then, gaze locked on Simon, he said, "Dinna make me regret taking ye along."

"Ye didna have a choice," Simon scoffed.

"There is always a choice."

"Quit your griping else I change my mind. And ye'll have to wear these over your head." Mac pulled several sackcloths from inside his saddlebag. "Dinna need ye running off to tell where we've gone. And trust me, in this, ye have no choice."

Six

EVERY CRACK OF THUNDER OUTSIDE THE CASTLE HAD Jenny wincing. Less than a day after the massive move, a letter arrived from Hamish that he was sending a contingent of his men home to gather fresh supplies and horses.

She should be grateful that he wasn't coming himself and that with the advance warning she could get the supplies ready and send his men on their way as quickly as possible—along with three from home whom she knew to be his staunch supporters. They'd woken up with wicked hangovers from the sleeping draught she'd had slipped into their drinks, and Dirk and several other men had pretended to wake up the same way, so as to put them off from thinking they'd been singled out. Not one of them seemed to notice the new people in attendance, which was perfect.

Jenny was trying to look at Hamish's demands as a blessing in disguise, since they gave her an excuse to send away the men who made her nervous. The problem was that every extra pair of hose, every bullet, every ration of grain that she piled into the waiting wagons felt like a betrayal to her cause.

There was no choice. If she refused to send her brother what he requested, then he would suspect her of treason and tear the castle apart looking for evidence. Risking their entire mission and the safety of her men was not worth the price it cost to her heart to load up the wagons. So she'd make certain they worked hard to whittle down the list of her brother's demands.

The place at the head of the table reserved for the laird sat empty, though she longed to symbolically take it for herself. Jenny sat to the right of her brother's seat and across—for the first time in months—from her mother.

Lady Mackintosh had not come down to eat with the clan in so long that Jenny couldn't clearly remember the last time. This time, her graying chestnut hair was swept up into a knot atop her head, with curling tendrils framing her face. She wore a plain gown but a gown nonetheless, a whale-boned bodice and full skirts over panniers. Though dark circles still graced the undersides of her green eyes, her skin was no longer sallow but held a note of life. She sipped delicately from her spoon and then tore off a hunk of bread to dip into the bowl of cold pea soup.

"Mama," Jenny started, hoping she wasn't asking too much of her mother too soon. "Do ye want to walk in the garden after we sup?"

Lady Mackintosh set down her spoon and glanced up at her. "Aye, that would be—"

A loud knock silenced her mother, and every head in the great hall swiveled in the direction of the archway that led to the front doors.

Her brother's men must have come early.

"Show them in," Jenny ordered the guards who stood sentry. They nodded, leaving the great hall along with her appetite.

Jenny set down her spoon and smiled tightly at her

mother. "Hamish's men will be on their way shortly, Mama. Go ahead and finish your meal."

Jenny stood from the table, prepared to meet the men in the entry hall and offer them sustenance before showing them their wagons. Ideally they'd be willing to turn and leave right away, but they'd likely prefer at least a night of rest. But as she drew closer to the archway, the voices she heard did not sound like those of men, but rather…a lass. A lad. And…nay. It couldn't be!

What the devil?

Jenny quickened her pace, concern and fear ripping into her chest. Her footsteps drew to a halt in the dimly lit entryway when she saw exactly who'd come through her door with Mac at his side. Toran MacGillivray Fraser.

Standing behind him was another stranger flanked by two adolescents. But she had no interest in those. Staring at Toran, she felt like she'd been punched in the gut. The last time they'd spoken, they'd been threatening to kill each other, and then he'd disappeared.

A day's worth of growth peppered his cheeks, giving him that rough look she found both intimidating and intriguing. The corner of his mouth twitched as though he wanted to smile but couldn't allow himself to do so. And his eyes…oh, the danger in those eyes as they swept over her. His look sent unwanted chills of excitement racing over her skin. This was wrong. Very wrong.

Jenny allowed herself half a moment more to study him before shifting her gaze to the individuals he'd brought inside her keep and Mac.

At Toran's side were a lad who appeared to be his

spitting image and a lass who looked very familiar but whom she was certain she'd never met.

Her gaze was drawn back to Toran's. Blast it all, but his damned blue eyes made her melt and rallied her ire at the same time.

"Mac, what is he doing here?" The harsh words snapped out of Jenny's mouth despite the fact that she was actually pleased to see he was still alive, if only because she wanted to be the one to kill him.

After her conversation with Dirk, the memory of those ice-blue eyes and the fear that he'd come back and bring with him a horde of dragoons had stolen away her sleep the past few nights.

Seeing him now, her palms slickened enough she wanted to slap herself into sanity.

"He's brought us Simon Fraser, Mistress."

"Ye're in the Mackintosh castle," Toran interrupted Mac's explanation with a cock of his head, but before she could retort and admonish her guard for having brought the enemy into their midst, he continued, "'Tis good to see ye too…my lady." The last bit was drawled in his scratchy brogue, as though he weren't certain how to address her.

Och, but why did he have to do that? She was grateful for his caution and irritated all the same.

"What are ye doing here, Fraser?" she asked again. "And who are the ragamuffins ye've brought with ye?"

The lass pouted in turn, and the lad puffed his chest. His frown mirrored Toran's, causing Jenny a flicker of guilt. The man beside them all who looked a wee bit out of place scowled at her. She instantly didn't like him. He struck her as one of those fellows who saw himself worlds higher than anyone else.

"Did ye think I'd deserted ye, the cause?"

She narrowed her gaze. "I believe verra much ye would and that ye did."

His jaw tightened. She crossed her arms protectively over her chest. He was going to have to do a whole hell of a lot better than that.

"This is my brother Camdyn and my sister Isla." He nodded toward the man. "My cousin Simon."

She studied the two young ones again, seeing now what she'd idly noted before and making sense of it. Though their clothes were dusty from travel, the fabric was of high quality. Camdyn wore trews and a frock coat and Isla a simple arisaid. Their leather shoes appeared sturdy and well made. Simon also wore clothes of good quality, but it was evident he didn't care so much for his appearance, somehow coming off as bedraggled in his expensive boots.

Toran's gaze roved over her, his brow rising, and she realized then she was dressed in a proper gown. He'd yet to see her in anything other than her trews and jacket. This was not her favorite gown, but she knew it flattered her figure. Made of soft green dyed wool, the whale-boned bodice accentuated her curves and pushed her breasts up, the fleshy parts thankfully hidden by a soft woven shawl made by a Mackintosh weaver.

When he didn't say anything further, Jenny dismissed the two men hovering protectively behind her. To Mac, she narrowed her gaze. "Go and get Dirk."

With her guards out of sight, Toran's shoulders seemed to ease some. "As I said, I'd not desert ye, Mistress." He whispered the title. "And I've brought ye three new recruits."

"I dinna recruit children. Nor sons of traitors."

Simon stepped forward, offense written all over his face. "My father is not a traitor. He has allied with the Jacobites, and has offered funding for your outfit." He pulled a bag of coin from inside his sporran and handed it to her.

Jenny didn't take it. "A bribe?"

Simon frowned harder. "Beggars canna be choosers."

Jenny scoffed. "I'm not a beggar, and I'd be just as happy if the lot of ye went back where ye came from."

Simon stiffened, and she reached for her hip, taking note that her sword was missing.

It was Toran who stepped between them in an attempt to defuse the situation. She crossed her arms over her chest and glared at him.

"Listen, I know ye wish to never see me again, especially not with more relations." He sighed, eyes sincere as he locked his gaze on hers and said with all seriousness, "My brother and sister need protection, and my cousin, he is not only their protector but a staunch Jacobite who wishes to serve ye."

Simon started to bluster, but Toran tapped him rather aggressively on his chest to get him to quiet.

She straightened, hugging herself tighter at the chest. "And ye brought them to me? Why?" She was unable to keep the surprise from her voice. "With a bag of coin like that Simon could start his own regiment."

Toran seemed unfazed by her disbelief. "Aye. He could, but he's a Fraser and son of the Fox."

She narrowed her eyes. "And ye think because ye tricked me before I'll fall for it again?"

"Nay. I dinna. But we've a mutual enemy—Captain Boyd. Isla and Camdyn are innocent in all this. Boyd willna hesitate to punish them to get to me. He is hunting me. He will hunt them too. Ye know it, lass," he said softly. The tone of his voice had her doubling back to his gaze, searching.

That was enough of an explanation. Bile rose in Jenny's throat as she recalled Boyd's breath on her neck, his hands roving over her body, and her eyes shifted to Isla. Had Toran seen Boyd's assault? Boyd would go after Camdyn and Isla without batting a lash. And the things he would do she didn't dare imagine.

"And"—he glanced back at his cousin—"where they go, Simon goes."

"And what of ye?" she asked.

"I can take care of myself."

"I'm not a caregiver of bairns, Toran, nor their governess."

This made the trio behind Toran glower all the more. And they had every right. The lad looked ready to burst into manhood, and the lass was only a few years away from lads clamoring for her hand. She was gorgeous, with hair the color of autumn leaves and eyes the same shade as her brother's, only lighter. She looked so damn familiar. And Simon…well, she could use the coin.

All the same, who the hell did Toran think he was

dealing with? She was a leader of a rebel army and a soldier in her own right! She was raising an army to defeat the English. She couldn't be in charge of his siblings while he—

"I won't leave them—unless ye make me."

Make him… She should. But the way he implored her with his eyes. Perhaps she was a fool, but for the first time since they'd met, she actually sensed a sincerity in him she'd not taken notice of before.

"What's this?" The words were harshly spoken, coming from behind her by Dirk. "Fraser," he fairly growled.

"Mackintosh."

Dirk had questions, she could read it on his face, but he kept silent, thankfully deferring to her for the moment.

"Would ye take the children and their guard to get something to eat, please?" She added the *please* in order to soften the request.

Dirk frowned harder but nodded to the two wee Frasers and Simon. They in turn glanced at their brother to gain his permission before going off with Dirk.

"Simon?" She held out her hand, and he placed the bag of coin on her palm, the weight of it staggering.

Dirk passed her a questioning look, but she nodded for him to go. There would be time later to explain to him her motives.

As soon as she and Toran were alone, Jenny's heart sped up, pounding so hard inside her body she was certain to crack a rib. The grand foyer felt suddenly smaller, the walls closing in around her and making it hard to breathe.

"If ye run again, I'll have my men hunt ye down, and I'll put the bullet in your chest myself. And they…" She glanced toward the corridor where his family had disappeared, hating that she had to make threats against children. "They will suffer."

"I dinna doubt ye, Mistress J."

"Good."

———

Toran watched the swish of her skirts as Jenny whirled, giving him her back on her way to what he presumed was the great hall. Her hips swayed gently as she walked, not in a way that some women intentionally moved to be seductive, but it seduced him nonetheless. He found himself watching, mesmerized. And then her head snapped around, emerald eyes flashing at him, as if she'd known exactly what he was doing.

"Are ye coming?" The command in her voice was full of confidence. The woman was used to giving orders, and he didn't doubt that any man put in a position to follow would do just that.

"Aye." He picked up his pace, still a little shocked that she'd allowed him entry, when a large part of himself had been certain she'd put him in the stocks.

She was more beautiful than he remembered. And not because she was now in a dress that accentuated the strength of her figure, showing off her shoulders, the long column of her neck. Truth be told, he wouldn't mind if she continued to dress in trews. Hell, in those he could see the roundness of her bottom, the muscled outline of her thighs. He'd die of joy right now if she came to him naked and covered in mud. It didn't matter. Seeing Jenny Mackintosh had been like a punch to the gut because he hadn't realized how much he'd *wanted* to see her. Damn if his body wasn't telling him just how much. He shifted as he walked, trying to hide the evidence.

Apparently, while he'd been asleep, his mind had determined that Jenny was… Toran shook his head. He didn't want to think about whatever it was his damned brain had decided she meant to him.

She was a rebel leader. And every time he looked at her, he pictured his mother begging for her life. Whether or not it was Jenny who was at fault, his mother had died, and somehow the rebels had been involved. He couldn't trust her.

And yet when her pistol had been pointed at him— more than once—she'd not taken the shot. When she had the chance to toss him out the croft door at Boyd's feet—she hadn't. When she could have left him and Archie on the side of the road—she'd taken him up on her horse and tended Archie's injuries instead.

He could still recall the heat of her body beneath his, the coiled anger that he wanted to tap. Mistress J was beautiful, sensual, and, he needed to remember, deadly.

"Sit." She pointed at a seat beside the head of the table and then took the chair at the head herself.

Simon, Camdyn, and Isla had found a place between Dirk and an older woman with similar features to Jenny. Her mother, perhaps. A fresh pang hit him in the chest.

If only he'd known that his mother had snuck off to side with the Jacobites. If only he could have somehow stopped her.

"Toran, this is my mother, Lady Mackintosh."

The lady reached across the table with her hand, and Toran stood to take it, pressing a light kiss to her knuckles. "A pleasure, my lady."

"Welcome to Cnàmhan Broch. We dinna get many visitors, especially handsome ones." The older woman winked, and a glance at Jenny showed the younger woman's horror at the exchange.

"And I dinna often have the pleasure of dining with beautiful women." He winked back at Lady Mackintosh and ignored the snort of disgust from Dirk. Beside him, he could sense rather than see Jenny's spine stiffening.

"Thank ye ever so much for letting us stay with ye," his sister said to Jenny.

Jenny pressed her lips together, and he prayed she wouldn't shoot his sister down with that viper tongue of hers.

"Ye're verra welcome," Jenny managed.

Toran nodded his thanks to her. Bowls of soup were placed before them along with hunks of bread.

"The pea soup is cold," Jenny said. "The way we like it in summer."

"Looks delicious," Toran said.

"'Tis."

A large hound with graying black fur and floppy ears bounded into the room then, as if he'd only just noticed they had newcomers. He stopped behind Toran, hackles raised as he growled.

"Dom," Jenny snapped, making a slashing movement with her hand.

The dog immediately stopped growling and sat less than two feet behind Toran, staring at him with large black eyes.

Jenny went back to her soup as the hound stood guard. Across the table, Isla and Camdyn grinned, while Dirk smirked and Simon had his eyes on Toran with a look that said he'd like to gut him. Nothing new there.

The meal concluded shortly after, with the hound still at Toran's back, and when he tried to rise from the table, the dog let out a low growl. Evidently Dom was going to be keeping a close eye on him.

"My lady?" Toran asked with a raised brow, though he knew he could take the dog in hand with a few bits of meat.

Jenny rolled her eyes. "Dom, come." She patted her hip as she walked toward the hearth where several chairs were grouped around a small round table topped with a chessboard. "Do ye play?" she asked Toran, indicating the board.

He did in fact play, but he'd only ever done so with none other than his uncle, the Fox, and it had been some time. "I've had the occasion."

"Would ye play me now?"

Good God, would he ever… But he knew she was speaking of the game, not her body. Thrusting carnal thoughts from his mind, Toran nodded, not trusting that his voice wouldn't rumble low with desire.

Toran held out her chair, and she took a seat,

smoothing her skirts beneath her bottom. He scooted her closer to the table before taking the seat opposite her.

"I'll allow ye to go first as my guest." She swept her hand over the board game.

"But I must insist that a lady go first."

She raised her brow in challenge. "So ye think me a lady?"

He grinned. "At least ye play one well."

A soft laugh escaped her. "Ye will not be able to win me over by making me laugh."

"I am not here to win ye over, my lady." Those simple words reminded him exactly of why he was here. This was no flirtation at a country dance; this was a deadly game.

Around them Highlanders took up places as though they had an evening routine. He couldn't help but wonder if it was all for show, or was this natural? Dirk took up a spot against the wall near the hearth, a dagger in his hand and a partly whittled piece of wood in the other. Other men took up games of cards or bones, and Lady Mackintosh claimed a seat near Dirk, arranging herself with an embroidery frame. Simon stood on the opposite end of the hearth, eyes on Toran, a silent reminder that he was there to spy for his father.

Camdyn pulled a stool closer to the game for his sister and stood sentry behind her, just as the strange old hound now stood sentry behind Toran.

"If ye will not accept the offer, sir, then we are obliged to flip a coin for it."

From her sleeve, she withdrew a silver coin, one he'd never seen before. Face up in the palm of her hand, it showed the royal arms of Scotland. She carefully turned it over, showing the profile of a young Prince Charles Stuart. This was one of the infamous Jacobite coins. Currency that could get one killed. Just for having it here in her hand, she could be hanged. Even his uncle who'd sworn allegiance once more to the Jacobite cause did not have the notorious coins on hand.

"Pick a side. The crown or the prince?" she said.

Was this a test? Why did everything she said feel that way? If he chose the crown, would she think he was siding with the English? If he chose the prince, then he was declaring himself a Jacobite in mixed company. There would be no easy excuse for it later.

So be it.

"The prince."

She grinned, obviously pleased with his choice. He must have passed her test. Jenny tossed the coin into the air and caught it again, pressing it down onto the back of her hand. When she pulled away, revealing the crown, he conceded. "Ladies first."

Jenny's face went blank as she studied the board, and then she moved her right pawn forward two spaces, freeing her rook for movement.

Toran mimicked her move on the opposite side of the board.

She moved her pawn, third from the right. And he did the same.

After the third time he'd copied her movements, she blew out a huff and glanced up at him. "Ye propose to win by moving the same way I do?"

"Does not any good soldier follow his leader?"

One delicately arched brow lifted as she studied him. "Is that what ye are? My soldier?"

"Does everyone always do what ye tell them?" he asked, genuinely interested in her answer.

"What kind of a question is that?"

Why my mother? "An honest one."

"The duty of a soldier is to obey orders."

He knew it wasn't a confession, and yet it felt that way all the same. Toran moved his knight into position. "Check."

Jenny countered by taking his knight with her queen. "Ye see, in any game, whether on the board or on the field, a woman can take down a knight in protection of her king."

"At the sacrifice of all those pawns in the way." He took out one of her pawns with his bishop.

"We all make sacrifices." She took his bishop.

"Some more than others."

"All give some, Toran. That is what we are made for. Whether it is the knight on the field or the grieving widow at home." She took one of his pawns, and he parried by taking her knight.

"Or the grieving parentless children. Ye're good at this."

"I've had a lot of practice." She kept her eyes on his, giving away nothing. "I will not give up."

"Neither will I. Check."

They grew quiet then, as she moved out of his way and he continued to chase her around the board, each of them losing piece by piece. Those around them had stopped what they were doing in order to watch, gasps coming from one or another watcher when either of them made a check. Finally, Jenny had him cornered.

She was a damned good player, he'd give her that, for he'd been trained by the best. Which meant this wee chit across from him could best the Fox. Sitting beside him were two orphans, the woman responsible had him in check, and he still didn't have the answers he sought.

"Ye're in check. Do ye surrender?" she asked.

Toran sat back in his chair, eyeing her across from him. The light from the candelabras and the fire reflected in her emerald eyes. There was a triumphant gleam to them and a flush on her cheeks. Her lips curved slightly, not quite a smile, and her breaths were coming only slightly faster than before. Was this what she'd look like if he kissed her? Bloody hell, he was more likely to put his blade to her throat than kiss her.

"I've no other choice," he mused aloud.

Her smile hitched a little higher. "Everyone has a choice. Ye could flip the table and toss all the pieces into the hearth, or ye could try one last time to best me."

"I'm not an irrational man."

"Good to know."

"I surrender to ye, my lady." *But only in this game.*

Those around them clapped, and someone called out, "Good game."

"A rematch?" she asked.

"Perhaps another time."

"I'll accept that." She picked up her coin from the

table and slipped it back into her sleeve. "Perhaps next time ye'll win, and this coin will be yours."

"I didna realize we were wagering." He went to open his sporran to pull out a coin.

"There is always a wager on a game, sir. But I dinna want your coin."

"What, then?"

"Your surrender was all I asked for, and ye have already given it."

The woman was sly, he'd give her that.

"I believe I surrendered to ye the night we first met."

Her eyes widened, and he realized he probably should not have said that aloud in such a public space, but in the heat of their exchange, he'd felt as though they were quite alone. Were all in the hall privy to her nighttime dealings, or had he given her secret life away?

"When was that?" her mother asked, clearly not privy at all.

The flush in Jenny's cheeks grew paler, but she spoke with ease. "At one of the festivals we attended with Da a few years ago."

"Ah," her mother sighed, and he could sense the sadness there. She'd lost her husband to this rebellion too.

Toran pushed back from his chair and stood, holding out his hand to Jenny. "My lady, if I may beg your hospitality for sleeping quarters for the four of us."

"Of course." She placed her hand in his—small and delicately boned and yet the palms were callused. She was not a recluse who sat in her tower all day gazing at the world working around her. But he didn't have to touch her hands to know that already. "Isla may have a chamber above stairs, and ye men can sleep with the men in the barracks." She glanced behind her at Dirk. "Will ye show them?"

"Aye," Dirk grunted as he pushed off the wall, the tip of his dagger conveniently pointed at Toran as his gaze fell to where their hands clasped.

Jenny jerked away, her face coloring once more.

"Isla, if ye will, I'll show ye upstairs. Mama, would ye care to join us? We'll have a cup of tea before we retire."

Toran hesitated in following Dirk. When Jenny sensed his stillness, she turned to him, seemingly reading his mind.

"Your sister will be fine," Jenny said. "Trust me."

Two simple words that carried with them a heavier weight than she could know.

Isla hugged him tight, smiling up at him. "I'll be fine, Brother. Jenny is kind."

Kind he wasn't certain of; however, he did know that the lass had heart. And he supposed for now that was good enough. Toran nodded to Jenny and patted Isla on the back.

"Be good," he murmured.

Isla rolled her eyes. "When have I ever misbehaved?"

Jenny's eyes crinkled with laughter at that, a private moment shared between the two of them that mystified him.

"Fraser," Dirk growled, yanking his attention back.

"Ye'd best go afore he bites," Jenny cautioned, and she wasn't talking about Dom.

Toran moved slowly toward Dirk, Simon, and Camdyn, watching the ladies as they exited through a small doorway to the right.

Out of earshot of Jenny, Dirk clapped a hand hard on Toran's back. "One wrong move from ye, and I'll run ye through myself."

Toran didn't doubt the man meant every word. "I gather one wrong move is not all it'll take."

Dirk grunted.

"What say ye we have a little friendly sparring match?" Toran offered, needing the distraction from thinking about Jenny undressing and climbing into a big bed all alone.

Dirk grinned and clapped him on the back again. "Kicking your arse would be a great pleasure."

Toran grinned in return. "Likewise."

Seven

"How old are ye, Isla?" Jenny settled into a chair in her mother's solar with a cup of warm tea clasped between her hands.

Her mother sat to her left and Isla to her right. They'd all kicked off their shoes and tucked their feet beneath them, their shawls discarded. And if Jenny didn't think it would offend her mother too much, she would have stripped off her gown, settling onto the chair in true comfort rather than with her back ramrod straight.

"I'm thirteen, my lady."

"Och, ye need not be so formal in here with me." Jenny wiggled her stockinged feet. "We're not even wearing shoes."

Isla giggled and sipped at her tea.

"Thirteen. I remember when I was thirteen."

Her mother glanced up, smiling at her over the embroidery ring. "I remember too. Ye were a spitfire."

Jenny laughed. "What about ye, Isla, did ye drive your mother to distraction?"

She shook her head sadly, settling her cup down on her lap as she looked toward the hearth. "My mother was... She was often distracted, but not by me."

Jenny's heart constricted; she'd not meant to upset the lass. "I'm sorry for your loss." Jenny frowned, wondering what it was that had her mother in such a state. She wasn't certain what she herself would have done without her own mother, and she felt extremely lucky to have her. The past couple of years since Hamish had left had been a challenge in more ways than one. "And your older brother?"

"Which one?" Isla grinned, the sparkle in her eye saying she knew which one Jenny was talking about.

"Toran."

"Ah, he was always away, fighting in this battle or that. Mama was too."

At this Jenny's interest piqued, but she sipped her tea and pretended not to be as intrigued as she was. She went so far as to tug at a thread on her gown and then ball it between her forefinger and thumb. "Has your clan had much issue with the rebellion?"

They were Frasers, of course they had. Jenny knew the history of the clans, had listened to her grandfather and father tell her stories about their battles past and who was on which side. The Frasers seemed to be warring within themselves with the chief going back and forth on his allegiance, leaving his people floundering for a solid foothold in something to believe in. In fact, their double-dealing chief was not one Jenny would trust, which made it difficult for her to trust the other Frasers now.

Isla met her gaze, a seriousness in her young eyes that belied her age. "Have not we all?"

There was so much sadness in her tone, so much gravity, that Jenny's heart ached for the lass. "Aye, ye speak the truth."

"What was your mother's name?" Lady Mackintosh asked, taking a sip of her tea.

"Moire MacGillivray."

Lady Mackintosh looked thoughtful for a moment but said nothing. Jenny, however, was more than a little startled. She knew the name. She knew it well. Her hand shook, causing the liquid in her cup to swirl up and over the sides. A droplet of warm tea cascaded over the back of her hand and down her forearm. Jenny set down the cup, licked her lips, prepared to ask Isla to say the name of her mother once more, but found the words stalling in her throat. Could it be that her mother had been...*the* Moire, who had been a staple member of their rebellion until her life had been brutally ripped from her?

The lass let out a yawn. "My ladies, I am so tired..."

"Of course." Jenny stood up so quickly she wavered on her feet, feeling a little dizzy at the movement. "I'll show ye to your room."

Down the hall she opened the chamber across from her own. A small fire had been lit in the hearth, and the washbasin was filled.

"Ye've water for washing, and it looks like someone brought up your bag. 'Tis rather small. Do ye have a nightdress in there?"

"Aye. Thank ye. We didna have much time to pack." Isla laughed shortly and then unbuckled the bag. "But 'tis not as if I owned much besides a couple of gowns." She pulled out a wrinkled white chemise. Was anything else in there that might give Jenny a clue as to why they were on the run? What they knew?

Though she shouldn't be, Jenny found herself even more intrigued by this family.

"Shall I brush your hair out for ye?"

"Thank ye. Ye're so nice."

Jenny laughed. "Dinna tell Toran."

"I will no." Isla grinned wide and then pinched her lips closed with her fingers as if holding in the secret.

Isla started to work herself out of her gown, filthy from their ride, undoing the ties at the front of her bodice. Jenny helped with the unlacing until the lass was down to her shift, and she passed her a clean night rail.

"I'll hang up what ye do have while ye wash and put on the clean shift," Jenny offered, opening the bag once more.

Isla didn't argue, and Jenny sifted through the meager contents, pulling out one gown, two shifts, and a balled-up pair of hose. There were a few hairpins, a worn book of fables, and a pair of slippers. She even slipped open the tiny book looking for an inscription or handwritten notes that might be a code but found nothing.

Perhaps if she could get her hands on Toran's satchel she might find something more useful.

Isla finished dressing and sat on a bench before the hearth. Jenny brushed out the lass's hair until it crackled. All the while Jenny brushed, Isla gripped her hands tightly in her lap.

"Am I hurting ye?" Jenny asked.

"Nay." Isla laughed tensely. "Just a little…nervous is all."

"Ye'll be safe here."

"I know." She nodded, smoothing her fingers over her brows. "I can tell. We didna feel so safe at our great-uncle's castle."

"Why is that?" Jenny asked it softly, not wanting to pry too obviously. She had about a hundred questions she was ready to fire off at the lass but instead was trying to remain calm so as not to give the girl any alarm. She was sharp, and Jenny had to remember that.

"I'm not certain how to explain it." Isla shrugged. "Just felt…unsafe. People were always watching. Uncle always waiting. The air was so…I dinna know, thick, I suppose. Angry."

Jenny knew that feeling. "And Camdyn? Did he feel that way too?"

"He was busy training." She shrugged again. "We didna talk about it overmuch. But I know when Toran came home, things seemed to grow tenser. He was not even home an hour before it was time to go. Neither of us argued. Even Simon didna argue, and he and Toran fight at every chance. My brother said we were going to a safer place. A place run by a brave woman. Is that ye?"

Jenny smiled. "'Hap 'tis."

"I think so." Isla turned abruptly, causing Jenny to nearly rip out her hair with the brush, and she flung herself against her. "Thank ye."

Jenny hugged the lass back, stroking her hair as she imagined an older sister might do. "Ye're welcome." She patted her awkwardly then, pulling back slightly and feeling the need to leave to process what she'd learned. "Sweet dreams. If ye need anything, I'm only across the hall."

Jenny slipped from the room, entering her own chamber with a great sigh. If only there was a way for her to sneak into the men's barracks without anyone the wiser.

A sound from outside her window had Jenny easing over to pull back the curtain and peer down below. Well, it would appear that there was a God after all. What looked to be all the men from the barracks were standing in a circle in the center of the bailey, chanting. A fight, no doubt. She couldn't see who it was, as the crowd pressed in around the combatants and not enough of the torch-light filtered through. Did it matter? They were probably fighting over a bet or a lost game of knuckles.

But that meant the barracks were clear—and her desire to search through Toran's bag was actually possible to fulfill.

———

Toran grinned at his opponent. He and Dirk had both discarded their shirts and boots, standing only in their trews. The men of the clan stood in a rocking circle around them, and somewhere in the courtyard some-one beat against a drum. Simon was taking bets—having staked his odds on Dirk, the bastard.

The fighting ring was illuminated by only the moon and less than a half dozen lit torches flickering in brackets on the walls.

Dirk had the advantage of a few inches in height, though Toran himself was a tall man. He more than made up for those inches in muscle—Dirk was well built, but Toran was bigger. Stronger. And, he prayed, faster.

The drum stopped abruptly, a signal that their fight was now to start.

Dirk held up his hand and beckoned Toran forward. So, Dirk wanted to see Toran's moves first and wouldn't toss the first punch. Well, he didn't fault him for that, for he'd been considering the same method. But now that he'd been invited to swing first, he couldn't refuse without looking like a fool.

Fine.

Toran stepped to the left and then quickly to the right, throwing out his arm in a hard right hook. Dirk blocked him and parried with two quick jabs to Toran's ribs. Toran gritted his teeth, letting out an oomph.

Ballocks but that bloody hurt! The man had a damned hard hit. Toran retaliated with a jab up, hitting Dirk in the jaw hard enough to snap the man's head back, stunning him for the few seconds it took to swing with his left, catching Dirk in the gut. The man stumbled back, shook his head, and rubbed at his jaw.

"Good hit, Fraser." Dirk smirked. "That'll be the last one ye get."

Toran grinned. "Challenge accepted."

Dirk lunged forward. When Toran moved to block, the man ducked and spun to hit Toran in the back. Though his move was quick and tricky, Toran was ready for him and dodged the attempt with a laugh.

"Ye're quick on your feet for a big man," Toran taunted.

"I could say the same of ye, ye bloody bastard."

Toran only chuckled at the insult. Dirk was getting frustrated, made even more so when Toran repeated his move and was able to land an elbow in the man's spine before he got out of the way. They whirled on each other,

Toran landing a punch in Dirk's belly while Dirk connected a hard punch to Toran's cheek. They grappled with one another, punching until Toran tossed them both to the ground. He pinned Dirk in place only to find himself launched in the air. Dirk scrambled toward him, where he'd landed on his back.

Leaping to his feet, Toran avoided being crushed by the weight of Dirk's tackle. They circled each other again, nostrils flaring, bruises forming in the places they'd been able to land blows.

Rather than feeling anger or even pain, Toran felt exhilarated. It'd been a long time since he'd been in a scrap like this. "Ye impress me, Dirk."

"Wish I could say the same. Wait a second, nay, I dinna."

Toran chuckled. "I know ye dislike me, and I dinna care. Your mistress likes me, and that's all that matters."

That was enough of a goad. Dirk lunged forward, a meaty fist cracking Toran in the eye. But he'd been expecting that as well. He started to fall backward and grabbed hold of Dirk's head. Toran brought his knee into the man's nose, the sound of cartilage crunching and Dirk's shout of pain a signal it was time to call it quits. No use in annihilating a man only to prove he was better—he'd already done that.

Toran backed away, hands up. "No more, man," he said. "I've already broken your nose. I can barely see out of my eye, and I'll be pissing blood for days."

Dirk let out a bellow that was likely to wake the whole village. It certainly set the dogs howling, and old Dom came barreling into the circle to stand between the two men, barking his orders for them to cease fighting.

Toran was ready to listen, but Dirk, blood dripping down his face, looked ready to tear Toran in two.

"This is nay over." Dirk spat blood onto the ground before stalking away, evidently not pleased even with Toran's surrender.

The men's barracks were barely lit. Shadows crawled across the ceiling, making it look like it would come crashing down on Jenny. She shouldn't be in here—she should be outside putting a stop to the brawl. It had only taken one glance as she sprinted across the courtyard to see that the two men fighting inside the circle were Dirk and Toran.

She'd paused only long enough to see that they appeared to be on equal footing before rushing into the unguarded barracks. As soon as the fight ended, the men would be going back inside to sleep and nurse their wounds, and she couldn't be caught there.

A fight between Toran and Dirk seemed inevitable. They'd been butting heads since the first night she'd spied the two Frasers on the road, and perhaps this was what they needed to knock it out of their heads and finally get along. At least she could hope. In the meantime, she stared around the barracks at the rows of cots, the clothes hung on the walls, the weapons stacked against the corners. How in blazes was she supposed to figure out which one belonged to Toran?

Jenny walked slowly down the center of the long chamber, staring from cot to cot, hoping something would leap out at her and scream *Toran*. It wasn't until she got to the very end that she saw what she was looking for—two satchels matching the one she'd seen in Isla's room, each on a separate cot.

Camdyn's and Toran's. She didn't have time to contemplate whose was whose; she would just have to look through both. Jenny made quick work of the buckle on one, looking over her shoulder every few seconds as she riffled through the contents. Just clothes, a ball of soap, a...paper! She pulled out the folded scrap. A note? She opened the paper to find something quite unexpected instead.

It was a drawing—a very indecent drawing of a naked woman—scratched in coal. The woman was lying on her side, arms up over her head, her legs pressed together, but not hiding the dark triangle at her thighs. Her breasts were large, and her mouth parted in an *O* of pleasure. Even for someone as inexperienced as Jenny was, the woman looked to be in the throes of...rapture.

A spark of something hot lit inside her. Not at the image itself but at the meaning behind it. What it would feel like to be in that same position, those same sensations whipping through her. She closed her eyes for a moment, trying to imagine it.

"What are ye doing in here?"

Jenny gasped, whipping around and tucking the picture behind her back, only to find herself face to naked chest with Toran. The muscles of his upper body glistened with sweat, and just looking at the dips and swells made her body ache. His nipples were small, dusky against his golden skin. Her eyes rose to his, taking in the trickle of blood down his cheek from where his brow was split in the brawl.

"I…" She glanced behind him. No one else had come in yet.

"What do ye have?" He nodded over her shoulder, but she shook her head, denying there was anything in her hands.

"Let me see it." He spoke softly, but there was an edge of danger in his tone.

Jenny let the paper fall, hopefully to the floor where she could kick it under the cot, but she must have flinched, moved in some way that he saw, because in a flash he was catching it before it hit the floor and stepping out of her reach.

Her mouth went dry as he regarded the image and then slowly raised those icy-blue eyes, one partially swollen, to meet her gaze. "Naughty lass. Were ye leaving me a present?"

Jenny's face felt like it was erupting into flames. She jutted her chin out. "'Tis not mine."

"And yet I found it in your hand."

"Nay, ye found it on the floor."

He tsked. "Where ye dropped it. Were ye going to put this on my pillow so I might dream of ye?"

She gasped and stepped back, forgetting in her fluster that there was a cot there. She flopped down onto it, catching her balance before she fell all the way backward like the woman in the drawing.

"I'll have ye know, lass, that is not my cot." He nodded to the one beside it. "So, if ye'd kindly fall on this one, I can show ye what it is ye desire."

His tone was teasing, almost mocking.

Jenny stood up in a huff and shoved him in the chest as hard as she could—he barely moved. "I didna bring that drawing for ye."

"Then who did ye bring it for?" Oh, but why did his voice have to be so low, his brogue so enticing? The sound of it seemed to travel from her ears straight to every single part of her she wanted him to touch.

"I didna bring it at all. It was in the bag."

"Oh? Ye were snooping." He peered behind her at the opened satchel.

She frowned. "'Tis my right."

"Ah. So it may be. Is this what ye were looking for, then?"

"Nay."

He chuckled, stepping closer to her. Though there was still at least a foot of space between them, she felt caged in. The heat of his very naked chest seemed to leach out from him to her own skin, everything feeling suddenly so incredibly warm.

"I need to go," she said.

"Ye probably should," he drawled.

"'Tis late. And ye need to…take care of your face."

He grinned. "What's wrong with my face?"

"Ye know."

"I'm glad ye care."

"I dinna care. Where is everyone else?"

He stroked his hand feather-light over her arm, sending a thrill running through her. "Dirk walked off. The rest are still out in the bailey. Ye'd best hurry out of here else they find ye."

She took his advice, skirting around him and rushing for the exit.

"And, Mistress," he called after her, "'tis verra unsafe to go riffling through a man's things. Death has come to some for less."

Jenny gritted her teeth, prepared to tell him exactly what she thought of his threat, but a few of the men had started to trickle inside. Their laughter died on their lips when they saw her, hopefully assuming she'd come for some important reason. But when they saw Toran standing at the end of the barracks, they ducked their heads and murmured formal greetings.

Saints if she wasn't mortified; she felt as though she could burst into flames. Through it all she raised her chin, meeting their gazes as she spoke.

"See that our guests are not in need of medical attention," she ordered Mac. "Where is Dirk?"

"He's gone to the loch, my lady, likely then off to see the healer."

She nodded, and more of the men filtered into the barracks, including Toran's cousin Simon with a leering expression.

"Mac, tell him I should like to see him first thing in the morning."

"Aye, my lady." Her guard bowed, and Jenny got the hell out of there as fast as she could.

Eight

THE DARK OF NIGHT, WHEN ALL WAS QUIET, WAS THE time in which Toran found his thoughts the loudest, and tonight was not any different.

He'd settled into his cot, surprised at its comfort. The bruises on his face and ribs had been dulled by the three drams of whisky he'd downed with the men who'd attempted to befriend him after Jenny had left the barracks. *After* he'd made certain she'd not found the coded message he'd yet to cipher. Sneaking past Simon was going to be an effort.

Jenny... What had she been doing with that naked drawing? The idea of her looking at it had aroused him too much. Seeing the flush on her cheeks, the way the pulse point in her neck leapt and her breasts rose and fell at a rapid pace beneath her shawl—the shawl that split apart at her throat, showing just a hint of the soft mounds it covered with every breath she took. It had required every ounce of willpower he possessed not to kiss her. Not to toss her onto the cot or simply bend her back over the one she'd fallen onto.

Had that been her aim? To seduce him so that he didn't ask questions? He shifted uncomfortably on the cot, something digging into his back.

From what he knew of her, he highly doubted that was true. Only everything about her had his head turning. Even her lingering scent had him lifting his chin to take in a deep draw of floral, spicy air.

It didn't matter if she wasn't *aiming* to seduce him, for it was happening naturally. And it was appalling. The woman had obviously been in the barracks to snoop through his things and happened upon the wrong satchel. The portrait must have belonged to Camdyn, which meant he had some talking to do with the young chap about taking precautions with the lasses.

His brother slept soundly beside him, not in the least aware that Jenny Mackintosh had found his private image. The lad would be mortified. But not half as mortified as she'd been when Toran had spied her looking. It had been fun to tease her, to taunt her and watch her flounder. She had been trying so hard earlier to seem calm.

Knowing sleep wouldn't come, Toran rose to do what he did best—and to make good on his original vow when he'd first uncovered her identity. Time to do some snooping of his own and to see if he could figure out the missive he'd stolen off the dead dragoons.

Simon snored, laying flat on his stomach, face buried in the cot. None of the men stirred as Toran crept past them. He feared the creaking of the hinges when he opened the door, but for safety's sake, they kept the joints well oiled. Not a sound was made as he opened it and stepped outside.

Morning mist covered the ground, and the sky was a hazy gray. A raven's wings flapped overhead, disturbed from its perch on top of the barracks.

The bailey was not guarded, though several men were up on the walls keeping watch, none of whom turned around to see him. The moon was still visible low in the sky, and heaped in the bailey were the sleeping forms of a few of the men who'd stayed up well past midnight preparing wagons for Jenny's brother.

That had to hurt the lass's pride. To be a rebel in charge of so many, and at the same time forced to aid her brother who sided with the English. What a blow. He shouldn't even care, and yet he did. He also cared to find out what exactly was *in* the wagons.

Toran snuck over to the three wagons, overloaded and covered with woven tarpaulins. On the far side, out of view of the men who slept and those who guarded the walls, he lifted one corner to peer inside. Hard to tell— all he saw were lumpy sacks piled high. He ran his hands over the sacks. Felt like oats and grains. At the other end were large casks, filled, he supposed, with wine or ale. How much of their stores was she expected to send?

If Hamish was anything like his *Sassenach* counterparts, he'd likely demand the whole of it, his clan's welfare be damned. Bastard.

Toran moved to the next wagon. It was full of fabric items. Hose, shirts, breeches, plain wool blankets. Unsurprisingly, no plaids. Most of the Scots who'd sided with the English had foregone their kilts in favor of more traditional English attire. There were a couple dozen pairs of leather boots as well.

The resources already stockpiled in these wagons were enough to cause the clan to suffer, he was certain.

The third wagon was not yet as full, and this was the one he'd feared. Crates of arrows and crossbows, broadswords with the traditional Highland basket that goes around the hand but missing the rear wrist guard that he and his men had fashioned onto their own swords to keep their wrists protected. Interesting that she didn't want to give her own brother that advantage. There were shields as well, but noticeably missing were any pistols or shot. So she was arming them, but not with the most sophisticated items.

Toran had to give her the respect she was due there.

He set down the flap, eyeing the men on the wall and those asleep to make certain he wasn't being watched, and then he slipped into the barn, waving away the sleepy-headed stable lad who rose his head from the hay and making his way back toward his horse's stall. Inside, using the light from the single torch nearby, he pulled out the coded message. Using the cipher he'd memorized in his dealings with Boyd, he decoded the message. And then decoded it again, shaking his head in disbelief.

The message wasn't from Boyd at all—but from his uncle. Though he used a cryptic code name, *Vulpes*, which was only *Fox* in Latin, there was no mistaking it, for in the message he was offering up Toran, Camdyn, and Isla in exchange for the Fraser men in the garrison. The men who Toran knew were dead. So before he'd even gone to the garrison, his uncle had been dealing behind his back?

Good God... And now those men were dead, their lives on his conscience, and his uncle would seek more than to simply hand Toran and his siblings over. He'd want them to suffer—suffer a traitor's death.

Given that the dragoons had still been in possession of the missive, Boyd wouldn't yet know, but it was only a matter of time before his uncle reached out again. Was that the real reason why he'd insisted on Simon coming? Not because he needed him to spy but because he wanted to give them all over to the English?

Bile rose up his throat. How could the man who'd raised him so easily betray him? With the bitter taste of it still on his tongue, he burned the missive in the torch, igniting the gutting words in hopes of erasing them from his mind, but of course they were seared there forever.

He sneaked out of the stables and stared up at the sky, hands balled into fists at his sides, nostrils flaring. Every inch of him wanted to go back into those barracks and to beat Simon until he was as bashed and bruised as Toran's mother had been. Betrayal lanced at his insides.

But he couldn't do that, as much as he wanted to. He had to pretend he didn't know in order to keep his siblings safe. He muttered a string of whispered curses and then headed around the back of the castle. He needed to find a way inside that was more discreet than simply walking in the front doors. As much as he wanted to murder Simon, he still needed to find out more about Mistress J and her traitorous clan. He wasn't quite certain what he was looking for, other than to get a better lay of the land and as many details as possible about what Jenny was up to.

The kitchen door was open, and the scent of roasting meat came through. He wandered inside to find a spit-boy dozing by the fire, a large pig on the spit that he was supposed to be turning. Several other kitchen servants slept nearby, but none stirred as he passed them by. He slipped into the darkened alcove, winding up the circular stair, feeling his way along the cold stone wall until his hand came to air, and then sliding along a stone stair and arch. At the top he found a corridor with the very faintest of light coming from somewhere.

Silently he trespassed over the rugs that covered the floor. A torch had been lit at the end of the long corridor, and he suspected this was where someone, or more some-ones, slept. All of the doors were closed, and when he held his ear to the wood of one, silence greeted him. The like-lihood of these door hinges being as oiled as those of the barracks was not as solid. Of all the handles he checked, silently pressing on the thumb latch, only one was locked. This either meant that only one person wished to remain in perfect solitude and safety and the others were less concerned or that only one person slept on this floor.

With no clues as to the inhabitants and not wanting to risk walking in on Lady Mackintosh, Toran decided to make his way up to the third level to learn more before potentially alerting the household to his presence. This corridor was also lit with a single sconce at the end of the hall. Again, all the doors were closed and not one locked.

Bloody hell.

His hands on his hips, he stared out the glass window that overlooked the distant loch. The moon and stars glittered off the water's surface, shining like diamonds.

The cold press of iron at the nape of his neck wrenched his mind back to the present. Someone had a pistol on him.

He raised his hands slowly in the air and started to turn.

"Dinna move. What are ye doing up here, Fraser?" Though her voice was a low whisper, there was no mistaking Jenny. Who better to be sneaking about her own castle than the infamous Mistress J?

He grinned, coming up with an easy lie. "I couldna sleep."

"And so ye thought it best to take a stroll through the castle?"

He shrugged. "Would ye believe I got lost?"

She snorted. "Ye were spying. I knew I couldna trust ye."

"No more than what ye were doing in the barracks."

"So ye admit it?"

"I was looking for something, aye. Or, rather, someone. My sister." Quick thinking on his feet. "She oft has night terrors, and I meant to check in on her."

Jenny scoffed. "I dinna believe ye."

"I wouldna blame ye for holding that opinion. I am all but a stranger here. But I assure ye, I mean no harm." He turned quickly, catching her off guard.

She faltered a moment but held the pistol steady, pressing the barrel to his chest instead of his neck. "One bullet is all it would take to fell ye."

"I dinna think so. I've had one afore." And it had hurt like bloody hell. He was running at the time, and glad for it, else things could have been a lot worse.

"Ye have?"

"Aye."

"I saw no mark of a lead ball in the barracks," she challenged him.

When he'd been only dressed in his trews. The scars on his torso were clearly from blades. "Ye wouldna have. The mark 'tis not on my chest or back."

"Where, then?"

Toran grinned slowly. "My arse. Want to see?"

She arched a brow then, and he would have sworn he saw a fleeting flash of interest in her eyes. "No, thank ye. Your sister is just fine. And she's not asleep on this floor."

"Below stairs?"

"Aye."

"Door locked?"

"Only mine."

"Why's that?"

"If I had a need to get in."

He nodded. "And the lady?"

"Ye're standing outside my mother's chamber now."

He glanced toward the locked door, noting that it was dark under the door. "Then we're in danger of being caught in the dark, in the dead of night, and ye only in your nightgown."

Jenny glanced down then, and so did he. He took in the thin white gown, the way the shadows and light played across the fabric. The moonlit illusion toyed him into thinking he could see the faintest outline of her nipples and the thatch of curls at the crux of her thighs that he desperately wanted to slip his fingers through.

If she were to cover up, he'd protest, but he didn't

THE REBEL WEARS PLAID   141

think she would. Covering herself would require taking her pistol off of him.

"Go back to the barracks," she hissed.

"And what if I want to stay?"

"There is nothing here for ye. And there's no bed here for ye besides." Her eyes shuttered, as if trying to hide her thoughts, but the slight flutter of those lashes was hint enough. He would not hesitate to climb into her bed if she asked, though he'd likely wake with her blade pressed to his neck, not that he couldn't easily disarm her as he had at the croft.

"What if I was looking for ye?" he countered.

"'Tis the dead of night."

"Seems we keep meeting like this."

"The first time was by accident, and now 'tis on purpose." Jenny licked at her lower lip. "But no matter the intent, I'd still tell ye to go back to the barracks."

He grinned, feeling a sudden rush of boldness. "I'll go back. If ye kiss me first."

"What?" The harsh word came out higher than the whispers they'd been exchanging, and she glanced frantically at her mother's door.

"Ye'd best hurry afore your mother wakes." He stepped an inch closer, enjoying how easy it was to distract her and telling himself that was the only reason he'd suggested it.

She pushed against him with her pistol. "Ye canna command me to kiss ye."

"Nay, I suppose ye're right." He wrapped his hand around the barrel. "Ye're Mistress J, so ye'll have to command it of me." Why was it so much fun to watch the play of emotions on her face?

"Ye're talking nonsense."

"Perhaps. 'Tis the middle of the night, and I did get my arse kicked earlier this evening."

Her gaze roved over the swollen parts of his face. "I have it on good authority that was your own doing." Her voice had softened, her outrage fading.

Toran let out a raspy chuckle and pushed her pistol down to her side. "Dirk has wanted to pummel me since he first saw me."

"That is true. And so have I."

"All right then. Instead of a kiss, how about I give ye a free shot?" He held out his arms to the sides and then tucked them behind his back to demonstrate the truth of his words.

"From my pistol?" She lined it up again.

"Your fist, lass. I'll ask ye kindly to stop pointing your weapon at me."

Jenny lowered her pistol and cocked her head. "'Tis clear I gain the satisfaction of having caused ye pain, but what do ye get out of it, Fraser?"

"Perhaps the satisfaction of feeling pain brought on by a beautiful lass barely clothed." Good God, why did he have to point out the state of her undress—again—and why did he so badly want her to touch him, even if with a fist?

Her mouth fell open at his comment. "I am more clothed now than ye were in the barracks."

"Well, if ye wish to take off your nightgown to even the

score, by all means I'll not stop ye." His gaze roved over her chest and the outlines of her breasts against the linen. Perhaps Dirk had hit him harder than he'd realized, for he'd nearly forgotten how much he was supposed to hate her.

"Ye're a rogue."

"Aye, verra likely." He lifted his gaze to hers.

"I'll nay be kissing ye, and I'll nay be hitting ye, either. Though I want to desperately."

"Och, lass, I want ye to as well." And he didn't mean the latter.

Ballocks, but he was in serious trouble…

———

Go back to bed.

The words shouted in her head, demanding she heed them, but Jenny's bare feet remained rooted to the floor. She'd been lying awake in bed and had gotten up to splash water on her face when a shadow had moved beneath her door.

Jenny had opened her door a crack when the shadow departed and watched him as he checked each door handle in the corridor. His footsteps were silent, and even the press of his thumb against her door handle had been quiet. She'd slipped out as silently as he had done once he'd gone up the stairs. She had followed. Toran wasn't the only one who could be silent. She'd watched him check each door and snuck up behind him as he'd stared out over the moors and Cnàmhan Loch, the same way she'd done a thousand times.

He had no weapon drawn and didn't seem to be in any hurry. So, while he was currently sneaking through her castle, she didn't think he did it with intent to harm. Not in the moment, anyway. If he were spying, as she suspected, whatever information he passed on would put them all in danger.

But she hadn't counted on the danger he posed to her senses, even knowing the threat he posed to her world.

She was too close to him, barely clothed. He was right, no matter how much she argued, that she was barely dressed. Her night rail was thin, the linen fine. If he were to tug on it, the delicate fabric would rend in two. Already a draft from the cracks in the window wound its way around her legs, circling up over her calves and thighs, pressing against her buttocks and the heated apex of her thighs. Her nipples were hard, and if the very faint light of the torch behind him were brighter, she was certain he would see the pebbled nubs jutting against the white fabric.

Worse still, she *wanted* to kiss him, to hit him, at the same time. It was utter madness, that was all there was to it. To feel what it was like when lips were pressed together in passion. To feel that desire she'd seen on the face of the woman in the drawing she'd found in the satchel. To hit him for making her think these thoughts, for wanting him. Men, desire, all the things that came with it—none of those were in the cards for Jenny, as much as she might want some part of that world. She couldn't. Wouldn't. The cost was too great, the cause too much a part of her. The prince's importance, getting the redcoats out of their lands, it was all so much more important than settling down to familial discourse or even succumbing to a moment of rapture.

Desires of the flesh were a distraction.

Hadn't she noticed that already? Every look he gave her. The very sight of him. The feel of him. His scent. All of it had her turning her head toward him like her hound on a bone. She wanted him, aye, to devour him whole. She wasn't even certain what all those feelings meant or the various ways in which people could do such a thing. But licking him, holding him tight to her body, it sounded so very wicked and so very delicious.

And judging from the intensity of his blue stare, he was thinking much the same things. There was promise in his wicked eyes—promise of delights she could only imagine—and it made her tingle all the more.

Jenny swallowed hard, knowing full well that her silence spoke volumes and yet unable to make her tongue work. Her throat was tight, her body tighter.

"Lass…" Toran inched closer, and she was powerless to step back, couldn't make her feet move. "Dinna look at me like that." His voice was guttural, filled with the same hunger she felt deep in her core.

What was one kiss?

Nay! She couldn't. And then she worried… Could he tell she wanted him desperately?

"I…" She cleared her throat, backing away from his advancing steps.

He reached for her, the backs of his fingers stroking over her cheek in a touch that was whisper soft. It sent another volley of shivers racing up her spine. Her hardened nipples tingled, and a place deep inside pulsed with need.

"Dinna come any closer," she managed, knowing that if he did she would give in. She wanted to, maybe just once, to feel what it was like.

"Why?" Toran asked, startling her from her internal thoughts.

Why indeed…

"'Tis not decent," she managed.

He grinned at her as though amused. "The lass who traipses across the countryside in trews, who snuck up on me in a nightgown with her pistol pressed to my heart, is worried over decency? Ye amaze me."

The words could have been mocking, especially coming from him, but instead, in that moment and in his tone, the words were overlaid with admiration. Her throat went dry.

"I've never met another like ye, Mistress J. And I can see now why men follow ye."

The words were meant as a compliment, she was certain, and yet she could hear how quickly they dropped off from what else he meant to say. What was it? Dare she imagine that he would follow her too?

"Tell me what ye were looking for up here," she commanded. "The truth this time."

"Ye."

He didn't hesitate when he said it, and given the expression on his face as the words came out, she wasn't the only one surprised.

"Why?"

Toran shook his head, ran a hand through his wild hair. "I canna say."

"Ye dinna seem like a man who acts without conviction."

"Ye're correct." His gaze met hers then. "Ye distract me from myself."

Was this another ploy? Was she going to find herself pinned to the floor again, him having disarmed her of her pistol?

"In another life," he began, his gaze raking hotly over her. "In another life, I'd have taken ye to bed by now."

"In another life, I'd have pulled the trigger."

With a chuckle, he reached forward to tug lightly at a lock of her white-gold hair. "I'd not let ye kill me, lass, but I might have let ye wound me, if only to—" He stopped himself abruptly, and she was glad for it.

Because she was swaying closer. "I might have let ye," she answered and then firmly took a step back and then another, putting distance between them until she was half a dozen feet away. She whirled on her heel, running toward the stairs, not caring if he stayed inside the castle or not. She only needed to get away from him. Away from the intensity, the thickness of the air.

When she reached her chamber door, she paused, looking over her shoulder to see him still standing in the archway. One crook of her finger and she knew he'd follow her into her bedchamber, lay her down on the mattress, and show her exactly all the things she desired.

And she'd let him.

So instead of breaking her promise to herself, her vow to her country, Jenny shoved through her door, shut it firmly, and locked it tight. As she did so, she knew that she was locking herself in rather than locking him out.

Nine

JENNY ROSE BEFORE THE SUN, IF YOU COULD CALL IT rising after the sleepless night she'd endured. She wished she could simply tell her mother she was wearing trews, but instead, she got herself laced into her stays and into the wool gown with the small side hoops beneath that made her hips look wider than they already were.

"Loosen my stays a touch, Sarah, I'm feeling too confined today." Her skin was still hot from her encounter with Toran the night before, her stomach too unsettled. Wearing anything even the least bit snug was a new kind of torture.

"Aye, my lady," Sarah said with sleep still in her voice.

"I'm sorry for rousing ye so early." Jenny had not been able to fall asleep after escaping Toran. She'd lain awake in bed tossing and turning until she couldn't take it anymore. When the clock on the mantel above her hearth chimed half past four, she'd decided enough was enough and risen, though she hadn't roused Sarah until five.

"'Tis nothing, my lady. I've a lot of work to do today."

"All the same, no one likes to wake afore 'tis time."

"What has ye waking so early?" Sarah asked.

A certain Highlander. But she wasn't willing to tell her maid the truth. "My brother's wagons."

"All loosened."

Jenny pressed a hand to her stomach and inhaled

deeply. "Thank ye. Do ye think 'tis too much to hope that fashion will change in the coming weeks?"

"Perhaps ye'll set a trend." Sarah smiled.

"I wish I could."

As Jenny stepped into the corridor, the rustling of skirts could be heard on the stairs. A moment later, her friend Fiona rounded the corner, flaming-red hair flying in wild wisps around her heart-shaped face.

"Fiona!" Jenny said a little too loudly, before pulling her friend into her bedchamber and shutting the door. "What are ye doing here? Were ye followed? Is aught amiss?"

Fiona hugged her tightly and then walked over to Jenny's newly made bed and collapsed onto it, the skirts of her riding habit tangling in her legs. "I've a message for ye." She tugged a letter from her sleeve and held it out to Jenny, who eagerly snatched the paper.

Jenny flopped down beside her friend. "Ye look exhausted. Have ye many more letters to deliver?"

"Yours was the last." Fiona's voice trailed off, her eyes closing. Despite everything she had the face of an innocent, with a smattering of freckles over the bridge of her nose.

Riding like the wind at all hours of the night to deliver messages and packages to rebel leaders took so much out of Fiona. "I'll leave ye to sleep then."

"I was hoping ye'd say that."

"Aye. Rest."

Fiona's eyes popped open, reddened from exhaustion, but she lifted up on her elbow anyway to look at Jenny. "Not until ye tell me what's in the message."

Jenny looked at the back of the folded missive, stamped in a familiar seal. *A. M.*

She pulled her *sgian dubh* from her boot, the one unfashionable thing she wasn't willing to give up, and slipped it under the wax to keep the seal intact.

Mistress J,

How are you, my dear friend? I am so very excited to report that I have finally gained approval from the powers that be to throw a party—and there will be a special guest of honor I'm certain you'll want to meet. The ship of my youth will soon sail, my friend, I think very soon, in fact. Perhaps on my birthday—the fifth of July. But in any case, I should very much like for you to celebrate with me.

Gather your flowers, have your gown made, don a new pair of slippers, and plan for an exhilarating celebration. An invitation will be sent shortly with details. I do so very much hope you'll be there to welcome me into a new realm of maturity. Pardon the dramatics, old friend, but you know me. I've often felt in exile in this dusty old place with only the birds and frogs for friends. I think I shall decorate with thistles and heather. What say you? Will you come?

Your devoted friend,
A. M.

Jenny grinned. The coded message from her anonymous informant, who had an inside contact in the prince's party, could not have been clearer. To any red-coat who might have intercepted it the note would read like a silly lass preparing for a coming-out party, but to Jenny it dripped with insider political information. Prince Charles was setting sail from France on the fifth of July to come to Scotland. *At last.*

"What does it say?" Fiona asked.

"He comes." Jenny beamed at her friend, who suddenly looked more awake. "We must double our efforts. If he is to land in two weeks' time, then we'd best be prepared to provide him with all that we've amassed."

Fiona's violet-blue eyes gleamed. "Can ye imagine a Scotland without the English in it?"

"'Tis hard to believe that over a hundred years ago our Scottish king united the two realms, and here we are fighting a foreign enemy all over again. Fighting men that should be our people. The hate never dies."

Jenny nodded solemnly. So many lost lives over a crown. "We're doing the right thing. Charles Stuart is the true heir to the throne."

"Aye. Of course we are." Fiona flopped back down on the bed, her eyes growing heavy once more.

"I'll leave ye to rest." Jenny stood up, went to the candle on the mantel of her hearth, and held the paper over the flame until it caught. The orange flames licked at the paper, devouring it. She tossed it into the banked hearth, watching as the coals slowly turned the paper brown and then burst into flames.

The unfamiliar lass who'd snuck into the keep in the wee hours of the morning was clever, Toran would give her that. Had he not been awake watching for any signs of Jenny leaving, he would not have noticed the other girl. She'd rushed along the side of the castle like a wraith, slipping silently into a side door.

Who had let her in the gate? Had she climbed the wall? Was there a secret entrance he didn't know about?

Before the rest of the men roused, Toran took off at a run along the wall surrounding the castle, checking for any signs of a secret entrance. But he found none. The guard at the postern gate denied having let anyone in, and the men at the front gate stared at him as though he'd grown two heads.

"Ye must have spied our Green Lady," they teased. "Our ghost who lives in the tower."

Toran rolled his eyes at them, turning his gaze toward the tower of the castle, the top easily two floors above Jenny's chamber. What a bunch of storytellers.

As he headed back to the barracks to wake his brother, he spied Jenny exiting the castle. She didn't see him or at least pretended not to see him as she checked the wagons and spoke with the guards on the wall.

The gown she wore today was simpler than the one she'd worn the day before, more appropriate for working, which only had him more curious about her plans. He was about to approach her when Dirk loomed in front of him, his face looking as bruised as Toran's felt.

"Ye're coming with me," the man said, his voice a near growl.

Toran bristled, wanting to shove the brawny bugger out of his way. "Where are we going?"

"Riding the perimeter."

Dirk was taking him away from Jenny, away from the castle—and away from witnesses. Either he wanted to kill him or he was going to encourage him to run and then kill him anyway.

"And my brother?"

"He'll stay behind and work with the rest of the men. Archie will look after him and put your other blasted cousin to work. There's training and other chores to be done."

Toran nodded slowly. Denying Dirk now would only start a fight. He could handle himself. If Dirk planned to take him out to the woods and do away with him, he could fight back and win. But hopefully he'd not have to.

"We're leaving now." There was no room to argue in Dirk's tone. "Get into plain clothes."

Rather than pick a fight, Toran relented. There was no easier way to get Dirk on his side than to let him think he was in charge, and Toran could damn well use some allies. He went back into the barracks and changed into buckskin trews and a clean linen *léine*, the same getup Dirk had been wearing. Nothing identifiable about him.

"Where are ye going?" Simon rasped.

"Dirk has requested I ride the perimeter."

Simon sat up, shaking his head. "Nay. Not without me."

Toran whirled on his cousin, just about to punch him on the jaw, which he deserved, when Archie's voice called out. "Simon, Camdyn, let's go."

Simon rose slowly, his face only inches from Toran's. "Ye're getting off easy today, but ye'll not be able to shake me so well next time."

"Aye, because it's me who runs things around here."

Simon growled and shouldered past him, and again Toran had to use great restraint not to attack the bloody traitor from behind. His only consolation was that Archie could handle him.

Toran followed at a distance behind his kin to the bailey. Horses were already saddled for them when they arrived at the stable. Dirk swung up on his and nodded to Toran.

"We're to go alone?"

"Aye."

So it was to be an execution. Well, that was a bloody shame. But at a nod from Dirk, two lads handed Toran the weapons that he'd left in the barracks. That was odd. Why would Dirk arm him if he planned to kill him? Was he wrong about the purpose of this trip? Toran raised a brow as he strapped on his gear, and Dirk rolled his eyes.

"We're at war," Dirk was saying. "Why the hell were ye walking around without your weapons?"

"I was taking a piss," he lied. He'd left them behind on purpose before, afraid they'd make too much noise as he was sneaking around.

Dirk grunted. "Dinna flatter yourself that the piddly worm between your legs doubles as a sword."

Toran grinned. "Facts are facts."

"Ye wish."

"I'm happy to provide references."

Dirk groaned and urged his horse forward. "Ye're a bastard."

"I'm glad we're friends," Toran taunted back.

"Go to hell."

"Will ye be there?" Toran urged his mount to follow, suddenly looking forward to a day of mockery with Dirk. The man was intense and obviously cared a lot about his cousin, his people, and the cause.

Did Dirk care a little too much for Jenny?

Toran couldn't think about that. Couldn't think about the previous night when he'd been so close to kissing her, close to taking her to bed. That had been a moment that couldn't repeat itself. He'd come here for two reasons—to keep his siblings safe and to get answers.

Perhaps this ride with Dirk could lead him closer to his goals.

They crossed over the moors in silence until Toran finally broke the quiet. "Have ye lost many in the rebellion?"

Dirk was quick to respond with, "Have ye?"

"Aye."

"We all have. What kind of bloody question is that?"

Toran just came out and said it. "My mother was killed by people she trusted. Torn apart after they'd all used her." His words were crude, but he spoke the brutal truth.

Dirk swiveled his head toward him, a look of shocked anguish on his hard features. "I'm sorry for your loss."

Toran narrowed his eyes, surprised at Dirk's reaction. "Her death could have been avoided."

"Dinna blame yourself, man. 'Tis the fault of those bloody *Sassenachs* and the reason we're not giving up."

Toran gritted his teeth at the man assuming Toran blamed himself or the English—though it was partly true. He'd wished he could have been there to save her a thousand times over. Dirk stopped and jumped down from his horse, squatting over the road and touching hoofprints.

"They look fresh," Toran said.

"Aye."

"Only a single rider."

Dirk nodded.

"I saw a woman sneak into the castle this morning. I didna recognize her."

Dirk didn't look at him, though the muscle in his jaw tightened. "Dinna concern yourself with her."

"Who is she? I dinna believe the ballocks the guards gave me about a Green Lady."

Dirk did look at him then, meeting his gaze with a stern stare. "Ye saw no one. And ye'd do best to remember that."

Toran nodded. "If she rides alone, she's in grave danger."

Dirk stood, chest puffed out as he approached Toran's horse. Toran leapt down, prepared for another brawl, this time without an audience.

"I dinna trust ye," Dirk said, stopping two feet from him, hands flexed.

"Likewise."

"If I had it my way, we'd never have picked ye up off

the side of the road. I see the way your cousin Archie looks at ye, his eyes wary. He doesna trust ye either."

Toran couldn't argue with that, save to say, "I saved his life."

"And what about the rest? Ye were willing to let them die. Saving a life doesna mean ye'd not be willing to risk it in favor of saving your own."

Toran laughed bitterly. "Ironic coming from the likes of ye."

"What's that supposed to mean?"

Toran gritted his teeth, not wanting to give too much away. Had Dirk been part of his mother's death? This close to the man's face, Toran made out the wrinkles of guilt at his eyes.

"I asked ye a question."

"We fight for the same thing—Scotland," Toran said instead. "And we've both taken a vow to protect our country, our people. We've gotten a bad start, ye and I. As much as I'd like to pound ye into the ground, that's not going to solve any of Scotland's problems."

Dirk pressed his lips together, holding in whatever retort he'd had ready.

"Ye dinna trust me. I dinna trust ye. But we've got to make the best of it because, like it or not, we're on the same side."

"Are we?"

Dirk was not an idiot. He'd deciphered from Archie's behavior alone that Toran was hiding something. "We are." Toran would have to do a damned better job keeping his doubts hidden.

Proving his worth, his *loyalty*, to Dirk was going to be hard. Proving it to Archie might be even harder, given how much he knew about Toran's responsibility for the deaths of Fraser men.

Guilt ate at him. This man had every right to hate him. So did his cousin. Hell, all of his clan.

And so did Jenny.

But likewise, Toran had the same right. Until proven otherwise, he believed Jenny and Dirk willingly sacrificed his mother to a horrible death. And his own clan, under his uncle's leadership, had switched allegiances so many times that the name Fraser had meant nothing to the men who'd torn his mother to shreds. Not to mention that his uncle had done nothing in retaliation, and now he was willing to sell Toran and his siblings to the highest bidder. As far as Toran was concerned, they'd all failed.

"Your mother," Dirk said. "She was a rebel?"

Toran bristled. "Dinna speak about her."

Dirk held up his hands. "I'm sorry. I meant no offense."

Toran swallowed hard around the lump that formed in his throat whenever he thought of his mother. Their eyes remained locked, hard and unblinking. God, how he wanted to slug the man. Not out of hatred but out of anger. Pummeling someone would feel so damn good and might release some of the tension he had building up inside him.

It was Toran who finally broke the silence once again. "We'd best move along if we plan to ride the perimeter."

Dirk let out a long-suffering sigh. "We're not riding the perimeter."

The truth was about to come out, then. "What are we doing?"

"Hunting *Sassenach*."

That was a surprise. The day just got a whole lot more interesting. "Where to?"

"They've been stalking Mackintosh lands for months, we think some of Cumberland's spies and some of Hamish's. Doesna matter. If we encounter any and we think we can take them, we rob them. If we canna, then we keep an eye on them to report their movements to Mistress J. Have ye ever robbed a redcoat?"

Toran thought back to his escape from the cottage, how he'd not only robbed but had to kill two of them in order to take their horses. "Aye."

"Then this should be easy for ye."

"Aye." In all the years he'd spent with his uncle and in his own double-dealing, Toran had learned about gaining the trust of another. Give them something they think they can hold over your head. Something they can become invested in themselves. Hunting *Sassenachs* had presented Toran with just such a certain opportunity. "There's something I could use your help with."

Dirk grunted.

"A couple of redcoats I felled after the raid on the croft."

Dirk flashed him an angry look. "What?"

"Aye. They were lurking in the woods behind the croft after Boyd and his men left. I hid their bodies, but...

maybe would be best to bury them in case they're found by their friends and bring more dragoons to Cnàmhan Broch."

"Ye bloody fool." But Dirk didn't deny him. In fact, he looked at Toran with newfound respect. "Lead the way."

Ten

"THE SUPPLIES ARE READY. A RIDER HAS BEEN SENT ahead to my brother to have his men meet ye in Perth." She returned Hamish's signed document to one of the three Mackintosh men who were still faithful to him. Those three traitors she was sending away supposedly at Hamish's own request, though truly it was to get them away from Cnàmhan Broch. "Keep his letter on ye in case ye're stopped by dragoons. They'll try to confiscate the materials, but hopefully knowing they are going to troops fighting for Cumberland, they will allow ye to pass."

"We'll endeavor not to be caught in their path, my lady."

"Good." Jenny smiled pleasantly even though it was an effort to arrange her face that way to people she knew to be traitors.

What they didn't know was that Jenny had already sent word through Fiona that the envoy was leaving, giving their exact route. Rebels who might be so inclined could attempt to confiscate at least part of the contents that way, but with strict instructions not to confiscate it all, lest her brother come northward with his troops. Just a teensy bit to sting his pride and boost hers.

With the prince's arrival in Scotland imminent, the more supplies they had for his rebellion, the better. She wasn't about to give everything she had to the other side. Sending anything at all was painful, but it was her only choice in order to keep the dragoons from descending on her castle like a horde of swarming flies.

"Godspeed," she said to the half-dozen men, three of whom were her own loyal men and would return to her once the delivery was made. "And if ye should come across any outlaws who wish to rob ye, dinna allow them to rob ye of your life."

"Aye, my lady, we will honor your wishes."

"Good. I shall see the three of ye back here in a fortnight. Dinna delay, we need ye."

"We shall be swift."

And then they were riding through the gate. Jenny climbed the stairs to the wall, ostensibly to watch them go. In truth, she was searching for Toran and Dirk. She'd pretended not to notice the two of them leaving, dressed as though they were going hunting. But she'd watched every movement, every surreptitious glance from Toran in her direction.

She knew where they were going, of course, as she had been the one to command Dirk to take Toran with him. The two men would prove to be the most powerful in the ranks of men, given that neither had been a clear winner in their scuffle. If the rebellion had any chance of success, they needed everyone on the same side, which meant Dirk and Toran had to work out their problems— away from prying eyes and the possibility of others taking sides.

The late-afternoon sun was covered by clouds, but still there was no sign of the men—only the swaying grasses and wildflowers, the long-limbed trees and lush greenery, the high-peaked mountains in the distance that kissed the gray sky. She supposed she wouldn't see either one of them until after dark, if at all.

The rest of her day moved quickly as messages came in from her rebel contacts. Jenny took a look at the tallies of supplies they had left as well as gathering a circle of women to work with her mother in darning more socks and shirts. It turned out that Isla Fraser was quite adept at making socks, and she joined the women, excited to be doing something useful for the rebels. Apparently all she'd been allowed to do when she'd resided with her uncle was sit and look pretty.

Jenny felt for the girl. What a bore it must have been. Jenny was lucky to have had a father who embraced a woman's talents in all things and to not have been boxed into a corner because of her sex. Women had so much more to offer than sitting prettily and doing what they were told. The pain of missing him was a great reminder of why she risked so much to keep his legacy and his dream alive.

She marched up to her room and changed out of her gown into trews, a shirt, and a frock coat, determined to train with the men. Now that her brother's spies were gone and her mother had said she was going to rest for the remainder of the day, she could do so comfortably at Cnàmhan Broch. It was not yet sunset, and she still had plenty of energy.

Jenny hurried down the stairs and out to the training field. As soon as the men saw her coming, they let out a raucous cheer. The only two perplexed by her presence were Archie, who by now had healed enough to participate, and Camdyn.

Jenny aimed the tip of her sword at Archie. "Ye, Fraser. Want to fight?"

He pointed to his chest, eyes going wide, and then glanced around at the other men as if expecting one of them to have an answer. They all just grinned, knowing exactly what was coming. Simon, the wastrel, even started taking bets, his coin on Archie.

Jenny laughed. "Come on now, ye're not afraid of a woman, are ye?"

"Nay, Mistress," he said, though his eyes looked worried.

"Then take up your sword and let us see what ye're made of."

The men clapped and formed a circle around the two of them, Camdyn looking ready to leap to her defense. She pointed at the lad and said, "Ye're next."

The lad looked crestfallen, and she couldn't help laughing even more. "Lad, ye're old enough to know the rules of a soldier. Never show your opponent your fears. Slap some color back into those cheeks if ye have to."

Simon leaned over, grasping the lad around the shoulders, and said something, obviously teasing him, for Camdyn grew even redder about the cheeks.

Archie faced her, wiping sweat from his brow with the back of his hand and holding his sword and small Scottish shield—his targe—upright. His mouth pinched with worry, eyes crinkled at the corners.

"First to draw blood?" she taunted, finding the lure of teasing him irresistible.

He blanched. "Mistress!"

"I'm teasing. Try not to cut yourself." And with that, she started to circle him. "Show me what ye've got, Fraser. Dinna hold back."

Archie nodded and tentatively tapped his sword to hers, the way a child might.

"What am I, a bairn?" She laughed. "Hit me for real, sir."

Archie tapped her sword a little harder, and Jenny decided to show him no mercy. She slammed her sword against his, feeling the jar of the blow all the way up her arm and stunning the man in the process.

"Ye're strong," he mused.

"Aye. Now fight me."

Archie didn't hold back the next time, advancing on her. They parried back and forth, knocking into one another, blocking, dodging, hitting, ducking. Sweat dripped down her spine, from her brow, and on her upper lip. She'd not had a workout like this in weeks.

She was only just getting warmed up. She jabbed her sword forward, one of her favorite moves, and caught the blade of his just above the hilt. With a spin of her sword and a sure flick of her wrist, his sword was in the air.

Archie didn't hesitate to duck and roll for the weapon, but she advanced on him, kicking it away. He pulled out his dirk, and while some of the men gasped, Jenny only laughed.

"Good move, soldier." She pressed the tip of her sword against his neck. "Ye might be dead, but I'm wounded, aye?"

Archie grinned. She reached for his hand and helped him up.

"I've never fought a woman before."

"Most men have not. On the fields of battle, they either believe me weak and easily overcome or are too scared to injure me. Works to my advantage either way."

Archie shook his head in that way people did when they were proven wrong. "I will never underestimate a woman again."

"'Tis good ye say so. We are stronger than we look." She glanced toward Camdyn. "Are ye ready, lad?"

He nodded, smiling broadly, excitement in his features rather than the fear that had shown there before. She liked that, could see in him what an eager Toran might have looked like in his youth.

The lad took up his sword, in position to circle her, but just as he lunged forward, a bellow rent the air.

Toran pushed his way into the circle, standing between the two of them. "What the bloody hell is going on here?" A fierce glower covered his dirt-smeared face, cheeks flushed as though he'd been running from wherever it was he'd been. His wild dark hair flew in all directions, and she had to resist the urge to smooth it out and then to follow that by smoothing the angry lines on his face. She scanned his plain clothes, covered in dirt as though he'd spent his day rolling in the pen with the pigs.

Jenny frowned at him, jutting her chin forward a notch. "A lesson. And I could have run ye through just now. Have ye never learned not to jump into the middle of a sword fight?"

He ignored her rebuke. "What kind of lesson?"

Jenny cocked her head to the side. The man was refusing to see what was actually going on here, and once more he was underestimating her. "Have ye never trained afore, Fraser?"

Toran's mouth dropped open a little in surprise, his widened eyes ridding him of some of the angry wrinkles at their corners. "Ye canna mean to fight my brother."

Inside she bristled; on the outside, she remained befuddled. "Is he not trained with a sword?"

"He is," Toran scoffed.

"Ah," Jenny said, stabbing the point of her wooden training sword into the dirt. "Ye're no' worried over your brother. Ye think me feeble." She glanced around at the men and started to move in a wide arcing circle, dragging the tip of her sword behind her. "Ye only just missed me kicking Archie's arse."

"What?"

"Did we not meet at the point of my pistol? Why is this news to ye?" She pursed her lips as she moved, causing Toran to turn in a circle as she walked around him. "I have an idea. How about ye take Camdyn's place?"

"Me? Fight ye?"

"Aye," she answered as she finished drawing a circle enclosing the two of them.

A grunt and scuffle behind her revealed Dirk pushing forward. He too was covered in dirt, and she wanted desperately to ask what or whom they'd found. The hunt often yielded a prize or two, and clearly, they'd unearthed something.

"Come on, Cousin, what's a wee spar with a lass?" Simon goaded, and Jenny ignored him, with half a mind to call him into the ring next.

Toran sized her up, his gaze raking her from head to toe. She felt suddenly self-conscious, more than she ever had before. In fact, he was the only one she'd ever met who had the ability to make her feel this way.

A rush of heat filled her that had nothing to do with the exertion of fighting. She became aware of the sweat beneath her arms, the way her hair was damp and sticking to her forehead, temples, and neck. Her cheeks must be ruddy from exertion, not to mention that the exercise and sweat had likely taken away any bit of floral scent she had from her perfume. But that was reality, wasn't it? A reality for her, a soldier. Not a lady.

"Well?" she asked, letting her irritation slip into her words. "What are ye waiting for?"

A training sword was tossed in Toran's direction, and he caught it without looking, the wood hilt slapping against his palm, and causing a few appreciative murmurs from the men standing around them. Toran flipped his sword on his fingers, letting it twirl in a full circle before taking the hilt in a firm grasp.

This man was much more skilled with a sword than his cousin. Archie had been easy to best, but she knew by the glittering look of challenge in his gaze that Toran was about to take her to task. A shiver of excitement ran through her limbs. As many years as she'd been practicing, not one man had ever looked at her that way—as though he wanted to kiss her and spar with her all at once. Men always held back at first, something she could use to advantage, but from the look of it, Toran wasn't going to spare her a thing.

The notion thrilled her as much as it gave her pause. What was going through his mind? That he wanted to beat her? Or that he wanted to have some fun? To see what she was made of? The thrill of it made her limbs buzz, her fingers tingle.

Neither of them spoke, concentrating as they moved in a slow circle inside her makeshift sparring ring. Jenny blew out a long, slow breath, centering herself. With sword in hand and targe on her left arm, she studied the man in front of her, the way his muscles moved as he stepped, fluid and exact, the way he held his weapon, as though he'd been born with the sword in his hands.

He wouldn't be the one to make the first move, she could tell. Just like in their game of chess. Jenny never liked to go first. That meant her opponent had a moment to evaluate her and decide how best to react, an advantage she preferred to keep for herself.

Toran was grinning and she smiled back, flashing him a wink in hopes of distracting him, only for the second that it would take. She shuffled forward, feinted to the right, and doubled back to the left, slamming her targe and sword against his at the same time. The force of the double strike would send a jolt skidding up his arm, just as it did to her own. With her blow released, she leapt backward out of his reach, but that didn't stop his advance. She blocked his attack, slamming her sword against his, and then the dance began, parrying and attacking in fluid motion, the *thwacking* sound of their wooden swords a beautiful music to her ears. She was laughing as excitement thrummed in her veins.

She'd thought fighting with Archie had been fun, but with Toran...their movements felt natural and in line with one another, as if each could anticipate the other's move before it was executed. They were fluid, two rivers spilling into one swirling mass of water. Melding, connecting as one.

Sweat was pouring off them both, and her arms were starting to ache and shake from the exertion, but still she didn't quit. The men around them were silent, afraid to break the spell. But Toran was in for a surprise. Jenny had yet to show him her best moves.

As he attacked, she ducked, swiveling to the left, angling her head toward the ground. She swiped her foot toward his ankles and yanked back, quite literally sweeping his feet out from under him. Toran tried to catch his footing but fell to the ground with a surprised *oomph*. He was quick to roll, leaping to his feet, a wide grin on his face.

"Fancy footwork," he said.

She only snorted in answer and attacked him with a hard back blow, their swords twisting this way and that against one another. She feinted right, hitting left, and ducked to sweep his feet out from under him again, but he dodged her at the last minute, sending her skittering to her knees.

"Not so fast, Mistress. I'm a quick study."

Letting out a growl, she leapt back to her feet, twisting

around, only to be stopped by his arm around her waist. He held her back flush to his chest, his targe pressed to her breasts, his sword coming toward her neck. She blocked his weapon and kicked back against his leg, causing him to issue a grunt of pain as she connected her bootheel with his shin. His grip loosened enough that she rounded on him, but before she could make her final blow, he held up his hands in surrender. He didn't drop his weapons though.

"Not so fast, soldier," she taunted and swung her sword toward his neck. "Dinna make it easy for me." He blocked her, over and over, until he was able to finally stand up. She couldn't help but look on that strength of will with some admiration.

Toran stood there before her, chest heaving from exertion, sweat trickling down the column of his strong neck, dark hair plastered to his temples. The expression in his eyes was one of pride and admiration as well. He didn't raise his weapons to her again and instead said, "A truce, Mistress?"

Jenny shook her head slowly, meeting his eyes with all the seriousness she'd felt in the lesson she'd just provided him. "I never give up."

"I am seeing that."

"A good soldier never leaves a fight."

"Unless 'tis with his peers and the only way for both to come out alive and ahead is by calling a truce."

She pursed her lips at him, willing to concede. "Ye have a point."

"I am at your service." He bowed forward, and she

took the opportunity to press the tip of her sword to the top of his bent head.

"I win."

"So ye did." He straightened, stabbing his sword into the ground and holding out his hand to her, a grin curling his lips.

Jenny did the same, reaching for his hand, feeling the largeness of his palm sliding over hers, the strength of his fingers clasping around hers. A shock ricocheted from that grasp up her arm, sending gooseflesh to rise over her skin, hardening her nipples. Their hands were sweaty, slick, and hot as they rubbed together, callus to callus.

God, the feel of him. She wondered what it would be like for him to touch her in other places. What would happen if they were back up in that darkened corridor with no one around? This time if he'd challenged her to kiss him, would she?

"I could shake your hand, my Mistress J, but I would not be a gentleman if I didna kiss the hand of a lady." And then he was bending forward, his lips pressing to her scraped knuckles, warmth fanning deliciously over her skin.

Jenny's mouth went dry, and she forced a tight smile on her lips when all she wanted to do was gasp. To tug him closer and finish what they'd almost started so many times—a kiss.

She yanked her hand away, forcing herself to remember her vow. The prince was coming soon to Scotland; she could not waver now. She had to prepare for battle, prepare to take a knee before her rightful king. However much Toran caused her to forget, she couldn't allow him to distract her from that.

"Good fight, sir," she said. "I am impressed."

"As am I. 'Twas an honor to be chosen."

"Let us not forget that ye stepped in."

He winked. "And a pleasure it was to have done so."

From the corner of her eye, she watched Dirk huff. Though they weren't at each other's throats at the moment, it was clear the men still did not see eye to eye.

"Continue on, lads," she said, tearing her eyes from Toran and forcing herself to concentrate on the men's training. "Ye too, Fraser."

Toran grinned as he backed away from her and called his brother over to parry.

Jenny took up a stance along the perimeter, watching the men fight, her heart still pounding. Though she was no longer exercising, she couldn't seem to catch her breath. Her hand still burned where he'd kissed her, and all she could think about was his large palms sliding over her skin, his warm lips pressing to hers.

This was ridiculous.

Perhaps she should just bed the man and be done with it. Like a sweet, the more she pined for a treat and denied herself, the more she wanted it. Was desiring a man the same way? Could she get over the craving once she'd had him?

Jenny's gaze followed him on the field, watching the way he talked to his brother, all seriousness and calm. He was a good teacher. And damned fine-looking. His buckskin breeches hugged his arse in a way that made her itch to grip him, to squeeze and rub. Blazes, she was going to hell for thinking such things. Where had that thought even come from? She'd never touched a man's arse. Never even thought about it. But Toran's…

Dirk sidled up beside her, drinking deeply from a waterskin. "Did ye know he killed a couple of redcoats the day he deserted us?"

Jenny stared at her cousin in shock, all thoughts of arse rubbing gone. "Nay."

Dirk grunted, took another long sip. "'Tis probably safe to say he's one of us. If he wasna before, he is now."

Eleven

TORAN DIDN'T JOIN THE OTHERS IN THE GREAT HALL for the evening meal. In fact, he didn't join them for the next three nights running. Instead, he volunteered for guard duty on the wall, and during the day he kept himself busy both with training and hunting *Sassenachs* with Dirk. He barely slept, and even the few times he tried, it was all for naught.

He told himself that he was keeping busy to gain the favor and trust of the men. But in truth, he was avoiding Jenny. She was also the reason behind his lack of sleep. Every moment that passed, he questioned more and more whether she could have truly been involved in his mother's death. She was obviously able to defend herself, but cold-blooded murder now seemed beyond her. Even condoning it. She was so protective of everyone within her clan and each of her rebels. Until he found out the truth, it was probably best he didn't keep enjoying her company. The more distance he put between them, the better.

The problem was he genuinely liked her. It went way beyond the desire to press her hot body to his and toss them both down onto the nearest surface where he could give her screaming pleasure. Nay, he liked her passion, her determination, her strength, her humor. The lass had already surprised him in so many ways, and, damn it, but he admired her too.

It was no wonder the men fancied themselves half in love with her. Hell, if he spent any more time with her, he might get there himself. Jenny was beyond any man's expectations of the perfect lass. She looked damn fine in trews or a gown or a night rail. And the way she handled a sword... Good God, it was as if his image of the ideal woman had been sent to the heavens and dangled before him as the ultimate prize. One he'd never win—because he should hate her.

His conviction to seek his vengeance was wavering. And that was a problem. He couldn't simply forget his mother or what she'd suffered because he was distracted by a lass.

To make matters even more confusing, his siblings liked her too. They had found their places in the Mackintosh clan over the past few days. They were happier than he'd ever seen them before, which perplexed him. How could she possibly be so compassionate with Isla and Camdyn—with him even—if she were malicious? Even bloody Simon was smiling occasionally, which Toran was certain he'd never seen before in his life.

Toran was supposed to hate Jenny. He was supposed to wrap his fingers around her throat and say, "Got ye," before he snuffed out her life. And yet here he was avoiding her because he *didn't* want to wrap his fingers around her throat, he wanted them around her breasts, her arse, dipping inside her warm, tight channel. He didn't want to end her life, he wanted to enhance it. To give her pleasure and happiness. He wanted her crying out not in pain but in rapture.

She couldn't be guilty. That was what was eating away at him. And if she wasn't, then who was?

Bloody hell!

He slammed his hands down on the stone of the wall, hoping the movement would jar him from his thoughts.

"What is it?" Simon approached from a dozen paces away.

"Nothing. A damned midge." He swatted at nothing, hoping his cousin believed his lie.

"Ye were gone an awfully bloody long time with that dolt."

Toran slid his cousin an irritated glance. "Did ye miss me so much?"

"Tell me what ye did."

"None of your damned business."

Simon grunted.

"What are ye doing here, Simon?"

"Asking ye what ye were doing."

"Nay, not here as in standing in front of me but here at this castle. If ye're here to kill me, get on with it. In fact," Toran held out his arms to the side, "I'd like to give ye that opportunity right now. Kill me, ye slimy bastard."

Simon shook his head, a sneer on his lips. "I'm not going to kill ye."

"Nay? Ye'll leave that to your da? To the dragoons?"

Simon stopped smirking.

"Punishment for getting the lot of them killed, eh?"

Simon cocked his head. "Ye dinna know." It wasn't a question, and clearly Toran did not know.

He ground his teeth, trying to form words, when the

rage inside him was building up to a boiling point. But he wasn't going to give away what he'd found in the missive. It was imperative to keep Isla and Camdyn as far away from this as possible. "Know what?"

"They're not dead."

Toran reared back. "What are ye talking about?"

"The men at the garrison?" Simon shook his head. "They are not dead."

"Impossible."

"Ye're a fool, just like your mama. And fools get themselves and the ones they love killed." With that, Simon turned his back, prepared to march away, his head held high as though he'd just won some victory.

Not so fast.

Toran grabbed him by the shoulder, wrenched him around and slammed his fist into his face. The two of them fell to the ground, grappling with one another and landing blow after blow.

Toran was going to kill Simon, right then and there, and be done with it. Send the body back to his darling uncle and tell him to bugger himself.

Shouts from behind echoed in his ears, and then he was being wrenched off Simon, his blood still pounding through his veins, the need to kill strong in his fists. Dirk stood between the two of them, his fists curled into each of their shirts to hold them in place.

"Ye're a bloody madman," Simon growled around Dirk, perhaps the most ironic thing Toran had heard to date.

"Stay away from me and my family," Toran warned, jabbing his finger toward Simon.

"I *am* your family."

"Not anymore." Swiping at his bleeding lip, Toran marched down the stairs and toward the barracks, wishing there was a tavern close by where he could drown his sorrows.

"Back to your post, Toran," Dirk ordered. "And ye, Simon, get the hell back to the barracks."

Simon muttered a string of nasty curses as he trudged away, but Toran refused to be moved by them.

"Are the two of ye going to be a problem?" Dirk demanded.

"Nay." Any problem he had, Toran would handle it himself.

"Mistress J will be most displeased," Dirk warned as he disappeared to his post on the wall.

Mistress J. Jenny Mackintosh. *Mo chreach*, but he couldn't get her out of his mind.

Evidently no amount of time away from her was enough to lessen his interest. He dabbed the blood on his swollen lip with his thumb. When he'd met her nearly a sennight ago, he couldn't believe his good fortune at coming face-to-face with the woman he'd always believed responsible for his mother's brutal murder. And in all that time he'd not confronted her because a large part of him did not believe her guilty. Or was it that he didn't want her to be?

The thing was, he wasn't so certain anymore. If his mother was as staunch a supporter of the prince regent as he'd believed, then perhaps her conviction had run as deep as Jenny's. Jenny valued each man in her company.

Took care of them. Hell, she'd taken care of him when he'd been a dangerous stranger. Could a woman guilty of murder still hold her clan and company so close? And why would they murder one of their own and claim them to be a traitor? Something wasn't adding up.

He shook his head. The evidence and testimonies presented to him thus far pointed to his mother being murdered by Jacobite rebels. It wasn't as though his mother had sacrificed herself. That was a basketful of ballocks that needed to be burned.

Moire's death was Jenny Mackintosh's fault.

"How's the view?"

He whirled around at the sound of her voice behind him. No doubt she'd been informed of his fight with Simon. Toran gritted his teeth. She was so beautiful in the moonlight, silver slices dotting her eyes. The white of her teeth showed between full lips, which now parted in a genuine smile.

"Vast."

She came up beside him, leaning her elbows on the stone and letting out a soft sigh as she rested her chin in her hands. "Are ye all right? I heard about your run-in with Simon."

"I'm fine."

"Good. A little beating canna get a warrior down."

"'Twas not a beating."

She laughed, clearly teasing him. "I love looking at it. Our Scotland."

"Aye." Why was she here? Why wasn't he walking away?

"To think her beauty could be marred by so much hate and violence." The smile disappeared, and she glanced up at him, a note of sadness in the turn of her mouth. Not the mouth of a killer. Not the conscience of someone capable of such crimes.

"'Tis a tragedy."

"And yet we've suffered it nearly a thousand years."

"Ye think we'll suffer it another thousand to come?" Toran should leave. Every word out of her mouth slowly plucked away at his armor, and soon he'd be completely disarmed. And yet this was the conversation he'd been avoiding.

She shook her head. "Nay, Prince Charlie will unite us."

"Ye truly believe it."

She glanced at him, arching a single brow. "Ye're supposed to as well."

"I want to," he confessed, watching the play of her thoughts carry across her face. "I'm not turning tail, if that's what ye think."

Jenny rounded to face him, her elbow resting casually now on the stone, eyes assessing him carefully. "Are ye avoiding me?"

Saints, but she didn't hold anything back, did she? "Nay," he lied.

"Ye know your right eye squints just the barest bit when ye lie."

He grunted.

"Why are ye avoiding me? No one likes night duty. Especially when they've been as busy as ye have during the day."

"I'm not avoiding ye."

"I've as much a stubborn streak as ye have, Fraser. I can go all night."

Dear God, dinna let her say more things that have me thinking of bedding.

He cleared his throat and shifted his gaze to the center of her forehead when he really wanted to stare at her breasts. "I'm certain ye can."

"Will ye make me?"

"Is that an offer?" He couldn't help the words slipping out.

That single, delicately arched brow rose again in question. "Ye do have a habit of propositioning me, sir."

This time, he let his eyes fall. Toran raked his gaze over her, taking in the way her breasts pushed up out of her dress, the shawl parted open enough to reveal just the barest hint of porcelain skin. He had to clench his fists to keep from running his fingers across the swells to see if they were as soft as he thought they might be.

"I canna help it. Ye're a passionate woman, Jenny." God, he hated himself for saying it, for wanting her.

"I have no' given ye leave to use my given name in public." The words in any other tone than the one she used could have been a rebuke, but spoken as low as they were, as huskily, they came off entirely different.

"I am willing to take any punishment ye might give."

Her gaze moved to his lips, staring the way she had the night he'd encountered her in the corridor. There was no mistaking what she was thinking about. *Mo chreach*, but he wanted her to want him. At the look she was giving him, he felt his blood heat and funnel southward. The air around them thickened, as did the appendage in his trews. This was the one flaw in wearing them versus his kilt. His kilt and sporran might hide his arousal, but the breeches gave no leeway to his thickening shaft. If she were to glance down…

"I should think ye would quite enjoy any punishment I were to mete out, meaning it was no' a punishment at all."

He grinned. "'Haps."

"Perhaps the best punishment would be to leave ye to suffer in your brooding, sir."

"I suffer many things, Mistress."

"As I said."

Toran leaned forward, dragging in a lungful of her intoxicating scent. "Ye'll kiss me one day."

"Upon your death, I'll place a kiss right here." She reached up and pressed a delicate fingertip to his forehead.

"Will ye be the one to mete it out?"

"Ye're impossible." Her lips curled with mirth.

"Ye mean incredible."

"I think ye're unique, Toran. Whether ye're incredible has yet to be determined."

"In time ye will find just that."

"I would expect nothing less."

He leaned against the wall more casually, not wanting her to go. "Tell me your plans."

She shook her head. "So forward."

"Come now. If I am to fight for ye, the least ye can do is tell me what I'm fighting for."

"Ye're too curious for your own good. Besides, I've no' shared them with everyone else. What makes ye special?"

He leaned a few inches closer. "Does Dirk know?"

"Will ye try to beat them out of him?"

He shrugged. "Perhaps."

"I canna allow it."

"Ye're both verra close."

She raised both brows at him now, a knowing smile curling her lips. "What are ye getting at, Fraser?"

She only used his surname when she was irritated or taunting him. In this moment, he thought it might be a bit of both.

"He cares for ye a great deal." He let all the playfulness fall from his face as he studied her, wanted to know if she returned Dirk's affection.

"We are blood, Toran. Cousins. Like brother and sister. Like ye and Simon and Archie. We fight for the same cause."

"And that is all?"

She let out a short laugh. "Ye want to know if we're lovers." It was a statement rather than a question.

Fine, he'd be honest if it would gain him an honest answer from her. "Aye. I want to know."

She crossed her arms over her chest, a sign she was closing off to him. "Perhaps that is none of your business."

"Ye're right, 'tis no'. But I still want to know."

"And if he is?" She cocked her head.

"Then I'll challenge him."

"For what? A place in my bed?" She stiffened, and he sensed he was losing her.

"No' if that's who ye'd prefer."

Her frown deepened, and he regretted his line of questioning immediately. Jealousy was not attractive on anyone, and it didn't suit him at all. "I'm sorry, lass. I take it back."

"Ye canna take back that which is already spoken."

"I can try."

"Listen well, Fraser. Dirk is my cousin, my second-in-command, and my dear friend. I love him like a brother. I would kill for him, and he the same for me. I have no lover, and I dinna intend to take one. I am fighting for my country, and I have no time for distractions of any kind, especially no' from ye." She whirled around then, giving him her back as she stomped away, her gown swishing in short bursts that seemed to mirror her irritation.

"Those are words ye may wish to take back some day, Mistress, and then ye will see what I mean," he grumbled under his breath.

He could sense the whip of her anger in the air. He didn't doubt she was thumbing her nose at him as she moved out of sight.

Toran turned to face out over the wall, irritated at himself for making her angry, for not grilling her about his mother.

Mo chreach, the fire in her was mesmerizing and clearly made him forget himself. And he was pleased to have found out that she was not falling into Dirk's arms every night. She might love the man like a brother, but it was plenty obvious to anyone with eyes that Dirk felt quite a bit differently.

"She might slit your throat while ye're sleeping, Fraser. Be careful." The called warning came from another soldier on watch duty, followed by a snort of laughter and every other warrior within hearing distance laughing their bloody arses off.

Though they jested, Toran didn't doubt they were right. Probably why he wasn't ready to confront her, to find out that she might actually be capable of murder. And yet that very thought just didn't sit right with him. Toran believed himself to be an excellent judge of character, and there was nothing in Jenny that made him think she could be guilty of any heinous crimes, especially what was done to his mother.

The lass was all fire and ice, aye, but not evil. Holy hell, he wanted to melt her and douse her in wet heat at the same time.

And blast it all, he'd been so distracted he'd not told her what he and Dirk had found.

Twelve

JENNY SHOULDN'T HAVE GONE UP TO THE WALL. SHE should have let the idiot keep on brooding as he'd been wont to do the past several nights, but she couldn't help it. When she heard about the sudden brawl between him and his broody cousin, her feet had moved of their own accord. And she was halfway up the stairs before she'd even realized exactly what it was she was doing.

Blast it!

Seeing him standing there, staring out over the land, she had found it an effort not to run her fingers over his swollen eye, to wipe the droplet of blood from the corner of his mouth. Luckily for her, the man had the ability to make her temper flare as much as he made her desire ignite. What was she to do with him?

And what the bloody hell was that line of questioning?

Dirk? Her lover?

She'd been considering allowing Toran to kiss her, dragging him into bed before they went off to war. It would have just been to assuage the want and in the hope it would keep her from thinking about him when the enemy was closing in, but the arrogance! Oh, she wanted to slap him. She wanted to punish him. And they were both right; the perfect punishment for him was for her to walk away and leave him there. Except it was a heady punishment for her too, one she wasn't certain she'd survive.

Toran was jealous.

The notion struck her so hard, Jenny stopped short in her steps and stifled a gasp.

All the feelings and emotions she'd been battling he must have also been… She shook her head and kept marching forward. This was ridiculous.

Jenny found Dirk outside the barracks. "Gather a few men. We're riding tonight."

Used to her sudden nighttime rides to seek new allies, he nodded. But this time he also asked, "A missive has been sent?"

Jenny shook her head. "I want to sit in at the taverns and listen. Dress for the occasion."

"Did Toran speak with ye?"

Jenny cocked her head, certain what she and Toran spoke about would not be anything Dirk would be privy to. "About?"

"What we found."

"Nay."

"All right, we'll share at the tavern."

Jenny nodded and then hurried inside.

With her mother and Isla safely tucked into bed, Jenny was able to slip easily into her chamber and change into her trews, *léine*, and frock coat. She tucked her hair up under her cap and slipped the white cockade of the rebels into her coat pocket. The symbol was enough to get her arrested and executed if spotted by the dragoons, as much as it was a symbol of unity among rebels.

She pulled on her boots with trembling fingers, her nerves still on edge from her conversation with Toran.

Outside, the torches had been doused near the place where the horses stood, and she could make out four mounts and three men. The closer she got, she could see exactly whom Dirk had chosen to ride with them: Mac, Archie, and Toran.

Jenny narrowed her eyes, but Dirk's subtle nod caused her to hold her tongue. This was a test for their new recruits, and she found herself applauding Dirk's initiative as much as she hated the idea of Toran's company. The true test would be if she could actually concentrate on the evening with him there beside her.

"Where to first?"

"Mack's."

This was the local tavern she'd first gone to when her brother left, to gauge the sense of loyalty and purpose among their people. With the increasing numbers of dragoons on their doorstep and rumors surely spreading of Prince Charlie's impending arrival, she was certain there would be much buzz over ale and whisky.

The ride to Mack's was short, and they tied their horses up outside, their plain saddles not giving anything away. As was their usual, Dirk took the lead and Jenny followed, head down, keeping her features in shadow. The rest of the men walked behind her, almost hiding her from view should anyone be looking.

Inside, the tavern was crowded, and a mix of pipe and hearth smoke clouded the air. Through the haze, Jenny spied an empty table in the far corner and nodded for Dirk to lead the way. Though the table was in the corner, there were men drinking in clusters around it, but it was off to the side enough that it warranted them a measure of privacy if they kept their voices low.

Toran waved his hand in the air, which brought over a sweat-drenched serving lass with circles so deep beneath her eyes Jenny wanted to offer her a bed to rest in at Cnàmhan Broch. Her gown was threadbare, her apron stained, but she had a pleasant smile when she greeted them.

"What'll ye be having?" she asked, her voice raspy from overuse.

"Five ales and five whiskies," Dirk replied.

"Any food for ye? We've got a little bit of stew left."

"Not just yet," Archie answered.

They must have practiced, the four of them, for it was normally Dirk who did the talking so Jenny didn't have to.

They bent their heads, pretending conversation as they listened to those around them. At first she only picked up on the mundane talk of work and horses, drinks and women, but then something new caught her ear. She tensed and underneath the table felt Toran's thigh press to hers. He'd heard it too.

"Redcoats were knocking on me door earlier this morning, they was," a man said, slurring. "Tried to tear off my daughter's dress until she told him she was on the flux."

Jenny swallowed hard, pressed her own thigh back to Toran's.

"Where's Mistress J when ye need her?" one of the men he was speaking to murmured.

"Aye. She'd have kicked his arse back down to hell."

If only she was given the chance. Jenny's heart ached. She would have loved to go in there and run her sword through every dragoon who dared to touch a Scotswoman without her permission. Was it Boyd again? How many women had he tormented?

"Where did they go off to?"

"I dinna know, but I've a sense they'll be back. One of them was eyeing Molly with a greedy eye. I've a mind to send her to my cousins in the isles."

Unless they fought, unless they stuck together, even the isles wouldn't be safe.

They listened to more of the same, and in a low voice, Jenny asked Dirk and Toran, "Did ye come across any of them? Alive?"

Toran tapped her thigh with his, and she resisted the urge to reach under the table and grab his leg, to massage the thick muscles and pretend that none of this was happening, that Prince Charles Stuart was already reigning as regent over Scotland and England, uniting the kingdoms in peace.

"A lot of fresh prints," Toran said. "They are everywhere."

"Seem to be going circles 'round each other," Dirk added.

"They are swarming the lands. Looking for something."

"Me," she said.

"They burned the croft down."

There was only one croft she cared about. A chill ran down her spine. How relieved she was she'd had the forethought to get them the hell out of there.

"And the neighboring crofts?" she asked, worried about those who'd helped conceal them.

"Harassing them."

She wasn't surprised. "They won't stick with harassment for long. They will become violent."

"Aye."

"The men all need to be armed. The women trained to defend themselves," said Jenny.

"The men are armed," Mac added.

"And I'm happy to train the women." Toran's thigh had found a permanent place pressed to hers now, and she got a certain measure of comfort from the strength of it.

"I'll help ye," Jenny added. "That'll be our next message."

They stayed another hour, listening until the tavern started to thin of guests and those remaining behind were too inebriated to be useful.

Outside, the summer night air was chilly, and a swift wind blew, threatening to pull off her cap and unwind her knot of hair. Jenny jammed her cap back down on her head, feeling a chill of trepidation race up her spine. The hairs on the back of her neck were suddenly standing on end.

"Dragoons." She'd barely gotten the word out before the stomp of hooves and chink of metal echoed in the twilight air.

Somehow over the past two years, she'd gotten a sixth sense for the bastards.

"Keep moving," Toran said, his hand on the small of her back. "Get on your horse."

Dirk, Mac, and Archie made quick work of untying their mounts.

"You there." The voice was unmistakable, taking her right back to the courtyard outside their croft, his fetid breath on her skin, rough hands on her body.

Jenny's hand went to the pistol tucked into her belt beneath her frock coat. She wanted to shoot him dead.

"Leave it. Get on your horse," Toran instructed under his breath. "Ye know he willna balk at killing ye."

Not if she got to him first. She hesitated another moment, but Toran whispered her name in warning. She bristled, knowing running was the right decision for now. They were not prepared for an engagement.

Jenny leapt up onto her horse, the saddle sturdy beneath her buttocks, the warmth of the mount's sides seeping into her calves.

"Stop!" Boyd's bellow rent the air.

"Ride," Jenny ordered the men.

They urged their horses into full gallops, leaning over their necks to gain speed. Her cap flew off, hair pulling free of the knot and whipping around her head, threatening to blind her. Behind them a shot rang out, and she waited to feel the shock of a bullet crashing through her skull, but there were only the wind and the pounding of her heart.

None of the men fell off their horses either. Boyd had missed. Thank the saints. They rode harder. The redcoats chased behind, shouting words that carried off on the wind, sounding more like the bellows of angry animals. Another shot. She waited. Nothing.

It was dark out, but still, a man like Boyd didn't make it to where he was by missing. Was he missing on purpose? He didn't want them to fall, he wanted to follow them. He wanted to know where they would go when they were running scared.

Jenny yanked the reins to the right and veered sharply off the road, and the men followed. There was no way in hell she was leading them anywhere near Cnàmhan Broch.

They crashed over fields, trampling crops, leaping fences, scattering herds of sheep and cattle in their race to get away. No matter how many sharp turns she took, the dragoons remained close behind. Their long months of chasing Highlanders had taught them some of the tricks. She hated that.

She veered again, to the left this time, taking the men up over a crag. The terrain was treacherous, especially in the dark, but the horses were used to it. She and her men were used to it.

The English, hopefully, would not be.

Up they rode, until they crested the top, and raced along a narrow goat path that was dangerous to ride even in the light. She heard a scream behind them. Someone had fallen. Not one of their own. They didn't stop. Another crack of a pistol shot. More waiting to see if the bullet struck its mark. More misses.

They rode down into another valley, far now from home, and the first hints of light were coming out hazy purple on the horizon. Dawn would be there soon, and they'd have no way of hiding.

They slowed and dismounted to let the horses cool off. It seemed certain now that the dragoons had not followed after the injury of their man. It would seem they did have some integrity or compassion for their own. Not that it mattered. Their crimes against the Scots were extensive enough as it was. Was it too much to hope it was Boyd who'd fallen?

"I know where we can hide for the day," Toran said, and Archie glanced at him, giving a short nod. "The Fox Hole. A fortress that used to belong to the Frasers, but it's been in ruins since I was a lad."

"Where is it?"

"We're not far now."

They remounted, following Toran's lead. Jenny realized she was trusting he'd not lead them right back to Boyd. Some two hours later they arrived at the castle ruins.

Ominously, three crows sat on the half-crumbled wall of the left tower, turning to look on them as they approached. The right side was a pile of rubble. There was no roof on the tower, and the walls looked to have been dismantled by a volley of cannon fire. They drew closer, and the birds flew off one by one. Jenny had the mad thought that they were going to tell the English what they'd seen.

"We'll be safe here until tonight," Toran said, dismounting. "And then we can work our way back to Cnàmhan Broch."

"Do ye think Boyd has gone there already? When he takes note of me missing..." Jenny eased off her horse, stretching out the kinks in her muscles.

"The clan will make excuses for ye. Saying ye're sick,"

Dirk said. "Ye gave them all the answers, J. Trust them to see it through. Besides, he knows what ye look like. To him ye're Mrs. Mackintosh, resident to the croft he burned, not a lady nobly born."

"My mother," she murmured. Toran stiffened, and she reached for him without thinking, pressing her hand to his. Then she yanked it back when she realized what she'd done.

He cleared his throat. "Let us make our beds and sleep as much as we can. We can keep the horses in the stables. It might not have a roof, but we can jigger the door into place."

While the men took care of the horses, Jenny walked up the crumbling outer stairs of the castle, entering into what had once been the great hall. The main level's stone floors had kept its structure at least, supporting their weight, unlike the floors above that had caved in. The furniture, rugs, tapestries and other decor had long since been pillaged by locals, and the roof was gone. In the moonlight, it was evident that some of the walls were charred black with soot. A fire must have consumed the place during whatever attack had happened here. There was a flap of wings, more crows who'd been inhabiting the inside taking flight at her approach.

Such an eerie place. Though she was glad for the crows' departures. If they'd stayed, that was a sure sign of death to come.

Jenny found a spot near the far wall where she could see the entrance but she herself would hopefully remain in shadow.

When the men entered, they each found their own places in corners and behind piles of rubble. Archie, Mac, and Dirk fell asleep almost instantly, whereas from his spot a dozen paces away, Jenny could see Toran watching her.

"Go to sleep," she ordered.

"Ye first."

"Stubborn man."

"I am not ashamed of it."

She tried to glower at him, but the effort was too much. She was exhausted. Toran stood from his spot, coming closer and sinking down beside her.

"What happened here?" she asked, full well knowing the answer, for it was the same everywhere across their land.

"Dragoons." He rested an arm on a bent knee. "Burned it after imprisoning my great-uncle some thirty years ago. Archie and I used to come here to play when we were lads."

"'Tis glad I am that ye remembered it."

"'Tis glad I am ye didna shoot the bastard, even though ye would have likely hit your mark."

"Better than he."

"Aye."

"He escaped death tonight, to be sure." Jenny paused. Now, in the quiet when they were alone, was as good a time as any to bring up what she'd been wanting to ask him for some time. "Dirk told me about the men in the forest. The dragoons ye killed."

"A casualty of this war." He let out a soft sigh. "And I needed a horse."

"I thank ye all the same."

Resting his wide, warm palm on her arm, Toran said solemnly, "Thank ye for taking care of my siblings. Ye could have turned us away."

"I dinna fault children for the sins of men." And she was serious. "Besides, ye'd be surprised at the power of children, their memories, their pacts."

He eyed her. "Ye speak as if from experience."

"Maybe I do."

"Can I ask…" His voice faded out, and he looked away. "Simon said something to me last night, and I've got to know."

"What is it?"

"The Fraser men at the garrison… He said they were not executed."

There was such anguish in his voice. Guilt must have racked him at leaving his comrades behind.

"'Tis my fault they were there, and I thought—" He cleared his throat. "I thought them dead."

Toran seemed to relax beside her. She couldn't imagine the stress of having believed he'd killed his own men. He leaned closer, their shoulders brushing and hazy predawn light filtering through the roofless castle. She stared into his eyes, allowing herself just the tiniest moment to sink into their depths and dream. The more time they spent together, the more she wanted to. There was something intoxicating about him. A sweet she wanted to devour.

Before she could decipher what was happening, his lips brushed ever so gently across hers. Jenny gasped, mesmerized at the soft warmth and the jolt of awareness that spiraled through her. Just when she had the where-withal to press her lips back, his mouth left hers much too quickly.

"I'm sorry, lass," he whispered, eyes on hers. "I shouldna have done that without asking."

She flicked her gaze from his eyes to his lips. And threw caution to the wind. "Dinna be sorry."

"I've been wanting to do that for far too long."

"And I've been wanting ye to." She shouldn't. She could feel herself getting caught up in the whirlwind of things she'd forbidden herself. Clan and country first. But resisting Toran had been a test she seemed doomed to fail.

He leaned in again, and she tipped her face up, meet-ing him halfway as his lips connected to hers. He took her hand in his and pressed it over his heart, the thump of it beating beneath her trembling fingertips.

"Ye feel that?" he asked. "'Tis what ye do to me every time we cross paths."

"Ye've a way with words. Do ye speak to all the lasses like that?" she teased, smiling and wishing he'd kiss her some more.

"Nay."

He couldn't know how much that single denial made her want to swoon. She let her eyes close, reliving the soft kisses, his words, and breathing him in. He smelled of adventure—horses, leather, the outdoors, a subtle spice, and a faint hint of sweat.

"Will ye let me kiss ye some more?" he asked.

This was the chance she had to deny him, to tell him again that her life's goal was to see the prince returned to his rightful throne—and nothing else. Changing her purpose on the flap of a crow's wings was to be untrue to herself.

And yet denying him, letting him go, seemed also to be a betrayal to herself.

How could she have both?

It was impossible.

But right now, in this ruined castle, in the dark, with their enemies at bay and no warring or planning to be done, when she should be sleeping, she could allow him to kiss her some more. To indulge in a moment she might remember when things turned bleak.

"Aye," she said, her mouth forming the affirmation before her mind had fully comprehended or determined what she wanted.

Toran's hand slid over her cheek and tucked behind her head, tugging her closer as his lips pressed firmly to hers. The soft, tentative kiss they'd shared a moment before was replaced by this heady melding of lips.

Jenny sighed, her hand pressed to his heart, curling her fingers in his shirt, wanting to hold on forever. Their mouths moved to better fit, his breath on her cheek, her heart pounding in her chest.

When she thought their kiss could not grow any more intense, he licked her.

Well, not a lick exactly. More like a swipe of his tongue. A flick over her lips that had her gasping. He did it again, running the hot, velvet heat of his tongue over her lower lip and then the top, curling inside her mouth before darting away. It was fascinating and intoxicating, and it sent shivers racing all over her body.

She tugged harder against his shirt, pressing her body against his, and then he was dipping his tongue inside, touching the tip to hers, and she was emboldened to do the same thing.

A hot flash of desire sparked as the tip of her tongue tentatively touched his. Shivers ran rampant over her flesh. How was it possible that kissing him could get better and better?

Her heart was pounding, her body trembling, and heat licked at places she didn't even know could feel... let alone feel so good.

A throb started between her thighs, and she arched her back, wanting to be closer to him, wanting him to touch her.

At the same time, she was very aware of where they were and the other men not too far away. Toran's hand slid from her face, his fingertips brushing over her neck to her collarbone, his palm flattening just above her breasts. She clamped her mouth closed to stifle both her gasp and her enthusiastic surrender.

Toran stilled, feeling her body stiffen. He was pulling away then, and she wished she could pull him back, wished she could tell him to continue kissing her. But the truth was she should have been the one to pull back, to put a stop to the madness.

"Was that your first kiss?" he murmured.

She blinked her eyes open, staring into the blue

depths of his soulful eyes. Suddenly self-conscious, Jenny asked, "Was I terrible?"

In the hazy light, she could see him grin. "Nay, ye're a fast learner. A guess, really."

She didn't believe him. "I've had plenty of opportunities to kiss, I'll have ye know."

"I dinna doubt it." One eyelid slowly drifted closed in a lazy wink. "Ye're a discerning woman, and I am honored to have been chosen as your first."

Jenny frowned, wishing she hadn't run away every time Hamish's best mate had attempted to kiss her in their youth. Or Annie's brother, for that matter. With practice she could have knocked Toran clear out of his boots.

"Dinna flatter yourself, soldier. I merely decided it was time to put the task of kissing behind me."

"Ah, I see. And as your loyal vassal, I aim to serve and please ye, Mistress J. By any means necessary."

He stroked over her collarbone again, and she resisted the urge to shiver, having forgotten that his hand was still pressed so close to her breasts. She swatted him away with a huff, turning to face away from him.

Despite her attempts at irritation, her blood still sang with pleasure, and Toran chuckled.

"So much bluster." His whisper fanned over her ear, and he gently bit the shell of it, sending another volley of pleasure racing through her body. "One day, Jenny, when the world is no' tearing itself apart, I hope you can revel in the pleasure of kissing."

She turned sharply to face him then. "What makes ye think I wasna reveling?"

"Ye're upset about it."

"I am no." And it galled her that the man could read her so easily.

"Nay?"

"Nay, no' at all," she insisted. *Lied*.

"All right. Ye know your own thoughts much better than I would."

"That is a fact, sir." She'd not been particularly subtle, huffing and turning, but it was more frustration than anything else.

"I wish ye a good night, Mistress J."

"Ye need no' call me that when we are alone."

"Do ye foresee us being alone more often?"

She rolled her eyes, but it was with a smile. He was lightening the mood, making her feel less unnerved. The man had a knack for it, she'd hand it to him. She'd nearly forgotten where they were and why.

"I'll take the first watch," he said. "Ye sleep."

She wanted to argue, but there was no denying her exhaustion. "Good night, Toran."

"Sweet dreams, Jenny."

She curled up on her side, away from him, afraid that if she were to face him she'd watch him all night. And she'd thought he might move away from her, but he didn't. And as it turned out, facing away from him was a worse kind of torture than if she'd actually been facing him, for she couldn't see when she wanted to, and her mind continued to conjure up all sorts of thoughts. How did he look when he was concentrating on the wind? Would his eyes get droopy?

Was he…watching her?

Thirteen

THEY ARRIVED BACK TO CNÀMHAN BROCH IN THE dead of night, a full twenty-four hours after they'd left. The castle was in an uproar over Jenny's disappearance. First and foremost among the frantic was Lady Mackintosh.

She came running out to the courtyard from within the castle, wrapping Jenny up in her arms, Dom loping slowly behind her. Camdyn and Isla too were tossing themselves into their brother's arms, and Toran's low voice rumbled soothing words that Jenny couldn't make out.

Her mother pressed her hands to Jenny's face and searched her all over as if checking for injuries.

"I'm fine, Mama."

"Where have ye been?" Her eyes were filled with worry, and as her gaze traveled the length of Jenny's clothes, taking in her appearance, she grew paler. "I had wondered," she started but stopped. "Come inside."

Had wondered what? Jenny hadn't made much of a secret about changing her clothes and training with the men, which was something she'd done even as a child, but she had tried not to do it so much in front of her mother. Had her mother figured out Jenny's role in the rebellion? Jenny looked back at the men who'd come home with her, giving them a solid nod. They knew what to do and would inform the rest of the men of what they'd discussed at the inn.

They'd make certain those who lived near the croft were protected.

Right now, she had to deal with her mother, and it seemed like the scariest thing she'd ever had to do. Would her mother take to her bed again? Would she forbid Jenny from her duties? Worst of all, would she believe that Jenny had joined Hamish in his betrayal?

Her mother's small, cold hand trembled in hers as they raced up the winding stairs to Lady Mackintosh's solar.

Behind the safety of the walls, her mother pulled her to the small nook in the window and sat her down on the bench across from her own, their knees brushing, their hands still clasped.

Her mother's expression was stern. "I am glad ye've returned unharmed, but please, my daughter, tell me ye were not doing something for Hamish? Tell me ye've no' switched sides?" Tears sprang to her mother's eyes.

Jenny's heart thundered, and she felt sick to think that her mother could believe that.

"Nay, Mama, I have no'. I do Hamish's bidding only to the brink of which no' heeding him would bring danger to our clan. But I was no' missing last night in service to him, Cumberland, or any other of King George's men."

"Then who? Have ye been…compromised?" She scanned Jenny's body as though there would be clues.

Jenny thought of the kiss she'd shared with Toran, how she'd wished it had kept going, at which point she would be very much compromised.

"I am not compromised, Mama, I promise. I was

doing my duty for Prince Charles. I am sorry I didna tell ye sooner, but I didna want ye to worry."

Lady Mackintosh's brow wrinkled. "Your duty?"

"Aye." Jenny bit her lip, chewing on it nervously. How much should she tell her mother, and how much should she keep to herself? At this point, it seemed best to tell her mother all. "I have been gathering men, weapons, coin, supplies, anything that might aid the prince in the rebellion. He is coming soon, Mama. Hopefully all that I am doing will help him regain his throne. I—" She swallowed hard. "I know Da would have wanted this, and I have been aiming to carry on his legacy."

Her mother sat back, letting go of Jenny's hand to swipe at her tears, and then placed her hands over her heart. "Ye always were your father's daughter. But I'd be lying if I said it didna terrify me. I dinna like it."

Jenny smiled sadly. "He made a rebel out of me, Mama."

"He did. He'd be so proud of ye." Her mother leaned forward and gathered Jenny in her arms, holding her tight. "I'm proud of ye. And terrified too."

"I'll be safe, I promise." Emotion whirled inside Jenny, along with relief that her mother accepted her, supported her. She'd feared so much that her mother would reject her way of life, would demand Jenny cease her efforts or, worse, put a stop to them herself.

"But what of Hamish?" Lady Mackintosh held her daughter at arm's length, watching Jenny with fearful eyes.

"He knows nothing, and I think 'tis best we keep it that way."

"Oh, aye. Who else knows besides Dirk, Toran, and his cousin?"

This was going to be the hard part. "Most of the clan, Mama. They have been helping me. And until now we had safe quarters some distance from here, but we were compromised by dragoons and forced to flee." She paused to collect herself. "About a sennight ago, I moved everything here to Cnàmhan Broch."

"Oh." Her mother said the word as an exhale, her eyes darting toward the window and a flicker of fear crossing her features.

"I know it is not ideal, Mama, and I'm sorry for no' telling ye of the danger sooner. I will find another place if ye wish it, but I thought it best if the men and arms were hidden behind walls where they could be defended. That we would be safer hiding in plain sight rather than traipsing through the forest." She squeezed her mother's hand. "When I sent Hamish the latest shipment, I sent with it the last three men left of his that I knew we couldna trust."

"Ye were right to do it. All of it. I used to help your da, did ye know? Everyone, and everything, is safer behind the walls. I am concerned over Hamish though. He's bound to come home one of these days. What if he should find out?"

Jenny pressed her lips together. "I have been doing everything I can to keep him away. 'Tis one of the reasons I continue to do his bidding when he requests supplies."

"I see. I canna tell ye what a relief it is for me to hear ye've no' switched sides. I feared the worst."

"Och, Mama, I could never back away from our heritage, from what Da and Grandda sacrificed, what all of our people have sacrificed. I have wanted to tell ye what I was doing for so verra long, and I am just so grateful to finally get a chance to share it with ye."

"Oh, my darling lass." Her mother pulled Jenny into her arms once more. "I dinna know what I would have done without ye. Ye've been my rock in everything. The loss of your da, your brother's choice. Ye're the reason I stepped outside my room. I saw ye, in the bailey below, ordering the men about. And I thought, that's my daughter, so strong and taking care of so much. I need to help her. I want to help her."

"Och, Mama. I dinna know what I would have done without ye either."

"But I worry about ye. That ye're spending so much time on matters of the country that ye're no' taking care of your own happiness."

Toran's words echoed in her ears. *One day, Jenny, when the world is no' tearing itself apart, I hope you can revel in the pleasure of kissing.*

It was a bitter realization that she wanted that very same thing and an equally bitter kernel of truth to know that she would likely never get the chance.

The prince would be landing in Scotland on the fifth of July, and though the Highlands had been swarming with dragoons up to this point, things were about to get even more harrowing. The rebellion would gain momentum from here, and this time, they'd rid Scotland of the blasted dragoons for good.

There was danger in rebelling. Danger in fighting. Already she'd felt the harsh touch of a dragoon on her person from which she'd been able to escape, but that didn't mean she'd get so lucky the next time. Boyd was looking for her, and she knew he wouldn't stop until one of them was dead. Jenny didn't plan on giving him the satisfaction of stealing her breath, which meant she had to finish him first. The best place to do that would be on the field of battle.

"Ye've grown still." Lady Mackintosh's tone was soothing. "What is it?"

How much should she divulge to her mother? She didn't want to overly worry the woman, and telling her about Boyd was going to do just that. Then again, her mother already knew that they'd been on the run from someone. If Boyd came to the castle when Jenny wasn't around, her mother needed to know the danger.

"There is an English officer, Captain Boyd. He... He is a dangerous man, Mama."

"Did he hurt ye?"

Jenny shook her head quickly and met her mother's gaze. What happened in the courtyard of the croft was a bit too much to share. "Not yet, but he wants to. He wants to hurt us all. But I fear the day is coming that he will be knocking on our door, and when it comes, I dinna want ye to answer."

Her mother narrowed her eyes. "Ye canna think I would let ye willingly sacrifice yourself."

Jenny pressed her lips firmly together. "Dirk and I have a plan for Captain Boyd, and in order to see it through, I beg ye not to get yourself involved." This was not entirely a lie. They both wanted the man dead, but the plan… Well, that had yet to be solidified.

"What about Toran Fraser? Is he a part of the plan?"

"Aye, as is his cousin, Archie." The lies came too quickly, too easily.

"Moire would have been so proud."

Jenny flinched. "What?"

Lady Mackintosh let out a great sigh. "Toran, he is Moire's son."

Jenny blinked, her mouth going dry. If her mother had hit her in the head with a chair, she could not have been more stunned. She parted her lips to speak, but no sound came out, and she found her mouth opening and shutting again like a fish out of water. "You knew all along who he was?" Her words were raspy, as she forced air from her lungs and wrangled her lips to help form the words.

Her mother let out a long sigh. "Aye. Isla is the spitting image of her mother."

Again, Jenny was floored. She should have recognized her too, and yet she'd been blind to it. She swallowed as her mind worked back to the very moment she'd met Toran. Had he known that she was acquainted with his mother? Did he purposefully keep that connection a secret? He must have… "Why did ye not say anything?"

Her mother shrugged. "If he'd not yet divulged the information… I wasna sure how much he knew of his mother's involvement…or what happened to her."

Jenny's heart did a flip at the horrific memory. God,

part of her hoped that Toran wasn't fully aware of the brutality of his mother's death. That was something one did not recover from. "I'm not sure how much he knows either." Jenny squeezed her mother's hands. "Promise me, Mama. If Boyd comes, ye'll stay away from him. Ye'll protect Isla. I canna lose ye, the way Moire was lost to us, and he shouldna have to bear another of his kin being executed by that bastard."

Lady Mackintosh nodded, swiping at the tears falling freely. "Of course. But promise me ye'll no' make yourself a sacrifice? I still remember when…" Her voice grew choked, and Jenny knew well the memory that had to be plaguing her mother's mind. Her mother's dearest friend, Moire, had sacrificed herself for Lady Mackintosh's safety, and the pain and brutality of that loss had never faded.

Knowing that Moire had been Toran's mother changed so much… Every interaction Jenny and Toran had now held so much more meaning. And made her question his motives too—and wonder why exactly he was here.

Jenny pulled her mother back in for a hug, unable to face her, because she knew the request her mother made was not one she could necessarily honor. "I will no' be lost to ye, I promise." And that was probably the worst lie of them all, for she could promise no such thing. But she could wish it, hope for it, pray for it, keep her mother believing.

"Your da would be so proud," her mother whispered, patting Jenny's hair. "Now, enough of these tears." She drew in a ragged breath, swiped at her eyes one more time, and then stood, her back ramrod straight, her expression determined. "We've work to do."

"We?"

"Aye. There's easily twice as many socks left to knit as Isla and I did last week. We canna make less socks for Hamish's lot than we did for our own men. There is also training. Ye may be training men, but I can spend an hour a day training the women who work in the keep to protect themselves."

Jenny stood and grinned, excited to have her mother on her side. If only she had told her sooner, perhaps the past two years would not have been so steeped in misery. Alas, she could not go back in time, and to dwell on the past would put a damper on their bright future. "Isla will be so pleased to help ye. And I can gather the rest of the women for ye as well. See that the kitchens make ye all a hearty meal."

"And welcome Toran in to dine with us this evening." Lady Mackintosh winked at Jenny.

"Mama?" Jenny narrowed her eyes.

"I saw the way he was looking at ye in the courtyard. The lad is enamored."

Jenny shook her head. "Mama, I've no time for flirtations. I've a country that needs mending and a prince I've devoted my life to."

"Everyone has time for flirtation, love. Do ye nay recall the love between your grandda and grandma? The love I had for your father? Love is what keeps us on the right path when violence and horrors threaten to undo us."

She had a good point there. The idea of having someone to lean on, some way to escape danger if only for a minute was more than appealing—it made her heart ache. But how could she possibly?

Jenny thought back to those moments in the ruins where he'd held her close, worshiping her mouth—how the world had melted, how the redcoats had been the furthest thing from her mind. How when she'd finally been able to sleep it had been deep, a kind of rest she'd not reached in years. When she'd woken and seen Toran close by, she'd been filled not with heart palpitations and panic like she normally was but with a sense of calm and purpose.

"Ye may be right, Mama."

"Invite him."

Toran waited until Simon left the barracks before sneaking back inside. He'd waited too long already to seek out information. Kneeling beside his cousin's cot, he first lifted the thin mattress, feeling underneath and then along the seam for loose threads. Finding nothing there, he sifted through his satchel and his clothes and still came up empty-handed.

He felt along the floorboards for a loose board and finally found what he was looking for near the head of the bed. Toran popped the floorboard loose and felt around inside the dark space, his fingers brushing against a leather-bound book. Toran pulled it out and sifted through the pages—a diary logging everything that Simon and the rest of the clan did during the day. Then his focus narrowed on how many notes in particular were logged about Toran's actions. The man was bloody spying on him, not that it was truly a surprise.

Toran shook out the diary, looking for loose pages or letters but finding none. He searched the hole again, finding it empty. Just the log. There was no evidence to indicate that Simon had shared this information with anyone, but Toran wouldn't put it past him. He'd known from the start that Simon was a foul egg.

Had the Fox and his horde secretly switched sides once more? Simon wouldn't do anything to jeopardize himself in a house full of rebels—but he would sell Toran out the moment he found the right chance. And given their past, Jenny might believe him, pushing Toran away and forcing him right into Simon's trap.

Well, Toran had one thing on his side—Simon didn't know he knew.

The invitation to dine in the great hall came from Isla, who found him on watch atop the wall, though she swore it was Jenny who'd asked him to come. Toran had been prepared for another long night standing watch up on the wall, hoping the chill night air might douse some of the heat he felt when he thought of her.

He'd been a bloody fool to kiss her.

But it had felt so damn good. Having learned that the

men he'd never meant to die had lived was such a palpable relief off his shoulders, he felt drunk with it. The lass's lips were sweet as honey, soft as silk, and her boldness and enthusiasm had not disappointed him. Ever since he'd met her, he'd wondered at the passion that boiled beneath the surface of her brisk demeanor. And good gods, had she shown him.

It didn't seem to matter to either one of them that Dirk, Mac, and Archie had been sleeping only a few feet away. It was a mistake he was certain to hear about once the men had him alone, for if they'd woken, even just to roll over in their sleep, there was no way in hell they hadn't heard their soft murmurs or Jenny's gasps of pleasure when he'd pressed his mouth to hers. The sound fairly echoed in his ears even now.

He'd been on the verge of asking her about his mother, to get answers once and for all. So he could force away the confusing thoughts plaguing his mind. So he could know that wanting Jenny wasn't a betrayal of his mother, himself, and his clan.

Toran had never been a man afflicted by nerves, rarely worried over what a lass thought, and the fact that he couldn't seem to get beyond all of that now was like a kick to the ballocks. How had she so skillfully slipped beneath his defenses?

He entered the great hall, scanning the room for the woman in question.

She stood by the hearth beside her mother, Isla, and several other women. She was dressed in a plaid gown, this one a touch more formal, low-cut across the bosom and with no shawl draped over her shoulders, and he was able to take in the sight of her silky flesh, her skin sprinkled with a faint dusting of freckles, like spice sprinkled on cream. Her hair was swept back in a loose knot, light-golden tendrils curled and falling delicately around her.

The men seemed to be standing on the perimeter of the room, not approaching, but Toran ignored that subtle cue, walking straight up to the circle of women and giving a slight bow.

"My lady," he said first to her mother, taking her hand and kissing the knuckles. Then he reached for Jenny's hand too, and she stared at his outstretched arm as though he had a trap on the end of it instead of fingers. Finally she took his hand, and he kissed hers too.

"Such a gentleman," Isla teased, and he passed her a wry smile.

"I must thank ye for the invitation to dine. The idea of walking the walls tonight is much less appealing."

He spotted Dirk eyeing him from a dozen paces away, his brow furrowed and an irritated downturn to his lips. That man obviously wished Toran was still on watch, twenty feet above. The look was not unlike the glower he'd gotten from Simon when he'd left the barracks, though Simon wished him twenty feet under.

"We are glad ye decided to join us," Lady Mackintosh said. "And I must offer ye my gratitude for keeping Jenny safe last night." She seemed on the verge of saying something else but then bit back whatever it was.

"'Twas my duty to see to her safety, but alas, it was she who kept us all from collecting dragoon lead."

Lady Mackintosh blanched slightly at his words.

"We are alive and well." He beamed a smile, winking at the older woman in hopes of distracting her from the scare he'd inadvertently given her.

"And I am glad for it. Ye are most welcome to our table, sir. Would ye escort my daughter to her place?" She beckoned Dirk forward. "And I shall take the arm of my sweet nephew."

Toran glanced down at Jenny, holding out his elbow for her to loop her arm through. She hesitated a moment and then hurried to oblige when her mother started to say something.

As they walked toward the table, he bent his head toward hers, enough to keep their conversation confidential but not enough to be inappropriate. "Did the invitation truly come from ye, Mistress J?"

He watched her smile, her eyes fixed straight ahead. How very much he wanted her to look upon him, to see that light and fire reflected in their depths. He settled instead for finding a pattern in the freckles of her skin, swearing he could connect the dots on her shoulder into the shape of a musket.

"I suppose it did, though the idea was entirely my mother's."

Toran let his gaze slide from her shoulders along to her neck, eyeing the dip at the base of her throat. He wanted to touch it, to lick it. "Ye wound me."

Jenny's cheeks flushed the barest hint of pink. "I didna wish to take ye away from the task ye seemed so excited to maintain."

"My watch on the wall?"

"Aye." She touched the spot on her neck where he'd been staring.

"To tell ye the truth, I'd much rather watch ye."

They reached the table, and he pulled out her chair for her, tucking her into place, letting his fingers brush just lightly enough on her shoulder to feel the silken skin but not to gain her attention. Still, he could swear he heard her slight inhale. He started to move down the trestle tables to eat with the men when she called him back.

"Where are ye going?"

"To sit with the men."

"My mother wishes for ye to sit here with us."

"And ye? What do ye want?" The question was loaded, and he could see the intensity of it weighing on her. He leaned his head down closer and whispered, "Tell me."

"Perhaps that is a question best left until after the meal. I shall require a walk and an escort." The words were said so softly, he could barely make them out.

Toran raised a brow. "Is that a request, my lady?"

"Aye, if ye're no' otherwise engaged."

He slid into the chair beside her. "I am free. Ye may do with me whatever your heart desires." His gaze dipped to her lips, and color touched her cheeks.

"Ye're verra generous," she said with a flash of emerald eyes meeting his. "Perhaps my desire will be to lighten ye of your coin purse or your favorite weapon."

"I must protest, but if ye desired them overmuch, I suppose I could part with both. Though I'd like visitation with my weapon of choice every now and then."

She let out a soft laugh, a sound that gained the attention of several of those around the table. The sound was beautiful, a tickle to his ear that made him want to encourage it over and over, to give her that measure of happiness. Jenny was not a lass who laughed often, at least not in the few weeks he'd known her. She was serious, dedicated to the many people counting on her. He was curious some days to know how the hell she was still standing.

The servants appeared with food, serving them all portions of poached salmon drizzled in whisky sauce, and stewed vegetables, accompanied by thick bread, steaming hot, and pots of golden butter.

Hungry, most of them ate quickly. Toran couldn't help but notice, however, that Jenny barely ate at all.

"Are ye feeling unwell?" he asked.

"Nay, why?"

"Ye've barely touched your food. Do ye no' like salmon?"

She stared down at her plate as though she'd only just noticed. "I'm no' verra hungry, I suppose."

"Would ye like to walk now?" He was willing to miss the rest of his meal in order to take a walk with her. Hell, he'd miss a week's worth of meals or more if she'd let him kiss her again. A lifetime if she told him she wasn't guilty… "Though we may start tongues wagging."

"They can wag all they like." She turned to her mother. "Would ye excuse us, Mama? I need some air."

Her mother's expression was blank as she nodded and waved them away before turning to engage Isla in conversation.

Toran stood, offering Jenny his arm again, but she walked away ahead of him. On second thought, that was for the best. Everyone was already watching them leave the great hall. No need to start rumors about how intimate that joint leave-taking might be regarded.

Outside the sun had not yet set, though the sky was a dusky shade of blue. The moon had already risen, a silver crescent fighting for light with the fading sun. On the walls that surrounded them men stood at their posts, staring out over the moors and the loch beyond.

He followed a pace behind Jenny, acting truly as her guard rather than her escort. They rounded the courtyard and the side of the castle, passing by the outbuildings and then beyond them to the gardens and orchards full of vegetables, herbs, and nut and fruit trees.

Jenny paused on a path and turned to face him. She had that haughty expression, the one she wore when she was bossing him around. "Are ye coming, Fraser? Or will I have to wait all day for ye?" She raised a brow, teasing him.

"I was content to watch ye walking, Mistress." He let his gaze travel over her body rather rakishly as he came closer, only to have her swat at him playfully.

"Ye're a rogue. And when we're alone, ye dinna need to call me that. I like it when ye say my name."

"And I like it when ye say mine."

She smiled at him and turned to continue walking, waiting for him to step in beside her before she moved forward.

They traversed in silence several moments before she

spoke. "I told my mother about what I've been doing—about the cause. I was so nervous that she would try to force me to stop that I never considered she'd support me."

"That is good news."

"Aye." She smiled sadly and plucked a pear from a tree as they passed, rolling it between her palms. "My mother has been through so much. I dinna say that to take away from anyone else's pain, for we've all been through much, I know. We've lost so many already, and the battle has yet to truly begin."

Toran's gut tightened. The words were on the tip of his tongue. *What happened to my mother?*

Instead he said, "Why do ye believe in the Stuart crown?"

She jerked her gaze toward him, shock at his question in the widening of her eyes.

"I mean nothing by my inquiry, Jenny. I but wonder where your heart lies."

"My grandfather and my father fought in the first rebellion. They both lost their lives for the cause. Too much precious blood has been shed to turn back, all because pretenders wish to hold onto the crown. Ye know this. I know this. How many more Scottish lives will we lose before we win? I canna bear to see my children or my children's children having to fight off redcoats when they only wish to live a happy, peaceful life."

He heard her words, heard her mention of children. So she might someday want children? A sudden desire to bring those children into the world with her stirred in his gut. "Ye fight for a brighter Scottish future."

"Aye. I fight for our people." She paused her steps, bit into the pear, and then passed him the fruit.

Toran took it from her, happy to have his lips on something that had touched hers.

"What about ye?" she asked. "Why do ye believe Prince Charles should regain his throne?"

The toughest question of them all.

"I didna always, ye were right about that."

"What changed your mind?"

"Seeing my people die." Toran didn't tell her when or whose death it had been that had set that stage. "Seeing the spirit of those who lead others." He didn't tell her she'd played a part in that. "Camdyn and Isla mean everything to me. I canna imagine them living in a world such as this. I canna imagine them suffering what our mother suffered." His voice trailed off. Now—now he needed to say something.

The words were on the tip of his tongue, ready to spill off, but then she looked up at him with those wide blue eyes, her lips parted, and all he could think of was pressing his mouth to hers. Forgetting about everything else and just being with her. She made him feel alive the way no one, and nothing else, ever had.

Toran cleared his throat, passed back the pear. "I'm no' proud of some things I've done. Choices I've made."

"We have all done things we regret." She bit into the fruit, licking the juice from her lower lip.

"Aye, but I fear my secrets will haunt me even in death."

"Then ye'll have to make up for them now."

"I dinna believe I can."

She patted him on the chest, offering him the last bite. "Ye're already doing it."

Jenny's eyes were locked on his, and he had the distinct impression that she knew all about his past and could see right into his soul. It was not the first time he'd looked at her and imagined she could see him for who he really was. And she wasn't running. That was the most fascinating part.

Without thinking, he tossed the pear core aside and dipped his head toward hers, capturing her mouth. When she didn't pull away, he grasped her waist in his hands and tugged her flush against him. One more kiss before it all ended…

She kissed him back as eagerly as he kissed her, arms coming up around his neck, the taste of pear on her tongue. Toran explored every part of her mouth. He stroked down her back to her waist, remembering how it had felt to have her plump breasts pressed to his chest and longing to touch them. His hands spanned her middle, thumbs only a few inches away from the lushness of her breasts. He only had to move a fraction of an inch per breath and then he'd be there.

"Oh, Toran," she whispered against his lips. "Ye make me feel like I'm floating."

He chuckled, sliding his hands back around to her spine to keep her close. "Ye make me feel the same way, lass."

She tucked an errant lock of hair behind her ear, her wistfulness changing to sadness. She put a hand to her chest. "We canna ever be more than this."

"Right now." He found himself speaking the very phrase running in his mind.

"Toran…" Her eyes were pleading, and he couldn't decide whether she wanted him to beg to have her or to simply give in and let the moment pass.

"I dinna like to consign myself to a fate I canna know," he said instead.

Jenny smiled. "Dinna let your rebel leader hear that, else she may think ye unreliable on the battlefield."

"I am her servant."

"Ye are her soldier."

"Aye." Toran brushed his lips tenderly across hers once more, not taking it any deeper, though he desperately wanted to.

"We should get back," she whispered. "We've still much to do."

Reluctantly, he let her go, following her back to the castle, kicking himself for abandoning his line of questioning once more. When they were within a dozen feet of the rear entrance, Jenny stopped, pressing her hand to his arm before jerking it away again as though she had been singed. "Please, Toran, dinna kiss me again."

What the devil? He didn't bother to hide his shock. "That will be a hard promise to keep, but one I shall if that is your wish." Why did it feel like a hundred stones were pressing against his chest?

She licked her lips, her eyes cast down, and then she finally raised them to meet his. "When it is over."

When it is over. He rolled her statement over in his mind.

"Let us have something to look forward to."

He understood then. She would be willing to kiss him once the prince was on the throne, when he'd proven himself loyal to the Stuart line and worthy of her affection. Would he be able to?

"Is that a promise, lass?" he asked, taking her hand in his.

"Aye. I vow it."

He raised her hand to his lips. "I vow to kiss the hell out of ye when all this is over."

She smiled. "I shall hold ye to it." And then she turned and raced into the castle, leaving him feeling a little stunned at the promise he'd just made to the woman who should have been his enemy.

Fourteen

Mistress J,

Oh, can you believe it! The day is upon us! I hope to see you at the Glen, where Finnan will be awaiting a dance with you. He is ever so bonnie. Do you remember that august moment, not so long ago—we might have only been nineteen at the time—where we stared up at the stars and declared ourselves aligned with the angels? I still think about that.

I cannot wait to see you, my angel friend.

Devoted,
A. M.

WHEN FIONA ARRIVED AT CNÀMHAN BROCH THAT morning, supposedly to take tea with Jenny, she had Annie with her.

"Do ye know what this means?" Jennie held up the note. "*He* is here. Arrived on our shores, and we should meet him soon! The nineteenth of August at Glenfinnan."

"I like that she's calling ye an angel. Anyone who's been at the point of your pistol will no' agree," Annie teased.

"Prince Charlie's angels, that's what we all are, working toward our cause and helping our prince." Jenny twirled in a little circle that ended with her thrusting a pretend sword into the enemy.

Fiona snorted. "More like Prince Charlie's hellions."

Annie and Jenny both laughed at that and then flopped down in their chairs at the table, sipping delicately at their tea.

"I have so much to do," Jenny said. "We'll have to leave here in a sennight if we're to arrive in time to watch the prince declare his claim to the throne. And my mother and I've been spending several hours a week training the crofter women how to protect themselves when we're gone."

"How is your mother?" Annie eyed the closed door behind them.

"She knows all, and she supports me. In fact, I think it has helped her in dealing with my brother's betrayal."

"Will she wish to attend?"

"The battle?" Jenny shook her head. "Nay, she'll remain behind to keep the castle in order in case my brother or any dragoons come by." She told her friends then about the close call she'd had after the tavern visit.

"Ye could have been killed," Annie said, her face going pale.

"Ye take too many risks," Fiona added with a shake of her head.

"This coming from the two of ye? We have all taken many risks that could get each one of us killed."

"Aye, but ye're the only one who's come so close so far."

Jenny frowned. "I dinna know what else I can do. I canna stop." She glanced at the letter again, the carefully crafted message that sounded so much like society lasses gushing about an upcoming ball. "I canna let anyone down."

"Aye, we've all come so far. And we made an oath, one we intend to honor," Annie added.

"Will the two of ye come with me to Glenfinnan?" Jenny asked.

"I will be there," Fiona said. "I have had a missive from A. M. myself."

"As have I," Annie confessed.

"The same one?"

"Aye," they both said in unison.

"We shall meet upon the road then and travel together. There will be safety in numbers, especially if the English have caught wind of this."

"Will ye be bringing the supplies?" Annie asked.

Jenny nodded. "I think I should."

"Aye."

The door to Jenny's solar burst open, and Isla rushed in, stopping short when she noticed they were not alone. The poor lass looked ready to retch or run at having burst into the room without knocking.

"Oh, I'm so verra sorry." Her cheeks burst into flames of red, and she started to back out of the door. "I was looking for my knitting."

"Who is this?" Annie said, with a kind smile in an attempt to calm the lass.

"Come in, Isla, meet my friends, Annie and Fiona."

Isla dipped a curtsy to them both, and each of them fussed for her to stand and not bow to them.

"Would ye care to join us for tea?" Jenny asked, eyeing each of her friends, who gave wordless affirmations. It was best they not appear too conspiratorial. Knowing who her brother was, Isla couldn't be too much in the dark, but all the same, it wouldn't be worth scaring the poor lass if she was oblivious to everything going on around her. "Ye seem to have something on your mind."

"Aye, thank ye so verra much." Isla grabbed one of the stools and scooted close.

"I'll go get an extra cup for tea," Jenny said.

"Oh, I can go," Isla gushed.

"Nay, stay here and have a biscuit. I'll be right back."

She exited the solar, slipping down the back stairs toward the kitchens but pausing on the stairwell when she caught sight of Toran in the courtyard. He was leaning casually against the wall by the gate, chatting with a few of the men. They were obviously jesting about something, all laughing, and she found herself mesmerized by the easy nature of it. The normalcy. This was a rare moment of joy in times of worry.

The men abruptly stopped laughing, their bodies jerking to stiff pillars.

It was then she saw the riders coming down the road, the same moment the men on the wall gave the warning signal. The red coats of their impending guests shone brilliantly crimson in the summer sun; their golden buttons flashed. And though she couldn't hear from this distance, she could from memory add in the chink of bridles, swords, and spurs.

Dragoons.

Jenny would bet her right arm that Boyd was at their head. *Bloody bastard.*

She hurried back up the stairs to warn the women, but

by the time she burst through the door, her friends were already at the window, their faces pale.

Jenny pulled A. M.'s note from her sleeve and tossed it into the banked fire still smoldering in the hearth, where it crumbled to ash.

"Isla, go to my mother. Dinna go outside at all. Lady Mackintosh will keep ye safe."

Isla didn't argue as she rushed from the room and headed toward the stairs going up.

"If Boyd sees me here, we're lost," Jenny said. "He knows me for the wench at the croft and the rebel at the tavern."

"Then let me pretend to be ye, he willna know that I'm untrue," Annie said. "Go with your mother and Isla."

Jenny worried her lower lip. "Nay, he'll kill ye if he finds out, and I canna risk that."

"He canna kill a lady without cause."

"He will think he has cause, this I know."

———

Bloody bastards.

Toran grabbed Archie by the arm and gestured for Dirk to follow him into the barracks as the rest of the men hurried to go about their duties—farmers rather than soldiers training.

In the dim light of the barracks, Toran turned to Dirk. "Boyd knows me. He believes me to be loyal to the English."

Thunder rolled over Dirk's features, and Toran

watched as the man vacillated between competing desires to kill him or question him. "And are ye?" he growled.

"Nay," Toran answered without hesitation.

Dirk frowned. "*Were* ye?"

Toran worked hard to keep his voice steady and to not show any of his frustration. In fact, he was surprised it had taken Dirk this long to force the story from him. "I admit to having been a party to both sides in the past."

Simon rounded the corner then, clapping slowly, a look of satisfaction on his face. "At last, the truth comes out. Father knew ye were a traitor."

"I should kill ye now," Dirk said to Toran.

"I'd rather ye didna." He fixed his stare on Simon. "Him, however, I'd help ye."

Dirk slanted a glower at Archie. "And what about ye?"

Archie frowned. "I've always been loyal to the Stuart crown."

"I should have known, with your uncle being the Fox," Dirk said to Toran. Then he glanced at Simon. "And ye, your da is known as a double agent. What's to say ye're not the same?"

Simon shrugged. "What's to say?"

"I know ye've something to do with this. Toran rushed his cousin, ready to put him down, but Dirk grabbed the back of his shirt, putting a falter in his step, though it didn't stop him completely. However, Archie joined, holding Toran back from finally killing his cousin.

"Is he speaking the truth, Simon?" Dirk asked. "Did ye have something to do with the dragoons coming here?"

"Ye're harboring a fugitive."

"Mistress J," Dirk said.

Simon scoffed. "Nay—Toran. He's the traitor. Allow me to escort him out the gates and save all of ye the trouble of having to scuff your swords. My father and I are loyal to the Jacobite cause, while this whoreson was willing to kill a dozen of his own clan."

Hearing Simon call his mother a whore was enough to send the rage billowing out of Toran like cannon fire. He shot forward, breaking free of Dirk and Archie's hold, and tackled his cousin to the ground. With his hands at Simon's throat, he growled, "I know about the ransom."

Simon paled, his mouth going into a firm straight line. "Give yourself up, and I'll make certain Isla and Camdyn are safe."

"Ballocks. I'll just kill ye and never think about ye again."

"Like the men ye thought ye'd killed?"

Toran reared his fist back and slammed it into Simon's temple. The jackal's eyes rolled back in his head, his body going slack.

Mac burst into the barracks. "What the bloody hell?" He glowered down at Toran. "The two of ye have cost us enough time. Shall I put them in a cell, Dirk?"

"Just the unconscious one."

Mac nodded, and Toran climbed off his cousin, watching as Mac lifted him up and carried him out of the barracks.

Toran wiped the sweat from his brow, still panting, and turned around to face Dirk and Archie. Both of them were looking at him incredulously.

"I intercepted some information," Toran said. "My uncle was going to ransom the men in the garrison in exchange for myself and my siblings. Simon was only biding his time."

"And ye didna tell anyone?" Dirk asked.

"Aye. Foolish, I know, but I thought I could handle it myself."

"In this outfit, we dinna handle things on our own." Dirk grimaced and looked away.

"Understood. There's no point in arguing the matter. The fact is if Boyd sees me, he'll be suspicious of ye all. I betrayed him when I saved Archie."

"Fine. Stay out of sight." Dirk bared his teeth, and Toran had the distinct feeling the man wanted to tear into his flesh. "Does Jenny know about your past?"

"Some of it."

"Ye'd best tell her the rest soon, else I'll be telling her and ye'll no' want to deal with my fury on her behalf," he warned. Rounding on Archie, he asked, "What of ye?"

"Boyd will recognize me since I escaped his prison."

"Fine, then the both of ye stay hidden. Probably best if ye go into the castle and keep the women safe. We'll try our damnedest to keep Boyd out. If he makes it far enough to get to you, it's because he's stomped on our heads."

Toran agreed, and Dirk marched out of the barracks with the two of them on his heels. When Dirk headed for the gate, Toran and Archie hurried for the castle.

"Is what ye said true about Simon?" Archie paused just inside the entrance of the castle.

"Aye," Toran said without hesitation. "I intercepted a missive from Uncle agreeing to terms with Boyd for the exchange. Boyd will get more than he bargained for with Simon added to our ranks, and he wants me dead. So does Uncle because I went behind his back."

Archie nodded. "But why Isla and Camdyn?"

"That I canna understand." He shook his head and pressed his fist to the cold stone wall. "Simon has been keeping track of everything I do. I think he's behind Boyd's visit today."

"He could be."

"God, I wanted to kill him."

"He'll get what's coming to him. Maybe we'll all forget he's rotting in a cell."

"Wishful thinking."

They made their way up the stairs and paused outside Isla's door. There was no answer when he knocked, but Jenny's door jerked open, and her beautiful head popped out, worry creasing her brow.

"What are ye doing in here?" she asked.

"Where is my sister?"

"She's safe with my mother."

"Dirk requested we keep ye safe."

"I dinna need ye to protect me. But my mother and your sister would likely find comfort in your presence."

He wanted to ask why *she* wouldn't find comfort in his presence, but since that night when they'd had their last kiss, they'd been avoiding each other. It'd been nearly two weeks since, each keeping busy with their own tasks, each doing their damnedest to pretend the other didn't exist. Only she was everything he thought about in the morning when he woke and the very last thought he had before he fell asleep. If he slept at all.

And Toran had done what he did best—keeping an eye on Jenny while she talked with her nonexistent friend, the one who snuck in and out of the castle—and found out exactly when the prince would be arriving, which was *now*. Charles Stuart was here, on Scottish soil. And at any moment, the woman was going to insist on meeting him, on bringing all of her planning to bear. Och, but he couldn't blame her. In fact, he admired her for it.

If Simon wasn't responsible for the dragoons on their doorstep, was this the reason why? They'd not seen even a shadow of a redcoat since their nighttime run, and now the bastards were here.

Toran walked closer to her. "I have my orders from your second-in-command," he murmured.

Jenny snapped to attention and then turned to speak to someone else in her room. "Annie? Fiona? Would ye show Archie to my mother's chamber? I need a moment alone with Toran."

He leaned a shoulder casually against the corridor wall even when he felt anything but. The healer he'd met at the croft passed him, followed by the woman he'd seen sneaking into the castle weeks ago. That one flashed him a teasing smile.

The two women hurried down the corridor with Archie. As soon as they'd cleared the stairwell at the end, Jenny grabbed the front of his shirt, dragged him into her chamber, and shoved him up against the wall.

"Ye're strong," he teased.

"What are ye doing?" She glowered at him.

"Boyd will recognize myself and Archie. We thought it best our duties be to the ladies inside." He didn't tell her about Simon, not just yet.

"I dinna mean what are ye literally doing. I mean what are ye doing?" She waved her hands between them. "This. Coming to find me. Ye're a distraction, Toran. There are redcoats here at Cnàmhan Broch right now, and instead of helping, I'm in here with ye."

"Ye canna help. He'll recognize ye." He narrowed his eyes. "With all due respect, Mistress J, ye're not going out there. I saw what happened to ye at the croft. I was there when he chased us over the moonlit moors. The man wants ye, and then he wants ye dead."

"Why did ye no' say anything about Boyd before?"

"I thought it was no' my place to ask. If ye were willing to share it, ye would have."

"I thank ye for no' saying anything." She crossed her arms in front of her. "What makes ye think he willna recognize Dirk?"

"Dirk wasna at the croft. And he was well ahead of ye when they spotted us outside the tavern."

"And Boyd would know ye and Archie because of your arrest?"

"Aye." He gritted his teeth. Boyd knew him for a hell of a lot more. Now was the time to tell her about his past, and he was still unable to find the right words. Especially since Jenny's temper was high enough that she'd likely run him through before even asking questions.

Jenny backed away from him, going to her window to peer out from behind the curtain.

"Boyd is like Cumberland's own spawn," she murmured.

"Aye." He drew closer, leaning on the opposite side of the window frame. "Your prince has arrived on Scottish soil."

She flicked her gaze toward him. "How do ye know?"

"I listen too, Jenny."

She grunted. "I suppose that makes sense, given your background."

He stiffened.

"If my uncle were a great spy and renowned double-dealer, I'd have picked up a thing or two as well."

Toran winced. "My lady—"

"Jenny," she corrected.

"I have need to tell ye something." It was now or face her blade.

"They are here." She pressed her face to the window, and he did the same. Now was definitely not the time to hope for her understanding. Later. When Boyd had gone, he'd sit her down and confess all.

The men on the wall called down to the visitors, the echo of their voices like a dusting on the wind. Jenny unlatched the window and let it swing open a little, the wind blowing in gently over his fingers where they rested on the casement.

"Open the gates in the name of the king," Boyd shouted.

"We've paid our taxes and committed no crime.

Our laird, Hamish Mackintosh, serves King George at Stirling," Dirk called down.

With each word, Jenny's brow wrinkled deeper. The men would try as they might to shove the dragoons off, but Boyd wanted in.

Boyd drew his pistol and pointed it at Dirk, up on the wall. "I said open up."

Jenny shivered beside Toran, and he wanted to pull her close, to hug her against his body and hold onto her until all of this was over. To tell her there was nothing to worry about and that the redcoats would soon leave them be. But how could he promise something he was unsure of?

"I willna let him hurt ye," he whispered. That much he would make certain of with every last breath in his body.

Jenny looked incredulous. "I am no' worried for myself."

"I know, but I am."

She didn't look at him, her eyes wide and fixed on the gate slowly being opened. Her brother had thought the use of a gate to be entirely too old-fashioned, and perhaps it was, but it was for their safety, and she was glad now that she'd insisted he not tear it down.

"Go and hide the women," Jenny said. "If they will take one, it will be me."

"I'll not leave ye."

She glanced up at him then, her expression earnest. "Sometimes one sacrifice is better for the greater good than all of us perishing. A great woman taught me that."

Toran's gut soured. Did she mean his mother?

"Go, Fraser. That's an order."

Toran ground his teeth and planted his feet, crossing his arms over his chest. "I'm not leaving ye to sacrifice yourself."

She shoved against his chest. "Go!"

"Nay." He grabbed her hands, pulled her close. "I already lost one woman who meant the world to me in this war. I'm not losing another."

Her face crumpled in grief, and she looked ready to argue with him. He was so bloody ready to press his mouth to hers, to tell her that she belonged with him, that he couldn't even consider leaving the room.

But they were both distracted once more by the men in the courtyard. The voices had grown louder. Not because there were more of them, but because they were closer.

The courtyard had completely cleared save for Dirk and a handful of Mackintosh men who stood at the head of the dozen mounted dragoons, including Boyd.

"Where are your weapons?" Boyd demanded. "By our right, we've come to divest ye of any excess arms."

Dirk kept his hands at his sides as he spoke. "They've been sent to Laird Mackintosh to serve the king. We keep only what is necessary to fend off any outlaws."

Boyd narrowed his eyes, clearly disbelieving. "Where do the men sleep?"

"In what was once the barracks." Dirk nodded toward the building.

Boyd dismounted and started marching toward the barracks and stables, likely to investigate their weapon hoard himself. He waved at his men, who dismounted and joined him in the search. They shoved open the doors of various outbuildings. They were going to toss the place. Toran knew the drill. He'd witnessed it plenty of times. They would be entering the castle. They would commandeer anything they wanted. And if they found any guns, they'd line the residents up and either shoot them or take them to the garrison where they would wish they'd been shot.

"Ye need to leave, Jenny. And so do the women upstairs." His voice was calm, deadly serious.

"What?" She looked at him, confused.

"Boyd is coming into the castle. He'll find ye. He'll find everything. 'Tis what he does."

"How do ye know this?"

"I know it because…I've been with him when he's done this before."

She backed away from him then, shock and outrage on her face. "Ye brought him here." She pointed at him, accusing and angry.

"Nay," he adamantly denied, shaking his head. "I would no' have done such a thing."

"I dinna understand."

"I want to explain it to ye, but I've no time right now."

"'Tis no' just the women who we harbor here," Jenny said. "Have ye forgotten about everything we've been doing? Collecting?"

Ballocks!

"Where is it all?"

She hesitated, as though she didn't want to tell him.

She no longer trusted him, and that tore at his heart. Finally, she said, "In the tower room."

"Hidden?"

"Aye. But if they are looking, they will find it."

"All right, then we need to create a diversion."

"Such as?"

"Your mother. Most of the Highlands knows she's been ill. We need to have her more than just sick of heart. Perhaps a case of the measles is in order."

"And she's been quarantined in the tower."

"Aye."

"I'll move the women there. Ye find a way to make certain Boyd comes nowhere near us."

Toran agreed. "'Tis the least I can do."

"And when he is gone, we will talk."

"Aye, Jenny. We will."

He turned and left then, feeling a heaviness in his chest. *Mo chreach*, but he hoped this would not be the last time he saw her. Their plan had to work.

Toran hurried down the back stairs to the kitchen, where he found the staff huddled in the pantry, hiding. "I need a message to be spread among everyone who works at the keep. 'Tis from your mistress."

The women perked up, nodding, though fear still filled their faces.

"Lady Mackintosh has been struck with the measles these past five days and is in quarantine in the tower. Make certain all know it. We canna have the dragoons going up there."

"Aye, sir."

"But I just saw her this morning..." One of the maids,

not very quick to catch on, started to say before Cook swatted her. "Oh, I see. Aye, I'll not say a word."

Toran grimaced. "See that ye stick to the story, else they will burn this castle to the ground and not one of us will be walking away alive."

"Aye, sir." They nodded vigorously and dispersed, not once questioning. Their loyalty to their mistress was admirable and made him swell with pride.

The English had yet to infiltrate the castle, but he could hear them making a ruckus outside.

From the nearest window, Toran peered out, observing Boyd in the center of the ruckus, pointing to his men, giving orders.

A loud moan echoed through the courtyard, eerie and otherworldly. The men all stopped and turned to stare up at the castle.

"What was that?" Boyd asked sharply.

"The Green Lady," one of the men said with a shiver. "She haunts us."

A maid ran around the side of the castle with a bundle in her hands, making for the front stairs to the tower.

"You there, stop!" Boyd demanded.

The woman stopped short, nearly toppling backward. "Aye, sir?" She turned slowly, terror on her features.

"What have you got there? Where are you going?"

The maid did a fantastic job of glancing back up at the castle tower, her eyes wide with worry as she tapped at her bundle.

"Herbs for my mistress, sir. She's been near death's door with the measles these past several days."

Boyd stiffened, and the men around him backed away from the clansmen they'd been harassing.

"Measles?"

"Aye. We've been trying everything we can, but nothing seems to ease her suffering." The lass lifted her arm, wiping her eyes with her sleeve. "Me own ma just passed last week from it. An outbreak we've had. Three of the wee ones and Sarah's grandda."

Boyd took another step back at the mention of death and outbreak.

He glanced sharply at Dirk. "Is this true? Why did you not warn us?"

"Aye, 'tis," Dirk said, not missing a beat. He shook his head sadly and crossed himself. "I thought ye'd already know. We've been spreading the word to all those around."

"Seeing as how you're dealing with this, we'll be on our way." Boyd edged closer to his horse. "But do not think this is a reprieve. I expect, as loyal servants of King George, you will send a message to the garrison and let me know when all is well so I might return."

"Aye, of course," Dirk said.

Toran counted the seconds until the English mounted their horses and withdrew as swiftly as they'd come. He took the stairs two at a time until he reached Lady Mackintosh's room.

He raised his hand to knock, and Jenny threw open the door before his knuckles touched the wood.

"We did it," she said in a high whisper, and then she tossed her arms around his neck.

Her body crushed to his, the scent of her flowing

around him, her lush breasts pressing against his chest, and he couldn't help but envelop her in his arms.

"'Twas your servants who deserve the credit. I only delivered the message. They came up with the specifics of the scheme themselves."

"We are safe for now," she murmured against his shoulder, still holding tight to him.

"Aye, safe for now." He drew in one last longing breath and then eased away from her grasp. "I just wanted to make sure ye were aware the English had left."

"We are." She smiled up at him in a way he'd not seen before. Conspiratorial, proud. And he longed to see that same look on her again.

But not until he'd told her the truth. In their celebration, she'd momentarily forgotten her mistrust of him, and he'd basked in his reprieve for however short it was.

"I've a need to speak with ye about something. 'Haps another walk in the gardens after the evening meal."

"Aye. We need to." Her eyes narrowed slightly, but before she could say more, her friends called her back into the chamber.

Toran rushed down the stairs, pausing in the middle when he thought of maybe returning to her. He forced himself the rest of the way down instead. Tonight he'd tell her the truth. All of it.

In the barracks, Camdyn lay on his cot, his face pale. When he saw his brother, he exhaled visibly in relief. "I was worried," he said.

"'Twas a close call and will no' be the last," Toran said. "I know that's no measure of comfort, but it is the truth."

"I know, and I'm glad ye give it to me straight."

Toran sat down beside his brother, listening to him tell a tale of how he and the other men had hidden beneath their cots with swords, ready to cut into anyone wearing red. While Camdyn spoke, Toran caught snatches of conversation from the men around them who spoke about times past when the dragoons had come to their doorstep.

They started to talk about one woman, a great friend of Lady Mackintosh, who'd joined the rebellion. Toran slowly turned toward the conversation, listening intently, as did Camdyn, who knew about his mother's involvement in the rebellion. Both of them hungry to learn if this woman they discussed was their mother.

"Och but she had hair as red as fire," an older soldier said. "I flirted with her over a pint one night, and she nearly unmanned me with her dagger when I leaned in for a kiss."

"What was her name?" Toran asked, his voice hoarse.

"Moire."

Toran felt all the blood draining from his head, and he had the overwhelming urge to retch.

Beside him, Camdyn sat back hard.

"Och, but she was a firebrand," the older man said wistfully.

"Aye, she was a great mentor for our mistress," Mac said. "Used to accompany us on our routes."

"What…happened to her?" Toran forced himself to finally ask.

The room grew somber, those present hanging their heads low. It was Dirk who spoke, emotion filling his voice.

"The redcoats caught up with us on the road."

Toran narrowed his eyes. This was not the story he'd heard.

"She was so brave… Telling everyone to run and that she'd distract them. Jenny and her fought that night, but Moire"—Dirk shook his head—"she had it in her head that she was going to save everyone. And she did. She saved the weapons and coin too. They…they killed her."

"Dragoons killed her?" Toran stiffened.

"Aye."

"Ye're sure?"

Dirk narrowed his eyes and sat forward. "What kind of bloody question is that?"

Camdyn sat in stunned silence, and Toran was glad for that. "We heard she was killed by the rebels."

His mother had been a part of the rebels, he knew, because his uncle had been very vocal about her abandoning her clan. How much she'd kept from them. Did this mean she'd willingly gone to her death? If that was the case, then it meant that Jenny was not to blame for his mother's death. That his burning need for revenge had been concentrated on the wrong person.

Nearly every man in the barracks erupted in a roar of fury.

"'Twas that bloody Boyd," Dirk growled. "When I get my hands on him…"

Toran felt like he was going to retch. All this time, the man he'd pledged allegiance to had been the one responsible for his mother's death…and Boyd had to have known. Had to have been laughing behind his back as he reveled in the murder. What a bloody fool Toran had been. It had been the reason Toran had been so willing to lure the Fraser rebels to the garrison so he could question them in their part...except there had been no part.

Guilt riddled him, and he felt completely powerless. All the lives put in peril at his own hand—his own people's lives—because he'd believed lies.

Toran sat up straighter, rubbing his hand through his hair and then over his face. Nausea swirled in his gut, blurring his vision. Perhaps he should give himself up now. Surrender as an enemy and allow Jenny to take a sword to his neck.

He needed air.

"What's wrong?" Camdyn asked, following him.

Toran glanced at his brother. "Came close today."

Camdyn patted him on the back. "I've always wanted to be a soldier, like ye. Like our da. But I never knew that even our mother... I mean, I just didna understand."

"Ye're already a fine soldier, lad. And she's a woman ye can be proud of. Dinna believe anything but that."

Camdyn smiled, needing that comfort. "What of Uncle? Do ye think he's looking for us?"

Toran shook his head, cursing himself for the lie. "Nay."

Toran would bet every coin to his name that his uncle wasn't going to bide his time much longer. The man never could stomach waiting on anyone else. He'd be irritated that Simon was taking this long. He might be declaring himself for the Stuart return now, but the Fox could only be counted upon to vacate one den for another when cornered. And that was now.

Toran decided that Camdyn was old enough to share some of his thoughts. "I fear Uncle will align himself with Boyd soon."

Camdyn nodded, as if he'd been expecting that. "What happens when we get out on the battlefield and Uncle is there?"

"We face him. We have made our choice, and by then he will have made his."

"They say clan and country first. What if your clan is at odds?"

"Our clan is not. Me, ye, Isla, Archie, we are Frasers who stand on the side of right." As the words flowed off his tongue, he knew them for the truth they were.

"The right side."

Toran clasped his brother's shoulder and squeezed. "The prince's side. Mistress J's side."

Camdyn grinned. "Ye like her."

"Everyone likes her, look around." He indicated the men seated in groups around them.

"Nay, I mean ye *really* like her." Camdyn waggled his brows.

Toran ruffled his brother's hair. "I'll not be letting a lass distract me from our mission."

"Ah, so ye admit it, ye like her."

"I find her...intriguing."

Camdyn's grin grew wider. "Who wouldna? She's incredible."

"Dinna get your hopes up, lad. Ye're too young for her."

Camdyn touched two fingers to his jawline, running

them up and down the bone. "I am edging into manhood, Toran, ye'd best look out. We both know I'm the better-looking Fraser."

Toran laughed aloud at that. "Full of yourself too."

"Only because it's the truth."

Toran playfully shoved his brother backward, and Camdyn rose to the unspoken challenge. They started to wrestle, Toran letting him get in a few good licks before pinning his brother to the ground and looming over him.

"Ye almost got me."

Camdyn laughed. "One day the roles will be reversed. Just ye wait, Brother."

"I look forward to it."

Fifteen

JENNY STARED UP AT THE PURPLISH SKY. THE COLOR would be striking for a gown.

Beside her, Toran stood quietly. They'd walked together toward the vineyard, and the scent of wine grapes filled the air.

"Ye said ye wanted to tell me something." What was this feeling of dread in her belly? She couldn't face him, fearful of what he would say.

"My mother's name was Moire."

Finally, he'd decided to confess that to her. "Moire MacGillivray."

"Aye. Ye knew?"

"I only just learned recently. I'm so sorry for your loss." Tears filled her eyes as the memory of that day came back to her.

"Tell me what happened."

Jenny nodded, understanding how much he needed to hear it. "We were in the middle of the road, wagons loaded with the weapons and provisions we'd stolen from the redcoats." Her gaze dropped to her hands. "In the distance, we heard the marching of the dragoons coming to find us, to fight us. I said we needed to run, to hide. But your mother...she wanted to stay and fight, told the rest of us to leave. That she would be a distraction so we could get away. I begged her not to. But she shoved me to the ground and told me I would die if I stayed, and so would everyone else. That I needed to run to save the lot of them. I regret to this day not staying." She chanced looking up at him, taking in the anguish on his face and anticipating hatred, which thankfully wasn't there. "She was a brave woman. Perhaps the bravest I've ever known."

"She was." His voice sounded tight. "But that is not what I wanted to tell ye, Jenny. I have a confession that's been weighing on my mind, and I fear I canna stay here any longer without having told ye."

Her mouth went dry, and she stared at him, waiting, feeling her head wobble in a small nod.

"When my mother died…I got the news from my great-uncle and from Boyd. They put about that she'd been murdered by rebel Jacobites. That it was the rebels who did those heinous things to her. They sent her battered body to the castle in a pine box." His voice hitched. "*Mistress J* was carved into the box, and a note was…a note was with her body that said *Traitor*. My uncle was in league with Boyd at the time, and I didna realize. Shortly after that, he sided with the rebels, and I remained with Boyd."

She stiffened, that sense of dread in her belly growing worse.

"They set ye up, Jenny, for hate. And I confess that before her death, I was a King George loyalist."

"And after?"

There was a long silence, and then finally he let out a slow exhale. "My loyalty never wavered. Until recently."

"Ye mean ye sided with the *Sassenachs,* with Boyd and his murderous lot. The ones who killed her."

Toran flinched. "Aye. I believed that the Jacobites had

been so disloyal as to murder my mother. That they desecrated her body. Given that, how could I not seek retribution? I was told that the one responsible, the person who had my mother killed, was a female rebel. Mistress J, a leader of rebels."

His confession was a punch to her gut. This man standing before her, whom she'd kissed, whom she'd dreamed of a future with, whom she'd harbored and protected, was her enemy. Or at least he had been.

"Ye believed I had your mother killed?"

He nodded, his face tight.

"And now?" she asked, fearing the worst. "Ye canna be both a loyalist and a Jacobite, Toran. Ye canna switch back and forth if ye hope to gain anyone's trust. Ye canna stay here if ye think me capable of cold-blooded murder." *How will I ever trust ye again?*

"I am a Jacobite, Jenny." He got down on his knees, taking her breath away. "I swear to ye, my loyalties lie with the rebellion. Ye have inspired me to choose the side of right. My mother's side. And I believe ye were no' responsible for her death. I'm ashamed to have allowed those lies to have influenced me at all."

"Why did ye not choose her side before?"

He gritted his teeth. "My da was a loyalist. My whole life I was raised to be such. When my mother defected, I didna even know. It wasn't until just before her death that I found out, and I was in too much shock that she might have abandoned my father's ideals. And then when her body was sent… I was told that ye threw her to the wolves, and I believed it."

Her breath caught, and she gripped the sides of her gown to keep from striking him. Tears pricked her eyes, and she was close to screaming—both for the agony of him having thought such a thing and for all the lies he'd told her since the moment they met that she'd believed. How could he have shown her such affection if he believed her a murderer?

"I dinna believe it, lass. Not now."

"But ye did."

"I confess, I did." He grimaced. "But from the day I entered your service, your keep, I've been true to the cause, to the prince…to ye."

"How much of…us was real?" Jenny's knees wobbled, and she was close to collapsing. She squeezed them together to help keep herself steady. *Dinna fall down. Stay upright. Stay strong.* "I let ye kiss me… I shared pieces of myself."

She felt like she was being strangled. He wasn't the first man to have lied to her, and she was certain he wouldn't be the last, but that didn't make it hurt any less. That it was him at all was probably why it hurt so much.

"There is more."

Her fingers came to her throat as she listened.

"Simon—"

"He's in a cell. Dirk told me."

"Did he tell ye why?"

"Because he was sotted on nearly an entire cask of ale and attacked ye again."

"That is not the truth. Simon was sent by my uncle to keep track of my whereabouts in order to give the information to Boyd. They struck a bargain—the life of the men in the garrison for mine, Isla's, and Camdyn's. I didna believe it until Simon told me they were still alive."

Jenny shook her head. "That was days ago."

"Aye."

She opened her mouth to speak, but the words wouldn't come. Her throat was so dry, and she felt as though she was going to be sick. Her hands were cold, going numb where she clutched the skirt of her gown.

Finally, she was able to speak, her words coming out in a croak. "Ye need to leave, Fraser. Go back to the garrison for all I care." Och, but that was a heinous lie. She didn't want him to go back there, back to certain death, and that made all of this even worse. For she truly did care for him.

"Jenny, please—"

"Dinna call me that. I am nobody to ye. Dinna remember me. Dinna remember what ye saw here. If ye ever cared about me at all, ye'll forget me and my people, and ye'll never grace my presence again."

He was shaking his head, his face crumbling into despair like she'd never seen on another person. She read it in his face, that he regretted everything, wanted forgiveness, was willing to beg for it down on his knees before her.

"My lady, please," he pleaded, anguish on his striking features, his icy-blue eyes glistening. "I swear to ye now, on pain of death, that ye have all of my loyalty. I am with ye. I am loyal to Prince Charles."

"Your brother and sister will be safe here should ye

choose to leave them behind. Simon will be dealt with." She took a step back from him, feeling as though she might collapse. He might have hurt her less had he thrust his blade into her heart.

"What can I do to prove to ye that I am loyal? I'm begging ye."

What could he possibly promise her? The man had lied about his loyalties, betrayed his people. Likely more than once. Who was to say that he wouldn't do so again? What if he got them all killed? How could she trust him when he had proven to be so adept a liar?

Jenny thought of Camdyn and Isla, so young, so impressionable. The two of them had begun to make lives for themselves in the clan. They were a part of it. Isla had grown so close to Jenny's mother. If Toran decided to leave and take them with him, she would fight for them. They should not have to suffer his betrayal. Or their uncle's.

Jenny took another step back. "Go. Please."

Now she was close to begging, needing him desperately to get away from her so she could think. So she could come to grips. So she could mourn an imagined future that felt as if it had just been ripped out of her.

This was why she'd promised herself to stay faithful to Scotland. This was why she'd vowed that the only important man in her life would be her prince and future king. Because now she was gutted, all because she'd dared to give her heart away.

A choke rose up in her throat, and she worked to keep it down, to hide it from Toran.

She *had* given her heart away; she was in love with him. Hopelessly in love with a traitor.

Toran finally stood, his eyes full of sorrow. His hand floated toward her but fell back to his side when she didn't move.

"Go. Now. Please."

Toran nodded. "If that is what ye truly wish."

"'Tis."

"I'm truly sorry, Jenny," he said, ignoring her demand for the use of her title—a reminder of how close they'd briefly become. "When I first met ye, I thought to make my mother's death right in my mind. But when I saw how ye were willing to care for your men, how much ye were willing to risk for your country, I started to change. Ye showed me the way."

She was shaking her head now, not wanting to hear more, but he kept on talking.

"I didna give ye away to the dragoons when I could have. I brought Camdyn and Isla to ye. Why would I risk their lives if I meant to betray ye?"

He made a valid point, but she didn't want to hear it. Couldn't right now. "Why did ye not tell me sooner?"

He shook his head regretfully. "There were many times I wanted to, but it always—there is nothing I can say except I'm sorry. My excuses are only that, excuses. There is no explanation for why I kept it a secret save to say I was a coward."

"There is no room in a rebellion for a coward."

She might as well have run him through with her sword for the emotion that cut across his face. And it was cruel of her, purposefully so. They were battling here, but words and emotions were their weapons.

The man might have lied to her, might have been confused about which side was on the side of right, which made sense given how he had been deceived. But he wasn't a coward. A coward would not have broken his cousin out of prison. A coward would not have fought off redcoats. A coward would not have brought her to safety when he could have tossed her to the wolves. He'd risked his life for her already—more than once.

But she wasn't ready to forgive him.

"Ye dinna have to leave Mackintosh lands this night. But I do need ye to leave my sight," she said, relenting. That was as much as she was willing to concede to him now. As much as she could live with. For if he obeyed and walked off her lands and she never saw him again, she was certain never to forgive herself.

Toran bowed low before her, and she resisted the urge to reach out and touch the wild mane of his hair as it fell forward and over his face. But the moment was over too soon. He backed away a few steps and then turned on his heel, walking slowly back to the castle.

A stone bench was hidden from the view of the path beneath an arbor to her right. She shuffled forward and collapsed onto it, finally allowing herself a moment to break as the coldness of the stone soaked through her gown and tears poured from her eyes.

Her heart ached, a lancing of pain shooting straight through her chest. How was she to know whether he could be trusted? Allowing Toran to remain was too high a risk, and to let him back into her heart could be disastrous.

Was she willing to risk her heart, her plan?

Jenny swiped angrily at her tears. Why did she have to fall for him in the first place? Why did she have to insist on one last run that fateful night? If she hadn't, they never would have crossed paths. And then he would have likely been caught by Boyd. By the time she'd found him and Archie, the lad would not have been able to travel much further. The idea of the two of them in Boyd's evil hands was enough to send a chill up her spine. The idea of never having met Toran at all made her grief all the worse.

Footsteps on the garden path jolted Jenny from her thoughts. The sun had already lost its battle with the moon, blanketing the garden in darkness.

Jenny's heart skipped a beat. She used the cuff of her sleeve to wipe away any more tears and then stepped onto the gravel path with her dagger in her hand.

Annie and Fiona walked with purpose toward her, their faces covered in shadows, but she knew them well enough to make out their shapes in the dark.

"What are ye doing out here?" Annie asked.

Her friends surrounded her, their presence a warm comfort. "I wanted some air," she lied, shoving her dagger back into her boot.

Fiona let out a sigh and leaned her head against Jenny's shoulder. "Are ye all right? We…heard what happened."

"Ye were spying on me?"

"Not exactly," Annie said. "We were talking with Dirk about the upcoming *ball*, and we just so happened to stumble across the two of ye. We told Dirk we'd make certain ye were all right."

"Toran betrayed me."

Annie took Jenny's hand in hers and squeezed. "For what it's worth, he sounded as heartbroken as ye. And what if it had been your mama sent back in a box?"

"I canna believe it. Why would they make it look as though I'd killed her?"

"Because those bastards didn't want the entirety of the rebels to come down on their heads. They hoped to pull rebels to their side. Boyd is clever, and he wanted ye to come out of hiding to defend yourself," Fiona said.

"But we never even heard about how she returned... Oh God, I canna believe how much she was made to suffer." Jenny dropped her face into her hands as she sobbed. Her two best friends held her close as she cried, whispering soft words to calm her, but the tears kept coming. To be sure they'd been waiting to be shed for a long time.

She cried for the loss of her friend, for the loss of Toran and her broken heart, for the loss of their fathers and all their men and the ruin of the country.

When Jenny's tears subsided, Annie said, "I know just want this calls for."

"What?" Jenny wiped at the tears streaking her face.

"Sweets. I'll go raid Cook's kitchen and see if I canna find us something delicious."

"And wine," Fiona added. "Grab a jug of that too."

"What would I do without ye two? I'm so glad ye're here." Jenny hugged them both once more, and then they made their way back to the keep. "We've been through so much together. I pray one day, the three of us will be old ladies, sitting about the drawing room and sipping tea, reminiscing about our escapades."

"We made a pact," Fiona said.

"A blood pact," Annie added.

Jenny smiled. "Friends forever, rebels always."

Dirk waited by the back door of the castle, just far enough away not to hear what they'd said but close enough to be of assistance in the garden if he was needed.

"I'm going to go help Annie," Fiona said. "We'll meet ye upstairs."

Alone with Dirk, she didn't know quite what to say. Luckily, he filled the silence. "I thought we could talk about the upcoming journey."

"Aye, let's."

She shooed him back toward the castle, setting a brisk pace for them both and glad to be talking about something other than Toran. "It will take us at least four days to get to Glenfinnan with our wagons. And the nineteenth is in two weeks."

"The men are ready, as are our stores."

"Good. And we've plenty of supplies to present to the guest of honor."

"Aye." He stopped walking a moment, touched her arm, stilling her. "Are ye all right?"

Jenny swallowed around the lump in her throat. "I'm fine. Why?"

Dirk cocked his head to the side, and she wished like hell in the dark she could read his thoughts. "Ye forget we've known each other since we were both bairns."

She laughed a little at that. "Ye're like a brother to me, Dirk. Perhaps the only true brother I've got."

"Ye can tell me whatever is bothering ye."

"I know." Her eyes still burned from her tears.

"Did Toran finally tell ye?"

"Finally? Ye mean to say ye've known all along?"

"I had suspicions. They were only just confirmed recently. He's a good man, Cousin. Despite his past, I trust him."

"And ye said nothing to me?" She was still baffled by this fact, ignoring Dirk's conclusions completely.

"He asked to tell ye himself. I warned him if he didna do it soon that I would."

"And what about Simon? Why did ye lie about the reason for putting him in the cell?"

Dirk sighed heavily. "I didna want ye to worry over it. We were in the middle of a raid by dragoons."

She wanted to be angry, but the ultimatum that Dirk had given Toran had been a fair one. She found her anger deflating, marginally.

"Thank ye for looking out for me." She decided not to tell him that she hadn't forgiven Toran yet, that she'd told him to leave Mackintosh lands and then relented, fearing Dirk would make certain he actually did leave before she woke.

"I always do."

Jenny dragged her thoughts back to the cause, back to their fight to put Prince Charlie on the throne. Planning would distract her from her pain. "With the dragoons watching us, we'll have to be careful. Taking the entire load at once will be dangerous."

"I agree."

"'Haps we should hide some in the tunnels and pack the rest in wool or in the false bottoms of wagons."

"Aye."

"That way if we're stopped on the road, they will not see it."

"I can have our men start the work on the false bottoms tomorrow."

She nodded. "There's been no word from my brother either. Nor his men." Not even a thank-you. She'd half expected the three traitors to return with rebukes from her brother about the missing materials from his list.

"He's a selfish bastard," Dirk said.

"'Tis a shame, for he's fierce on the battlefield." They'd both been trained by their father and grandda. Both of them knew how to fight like a rebel, infinitely superior to the dragoons. Hamish, damn him, had taken that skill to the other side.

"Aye, but ye can best him."

"Do ye think it will come to that?" Jenny dreaded the day she came face-to-face with her brother.

"I canna say for certain, but the both of ye are fighting on opposite sides."

"The men here have no loyalty to Hamish anymore." Thank the saints, or she would have been dealing with more than those treacherous three.

"Aye, they've seen the way their families were treated by the dragoons, and they feel just as betrayed as the rest at Hamish's switch in loyalty."

"My da has to be rolling in his grave, bless his soul." Jenny crossed herself.

"He has ye to keep his legacy alive and keep the clan safe."

Jenny nodded, considering that. If she were the one to keep them safe, to keep them thriving, and her brother was now an enemy of their clan, then perhaps it was time she laid claim to his title formally. She was his heir apparent, and she could become Mackintosh laird, ousting Hamish and his traitorous claims on her people and their resources forever.

She chewed her lip, the thought rolling around in her mind like dice on a table.

"I had planned to make a trip tonight," she said, "but I think it would be safest for us all to remain behind the walls for the next few days."

"Aye. Do ye want Toran and me to take the rounds of the perimeter? See if the dragoons have truly left the holding?"

She shook her head adamantly. "No' Toran."

"Archie?"

"One of our own."

Dirk stopped walking then, and when she looked at him, she could see his disappointment, perhaps even a bit of censure in his eyes. "Jenny, they are our own."

"No' tonight," she said, ignoring how awful it made her feel to say such. "Take someone else."

Her cousin didn't agree with her, she could see it in the stiff lines of his shoulders. But neither did he try to argue. And for that she was grateful.

With his silence she turned to walk again, heading from the garden back to the castle.

Sixteen

JENNY DIDN'T CHANGE HER MIND AND FORCE TORAN to leave, nor did it appear that she had told anyone else about her brief order for his exile. She also didn't speak to him for four days, notwithstanding his attempts to make amends and not for the lack of others trying to interfere. The tension between the two of them was palpable, and the time for her to leave to meet the prince was growing closer. The idea of her riding off without him at her side unsettled him.

Aye, he knew Jenny was plenty capable of protecting herself; he'd seen it firsthand. But he still couldn't just stay behind. He had a mission to win her over, to prove to her that he was worthy, that she could trust him. Damnation! He had to prove that he was the man for her.

Dirk did tell him that they'd decided to keep Simon in the cell until after meeting with the prince so he wouldn't be able to foil their plans or put anyone in danger while they were gone. It would be then that he dealt with his bastard uncle as well.

Finally, one morning, he waited in the shadows between the barracks and stables for her to check on the men constructing her false-bottomed wagons. He started toward her, and as though she sensed him—as much as he always sensed when she was near—she glanced up. Panic flashed quickly on her face before it disappeared.

"I'm going with ye, Jenny," he said. "Dinna deny me."

Her frown deepened, and she watched him through eyes that left no room for guessing at her thoughts. Those in the courtyard paused, trying poorly to be surreptitious in their eavesdropping.

"If I choose to deny ye, that is my right," she said, crossing her arms over her chest and managing to look down her nose at him despite him being taller.

Toran bowed his head. "Aye, 'tis. I'm asking ye not to." He raised his gaze to hers, searching the emerald-green eyes for some sign and feeling himself getting lost in their depths. "I was going the wrong way until I met ye, and I've been lost without your direction. I'll get down on my knees right here if need be. Ye've punished me thoroughly, I admit it. Allow me to prove to ye I am true."

"There is no coming back," she said, eyes steady, back stiff. "If ye betray our cause, I'll kill ye myself."

"Should it come to that, I will hand ye the weapon of your choice. I swear to ye, ye can trust me. I am yours." He cleared his throat. "Yours to do with what ye will. I am your soldier."

There was a shift in her eyes at that declaration, giving him a moment's glimmer of hope.

"Ready yourself, soldier." And then she turned her back on him and marched toward the castle.

He wanted to run after her, to swing her up in his arms and thank her for giving him a second chance, but to do so would cause a scene—not to mention possibly inspire her to change her mind.

Toran glanced at those milling around the courtyard. Some stared at him with respect and others with expressions he couldn't determine. There was one face that didn't look too pleased at all, and that was Dirk's, which didn't surprise him in the least.

If he was going to win over Jenny completely, he needed to win over her cousin as well. No way could he have the man she was closest with looming over him and wanting him dead. Toran wasn't afraid of Dirk. Hell, when they'd grappled weeks ago, they'd been evenly matched. If Toran had actually put in more effort, then he would have bested the man.

Toran nodded in Dirk's direction, and to his surprise, Dirk nodded back.

Never before had Jenny experienced this unsettled nervous feeling. Not when Boyd had had his hands on her, not when they had been running from dragoons with bullets whizzing past her head. But when she was around Toran, when he had begged her in front of everyone to let him come along with her, to believe in him—when it felt like her future hung in the balance and she had to choose an irrevocable path for the rest of her life—her entire world turned upside down.

She made it into the castle before she pressed her back to the wall and let out the breath she'd been holding, only to drag another one in. Her heart pounded in her ears, and all she could think of was Toran's pleading eyes. His kiss. The fact that her soul seemed to reach for him.

She couldn't say no. Couldn't turn away.

And the idea of leaving him behind seemed impossible. She wanted him near her. And having him there beside her—or at least in her vicinity—would alleviate any worried thoughts she might have. About how he was faring, for instance, if he was thinking of her, if he'd decided to go back to Fraser lands or even cross over to the English side once more.

This would be a test for him. A test for them both, truly. To see if Toran was loyal as he said, to watch him interact with the prince, and to know for herself if there truly was no going back. Because when he'd declared himself hers—even if he'd corrected himself to say her soldier—she'd known what he'd meant. It had taken every bit of willpower she possessed not to run and throw herself into his arms, to feel the comforting strength of his embrace, to breathe in his scent, to kiss him.

Right there in front of everyone, he'd been willing to break, to bare his soul to her, and she'd seen it. Felt it in her heart, and it was changing her.

He was changing her.

Jenny pushed off the wall and went to her father's study, the room her brother Hamish had never bothered with. He had preferred to keep all of his machinations to the great hall, as if parading his traitorous notions on display.

The maids kept the chamber tidy and fresh. Shelves lined the walls, filled with her father's books and papers. Items her brother would have discarded like yesterday's rubbish if she'd not insisted they were important to her.

God, she missed her father. Missed the way he'd invite

her up to his study after supper and share stories of the past, discuss with her the politics of the day. He was content to have her read in the corner while he wrote letters, and on occasion when his hand cramped, he'd ask her to write them while he dictated.

Hamish had always been too busy with his horses or his friends, making merry instead of spending time in this chamber learning what it meant to be chief to his people. Her father and Hamish had never really seen eye to eye from the time her brother was a bairn. She supposed it made sense that when their father died, Hamish had run off to side with the English—a final defiance and insult to their father even though he was already dead and buried.

Jenny glanced toward his desk, could still see him there smiling at her, beckoning her forward to show her whatever it was he was working on.

That little seed that had started in her mind was blooming, its roots finding purchase in her veins. Her father had groomed her to be laird, even if he'd never said it outright. She knew what to do. Hell, she'd already amassed an army, armed and funded it. If she could do that in secret, imagine what she could do if given true power to make things right.

Hamish didn't deserve to be laird. He hadn't earned it, and he didn't care enough about his people to rule them. But she had and she did.

She ran her fingers along the shelves until she came to her father's favorite, *Gulliver's Travels*. She lifted it from the shelf, opened it up, and drew in the scent of old paper, memories rushing back. When she'd been about seven years old, she'd commandeered one of their skiffs and shoved it out onto the loch, taking an oar, prepared to row herself to Lilliput. Thank goodness her hound Dom's sire had been on the shore barking his head off, or she might have adventured to another land altogether in the afterlife.

Jenny relived her memories for a few moments more and then put the book back on the shelf and went to sit in her father's chair. Being laird, asking for the clan to side with her, to be loyal to her, seemed like a hard prospect. But already they looked to her for leadership. There didn't seem any reason for them not to agree to her taking the title permanently.

The next male choice in line would be Dirk, but he wouldn't take it from her. If that had been his aim, he would have stopped her from doing what she'd been doing two years ago, not followed her every step of the way.

Nay, her cousin would support her. And so would her people, she was certain of it.

But would her mother?

Lady Mackintosh still wanted her daughter to marry and marry well. But marriage didn't have to mean giving up her position of leadership, did it?

No, it did not.

Jenny pressed her hands flat to her father's desk, the place where he had often laid them once he'd made an important decision. She was going to do this. She would take her brother's place as laird. When Hamish found out, it would mean a battle at their doorstep, and she was prepared to fight him. But at the same time, she was also trying to fight a war for the prince. Perhaps it would be better to officially lay claim to the Mackintosh laird-ship after the prince had been established on the throne. Prince Charles would undoubtedly support her claim after all she'd done for him.

A soft knock came at the door, and she called out, "Enter."

Fiona slipped inside, looking as though she hadn't slept in days.

Jenny stood and hurried toward her friend, worried she might collapse right then and there. "What is it?"

"The prince… He didna bring French reinforcements."

"What?" Jenny's heart twisted in fear. "What's happened?"

"Aye. His ships were attacked at sea. One of them, the *Elisabeth*, was damaged in a storm and not allowed to make passage by the English. 'Twas the one filled with gold and weapons. All the ships but one have returned to France. So the prince is here, but he's arrived with noth-ing but good faith and a few men. They have made a base at Kinlochmoidart and go back on their ship, sailing out whenever the dragoons come near. They are taking no chances."

Jenny felt herself wavering on her feet. They needed the French reinforcements, coin, and supplies. She'd been able to gather a lot of supplies, and so had several other Highland leaders, but what she had amassed was nothing compared to what the English possessed.

They'd been counting on France and on the prince's connection. Without it, they would be sunk.

"Are they coming back? Sending more?"

Fiona shook her head. "I dinna know for certain. He hopes to gain supporters here and that the French will return and invade from the south." She collapsed into the same chair Jenny had sat in as a young girl. "But to make matters worse, many of those who said they'd back the prince are angry now. They're threatening not to help him, saying that since he failed to show up with the soldiers and weapons as promised, they dinna trust him to deliver himself to the throne."

Jenny leaned back against her father's desk, bracing her hands on either side to steady herself. She shook her head, disbelieving. "What of our friend, A. M.? Has there been any word?"

"I've had no messages."

"I will still go to Glenfinnan," Jenny said, determined.

Fiona looked incredulous. "Ye canna be serious."

"I will. With a handful of men, and I will leave behind the supplies. I want Prince Charlie to know we support him fully."

Fiona nodded as if she'd expected as much. "I'll be going with ye."

"'Tis probably better if we're no' seen together."

"Ye're right. But I willna be far behind or ahead of ye, that I can promise." Fiona stood, scrubbing a hand over her face in an effort to wake herself.

"Will ye not rest a while?"

"I canna. I have more deliveries." Packages, messages,

news… Jenny didn't ask how Fiona came by her information. That was her friend's mastery and should remain a secret from everyone, including Jenny. What she didn't know couldn't be tortured out of her.

"Be safe, my friend." They embraced, and Jenny squeezed her friend tightly, fearing what was to come next. The prince had already failed in his initial mission. Would the Scots rally? Would their supporters in England and Wales pick up arms, or would they stay true to King George?

Fiona startled her from her worries. "I shall see ye at the Glen."

"Aye, and we shall dance the night away with a man named Finnan," Jenny said absently. The two of them laughed. Not because it was particularly funny but because it eased the worry and tension that wound them both so tightly.

A soulful howl came from outside the door after Fiona had departed, and Jenny went to open it, letting in old Dom. Her father's hound padded across the floor and went to curl up beneath her father's desk, a task that was quite a feat for his size. Jenny crouched low, stroking a hand over the hound's back.

"I miss him too," she murmured.

Seventeen

TORAN LOOKED UP JUST IN TIME TO SEE A MASSIVE wool sack hurtling toward his head. He caught it before it decapitated him and let out a grunt at the weight and impact against his chest.

Dirk stood before him, lifting another sack and tossing it toward him as though he were throwing snowballs and not woven sacks packed full.

Again Toran caught it and placed it on the pile. They'd been doing exercises like this all morning, lifting and tossing the sacks to hone their muscles. Today it was sacks of wool; tomorrow might be cabers or boulders. It seemed as though Dirk was trying to challenge him in this exercise instead of another all-out fight.

Toran was willing to take that challenge.

Dirk threw the next sack a little harder, the impact taking Toran's breath. He chucked it onto the pile. The next one caused him to take a step back. Rather than toss it onto the growing mountain, he chucked it back at Dirk, hard as the man had thrown it at him. If he wanted to challenge him, fine, but Toran didn't have to take the abuse.

The man looked surprised, but then he grinned and threw the same sack right back at Toran. He leapt back to catch it, a grin of his own matching Dirk's. So this was how it was going to be. He was ready.

They danced in a circle, tossing the sack back and

forth until they were both sweating and a ring of men had formed around them.

Then Archie leapt into the center, arms outstretched to catch the sack in midair as it hurtled toward Dirk. He tossed it to Angus, who tossed it to Camdyn, and around and around they went. Toran picked up another sack, passing it back to Dirk, until it was stolen. Again and again until half of the pile they'd previously stacked was flying through the air and the bailey echoed with shouts of laughter and calls for men to pass.

But just as suddenly as the game began, it ended. Jenny appeared, dressed in her trews and frock coat, light-golden hair braided down her back. She was frowning yet utterly beautiful. Her face was drawn, and she scanned her gaze over the men.

"I've a need to have a word with ye. Both of ye." She pointed at Toran and Dirk and then turned to head back to the castle without explanation.

Toran tossed his brother the sack he'd been holding and hurried to catch up with Dirk. Seemed they were both in trouble if she was calling them inside together. Hell.

Perhaps that had been Dirk's plan.

The logical part of Toran's brain denied both those ideas. Jenny was clearly disturbed by something, and it wasn't the men throwing bags around.

She led them up the stairs to a dimly lit study with shelves lined with books.

"Shut the door," she instructed.

Toran did as she asked and followed Dirk to the center

of the room, mimicking his posture of standing with his hands behind his back at attention.

"I've had some news that will change some of our plans," she stated. "We're still going to Glenfinnan, so dinna try to argue that point. But it would seem the prince has arrived with few reinforcements and no provisions. He is spending time at Kinlochmoidart and also sometimes on his ship." She told them about what she'd learned from her courier. "I canna know more until we go and meet with him, but I do know this. We haven't come this far to give up. We didna sacrifice so much of ourselves and have others give their lives for us to pack it up now."

Toran nodded, but Dirk was shaking his head.

"Dinna speak yet," she said, holding up her hand. "I'm no' finished. We will go to Glenfinnan, but we will not bring the supplies as originally planned. And we will go with a small group so as to avoid raising suspicion with the dragoons. When I thought we might be leading those bastards to an army of Frenchmen, that was a different story."

"Without the support of the French?" Dirk started, but she cut him off.

"I'm well aware of the risks, Cousin. But without risk, we do no' succeed. The prince needs to know he has support here, and the more clans that show their loyalty, the more will join in. If he's forced to return to France, there's no telling when he'll be able to muster enough confidence from the Scots to return." She glanced at Toran, and he had the distinct feeling she was talking about him. He was a risk to her. Did that mean she believed in him?

Did that mean she needed him?

It was too much to hope for. The lass was fiercely independent, and that was one of the reasons he admired her so much. She didn't cower in the face of danger or shrink before a man simply because he was a man. Nothing seemed to intimidate her. And Toran found all of it...arousing.

So to think that this woman, who faced down dragoons and other demons, might need him—the thought had desire flooding his veins.

"Aye, J." Dirk's voice was tight. He didn't agree, but he didn't seem about to argue with her either.

Toran respected that about Dirk. The man clearly had opinions, but he was loyal to Jenny and willing to do her bidding.

Jenny turned to stare at him, waiting for his response. There was only one response Toran could give her. Only one he wanted to give her.

"Aye, Mistress J. I am but your servant."

Jenny gave a quick shake of her head. "Ye are no' just my servant, Fraser. Ye're a soldier and a Jacobite."

"Aye." He grinned, wanting to stalk across the room and bend her over his arm as he kissed the tartness from her tone.

"I will leave it up to the two of ye to decide who else comes with us. I want the party to remain small, like our nightly hunts. We'll also need to arrange for a new hiding place for our supplies. We canna risk a raid while we're away. We were lucky once that Boyd was afraid of the measles, but he'll be back soon enough, and he willna be stopped."

"When do ye propose we leave?" Toran asked.

"I want to leave in two days' time. I dinna want us racing across the moors and catching the notice of English scouts. I also dinna mind if we arrive a few days afore the proposed date to throw the dragoons off. If everyone arrives on the same date at the proper time, without the French troops to back us up, we may have a battle on our hands that we canna handle."

"Is there anything ye canna handle?" Toran forced himself not to wink at her.

Dirk made a gurgling noise of disgust, but Jenny swung her gaze to meet his, a brow raised. "No' that I've come across yet," she said. "Is that a challenge, sir? Would ye care to take it to the field or the board again? I daresay, if put to the test, I'm strong enough to sling wool too."

"I have no doubt that ye can." He grinned at her. "And this is why I'd follow ye to the ends of the earth if ye asked me to."

She stared at him, clear contemplation in her gaze, and he waited for her to completely rip his heart out. When she lifted her chin, staring down her nose at him, he imagined how her retort would cut. How he'd bleed slowly to death but no one would see it.

"I dinna require ye to follow me to the ends of the earth, Fraser. All that I ask is that ye remain loyal to your rightful king, that ye do your best to protect our people, and that ye kick *Sassenach* arse on the battlefield."

Toran placed his hand over his heart. "I swear to ye now that I can and will do all of those things."

"Good." Despite her formality, there was a flash of

longing in her eyes that he did not miss, just before she turned her back and dismissed them both.

———

Two days later, in the dead of night, Jenny mounted her horse in the same way she'd done at least a hundred times before over the past couple of years. Only this time, she was going to finally meet Prince Charles and pledge her fealty in person.

Armed to the teeth and with enough provisions to last them the journey, she, Dirk, John, Toran, and Archie were ready to depart. They'd left Mac in charge of the forces at the castle to protect those within. They'd already over-seen the hiding of their treasure. Jenny had wished her mother a good night, hugged Isla, and watched Toran shake his younger brother's hand. Camdyn looked up at him with such admiration, it was truly touching.

"Pray we dinna come across any redcoats this time," she said, making the sign of the cross over her chest. It would be a miracle if they didn't. The entire country was swarming with dragoons, especially now that Prince Charles had landed.

His initial arrival had been kept secret, but a secret that big had a way of finding its way out. And Jenny had received several warnings the day before that there were whispers of the bonnie prince having landed near Eriskay and then taken his French ship up the coast to Kinlochmoidart. A check with Fiona had shown those rumors to be fact.

She glanced to her right at Dirk, who gave her a curt nod. His lips were pinched in the torchlight, brows drawn together. Though he supported her, he still believed the risks of this journey were too great. She understood his reservations. There was a part of her that would rather have remained behind, reading *Gulliver's Travels*, but there was a reason she loved that book so much, and the adventure was part of it. She had a duty to her clan and a mission to carry out.

John and Archie nodded at her, their expressions controlled, though she sensed in both their gazes a light of excitement. At last, she turned to face Toran.

The intensity of his gaze was enough to knock her off her horse, but she held herself tightly in place.

What he'd said to her in the study still struck strong, and she wasn't certain how to decipher it. The feelings he brought out in her were too intense. She drew in a steadying breath, which did little to calm the racing of her heart. Not even looking away helped. She could still see him in her mind's eye, feel the intensity of his gaze on the side of her face.

They rode with her at the fore, centered between Dirk and Toran, with John and Archie at their backs.

Through the gate and onto the road they went, several of their guards having gone out the hour before to scout the roads and make certain no lingering dragoons were watching Cnàmhan Broch.

Only two had been found, and so the rebels avoided their path. Certainly Dirk and Toran would have liked to dispose of the redcoats, but that was something Jenny wasn't willing to risk. Dead or missing dragoons on

Mackintosh lands would just be asking for another visit from Boyd.

They walked their horses at a reasonable pace for about an hour before breaking out into a gallop to avoid the rumbling of the earth that would alert any hiding *Sassenachs* of their journey.

Several hours passed before they took their first break to rest and water the horses and get a reprieve themselves. They were silent as they went, each of them moving in a pattern they all knew well.

A half hour later, they were on the road again. When the sun rose, they continued on, staying off the roads as much as possible so as not to be noticed.

By midday, Jenny's eyes were heavy, her body exhausted, but still she clung to the reins and tried to keep upright. She'd barely slept in weeks, and the rush of excitement had left her body feeling depleted of whatever energy remained. The men, too, seemed to be dragging. She'd hoped they could make it to sunset and then rest for the night. But it was summer, and the sun was not due to set for hours yet. At this time of year, daylight could remain until nearly nine o'clock.

Maybe she could try to push it for another hour.

But even as she thought that, she felt herself sliding on her saddle. With a curse she righted herself, angry at the weakness her body was showing. She was the leader of rebels on her way to meet the future King of Scotland, and she couldn't even keep her seat.

"We should stop," Toran said, the first words he'd spoken in hours.

Jenny's back snapped straight, stubborn irritation lancing through her. "Not yet," she said.

He didn't answer, and when she turned to look at him, he only gave a short nod. But she could see what he was thinking in his gaze. Blast the man for seeming to be able to see right through her.

A quarter of an hour later, as they passed through a denser part of the forest, she slowed her horse and veered further off the road.

"This should keep us hidden."

The men murmured their agreement, dismounting to take care of the horses. She did the same, her eyes drooping as she wiped down her mount's flanks. She fed him an apple from her satchel and then tied him loosely to a tree so he wouldn't wander off. That done, she sank to the ground and leaned against a tree, every muscle in her body aching. She worked to stretch out her muscles, feeling the tingly sting of the knots slowly starting to loosen.

"I'll take first watch," she said.

"I'd be honored if ye'd allow me to do it, Mistress J," John said.

Her eyes fell closed as she nodded and murmured her agreement, grateful that he'd stepped in.

When she woke hours later, it was the dead of night, and she felt much refreshed. She glanced around their makeshift camp, making out three lumps on the ground, her men sleeping. And a single figure leaning against a tree. From the shape of his long, muscular body, the way he held himself, she knew right away who it was. Toran.

"Welcome back to the land of the living," he said with

a little chuckle. "Ye snored loud enough to lead every redcoat within a mile to our location."

Jenny rolled her eyes, stretched out the kinks in her body, and then stood to walk over to him, feeling a slight twinge in her bottom from where she must have put most of her weight while sleeping.

"I dinna snore."

"I thought about smothering ye but figured ye'd not appreciate my efforts at keeping dragoons at bay." Though she couldn't see him, she could picture the teasing smirk, the way his eyes would twinkle.

"My da told me about one of the men in their caravan during the first uprising who snored so hard it used to rattle the leaves from the trees. By morning, he'd be covered in a natural blanket."

Toran chuckled. "Did they smother him?"

"Nay, for his noise was enough to keep even the dragoons away. They feared there was a rare boar in the forest."

Toran laughed again. "Well, 'tis a good thing I was only teasing."

"I dinna snore," she stated matter-of-factly.

"Och, nay, no' that. Ye snore like a prize champion, Mistress. I only meant I would never smother ye."

"Well, I suppose I should be grateful for that." She softly punched his shoulder. "I might not be so kind. Let's find out. I'll take watch while ye sleep."

Toran spun slowly from his spot, his hands grasping her hips as he framed her body with his, the tree at her spine. She inhaled sharply, surprised at the sudden movement and very, very interested. Every inch of her skin lurched, reaching for him, wanting to feel the hot press of his body against hers, his mouth capturing her lips.

He stared at her a long time, his face covered in nighttime shadows and the pools of his eyes reflecting the barest of light from the stars. It made his gaze glisten and sparkle. They remained still, chests heaving, eyes locked, and she waited for him to kiss her. But still he didn't move, just kept his hard, heated body pressed so intimately to hers. And when he finally did move, it was to step away.

Toran raked his hand through his hair, as dark as the midnight sky. "I've seen no one come this way since my watch. John saw a few people, but they looked like harmless Scots. Merchants or farmers, wandering home from a market or some such."

Cool night air replaced where the heat of his body had warmed her, and she had to clench her hands into fists at her sides to force herself not to reach for him and tug him back. She felt the loss of him keenly, the tease of him being so close.

She wanted him, and he knew she wanted him, but he wasn't going to make the first move. The man was going to let her make the next move.

But taking any further steps was terrifying in so many ways. They had a mission. They had a country to recapture in the name of their people. A new sovereign to support. Dragoons who wanted them dead. Every time she convinced herself that being with Toran would be all right, her duties surfaced to squash any such hopes. Every time, she had a cruel reminder that she couldn't have what most other women wanted—or already had. She couldn't have a man to herself, love, a family.

This war was her love, this country her husband, and her family were her men and every other rebel fighting for freedom. When a man was laird, he had a wife to breed, and he could go about his duties, protecting his line. But Jenny...she was certain that she wouldn't be able to rule without fear that her husband would try to take her place.

So she didn't say anything, only watched him put distance between them. Five feet. Ten. Knew he was waiting for her to call him back. Felt the slump of his shoulders in her heart rather than seeing him in the dark. And her soul matched that disappointment.

With a great sigh, she worked to focus her attention on their surroundings and not twenty feet in front of her where Toran sat with his back against a tree, masculine even in sleep.

Jenny stared at the trees, their black sharp angles swaying in the breeze. Shadows danced, and as hard as she focused, the dark shadows always formed into menacing shapes that left her nerves rattled. Every bounce of darkness was Boyd, every low skulking shadow a wolf ready to pounce.

She forced herself to breathe deeply, to shove aside all the night terrors of her imagination.

The truth was no one knew they were here. They'd not been followed, else they would have been attacked by now. While prowling outlaws and devilish redcoats might be skulking about, it was doubtful they'd run into them now. Even if a patrol passed on the road just beyond their camp, they wouldn't see them. The horses slept quietly, and the men didn't snore, sleeping too lightly to make any noise.

Jenny leaned against the tree that Toran had vacated and started ticking off the mental list she'd made of their journey and how she'd present herself and her men to Prince Charles.

As the hours passed, her confidence grew. And when the darkest of twilight melted into a predawn gray haze, the men started to stir, each of them slowly waking and taking care of his business some distance away.

When they returned to camp, she reported that nothing had occurred and then went to make use of a bush herself before they took off again.

Toran was watching her with clear interest in his eyes when she returned, a subtle curl to his lips that made her palms sweaty.

Unbidden, a thought went through her head that had her blushing. *When this war is over, oh the things I'll do with him…*

Eighteen

THEY MADE IT HALFWAY THROUGH THE DAY BEFORE they spied any flashes of red in the forest. Jenny caught sight of them first, but perhaps only a half second before Toran was reaching for her reins and they all stopped short.

Without any sightings in hours, they'd gone onto the road to ride harder. And that was when the flash of red was visible through the trees where the road curved sharply to the right.

"Ballocks," Dirk cursed under his breath.

The redcoats did not seem to have noticed them yet, but it would only be a matter of seconds before they rounded the curve and saw them in the center of the dirt-packed path or heard them clomping through the forest.

Jenny was dressed in her rebel garb, easier for riding, and they were all fully armed and bedraggled looking after nearly two days on the road. Whatever lie they were to come up with would be questioned, as the five of them looked every bit up to the mischief the dragoons would assume they were getting into. And they'd be right.

Without another moment's hesitation, Jenny hefted a leg over the side of her horse and flung herself facedown across Toran's lap. "I'm your wee brother and ye're taking me home after finding me out carousing with my pals. These are your cousins, and our ma is really worried about me after I got stuck in the wrong crowd."

"What the bloody—" Toran started to say.

But there was no time to talk. The dragoons rounded the bend and caught sight of the group, pulling up short, shouting and reaching for their weapons.

"Ho, there!" they called. "Halt."

"Ye heard her?" Toran asked softly of the men, and they grunted in affirmation.

They did not halt, their horses moving slowly down the road.

"I said stop right there," came the shout of a man, his English accent full of misplaced authority. Not Boyd, thankfully.

They were far enough away from Mackintosh lands and Boyd that Jenny prayed the men wouldn't recognize Toran or Archie from their daring escape from the garrison. But more so, she prayed that this ruse would keep them on their way without incident.

Toran's horse stilled. "We aim to cause no trouble," Toran called out in a meeker voice than she'd ever heard him use before.

"We'll be the judge of that," answered the dragoon. "What are ye doing out here?"

Toran slapped Jenny hard on the rear, and she gritted her teeth. "My wee brother got into a bit of trouble with some lads. Seems to have drunk himself into a deep sleep, that is when he's not retching his guts out."

There were a few grumbles and something she took to be an insult given Toran's stiffening tension beneath her.

"My cousins helped me fetch him back, and we're

headed home. My mother is quite beside herself," Toran said, sounding quite believable.

"Beside herself for raising such a foolish no-good troublemaker. Let us take him off your hands and teach him a thing or two about respecting one's mother." The dragoon's laughing comment was made with a cruel edge that had Jenny's blood running cold. Was it possible this man was *worse* than Boyd?

Toran let out a strained laugh. "I thank ye for the offer, but I assure ye, he's needed at home and already likely to get the belt when he gets there."

The redcoats snickered. "I've a better idea. Let us give him the belt now, and then we'll let ye be on your way. The last thing we need is a bunch of wayward drunken Scots cavorting about our countryside."

Her countryside! She wanted to shout and rave at them but kept her teeth firmly clenched against each other, else she give them all away.

Toran let out a laugh. "I think my ma deserves first crack."

"I think your ma deserves a cock in her arse," growled a dragoon, which only had Toran stiffening even more beneath her.

To talk of his mother like that after the awful way Moire had died was tantamount to drawing swords. Dear God, let him take a moment to push the vulgar words aside.

Jenny pinched his calf in hopes of keeping him in check, but she could already feel that this unfortunate meeting with the dragoons had turned from bad to worse.

From what she could make out, there were four horses in their party to her five. They could easily take the redcoats on, but not without consequences and perhaps alerting other dragoons in the vicinity to their whereabouts.

"Now, kind sirs," Dirk said. "Let us leave his ma out of this. We ask that ye allow us to pass to get our wee kin home. Ye recall what it's like to be a wee lad, nay?"

"We were never filthy Scots. Perhaps ye'd like to take the punishment for your *wee kin*," he mocked their brogue, "yourself."

"There's no need for that," Dirk was saying.

"We'll be the judge of what's needed. Give us the lad now." Their voices were sharp and edged with danger.

Now that lines had been drawn, there was absolutely no way these bastards were going to let them go without giving Jenny a thorough beating.

She started to shift, but Toran pressed his hand firmly against her rear, causing her to still.

"I'll do it," Toran said to the dragoons. "He's my brother. I'll take his beating if ye give us your word ye'll let us pass when ye're through."

Jenny's throat went dry, and she wanted to scream. This was not the way he needed to prove his loyalty. This was not what she'd wanted when she'd laid across his lap and trusted he would handle the English. This was utter madness!

She pinched him again to show her resistance to this futile plan.

"All right," sneered the dragoon. "Get off that horse and strip off your shirt."

Toran transferred her to Dirk's lap, and it was the hardest damn thing she'd ever done to keep her eyes closed and her mouth slack, her body flopping, when she wanted to protest, to fight.

She heard Toran's feet hit the ground, boots crunching as he walked to meet the bastard redcoat.

"If even one of ye makes a move to protect your kin, I'll have ye shot," the dragoon was saying. "Get against the tree, filthy Scot."

Jenny blinked open her eyes very slowly to slits, hoping no one noticed. All the dragoons' eyes were firmly on Toran, who had pressed his bare chest to the tree and wrapped his arms around it. The muscles of his back rippled in the sunlight and exposed scars of battles or beatings past. She couldn't breathe. Her heart was pounding so loudly, surely they heard it and knew she wasn't sleeping.

Stop! She wanted to scream. *Bloody stop! Beat me instead!*

Tears threatened, and she held them at bay. If even one fell, she wouldn't be able to wipe it away, and the moisture would only blind her to what was happening. Dirk's hand pressed firmly to the small of her back, a measure of support she couldn't seem to take any comfort in. Yet she was glad he held her down, for she wanted nothing more than to leap from her prone spot and draw her sword.

Perhaps that was why her cousin did it.

The dragoon's black boots hit the ground, and he walked slowly toward Toran, his riding crop tapping against his leg. The first slap was hard, and she clenched every muscle, including her jaw to keep from screaming. The crop sang through the air again and snapped against the golden skin of his back, bringing with it an angry red stripe.

Five more cracks of the crop brought five more bright red stripes across his skin.

When the dragoon paused, Toran started to pull away from the tree, and she breathed easy knowing the beating was over.

"Oh no you don't, savage. We're just getting started. Take off your belt."

"What?" Toran asked, his voice tight. Not since they'd met had she heard this tone from him. It was a new level of dangerous that snaked down her spine. He'd not yet turned around, and she feared what would happen if he did.

"I said take off your belt." The audible click of a flint-lock pistol cocking made Jenny want to throw up.

Beneath her Dirk's legs stiffened, and his horse side-stepped so her view was only of the men's feet. The dragoon swung on him. "Move and I'll shoot ye in the head."

Dirk managed to relax, but Jenny couldn't.

Toran didn't move, and the crop whipped against him. Jenny bit the inside of her cheek so hard that she tasted the familiar metallic tang of blood.

"Take off your belt or I'll have it cut off and you can ride home with your ballocks hanging out."

Toran was slow to take off his belt and pass it to the bastard. Once he did, the dragoon snapped it hard against Toran's back, muttering a derogatory expletive as he did it. Jenny lost count of how many times the bastard hit Toran, but with every crack, her nerves frayed more, and she was grateful to not be able to see him. By the time the man let the belt drop to his side, he was panting, and she could see droplets of blood sprayed against the ground.

Not a single sound had passed Toran's lips as he stood there taking the beating that had been meant for her.

Jenny was on the verge of sobbing or vomiting, her mouth filled with blood from the effort to keep herself silent. Her back was covered in sweat, and Dirk's hand was still pressed firmly in place. When she'd not found comfort in his touch before, she did now.

The belt fell to the ground beside the blood-spattered boots of the dragoon, who walked away.

"Be gone with you," he said in a near wheeze as he got himself back onto his mount. The clomps of their horses thundered in her ears as the dragoons disappeared back down the road.

None of them moved, not even Toran. When Jenny pushed away from Dirk, she could see the mangled mess of his back and how he pressed naked to the tree, eyes closed as if in a dead faint.

Archie was the first one to drop to the ground, running toward his cousin, pressing his fingers to Toran's neck and calling his name.

Toran's eyes blinked open, and he stared at his cousin. A soft groan escaped his lips, the first sound he'd made since questioning the dragoon about his belt.

Och, but she couldn't imagine the pain he must be in, and she felt the phantom stings on her own flesh.

She jumped off the horse and started for him, but Dirk grabbed her by the arm and shook his head. No matter how hard she yanked, Dirk wouldn't let go. Toran needed her. This was her fault, and as she stared at his bloodied body, rivulets of red sliding from the gaping wounds and down his bare legs, she had no idea how the hell she could ever make it right.

The man had just taken a vicious beating for her, one that could still leave him dead if they didn't care for the wounds properly and infection set in. His back was torn apart.

They needed Annie, who was going to be at Glenfinnan, but that was at least another two or three days' ride ahead of them at a fast clip, which they wouldn't be taking now that Toran was injured.

"We need to go back home." Dirk's face was dark, his tone leaving no room to argue.

"Aye," John agreed.

Jenny stared at her men in disbelief, stared at Toran and Archie who hovered over him. Toran had dropped to his knees, his head hanging low. They were right. They were only a day and a half into this journey and still further from their destination than they were from home.

"John, ride back to Cnàmhan Broch and get a wagon. We'll quickly follow, but ye'll be faster alone and can meet us upon the road."

"Aye, Mistress." John took off at a hard gallop.

Dirk let go of her then, and she bent to pick up Toran's shirt, coat, and kilt. When he saw her intent to dress Toran, Dirk dismounted too and took the clothes from her.

"Allow me," he said softly, and she did, for despite wearing men's clothing, she'd never dressed a man in her life. She had no idea how to do it when he wasn't injured, let alone when his back was split open.

Jenny's stomach roiled as the men cleaned the slices in Toran's back. They shredded strips from his shirt, binding them around his torso. They slipped his arms into his frock coat for added protection and belted his kilt into place, hoping for a sense of normalcy should they cross paths with any more redcoats. Though the graying pallor of his face was alarming.

Toran fainted as they dressed him. Then they gingerly lifted him up onto his own horse, facedown. They turned around on the road, the three of them taking turns riding ahead to scout for dragoons, while the others remained with Toran to see that he didn't fall from the saddle.

When the sun fell, they made camp, forcing whisky down his throat. Jenny insisted on being the one to clean his back this time. She'd watched Annie often enough that she knew partly what to do. His shirt was stuck in places, and it took an effort not to scream herself as she peeled the blood-soaked fabric from his back.

She patted down his wounds with whisky on a scrap of clean linen while Dirk and Archie held him in place. Dirk tore an extra shirt of his into strips, and they wrapped Toran's body with it. They didn't bother with the frock coat again, simply wrapping him in an extra blanket.

The night was long, broken by Toran's moans of pain. When it was clear none of them could sleep, they each took turns to force the whisky down Toran's throat. When the faintest light of dawn arrived, they silently packed up camp and continued on their way. They just needed to get to Cnàmhan Broch, where they could care for him. The walls of her castle would keep them momentarily safe from any more bastard redcoats wanting to take out their anger.

Guilt ate at her. This was her fault.

They were halfway home when Dirk finally said, "Ye've got to stop blaming yourself, Jenny. Toran volunteered to take your punishment. Do ye know what would have happened if the dragoons had discovered ye were a lass? Far worse than what happened to him, and ye know it."

She did know it. She could still feel Boyd's hands pawing at her flesh, see the lecherous hunger in his eyes. The brutality of Toran's beating was not lost on her, and neither was the fact that he'd saved her from something unspeakable. She involuntarily shuddered, recalling the horrific fate of Moire, Toran's mother. The awfulness of what could have happened slammed into Jenny's chest. A fresh wave of nausea was replaced by a slow-dawning ache of respect and admiration for Toran and what he'd done for her. How could she ever repay him for how he'd suffered?

The following morning they met the wagon along the road, and Toran was placed facedown in the back lined with blankets. Camdyn, who'd insisted on joining John and several guards for the return, rode in the back of the wagon with his older brother, keeping him plied with both ale and whisky to stave off the pain and fever.

When they finally reached the castle, Toran's skin was beaded with sweat, and his pallor had turned a sickly gray. Worse than before, this was the color of fever and infection.

They carried him upstairs to the spare bedroom beside Jenny's at her insistence, and the clan healer was called to care for his wounds. Jenny hovered in the corner with Dirk by her side. He pulled her back every time she lurched forward to interfere.

"Let her do her job," he said softly, and Jenny was recalled to herself. Their healer knew better how to handle the task than she did. But that didn't mean she didn't wish to comfort him all the same.

Isla came into the room and froze, her gasp of horror audible. It was Jenny's instinct to get the wee lass out of there, but when Isla moved to her side and slipped her hand in hers, feet planted on the floor, Jenny knew it would take more of an effort to push her out than to simply comfort her. It was just another way for the lass to see the danger they were in, the brutality of this world with redcoats in it. Isla was a young and beautiful girl, and if she was ever cornered alone with English soldiers, there could be no doubt what would happen to her.

"They said he did this for ye," Isla whispered. "That he took a beating so ye wouldna have to."

There was no accusation in the young lass's tone or words, only statement of fact. "'Tis true."

Isla's grasp grew stronger. "He is verra brave."

"Aye, he is."

"Did ye watch it?"

The memory of those horrible infinite moments made Jenny's stomach roil. "Aye."

"Ye're verra brave too."

"I would have gladly taken it," Jenny said, "so he didna have to."

Isla's fingers squeezed around hers. "Ye care for each other." Again, just a statement of fact.

Jenny's chest constricted, throat growing tight. *Care for each other, aye, very much.* But she couldn't manage to form any words, so instead she simply nodded. Dirk caught her eye then, having heard the exchange. She expected him to balk, to grimace, but he did none of that. Instead, he simply nodded his approval.

Toran had been hit by bullets, had been sliced by daggers, and had even felt the pierce of a sword. He'd been in battles waged on fields and those in courtyards and taprooms. He'd sustained plenty of wounds, always coming out of them as though he'd been built anew.

And this one would be no different.

Despite his fever and delirium, despite the pain of his torn flesh, he still understood that this all would pass.

One thing, however, would not be the same.

He was no longer going to stay passive when it came to Jenny. The lass was lying to them both when she said she couldn't or wouldn't be with him. Every time she looked at him he felt her interest deep in his bones, the way she leaned toward him—but most of all the way she'd called out to him, stroked his flesh when she cleaned his wounds. She cared for him, more than she was willing to admit. But he had enough ballocks to admit it for the both of them, if that was what it took.

A battle between loyalists and Jacobites was inevitable. He'd be damned if they weren't going to be a part of it. They'd face things—together. She was strong, stronger than any woman he'd ever met, but the very reason why clans thrived was because people were always stronger together. He and Jenny—together they would be unstoppable.

"Jenny," he called, needing to tell her right now.

But he couldn't sense her near him, and in his hazy vision he couldn't see her. What he did see, however, was a hulking figure that could only be Dirk.

"She's gone to rest, Fraser." *Aye, 'twas Dirk.* "Ye'd best get well soon. Jenny is beside herself. Blames herself for your injury. Stubborn lass, she is."

"Aye," Toran croaked out, wanting to push up from his prone position, but even moving made it feel like the flesh that had fixed itself back together was ripping open again.

"Dinna move. Ye need not face me while I'm speaking to ye, I'll forgive ye this once," Dirk teased. "Ye're a bloody fool, Fraser, but ye saved us all out there on that road. Ye saved Jenny."

He had. There had been other options, but none that didn't see Jenny harmed and the rest of them having to fight and then go on the run. He'd taken the punishment in hopes the dragoons would see their bloodlust sated and then move on, which they had. However much it had hurt, it had been worth it.

"Bastards," Toran said.

"They were that. I'll never forget the man's face, and if we ever see him again, I'll hold him down while ye run him through."

This was a new dynamic with Dirk. The men had been dancing around each other, looking for reasons to fight, to battle out their differences. But now Dirk was giving him a level of respect Toran had never imagined possible.

Dirk cared about his cousin a great deal, and now maybe he knew how much Toran cared about her too.

"A solid plan," Toran managed to answer.

"Rest, my friend. We need ye. Jenny needs ye."

Jenny needed him. Sweet music to his ears because damn if he didn't think he could survive without her.

Nineteen

THE DAY AFTER RETURNING TO THE CASTLE, JENNY and her men set out once more to meet the prince, leaving Toran at the castle in the care of her mother and his sister. She wanted to be there for him, but she knew he would understand the importance of meeting with Prince Charles. Though they might not make it in time, now that they'd been set back, she had to try all the same.

Jenny, Archie, and Dirk rode hard for three days with only half the inventory they'd promised in the name of speed. A wagon would only slow them down, so they carried only what they could on their horses and the backs of three additional horses.

"We're too late." Jenny stared at the hill of Glenfinnan, riddled with the evidence of a great gathering minus those individuals who'd been there.

"Perhaps the prince is still nearby," Dirk offered.

Jenny nodded solemnly and followed her cousin on horseback to the nearest village and tavern. Archie remained with the horses outside while they inquired discreetly inside.

The meeting at Glenfinnan had been a success. MacDonalds, Camerons, MacPhees, MacDonnells, and others had amassed there to pledge their support. The prince had marched up a crag at Glenfinnan with his men, one carrying the royal standard and pipers behind him piping a royal ballad. At the very top, he'd claimed the throne of Great Britain in the name of his father, King James Stuart, and himself as regent.

Though she was fiercely proud of her prince, Jenny regretted not being a part of history. They inquired as to the prince's whereabouts but were not able to glean any information. Even rebels weren't sharing where the prince might be in case it dampened the brilliance of his claim.

The ride home was slow and arduous, the lot of them tired and disappointment draining all their vigor. But alas, three days later, they crossed through the gates of Cnàmhan Broch to the fanfare of the clan, though their shouts of excitement dulled when they took in the equally loaded horses from when they'd left. After updating everyone on what had happened both at Glenfinnan before they arrived and after, Jenny sought out her mother.

"How is Toran?"

"He is recovering nicely. He suffered a fever for several days as well as infection. But we were able to save him. He's resting now, but I'm certain he will want to see ye when he wakes."

Jenny wanted to see him too. That ache in her chest whenever she thought of him, that desperation to see his face and know he was alive, it gnawed at her insides. Scared her. Perhaps she'd do better to keep herself busy and avoid him, if only to save herself from putting voice to the emotions.

In the quiet of her father's study, she penned a letter to A. M. to let him know what had happened and to make certain the prince was aware of their continued loyalty.

A week later, she had her reply. The prince had personally sent a message to Jenny and Toran that he would make his way to Inverness and thank them both for their efforts and personal sacrifices as well as to collect their bounty. He requested that she continue in her recruitment of men and resources, since she was one of the most successful in doing so, and that when the time came, he would ask her to join him on the battlefield. The thought that he would visit, that he would acknowledge them, was what spurred her on in her nightly quest to gather more support for him.

Dirk had told her two days previously that Toran was well enough to begin watch again, so Jenny had put him on night watch on the wall rather than have him join them on their nightly recruitments. She was hoping to avoid him at all costs. Watching him suffer, knowing what he'd done for her, had changed her irrevocably, had touched her very soul. She feared meeting him again, what she would say and how she'd say it. How to tell him how grateful she was, how to tell him she was so sorry and to beg his forgiveness for having been the reason he was subject to such a punishment.

Was she a fool for having told him they couldn't be together until the war was over? Who knew if either of them would make it that far at the rate they were going? They'd spent the span of the month she'd known him in constant peril. Now that the prince had declared himself for the throne in his father's name, their situation was only bound to get worse.

The pessimism she was feeling was unlike her, and

she knew it had entirely to do with Toran—and with the need to face her own fears and feelings for him. So what better way to avoid them than by avoiding *him* altogether?

Aye, she knew it was foolish, and right now, she was willing to be a fool. At least when it came to her heart. Because she couldn't give up on her duty, either, and she saw no way to meld the two. Love and duty? She shook her head. How could she possibly?

Only now, at the end of the secret passage, stood the shadow of a man blocking the exit.

It wasn't just any man but the tall, muscular frame of the very man who occupied her thoughts most parts of the day and night. The one she'd only just finished convincing herself once more that she needed to avoid. Jenny paused, her heart thumping at the sight of him. How had he gotten in here? The men behind her didn't seem alarmed, as though they'd been expecting this intrusion.

"Toran," she said. He must have been waiting there for them, anticipating her nightly routine.

"I'm going with ye." His voice was steady, and she wanted to sink against him.

But she had to stand her ground, remain strong. "Nay." There was no way in bloody hell she was going to let him get hurt again because of her. Which meant he had to stay behind.

Toran stalked forward, stopping a few paces away from her. "Ye can go and I'll follow, or ye can let me walk beside ye."

"Or I can order ye back to the wall where ye should be."

The men behind her backed up a few paces in the pretense of giving them some privacy.

Toran stalked closer, and she stood her ground, thrusting her chin up. She passed her torch behind her, and someone took it from her hand so she could cross her arms defiantly in front of her.

"Dinna try to intimidate me," she warned.

"Och, lass, ye have the wrong of it. I'm trying to do no such thing." He stopped about a foot away from her, no discernable limp or slowness or stiffness in his gait to show that he'd been in bed for nearly a fortnight with severe injuries. His back had to still be covered in scabs and would certainly scar heavily.

"Then what exactly is your aim, Fraser?" She could smell him, that strong woodsy, spicy scent that belonged only to him.

"Ye're my aim, Jenny. *My* Mistress J," he said.

She didn't want to think about the implication in those heated words. The intimacy of them. "I am everyone's Mistress J," she corrected him.

"Aye," he murmured, "everyone's leader, but not everyone's woman."

She gasped at so public a declaration. "I am no one's woman, Toran Fraser, and especially not yours. I'll not be claimed."

He chuckled.

"'Tis not funny. I am serious."

"I know."

"Then why do ye laugh?"

"Because ye're not a verra good liar." He stepped back

then, taking all the air from the tunnel with him. "Shall we?" He swept his arm out as if they were simply going into the great hall for dinner and not to recruit for their rebel army.

Jenny was about to argue some more, but he'd already walked ahead, and the men behind her were getting restless.

"Fine. Just this once," she conceded.

He grinned at her, the grin of a man very satisfied to have gotten his way.

She expected him to try to corner her once they were on their way, to kiss her, and she'd already decided she would let him. Her lips tingled with the anticipation of it. But not once that night did he try. He didn't even ride beside her. In fact, he gave her more space than she'd ever had from him before, save for the way he was completely crowding her mind.

Was this his game? To toy with her head instead of her body? Oh, she just wanted him to kiss her already.

She spoke passionately at each place they stopped, rousing the crowd with stories of the dragoons' cruelty.

When they returned home that night, he volunteered to take the horses back to the stables, avoiding her again and only making her want him all the more.

He was right—she was a bad liar.

———————

Part of Toran's plan for the following two weeks, now that he was on his feet again, was to get Jenny to *admit* she wanted him and to show that he was interested in her—hell, more than interested. But she was not the type of woman who wanted a man to stake his claim on her. Nay, she wanted to come to him, and he understood that. He'd play it her way.

And not just because he wanted to bed her. *Mo chreach*, but he wanted to walk beside her in this life, in this battle, in all things.

For the first time in his life, Toran wanted a wife, and not just any wife. He wanted Jenny.

When they'd been confronted by the dragoons on the road, he'd known in that moment that he would die before letting those men touch her and that he loved her, that he would do anything for her.

He was fairly certain Jenny could live without him if she chose, but he was doing everything in his power now to show her she wouldn't *want* to live without him.

He had started by leaving a flower on her chair at the evening meal so she might find it when she sat down to eat. He fed her hound treats at every meal, and as a result, Dom followed him around the castle grounds like a loyal servant. Whenever Toran was invited to dine with the clan, he challenged her to a game of chess afterward, and she always agreed. While they played, he tried his damnedest to beat her, but each time she won. The lass was good, but he was starting to understand the way she played. One of these days, he was going to win.

In the mornings he greeted her at the bottom of the stairs with a full report, a task he'd convinced Dirk to allow him to do.

He had Dirk's full support, and the servants were now providing him with flowers to choose from. He'd begun leaving them not only when she dined at night but also at her door in the morning, tucked into Dom's collar, pressed to her pillow, threaded through the stirrup of her saddle. Anywhere he could possibly find, he planted one.

And he was fairly certain that his efforts were working. Or at least he hoped. Her smile for him grew brighter every time he saw her, and the one morning when she'd come downstairs and he'd been late, she had looked disappointedly around until he'd appeared.

Their nighttime recruitments had been fruitful as well, and updates on the prince were giving them all hope. Soon he'd be seated in Edinburgh and London, on the throne of the Kingdom of Great Britain, uniting England and Scotland. Already the prince's army had taken Edinburgh and defeated the government's army at Prestonpans. The prince was now planning to head southward with a large retinue, taking towns as he went, all the way to London.

As the leaves of autumn turned and the weather went from pleasant to cold, they worked steadily toward their goals.

Simon was still in the cell below the castle, though he was being fed well to keep him alive. Toran needed the man alive and planned to keep him to exchange for any rebel prisoners, just deserts for his cousin's plan to do the same with him.

On two occasions now, Mac had accompanied him to the outskirts of Fraser lands where, dressed in disguises, their hair darkened with soot and a beard full grown upon his face, they'd subtly asked about his uncle's doings. And he was right. The old Fox was working with Boyd. The Fraser chief had yet to make it a formal commitment, but Boyd and his men had been seen coming and going from Dùnaidh Castle steadily for months. The Frasers at the garrison, his uncle's men, had also been released, Toran learned. The exchange price he couldn't discern, but he was certain it was for his uncle's soul.

Toran had volunteered to take a wagon run to meet their informant A. M. who had arranged to meet them along the road at the request of the prince. The false bottoms were filled with supplies for Prince Charles. Toran, along with John, took the first wagon. Jenny sent Archie out the following week with the last of the supplies for Prince Charlie's journey southward into England. Everyone hoped that by year's end King George's supporters would have surrendered.

The redcoats had made no further visits to Cnàmhan Broch, and they had the weather to thank for that. The first snowfall came in October, which bothered none of them in the least, and continued on through the month of November, until the ice came in December. The clans were all Highlanders, and they were made of hearty stock. But the English could hardly stand the Scottish winter, keeping indoors and huddled around their fires for months.

Sassenachs weren't built for such a life, which made the work the rebellion was doing all the easier.

Twenty

"WE'RE GOING TO WAR." JENNY STOOD AT THE HEAD OF the table in the great hall and made her announcement after the room had cleared of all except her closest consultants and family.

Toran and Dirk looked shocked, while Archie, Mac, and Cameron looked excited. Isla looked worried, and Jenny's mother kept her gaze steady. Jenny'd already spoken to her mother earlier that day, and while Lady Mackintosh was worried and had at first balked at the prospect, she had, in the end, deferred to Jenny's decision.

"The prince's attempt on London was unsuccessful, and he has withdrawn to Glasgow. There's to be a gathering there, from which we'll march on Stirling Castle. We shall rally and defend our prince. This is the moment we have all been working for. We are strong, and the English will not expect it. The dragoons stationed in the Highlands will not be prepared, as they've spent the past two months hiding inside and away from a bit of nippy weather."

"Will ye be leading the men?" Dirk asked.

"Aye."

She slid her gaze toward Toran, feeling her belly warm with just that one glance. They'd been dancing on a fine edge for months now. She wanted desperately to pull him into her arms and say enough was enough, that she was ready for him to claim her, but still she held strong. To give in just yet could mean the end of all they'd worked for.

Though the look in his eyes was not the one she expected, not after how much he'd been in support of her lately. He looked shocked. He and Dirk eyed each other, a silent exchange in their expressions that had her wanting to slap them both.

"This is my army, and I'll no' send them off without me. If this were your army, no one would expect ye to stay home." She directed her statement at the two of them. "Can a woman no' fight for what she believes in, sir? I am willing to die for Prince Charlie's cause, just like any soldier. Are ye?"

Toran stared at her blankly a moment before his expression changed, softening to understanding and some other unrecognizable emotion. "Aye, Mistress J. 'Twill be an honor to follow ye into battle. Your passion and patriotism are exactly what this land needs."

She nodded. "Thank ye."

Camdyn stood then. "I am also a passionate patriot and wish to fight. The *Sassenachs* took my mother from me. Allow me the honor of bringing them to justice."

"Nay," Toran said firmly.

Camdyn ignored him, lifting his leg over the bench he sat on to come before Jenny's table and kneel on the floor before her, his hand over his heart.

"I pledge to ye, Mistress J, my honor, my loyalty. I am a loyal vassal of the Stuart crown, to our prince and cause, and humbly beg your permission to fight on the crown's behalf."

Jenny looked down at Camdyn. Sometime over the past few months he'd become a man. Over his head, Toran stared at her with a pained expression. She didn't need his permission to grant Camdyn the right to fight, but she wanted it all the same.

Camdyn beamed up at her, delight and admiration in his eyes.

"'Twould be an honor to fight beside ye, Camdyn," she said. "Ye're an excellent soldier, but for now, I need ye to remain behind to protect the castle and the women. I know that might be disappointing to ye, but trust me when I say that it is the most important job to keep our people and our home safe."

Though disappointment flickered in the lad's eyes, he nodded all the same. "I will honor your order, Mistress."

"Ye're more a leader than Hamish ever was," her mother murmured, making Jenny's heart swell at the same time a great sadness filled her. Her heart was like a well that was overflowing.

Her brother had no idea what he had left behind when he'd sided with the enemy. Or perhaps he did. But it was hard to believe that he would have chosen treachery over honor.

A calmness poured over her. Over the next two days, they set about preparing for war. There was only one thing still to do before they rode out, and that was to claim what was hers. After calling for the clan to gather in the great hall, she faced her people and accepted their pledges of loyalty. Toran was the last in the line of those who wished to pledge themselves.

He sauntered forward and without hesitation dropped to his knees before her. "For all the days of my life, to thee I pledge," he said. "I will honor thee, follow thee, fight for thee. I pledge my fealty to ye and to the Stuart crown."

Coming from him, it was a declaration that made her heart skip a beat. She swallowed hard, finding it difficult to make her mouth work. She held out her hand, and he took it, kissing her knuckles. For just the briefest of moments, she closed her eyes and reveled in it before muttering her acceptance and asking him to rise.

Toran took his place with the men, but even with him offering her that small reprieve, she found it hard to breathe.

"My father and his father before him were men of honor, men of integrity. They fought for our Scottish king in the first uprising. If either of them were alive today, they would fight again. They believe in the Stuart line as I do, as do ye. We are their living legacy, and we will honor them in death just as we honored them in life."

A resounding cheer filled the room, shaking the rafters. The clansmen tapped their fists to their hearts and then raised them in the air.

"To that end," Jenny continued, "it is with my father and grandfather in my heart that I must humbly ask that ye support my claim to my place as laird of Clan Mackintosh. My brother has dishonored us by siding with the English. He has allowed our enemies to infiltrate our lands and home. He dishonored the legacy left by our ancestors, who sacrificed themselves for us to be free from the oppression of the English. He robs us of weapons and provisions that are used to fight against us. Hamish is no longer worthy of the title."

Jenny's hands were clammy, but that was the only sign she'd been nervous about claiming what should have been hers all along. Ripples of excitement and pleasure wound down her spine, and the exhilaration of the people in the great hall warmed her heart and made her want to sing and dance. How long this had been coming, and now it was here. It was hard to stand still, hard to keep her face serious when all she wanted to do was shout with joy.

"I submit to all of ye that Jenny Mackintosh, daughter of Jon Mackintosh, should be named laird," Dirk shouted, followed by her mother bellowing, "I second the motion."

What had been bellows of pleasure turned to "ayes" for a changing future.

Jenny gripped her mother's hand, pulling her up to stand beside her, and hugged her tightly. Dirk came around the table a moment later and effortlessly lifted Jenny up to sit on his shoulder as he paraded her around the room, ending with her right in front of Toran. She slid down from her perch to face the man she'd fallen hopelessly in love with.

"What say ye, Toran MacGillivray Fraser," she said, "of a woman as laird?"

"I couldna be prouder of ye, Laird of Mackintosh," he said with a sweeping bow.

The crowd broke out into chants of "Mackintosh," over and over until the floor beneath her feet rumbled.

She wanted to ask him if he could love a woman in

a position of power, but one look at him was enough
to know that already. He did love her, and she'd seen it
before. Why hadn't he said the words?

As quickly as the question popped into her brain,
the answer did as well. Because he was waiting for her.
From the very beginning she'd told him that she would
be the one to set the pace. That they couldn't be together
until she said it was the right time. Now he stood there
so humbly before her, and yet she could feel the power
coming off him in waves. Toran didn't have to announce
his position or demand respect; he simply earned it.

He'd put himself forward and worked hard to gain the
respect of the people, even Dirk. Not once had he backed
down.

More than once he'd proven himself to be a man of
his word. Whatever his past had been, his stumbles from
grace, he'd found a place with her that had lifted him up
and kept him steady.

And she loved him for that. Loved that with him by
her side, she felt invincible.

"'Tis I who am proud, Fraser," she said softly. "'Tis I
who am grateful to ye. Ye've more than earned your place
here, and I'd like ye to help me lead the men to Stirling.
We've more than one contingent. I shall lead one, and I
hope ye'll lead the other."

Toran's eyes shuttered his reaction, and she knew it
was because she'd truly touched him.

She patted him on the shoulder, wanting to grasp the
front of his shirt and pull him in for a kiss but not yet
ready to make a public declaration of it.

"I will make ye proud," Toran murmured.

"Ye already do."

This time it was Toran who hoisted her up onto his shoulder and danced her around the room. A fiddle and then a pipe started up, and the dancing began. When Jenny slid down the length of his body to join in the dancing, every inch of her came alive, feeling his hardened muscles against the softer parts of herself.

From the look in his eyes, he felt it too, wanted to keep her snuggled close. But they were both tugged in different directions by the clan who wanted to dance with her too, their eyes staring longingly after one another.

Jenny danced two songs before having to break the clan's merriment with a sobering truth. "We need to rest. All of ye. For tomorrow we ride."

When Dirk started to leave the great hall, she called him back. The room emptied out around them, leaving them alone and standing by the hearth.

"I know what ye're going to say," he started, "and I willna let ye go without me."

Jenny sighed, her heart sinking. "I know. But I canna leave my mother and the rest of the clan alone with redcoats in the area. And there is another reason."

"Dinna say it." Dirk shook his head fiercely, his jaw muscle tightening.

"If I dinna return, I need ye here, Dirk. I need ye as my second, to continue what we started. Hamish canna regain control of the clan."

"Nay. I willna stay." Dirk crossed his arms stubbornly

and shook his head. This was one battle she wondered if she'd be able to win.

"I know 'tis a lot to ask of ye. Believe me, if there was any other way I could see out of it, I would find it. But, Cousin, ye have been my second from the beginning. How can I go into battle and leave the clan at risk?"

"And as your second, I should be by your side to the end. Ye willna die, no' with me there. And we'll keep guards behind to protect your mother."

Jenny thought of Moire's fate and how her mother would also be likely to toss herself to the wolves if she thought it was the only way to protect others.

"Your mother would want me to go with ye," he said.

Jenny was silent, knowing there was no argument against that.

"Name your mother as second, Jenny. Give her the strength to fight Hamish should his plans change and he comes to the castle. Give her the power to make right what is wrong, at least until we return."

It had never occurred to Jenny that she could do such a thing, given the older Lady Mackintosh's long grieving, but it made perfect sense. Her mother was the daughter of Jacobites, had been married to one, had long held the belief in the Stuart crown. Now was her time to shine in Jenny's absence.

"All right. I will ask her."

"Good. And ye'll allow me to join in the fight?" Dirk looked relieved.

"Aye. We'll split the contingents of men into thirds. But I need ye to choose men to remain behind. If ye're not going to be here, I need strong men to protect my mother and in case Hamish returns. Mac would be perfect to take charge of the remaining men."

"Aye, he would."

"I trust ye," Jenny said.

They parted ways, and she climbed the stairs on tired legs, her mind racing. They'd not been able to meet the prince at Glenfinnan, but this time they would be ready. She'd put a ball of lead into anyone who tried to stop them.

Jenny's door was ajar, and she approached with caution, pushing it open with a fingertip to see inside before she crossed the threshold. Toran stood at her hearth, gazing into the small leap of flames that danced in the grate. The fire had been stoked since she'd been in the room last, an hour before.

"What are ye doing in my bedchamber?" She crossed the threshold then and shut the door, afraid that someone might see him there.

He glanced at the closed door and then back at her. "I'd kept it open for propriety's sake."

"I think 'tis fair to say that no matter what, ye standing in my bedchamber will raise an eyebrow. 'Tis a far cry from courting. And ye've no' answered my question."

Toran dropped his elbow from where it rested on the mantel and approached her. He stopped a few paces away, leaving enough space for them not to touch but not enough space for her to find her breath. The man seemed to suck all the air from the room when he was near. Golden flecks of candlelight glinted in his blue eyes, and his gaze swept over her, leaving her feeling as though he'd plucked open every button, untied every lace, and slid every inch of fabric from her skin.

"I like being in your bedchamber," he teased.

She rolled her eyes. "Get on with it then." Her brusqueness belied how she was truly feeling, how she itched to leap forward and plant her lips on his.

"I'd argue for ye to stay away from the battle if I thought it would do any good."

"But ye know me better than that."

"Aye. So I wanted to instead remind ye of your promise."

"My promise?" She raised a questioning brow.

"Aye, lass." He moved closer, reaching a hand up to brush his fingertips against her cheek. She found herself leaning into his touch. "To kiss me when 'tis over."

She tried to keep herself steady on her feet, her fingers curling into his shirt. For months she'd resisted him, hidden from him, but this temptation was just too much. "I'll kiss ye now for good luck."

Slowly, he shook his head. "I fear if I kiss ye now, in such proximity to the bed, I might convince ye to let me warm ye for the night."

His tempting words slid over her skin like a caress, his breath faintly smelling of whisky and the heat of his hard body wrapping around her. She wanted to feel him consuming her. The man was intoxicating, with a potent power over her that left her without sense.

"I fear if I fall into bed with ye, I'll never come out of it," she admitted, feeling her face heat with the admission.

"'Tis the same for me, lass."

He leaned down, brushing his lips against her forehead. Jenny closed her eyes, savoring the feel of his breath on her hair, his lips on her skin. She tipped her face up to his and kissed him then, needing to feel him if only for an instant. She kept the kiss swift and brief and then leapt away from him, putting the coldness of air between them.

Toran chuckled. "I have a little more control than that, sweet Jenny. I'll no' be tossing ye onto the bed like a heathen."

Oh, but she wasn't certain she would mind that. To be tossed onto the feather ticking and then to feel the press of his hard body on hers… A shiver of awareness swept through her.

"Och, lass, dinna look at me like that." Toran's voice was low and gravelly, and the way he looked at her with such raw desire made every nerve in her body come alive with want.

"Like what?" she croaked.

"Like ye want me to give ye a proper kiss."

"If ye can keep it to just one," she drawled. "As ye pointed out, the one I just gave ye was lacking."

His lips curled in a slow, sensual smile. "I can give ye a proper kiss if that's what ye'd like, sweetheart."

Jenny squared her shoulders, chin lifted, and looked him dead in the eye. "I think 'tis only fair, given we are about to go into battle." She was fully aware that she was using a line most soldiers used on the women they wished to bed, but she didn't care. Clichés be damned, she just wanted him to touch her.

"Something to look forward to in the end," he murmured.

"Aye. A taste of what's to come."

Toran's hand slid around her waist, laying a path of fire in its wake, before pressing to the base of her spine and urging her forward.

Their bodies collided.

His other hand slid up her arm, fingers brushing her neck, thumb stroking her lower lip. Then he leaned forward, placing his tongue where his thumb had been, licking her lip before capturing it in his mouth and giving it a gentle suckle.

Jenny whimpered at the sensual move, winding her arms around his neck at the same time he captured her lips for a searing kiss. His tongue delved inside to taste her, sliding against her own with tantalizing, hedonistic purpose.

The way they were pressed together she could feel the swell of his arousal grow against her until it pressed hard and hot against her lower belly. Her nipples hardened, and the place between her thighs throbbed with need. She pressed herself tighter to him, hoping to fill that need with touch.

Toran's hand slid from the base of her spine to her rear, tucking her closer still until that hard part of him rubbed against the apex of her thighs. She gasped a moan against his lips.

He retreated and pressed again, backing her up as he did so until her back hit the wardrobe, rattling the wood. Something toppled to the floor with a crash. Neither of them tore their mouths from the other to look to see what it was.

Toran's hand slid from her buttocks to her thigh, roving lower until he reached the back of her knee. He lifted her leg to curve it around his hip, giving that hard part of him further access to the hot part of herself.

His hips rocked against hers in delicious movement, their mouths clashed, tongues teasing. A hand splayed across her rear and the other gripped her ribs, sliding higher until he was cupping her breast. Fingers stroked that turgid peak. She moaned again, and Toran groaned into her mouth, kissing her deeper still as he explored her breast.

This was no mere kiss, and yet she wanted more. Enough to make her want to beg him to take her to bed now, to forget what she'd said. They shouldn't go into war without having him laid out naked on her, their limbs entwined on the feather ticking.

She wished then that she'd not gone to dinner in her breeches but that she'd worn a gown, any gown that left her limbs naked beneath her skirts.

But perhaps that was as good a reason as any for her to keep wearing breeches, for he was in a kilt, and all they would have had to do was lift the hem of both their garments before his hard arousal touched her softer one, joining them together forever. But what was so bad about that?

The hand that had been fondling her breasts was sliding lower, delving into her breeches until he cupped her bare sex. She bucked against him, not realizing until it happened how very much she wanted him to touch her there nor what it would feel like for him to do so.

Goodness…it was magic. The pulsing need inside her leapt until she was gasping, frissons of heat and pleasure centered on his fingers spreading through her limbs.

He rubbed against her with expert strokes, dipping a finger inside her channel, in and out, round and round, until she was panting and sparks of bliss made her legs grow weak.

Jenny clung to him, her hips rocking in time with his movements until she felt herself breaking apart. Taken aback by the explosion of pleasure, her eyes grew wide, staring with shock and wonder into the blue abyss of his gaze. Toran swallowed her cry of rapture with a deep kiss, and she rode out the waves in desperate shudders, hips rocking against his hand.

Still holding tight, the only thing keeping her limp body upright, Toran let her leg fall back down, her foot hitting the floor with a thud. She clung to him, afraid to let go lest the rest of her drop down as well.

"That was beautiful," he murmured against her ear, tugging on the lobe with his teeth. "Your first?"

First what? First everything…save for his kiss. "Aye."

"That will keep me going—having watched ye fall apart, feeling your body shudder against mine. 'Twas beautiful, lass. Incredibly so."

It would keep her going too, perhaps even keep her from sleeping.

"Did ye feel it too?" she asked, wondering if he too had felt that explosion of pure ecstasy.

"Not yet." He grinned wolfishly, and every nerve in her body reached out to him. "But I will."

Jenny shivered. "When? Now?"

He chuckled. "Soon."

"Why not now?" It seemed only fair.

His eyes darkened. "God, ye dinna know how much I want to."

"Let me try. 'Tis only fair." She had no idea what she was offering, but whatever it was, it couldn't be too hard. He'd stroked her body the way a soldier oiled and cleaned his weapons, lovingly, thoroughly, until she'd shone from the care of it.

"Ye dinna know what ye're asking."

"Perhaps not all the ways of it, nay, but ye can show me." She reached forward, feeling the rock solidness of him against the wool of his kilt, taking in the way his eyes dipped closed and his lips parted. He licked his lower lip rapidly, eyes opening again to stare into hers. The black pinpricks of his eyes had dilated, thinning the blue. Even though he said nothing, she could see the hope for more in his gaze. "Let me give ye the same pleasure." Jenny stroked the long, hard length of him and watched Toran struggle to hold onto his control.

"I canna," he protested. "'Twould no' be right. I canna use ye ill."

"What is wrong about it? Is it using me ill for pleasure when I offer, when I want to give it? Was I using ye ill when I took it from ye? Do no' lovers give their pleasure freely?"

"Aye," he groaned, as she stroked slowly up and down, marveling at the hardness, the thickness of his appendage.

"Then let me, Toran," she purred. "Let me give ye the same feeling."

His hand came around hers, stroking upward, the fabric still a barrier between her bare palm touching his flesh.

She shifted her hand to remove the barrier of his kilt, but he stayed her.

"Let that be something else we look forward to."

"All right," she agreed, her voice throaty with power and need.

With his hand showing her how to stroke, she caressed him and then lifted up on tiptoe and pressed her mouth to his, sliding her tongue over his lips until he was kissing her back. A hand came overhead as he braced himself against the wardrobe, his own legs possibly as weak as hers had felt, and she had the sensation he was swallowing her whole. She wanted to be swallowed.

To be utterly consumed by this man.

His hips thrust against her, his arousal sliding at a faster pace in her grip, until he was groaning into her mouth, his body shuddering right along with the wardrobe behind her. A hot wetness pooled in the fabric in her palm.

"Ye're bleeding," she said, terrified and unthinking.

"No' blood," he groaned and then chuckled. "'Tis a man's seed."

"Oh." She should have known that, shouldn't she?

Plenty of people had rocked their bodies beneath blankets at camp, and she'd seen animals mate, but now that she considered it, she'd never seen what happened after. Jenny grinned. She'd done it. Pleasured this incredible man, had his seed in the palm of her hand.

"Fascinating," she murmured.

He exhaled against her hair. "'Tis ye who are fascinating, Jenny." He kissed her softly.

"Allow me to get ye a towel," she murmured and then ducked beneath his arm to go to the basin, where she dipped a cloth in water before returning to him.

He turned his back as he cleaned himself up, blocking her view of his nakedness and making her all the more curious to see what he looked like. What a man looked like.

When he was finished, he turned back around to face her and then tossed the cloth into the fire. "No need for evidence to make anyone accuse either of us of... wickedness."

She glanced down at the broken pot that had fallen from the wardrobe. Considering the noise they'd made, it was a wonder no one had come knocking on the door already.

"Is what we did so verra wicked?" she asked.

He stroked her cheek, tugging on an errant lock of hair.

"Nay, love, no' at all." He regarded her with a face full of intensity, his jaw hardening even as she saw desire flaring in his eyes. "I need to go, else I will nay be able to." He glanced toward the bed. "When this is over..."

"Aye." Jenny nodded, not wanting him to leave either. She cupped his hand to her face and then turned her head to kiss his palm. "Sleep well, soldier." She smiled at him, a little bit of sadness creeping in on her happiness.

"And ye too, Mistress J." He backed toward the door, his fingers still captured in hers. She was loath to let them go, feeling the chill of the air against her fingertips when she did.

He opened the door, peered into the corridor, and then ducked out of sight.

Jenny shut the door, leaning her back against it, her heartbeat still erratic and her mind a jumble of confusion. What they'd done had been incredible, beautiful, and so very wickedly potent. She wanted to do it again. Had to restrain herself from yanking open the door and calling him back.

When the battle was over, she was going to strip bare for him and tear off his clothes too. She wanted to see what he looked like, feel the weight of his hard member against her hand, bask in his touch, and cry out in rapture until both their throats were dry and hoarse.

With that she crawled into bed, tugging her pillow close and pretending it was Toran she snuggled up against. One could dream, after all.

And perhaps those dreams would get her through what was still to come.

Twenty-One

A SPLASH OF WATER CRASHING OVER HIS FACE WOKE Toran the following morning. Eyes jerking open, he found Dirk looming above him, his brow furrowed so hard he looked as though he'd eaten a dozen sour prunes and was in great need of a privy.

"What the bloody hell was that for?" Toran growled, shoving himself upward.

"I know what ye did last night."

An image of Jenny pressed up against the wardrobe, her cheeks flushed as her body trembled in his hands, flashed before his mind. *Ballocks…*

Toran wasn't going to give in to Dirk's inquiry, however. "What in blazes are ye talking about?" He wiped at the water on his head. Perhaps there was something else Dirk was referring to. With luck…

"Jenny. Everyone walking past her chamber could hear the two of ye."

Damn. "What business is it of yours?"

After reluctantly leaving Jenny's chamber, Toran had fallen onto his cot and into a fine deep sleep. He'd not slept so well in months, if ever.

"She's not your whore," Dirk snarled.

"I didna treat her as such either, ye bastard. I ought to call ye out for speaking about her that way."

"So ye admit it then."

"Admit what? That ye're jumping to conclusions

and making your laird into something she's not?" Toran retorted, leaping from his cot so he could face off with Dirk at eye level.

"Ye bedded her. I know ye did."

"I didna. If ye need confirmation, I suggest ye go ask her, though I'll bet she'll not take kindly to your questions."

Dirk let out a growl and shoved Toran hard, but he'd been waiting for it, his feet braced against the floor, and so he didn't budge.

Archie leapt between the two of them. "That's enough. Save it for the redcoats, ye bloody fools, else ye want Mistress J to leave one of ye behind? We've got bigger enemies and far bloodier battles to fight than this petty skirmish."

Toran gritted his teeth, his glower on Dirk. "Agreed."

"Fine." With a final scowl, Dirk stomped from the barracks.

"Ye're even more of a fool than I thought before," Archie accused, turning his fury on Toran. "What were ye thinking?"

"I didna lie with her," Toran said.

"Ye might not have taken her maidenhead, Cousin, but ye came close enough that it counts."

Had the whole damn castle heard them? He thought of the fallen pot, their moans, the way his heart had pounded—surely loud enough to let all of Scotland know what they had been up to. "'Tis only a business between me and her."

"'Tis all of our business when we're about to head off to war."

"Our…connection will no' stand in anyone's way, nor has it compromised the mission."

Archie nodded, watching Toran for what seemed like forever. There was so much still left unspoken between them. And Toran needed to make it right.

"I'm sorry, Archie," he said. "For what happened at the garrison this summer. I'm a bastard, and I dinna expect that ye'll ever forgive me, but I'll ask it all the same."

Archie was silent, the muscles in both sides of his jaw flexed hard enough to cause divots. Slowly, the tension in him dissipated.

"Ye are a bastard for so easily betraying your clan. There's blood on your hands, but they were determined to get into the garrison one way or another. If ye'd not supplied the information, someone else would have, or they would have gone in anyway without it. I could hate ye forever, but it would do no good. The fact is I owe ye my life. And if I'd believed rebels responsible for my mother's murder, I too might have taken the same path." Archie ran a hand through his hair. "Ye've changed, Cousin. For the better. I trust ye, and I forgive ye."

Emotion swept through Toran. He pulled his cousin against him, pounding him on the back. "Thank ye."

"Ye dinna have to thank me. That is what family is for. To forgive one another, to take care of one another."

"I'll thank ye all the same."

Archie squeezed him back, cautious not to slap him on the back as men often did.

"Speaking of family… What are we to do about Simon?" Toran broached the topic, though he'd be just as happy if his cousin rotted forever in the dungeon. They'd kept the Fox at bay by forcing his cousin to continue sending mundane updates.

"Uncle is going to come after ye soon. He'll eventually figure out that the missives ye send are untrue and demand to see the son he's been missing for months. He will believe that ye've figured out his plans if it comes to that. The Fox may have tried to toss ye into Boyd's clutches, but he doesna believe ye're stupid."

"Aye. I'd thought to keep him locked up until after the battle. But I dinna want to bring more danger to Cnàmhan Broch while we're gone."

"Why no' give Simon a taste of his own doing?"

Toran's brows rose. "Ye mean send him to Boyd."

Archie grinned. "Aye."

"Boyd willna kill him because of the alliance with our uncle."

"Exactly. He may torment him a bit though, which is no worse than what Simon was planning for ye. In fact, 'tis showing him mercy."

"I'll speak with Jenny about it."

When his cousin had gone, Toran ripped off his wet shirt and replaced it with a dry one. He picked up his plaid where he'd laid it to dry by the brazier the night before after washing it in the nearby loch. The wool was still damp in a few places, but he didn't care. He belted it in place, pulled on his frock coat, boots, and cap, and then donned his weapons. The journey south would take four or five days, depending on whom they met along the way and whether the weather cooperated.

Toran hurried into the castle, sneaking up the back stairs, hoping to catch Jenny before she exited, and was lucky to find her just outside her chamber.

"What are ye doing here?" she whispered, glancing up and down the corridor.

"I needed to speak with ye about something afore we go. 'Tis important, or I'd no' have risked it."

"All right." She reopened her chamber door and ushered him inside.

"'Tis about Simon. I want to send him to Boyd."

"Nay!"

"Hear me out. If we leave him here, my uncle will come for him, and that will only bring danger to your mother and the rest of the clan staying behind. If we send him to Boyd, the danger will be directed away from Cnàmhan Broch. Boyd will use him against my uncle, but he'll no' kill him."

Jenny shook her head. "Ye're right. Leaving him here is dangerous. But sending him to Boyd, he'll only divulge everything he knows about us. Better to send him back to his father. That bastard already knows what's going on here."

"Aye."

"The Fox would be a fool to retaliate while we're away. He's got bigger problems than to attack an empty castle."

"I'll speak with Dirk and have a few men take him to the garrison in the middle of the night."

Jenny pressed a swift kiss to his lips and then pulled back before he could wrap her up in his arms. "Get out of here."

Toran chuckled. "Aye, Mistress."

He sneaked his way back out of the castle and found Dirk, finalizing the plan for Simon.

Jenny was all business when she exited the castle, barely looking his way other than for a nod of respect, as if he were any other member of her regiment. Toran grinned. All right then, that was how it was to be. In fact, he preferred it that way. He didn't need any needling from the men or another icy bath to wake him in the morning.

And for her part, she didn't need anyone speculating about whom she was lying with or when. It was none of their business, but worst of all, he didn't want her losing the respect the men had for her because she was bedding a man—bedding him. He suspected that part of her allure was that she was seemingly untouchable.

That was a bit of lore he rather liked about her, and he enjoyed watching the men who admired her from afar. Toran stuck to the back of the line as he mounted, perfectly happy to keep up her ruse.

The first day of riding they took slowly, avoiding the roads as much as possible, as they had that first time they'd ventured out months before. They made camp that night by a riverbed surrounded by thorny bushes. They were fully aware that if the *Sassenachs* took it upon themselves to notice an army, there would be nothing the Scots could do about it. This was no small contingent of men.

Jenny had called upon all of her reinforcements, and now they were some four hundred men strong. It was a massive lot of warriors to be traipsing through the woods together, and there was no hiding their purpose. With that many bodies moving, that many horses, wagons full of supplies, even splitting into smaller parties the path they made could not be hidden.

The second day of travel was through the Cairngorm mountains, and they were slowed down by rain that made the terrain slippery and dangerous. They pressed on, but it cost them time. They still spent the majority of their daylight hours moving forward, but it would now be five days' travel instead of four.

Jenny stayed away from Toran as they rode and still when they made camp, and he did the same out of respect. He would wait for her to come to him again, even if nearly every waking and sleeping thought was of her. She plagued him in his dreams and even more so when she relayed updates to him and then rode back to the front, her bottom bouncing enticingly on the saddle.

Their entire party was with them now, as the dragoons didn't often come into mountain territory. They were too afraid of dying, which many of them did—some by accident and others less accidentally.

They made camp at the crest with the road down below. Their makeshift tents within the trees attempted to keep them dry but failed. The night was miserable and freezing. By the morning, most of the men were snapping at one another as they packed up. The only one who had a kind word to say to anyone was Jenny, keeping the peace and raising morale.

When no one was paying attention, Toran passed her a cup of warmed cider.

"Mistress J."

She took it, and the slight dip of pleasure in her eyes at the warmth against her cold, red fingers was exactly what he'd been hoping to see.

"Thank ye, Fraser," she said.

"Ye're welcome, Mistress."

She took a long sip, her throat bobbing, and she sighed in pleasure. A slight curve of her lips was all the smile he'd get, but Toran cherished it all the same.

They set out once more in silence. Nearly at the bottom of the mountain, Jenny held up her hand. Arms shot up down the line to still the men and wagons at the back of their caravan.

Five men deep, Toran peered around her trying to discover what it was she'd seen or heard.

There was no mistaking the sound of the English soldiers riding directly toward the mountain, their chatter about stealing a string of horses from a Scottish crofter making Toran bristle with anger. They didn't bother to be quiet, boasting loudly for all the trees and passersby to hear their vile deeds. They were oblivious to the Jacobite army hidden within the trees. Idiots.

In silence they watched two men in red coats ride past at a leisurely pace, a half-dozen horses tethered to their mounts. It took every ounce of her willpower not to lash out at the men and instead allow them to pass.

When they stopped to make camp for the night, they filled up the woods like a village of outlaws, campfires smoldering near dozens of makeshift tents, the men joking around about this and that, sharpening their weapons and eating. Toran didn't stop himself from finding Jenny this time. He sat down beside her, ignoring the glares from Dirk, who was rarely far from her side.

She passed him a flask, which to his surprise was filled with whisky.

"Good work today," she said.

"And to ye, Mistress J, our fearless leader."

She grinned and took back the flask. "I am not without fear, but I am determined to make it this time. And without ye having to answer to a dragoon's whip."

"I will not oppose ye on that." Toran's back still smarted every once in a while, though the scabs had long since healed. The skin was tight, itched at times and stung at others, still sensitive to the touch. The men were aware of that fact, and when they were trying to rile him, they didn't hesitate to smack him on the back. Especially Dirk.

It wasn't overly painful, not the kind of pain that would bring a man to his knees, but enough so that he grimaced a bit more than he would have otherwise.

"Only a couple of days now," Jenny said, handing back the flask.

Toran took a small sip of the whisky and then asked softly, "Have ye been to battle before, lass?"

The words were soft enough that no one had heard, but all the same she stiffened, her head whipping toward him. He'd been so informal by calling her *lass*.

"Mistress, apologies." He'd nearly lost himself in being so personal with her.

"I have no' had the pleasure as of yet, Fraser. A few

small skirmishes with dragoons, aye, but nothing like what we're about to encounter."

He was glad she admitted it. The woman had pride, but she wasn't so full of it she couldn't admit where she was weak.

"But with ye and Dirk and the men who've been to battle before, I should be all right."

"I am at your service in any way that ye need me. I know 'tis not a topic either of us wish to revisit, but I will remind ye I'm familiar with the English and their ways."

"I think that will be helpful, Fraser. Extremely so." She slid him a sideways glance, a teasing smile on her lips. "It would seem your wayward days are coming into good use for us."

"May this be a way for me to redeem myself, for I've been a fool." His tone had turned sober.

For that he would never forgive his uncle or Boyd. The two of them had played him for a fool. The Fox was too old to move as swiftly as he once had and had used Toran's anger as a way to still be in the game. No longer. The Fox could go to the devil for all he cared and take his wily son with him.

Suddenly irritated, Toran stood, passed her back the flask, and walked off into the darkness. It would be nigh impossible to find any semblance of privacy, given the number of men camping in their makeshift village.

Toran managed to find a thick tree facing a darker patch of the woods, the nearest Highlanders a dozen feet away. He was able to lean against the tree and think, unnoticed.

Or that had been his hope.

"What happened back there?" Jenny's voice was quiet. He'd not even heard her approach.

"Ye've a light step." He pulled a cinnamon stick from his sporran and began using it to pick his teeth.

"Ye canna be a rebel without one. Have ye another of those?"

"Aye. True enough." He handed her a second stick.

"'Tis spicy," she mused.

Toran grinned, thinking about what it would be like to kiss her now, with both their mouths tasting of cinnamon.

"So, are ye going to tell me?" she asked.

Toran pressed his lips together, not one to talk about his feelings. Before meeting Jenny he'd been the hard, silent type, but she seemed to bring out a different side of him. At first he'd feared that she was making him weak. But how could that be, when she herself was so strong? She'd not bring him down, only bolster him, and he likewise for her.

"I dinna much like talking about it."

"Ah," she murmured and leaned against the massive tree beside him, her shoulder touching his arm. "I'll not push, Toran, but know that I'm here if ye ever wish to talk."

He turned to the side, leaning his shoulder against the tree and looking at the shadows that framed her face.

"When did ye know ye wanted to be a rebel?" he asked.

"I didna come here to talk about me."

He grinned. "I know."

She sighed and turned as well so they faced each other. She ran a hand through her hair, pausing a moment. "When we were wee lasses, my friends and I—Annie and Fiona—made a pact that no matter what, we'd take up the cause. We would continue to fight as our ancestors had, as our sires had."

"A lifelong conviction."

"Aye. What is a conviction unless ye can make something of it?"

"Nothing."

"Exactly. And what of ye? What convictions have ye made, besides those I'm already aware of?"

"No one has ever asked me that." Toran tucked the cinnamon stick away, and she handed hers back to him.

"I am honored to be the first," she said.

"Keep it," he said, then referring back to what she'd said, "Clan and country have always been my focus."

"Until they were no'."

"Even that I'm no' so certain about."

She raised a brow in question.

"I might have been on the wrong side, for the wrong reasons, but I was still fighting for my mother, for my brother and sister. I wanted them all to be free from what I'd believed was a death sentence."

"And now? Do ye believe our fight is a death sentence?"

"For some, aye. But if our cause is no' one worthy of dying for, then it would no' be worth it at all."

Jenny nodded, her eyes cast down, chin tucked to her chest. "I have a healthy bit of fear for what's to come," she admitted. "I know the risks, and I know that there will always be an opponent out there stronger than me, faster, more skilled. I hope I dinna meet them. But that is not what has me scared most of all."

"What is it?"

"That would be meeting Hamish on the field."

Toran took hold of her hand, her fingers cold in his grasp. He rubbed the pads of his thumbs over her small knuckles. "Ye willna have to fight your brother."

She cocked her head, thinking. "What was it like when ye saw Archie at the garrison?"

"Like being gutted with a rusty, blunt knife."

"I was afraid ye'd say that." She and her brother had never gotten along as children and had been at odds as adults, and even now she hated him for the decisions he'd made. But all the same, the idea of killing her own brother didn't sit well with her. If she had to, if it came down to it, she could do her duty. But it wouldn't be without heavy scars.

"No one would expect ye to fight your brother on the field."

She laughed bitterly. "The thing is, Toran, that where I might turn away and show my brother mercy, he is no' likely to do the same. If I face my brother in battle, he will try his damnedest to cut me down. He will see me no' only as a political traitor but as having betrayed him personally as well. He will see me as the enemy, one who could topple everything he's lied, cheated, stolen, and killed for. He will need to show the English that he took my life to prove that his own was worth something."

Heedless of whoever could see them, Toran tugged her into his arms. She let him, circling his waist with her arms and laying her cheek against his chest.

"Bastard," he said.

"He is."

"I willna let him hurt ye, Jenny." He pressed his lips to the top of her head, breathing in her scent, hints of cinnamon swirling between them. "He canna take ye out of this world. Ye're too valuable to everyone." *To me.*

"I feel so ridiculous," she murmured against his chest. "I'm the leader of a regiment I recruited myself. I've fought dragoons, outsmarted them, and here I'm practically blubbering like a bairn over a skirmish with my big brother."

Toran chuckled softly. "'Tis no' just a skirmish, lass, and even the toughest of warriors sometimes have to break down—if only to build themselves back up again. Ye're stronger than ye know. Just look around ye."

She pulled away, peering into the woods at the dozen or so fires where men talked, slept, ate.

"Ye're their leader, Jenny, whether ye're blubbering against my chest or seated in the saddle of a fine warhorse wielding your musket. Ye dinna have to be this person or that, ye just have to be *ye.*"

She swiped at her eyes and looked up at him. "Ye're right."

"Aye," he said, not trying to curb the twang of arrogance. "Ye'd best heed."

She laughed. "Now ye're overly confident."

"I just want to be me, lass."

Jenny playfully swatted him, and he grabbed her hand, pulling it to his lips. They were warmer now from his touch.

"Soldier, seducer, nursemaid," she teased.

"Nursemaid?"

"Aye, ye attended your cousin, and the hugs and encouraging words ye just gave me were very similar to my nursemaid's when I was about six years old."

He chuckled. "I may be a soldier and seducer, but I would no' label myself a nursemaid."

"What would ye call it, then?" she teased.

"Let me see... I think I should like to call myself a healer." He winked.

"A healer?" One arched brow rose in question. God, he loved how expressive she was when she was letting her guard down.

"Are ye no' better, lass? Are ye no' healed from melancholy?"

"I suppose I am," she said softly, and he had to resist the urge to pull her into his arms.

"Ye see, the name fits."

She rolled her eyes. "I'm certain most things will fit in that big head of yours."

He tapped her on the tip of her nose. "Dinna be jealous."

Jenny's mouth fell open a little in mock outrage. "I am no such thing."

"If ye say so."

She huffed and gave a little shove to his chest, but he caught both her hands in his and pressed them to the place where his heart beat.

"Ye, sir, are baiting me." Her voice was a little breathless, and he liked the soft lilt.

"I may be," he drawled.

"Tease." She pinched him playfully on the muscle of his chest, just a few inches above his nipple.

"'Tis true. Shall I pinch ye back in the same spot?" He waggled his brows. "Make it even?"

She backed away from him, shaking her head, and he could just barely make out the curve of her smile. "I came over here to make ye feel better, Toran, and I am leaving with a lighter heart."

"Trust me, lass, when I say that I am as well."

Twenty-Two

GLASGOW WAS A CACOPHONY OF NOISE, BETWEEN THE pipers, horse hooves clomping on the cobbles, shouts of newcomers meeting with those who'd already arrived, and drums that beat with no particular coordination. It was glorious chaos, and to Jenny it almost seemed like a mirror of the battle that had taken place here hundreds of years before between Robert the Bruce's troops and the English. It was odd how often history repeated itself. The two countries united but always divided.

The prince was quartered with Sir Hugh Patterson at Bannockburn House following his return from battle, and Jenny still for the life of her couldn't understand why the prince's advisors had told him to retreat. Why had he not pushed onward to London?

She supposed it was because he didn't think he had enough troops. But from what she'd heard, the Welsh supporters of the Stuart line had rallied and marched on London thinking to meet the prince there.

The overcast sky gave way to drizzle and mist but nothing stronger. Jenny glanced at Toran, gathering strength just from his presence. And from the rest of her men, nodding at her with approval. To think back to two years ago when she'd gotten the idea to ride out into the night—that since then she'd been able to amass all of this.

When they reached camp of the prince's army, set up outside the walls of Bannockburn House, they weaved their way through tents and carts, passing by dozens of men and women she didn't know and dozens more she did, as they stood back to allow Jenny and her army to pass on the way to greet the prince. Prince Charles stood on the steps of the great manor house before a crowd of people, looking every bit as French as Jenny imagined the royals in Paris might look. His long ivory-and-silver frock coat shimmered, embroidered with cream-colored silk thread in what at first looked like everyday flowers but on closer inspection were in fact tiny white Jacobite roses.

He wore a powdered wig, and his cheeks were pink, but she guessed the color was from the excitement and perhaps the wine that he held freely in his hand. He was indeed as beautiful as witnesses made him out to be, with high cheekbones, plush rose-colored lips, and light-blue eyes.

At his side was a pretty woman a few years older than Jenny, her dark curls styled in delicate ringlets that hung to her shoulders. She wore an elegant gown of creamy silk, embroidered with roses. It made Jenny feel only slightly self-conscious of her trews and frock coat.

When Jenny was announced, the prince looked up from his conversation, his eyes scanning her with what could only be called amusement, and he beckoned her forward. The crowd parted, allowing her to come closer.

"Your Highness," Jenny said, starting into a low bow but then quickly changing to a curtsy despite her lack of gown.

The prince laughed. "*Ma chérie,*" he said. The prince had been raised in Rome and spent some time in France, but she had supposed that he would have spent all his time in the company of his own courtiers and developed their accents, for his was a mixture of Italian and French.

His eyes widened in recognition. "It is a pleasure to meet you, Lady Jenny, though I have heard that I should instead call you Mistress J. I still owe you and your clan a visit."

A giddy pleasure rippled through her at his use of her title and the fact that he respected her enough to say it as though it were a truth. And she supposed it was now, if the prince was declaring it so.

"Aye, I am one and the same. We'd be honored for ye to visit us." She felt the color rising in her cheeks. "I've brought ye over three hundred soldiers to aid in the fight as well as wagons of weapons, coin, and other provisions. Will ye accept our gifts, Your Highness?"

"I am more than honored, my lady. We are extremely pleased with your gift and to name you our royal subject." He took her hand in his and brushed his lips over her knuckles. "A formidable adversary you will be to our friends in the south."

"Not only those in the south," she said. Her stomach twisted at what she had to tell him. But it was like any wound that needed tending; ignoring it wouldn't make it better. "I must tell you that my brother Hamish, the former Lord Mackintosh, fights for Cumberland."

"Ah, well, I have heard this much. Brother against brother, father against son. And for you, sister against brother—this will be hard, no?"

"Aye, but I know I'm on the right side. When he meets

his maker, my brother will regret the choices he's made." She only hoped she didn't have to be the one to deliver him there.

"He will, my lady. You will be a valuable asset to Murray who commands my troops."

A man approached, speaking softly to the prince in an Irish brogue. One of his seven men of Moidart, no doubt—men who had come over from France with him, a mixture of English, Scottish, and Irish subjects.

Dismissed, Jenny returned to her men to find Annie and Lady MacPherson, her mother, sitting with Dirk inside her tent. Jenny embraced her friend and then looked for Fiona, but their third was not yet present.

"Jenny," Annie said, gaining her attention. "We've no' many men in our contingent, and they all get along well with yours. We all fight under the direction of General Murray." She gestured at the dozen MacPherson warriors who mingled with the Mackintoshes.

"Aye, I'm glad."

Their rest in Glasgow was not long. They stayed a few days, their time filled with hours of training, the regaling of tales from the battles of Prestonpans and Derby, and Jenny's nerves growing thinner and thinner. She met often with Murray, learning as much as she could about battle tactics. While she would take direction from him, her men were to take direction from her. And so after her meetings with Murray, she gathered her men to discuss the tactics they would take in the coming days—in particular that the prince had informed Murray the Mackintosh army was to be at the frontline of the battle.

She longed for a moment alone with Toran. Even a brief conversation would have been nice.

And then the horn blew—a sound they'd all been eager to hear.

It was time to march into battle.

Jenny's heart thrummed like the pounding of imaginary drums as they made their way toward the battle point. The moment of attack had been chosen, a strike when the English would be least expecting it. A surprise attack. She and her three hundred men were to march under Murray's leadership, alongside the Mackenzies, Farquarsons, MacDonalds, MacPhersons, Frasers, Camerons, and Appins, their weapons bared. To their rear were the Gordon, Atholl, and Ogilvy clans. All had come dressed in Highland garb, swords gleaming and sharp, muskets loaded—if they had them.

Their caps were adorned with white rosette cockades, pinned to show those loyal to King George just whose side they were on—the Stuarts. Not a *Sassenach* would get past her nor a traitorous Scot, and none would take her life. That was the vow Jenny had made to herself, no matter how unrealistic the first part might be. She was going to do her damnedest.

The prince had not joined them on the battlefield. He was instead nursing an ague at Bannockburn House with Lady Clementina for company, the woman Jenny had seen beside him when she first met him. Annie had been asked to aid him as well. While he might not be there in the flesh, he was there in spirit. Jenny swore that she'd be among the leaders who presented the victory to him.

Most of her men were on foot, while the rest were on horseback. Being on the frontline, with the English using their cavalry to fight foot soldiers, Jenny and her men would have to rely on the unpredictable tactics they'd practiced.

She was flanked by Toran and Dirk, with Archie at the rear, as though they formed a shield around her. Both Toran and Dirk had fought to stand in front of her, but she'd not let them. She knew what they were up to, not wanting her to be hurt, and she could appreciate that. But she wasn't going to be the type of leader that stayed hidden in the background.

Most of all, she feared the moment when she finally came face-to-face with her brother. She'd rather face him on Mackintosh lands where the rush of battle made their judgments not about life and death but instead about negotiation. A negotiation that she might be able to swing toward her favor on their own lands with the elders there to back her up.

Boyd, however, she would gladly meet on the field of battle. She was certain that black-hearted bastard would revel at the idea of cutting up Scots.

At last the time came to make their presence known to their enemies. The Scots stepped from the shadows, eight thousand strong, to surprise the *Sassenachs* on their stolen ground. Flashes of red, gold, and white went by in blurs as the English scrambled to get themselves into place, tossing on coats, pulling on boots, grappling with reins and weapons.

As they stared at the faces of their enemies, their breaths puffs of clouds in the frigid air, thunder rumbled overhead. The skies that had been mostly gray and threatening now unleashed, pelting against their faces. Jenny smiled. This was Highland weather at its finest. If these bastards thought they could simply come onto Scottish soil and steal their holdings, their very lives, then they had better be ready for the Highlanders to steal them back.

The battle was fierce, and throughout the melee, true to their word, Dirk and Toran remained by Jenny's side, fighting shoulder to shoulder. More than once Jenny raised her father's sword high, saving one or more of them from English blades. Their enemy fell quickly, none having been ready for the battle—men half-dressed and fighting in bare feet.

As the rain pelted down on them, the English forces broke. Loud cannon fire erupted with the thunder, and the screams of those dying and being torn apart shook the earth. Seeing that they were on the losing end, the English generals called their men to retreat.

The Jacobites gave chase to the retreating English forces, some of the men looting the bodies of the dead loyalists along the way. And it was only belatedly that she noticed Dirk was nowhere to be seen, having joined the men who chased after the retreating rebels, while Jenny and Toran took their contingents to fight the dragoons who remained behind.

"We have to find Dirk and the other men," Jenny said.

Toran searched the fallen with her for what felt like hours. The ground was littered with men in red coats, some of them reddened by dye and others by death. None were Dirk or any of her men, which relieved Jenny at the same time as it sent a chill down her spine. Pray God none had been taken captive by King George's men.

And then she came across a familiar face—one of the men she'd sent to be with her brother, a loyalist she'd been glad to see the back of. He lay dying on the ground, clutching a gaping wound in his belly. She knelt beside him, an enemy, but a man she'd known all the same, and offered up a prayer for his soul.

"Traitor," he sneered, choking on blood that burbled in his throat.

"Where is my brother?" she asked.

His lips peeled back in a smile, teeth gleaming red. "Where he belongs."

"What does that mean?" A sense of panic lodged in her throat.

"Taking back what ye stole." The man started to cough then, spraying blood against her cheeks.

"Enough riddles," she said, swiping at the warm droplets. "Where is he?"

But the man did not answer, his eyes rolling back as death took him. Jenny shuddered, staring into his death mask and willing his words to make sense. The only thing she could surmise from them was that Hamish was heading to Cnàmhan Broch to take back the castle. She prayed she was wrong.

When darkness fell completely, Jenny and her soldiers retreated themselves. They followed a horde of other Jacobite soldiers nearly a mile to Dunipace, to a castle, barely lit, its walls and towers jutting toward the sky like fingers reaching from a grave.

They were ushered inside. Jenny recognized several clan chiefs but in her exhaustion could do barely more than nod. They were shown to the great hall, where men dined on a pottage that smelled like peas and pork and that made Jenny's belly rumble with hunger.

She collapsed onto a bench, held upright only by her hands flat on the table. Toran sat beside her, his hand resting on her elbow.

"Are ye all right?"

"Tired. Worried." She could speak in no more than single words. "Some of our men are missing, and Hamish… One of his men said he's going to take back what is his."

"We'll find out what happened to the men in the morning, I swear it. And your brother, he willna have gone from battling to seizing. He's resting tonight as are the rest of us."

Even as he said it there was a commotion at the door. Every man and woman in the great hall reached for some sort of weapon.

"'Tis MacDonald," someone called out. "He comes with good news."

Jenny perked up at that.

The men in the corridor shuffled into the great hall so everyone could hear what MacDonald had to say.

"We are victorious," he announced, and cheers went up around the room. "General Hawley, coward to King George, ordered his men to retreat to Edinburgh. The prince now resides in the house that Hawley vacated, the remainder of our armies with him. He bids you rest tonight and join him there in the morning."

Jenny sagged against Toran. Surely Dirk and the rest of her men would be there. They were resourceful, strong. They'd not have allowed themselves to be taken by King George's forces.

"We'll find them there in the morning. Dirk is a good leader, and I'm certain he'll have fallen in with the prince's men when called to do so," Toran said, echoing her thoughts.

"Aye," Jenny said. "I'm sure ye're right."

Bottles of whisky were passed around, but Jenny declined. Even one sip would see her falling asleep in her soup. She was no longer hungry despite having been starving only a moment ago. Instead, she stood from the table.

"I need to find a bed," she said.

"I'll come with ye—to guard ye," Toran quickly added.

Jenny tried to smile, but she was so exhausted she was certain it was more of a grimace. Happy to let Toran choose the accommodations, she followed him blindly through the castle until he opened the door to a small, cozy room where a single cot sat against the wall. There was no light other than the torch from the corridor.

"I'm so exhausted that if ye'd like the bed, I know I'll have no problem passing out on the floor," she said.

"Och, nay, my colonel. I insist ye take the bed."

Jenny fell in a heap upon the dusty mattress and was asleep before she could even say thank ye. But she woke shivering some time later, her teeth chattering in the tiny, cold room. They'd no hearth or even a brazier to keep them warm, and though the window in the chamber was small and shuttered, it was letting in a mighty draft. She searched the cot for a blanket and found one, but even wrapping it around her body thrice did nothing to alleviate the chill that she felt deep in her bones. She glanced down at the floor where she made out Toran's snoring shape, his teeth not chattering at all. The man had to be a human fire.

The more she thought about how warm he seemed to be, the more she wanted him up there on the cot to warm her up as well.

"Toran," she whispered.

He muttered something in his sleep.

"Toran. Come up here. I'm cold." He murmured something else unintelligible, and she reached out to shake his shoulder. "Please, I'm freezing."

"Is that an order, Mistress J?"

She could hear the laugh in his voice.

"Aye, an order to warm your leader lest she catch a cold."

Toran effortlessly rose from the floor and scooped her up in his arms before tumbling them both back onto the cot, where he cocooned her in a wealth of heat. Her back was to his chest, a heavy arm laid across her waist, and a thick, muscled leg over her own. She was surrounded by

Toran and his glorious heat. Even her head was growing warm, tucked against his neck.

As her body thawed, Jenny fell into a deep sleep. She woke with the rising sun, every muscle feeling as though she'd been trampled by a horse. Toran was still folded around her, and she couldn't bear to move and feel the cold again. Not when being in his arms felt like heaven.

She wasn't certain her muscles had ever ached this much from a fight. Granted, she'd also never fought as hard or as long as she had yesterday. She rubbed at her neck and shoulders in an attempt to ease the tension. From behind her a strong hand clasped over one shoulder, rubbing at the knotted muscles. She bit her lip rather than moan aloud in relief.

"What ye need is a hot bath," Toran said.

"That would be heaven right now. But alas, there are no hot baths to be procured."

"Then I suppose ye'll have to make do with my gentle touch." He spoke softly beside her ear, his warm breath tickling her skin.

"There are much worse things," Jenny mused and then laughed.

"Och, lass, ye wound me." His hands stilled, and every fiber of her body screamed out for him to continue touching her. "Should I stop?"

"Nay. Dinna stop."

Twenty-Three

TORAN'S HANDS WERE LIKE MAGIC SKATING OVER HER skin, loosening her aching muscles. Every inch of her tingled from the release of tension and then from the simple act of his touch.

His lips skimmed the side of her neck as he rubbed his thumbs into her lower back, having lifted her shirt enough to slip his hands beneath to touch her bare skin. One of his large thighs was draped over her legs, trapping her. But she didn't feel trapped. She was very much where she wanted to be.

The battle had ended in victory for them. And wasn't it this moment that she'd promised to herself, to him, if they should win?

Jenny rolled in his arms, coming face-to-face with him in the near dark. She pressed her lips to his, her breasts to his chest, her hands on his shoulders. Her legs were still trapped between his, and she rocked into him, wanting to feel him flush against her.

"Jenny," he groaned against her lips when she teased the corners of his mouth with her tongue. "I want ye."

"I need ye," she answered. "Make love to me, Toran."

Rather than answer her, he nimbly rolled her onto her back, covering her body with his. He rested a hand on her hip, tenderly massaging as he deftly shifted his legs between hers. He slid his palm down her thigh, hooking her knee in his grasp and up around his hip. He swayed his pelvis against her.

Goodness, but that felt good. As if her entire body hadn't been coming alive before, the press of him so close to the center of her had her back arching so she could get closer to him. His kiss was tender, and his hand rising up her shirt to stroke her breast sent her heart into a tailspin. Her nipples grew into hard, aching points. Jolts of pleasure coursed through her when he brushed the pad of his thumb over one before rolling it between his fingers. Jenny had never believed that a woman's nipples could be used for anything other than feeding bairns, but Toran was introducing her to something new.

Oh, what pleasure he was bringing her. She lifted her other leg around his hip, and he shifted, the hardness of his arousal pressed alluringly to the damp folds between her thighs. She wanted to remove her trews, to feel that thickened shaft of male flesh sliding along her naked skin.

Toran gently swayed his hips back and forth, pressing his erection against her sex and sending sensations spiraling throughout her body, so much so that she was finding it hard to decipher a single thought.

Toran's lips slowly drifted lower to her neck, his tongue flicking out to taste her skin where her pulse beat hard. And then lower still, to her collarbone, his teeth scraping gently over the slope of her bone. He lifted her shirt, revealing her breasts to his gaze, and she sat up slightly so he could remove the garment properly. When she fell back against the bed, he was staring down at her in wonder, his hands tracing lines from her collarbone to her breasts and along her ribs.

"Ye're even more beautiful than I imagined."

"Ye imagined me without a shirt on?" she asked, a teasing smile pulling at the corners of her lips.

"Och, lass, I've imagined ye without a stitch of clothing on and lying beneath me as ye are right now."

Jenny felt her face flush, heat rising from her chest up over her neck and cheeks.

"Ye're so damn gorgeous." He leaned down to kiss her again, the roughness of his shirt scratching against her sensitive skin.

Jenny tugged at his shirt too until he practically tore it off, tossing it to join hers on the floor. When his body joined with hers again, she gasped at the feel of his heated flesh on hers and the tickle of the hair on his chest. The feeling was exquisite, sensational, and she never wanted it to end. She pressed her hands to his ribs, letting her palms slide upward, stroking over the contours of his body, delighting in his very male flesh.

Toran slid lower, his mouth coming to her breast, tongue darting to flick over her nipple. She bucked and gasped, not having expected the incredibly wicked sensation to jar her so much. He swirled his tongue and then sucked her nipple into his mouth, and she thought she might actually float from the pleasure of it.

Jenny thrust her hands into his hair, arching her back and lifting her hips in time with the sway of his. Everything felt so good she wondered if she were in a dream or truly experiencing all the pleasure that Toran had to give. He kissed between her breasts, sliding his warm velvet lips to her other breast before teasing and toying with her nipple until she was panting, tiny mewls of pleasure escaping her throat.

But he didn't stop there. Toran was kissing his way lower, his lips skimming over the quivering flesh of her belly, tongue circling her navel until he came to the ties that held her trews in place. With his teeth, he tugged, and she giggled.

"What are ye doing?"

"I am showing ye my skill, my prowess as a lover."

"I am impressed."

"Ye have no' seen anything yet." And then he tugged in earnest, proving to her that her trews could be removed by his teeth alone.

The cold whisper of air on her bare flesh was quickly replaced by heat as Toran kissed his way up from her bare ankles to her calves, tickling behind her knee with his tongue and then skimming his heated kisses over her inner thigh. Her calf rested on his shoulder, and she felt so incredibly wicked in this position, her sex bared for him to see, the hooded, hungry look in his eyes. He looked as though he wanted to devour her.

And then he did, taking his wicked mouth from her inner thigh to press a heated kiss to the center of her curls.

Jenny bucked upward, trying to sit up, to protest, but Toran grunted against her throbbing flesh. His tongue darted out to lick at a certain spot that had her falling backward, even as the flat of his palm pressed between her breasts urging her back onto the cot.

"Let me kiss ye," he murmured between her thighs. "Let me love ye."

Jenny sighed in answer, finding words too difficult to form, and allowed her brain and body to succumb to the pleasure of his wicked tongue. His tongue dipped between her folds and stroked softly along the length of her. A hand behind her head, she tugged at the railing of the cot to keep herself from bucking completely off the surface. He fluttered over a sensitive knot of flesh that made her cry out, swirling around it and then suckling gently, bringing her just to the brink of rapture before pulling back and starting all over again.

He tormented her this way, over and over, her thighs shaking, breaths rapid, until finally he didn't pull back but took her right over the edge. Jenny cried out, hands letting go of the cot and thrusting into his hair as she tugged him closer, then pushed him away, and then tugged him closer again.

Toran didn't pause to let her come down from her climax but instead divested himself of his plaid in record time and settled the heat of his body between her thighs. He gripped his shaft, sliding the tip over her still-quivering, wet flesh before notching himself at her entrance. Her knees fell open in response.

"Are ye certain ye want this?" he said gruffly.

"Aye. Please."

"There is no going back."

"I have no intention of going back."

Toran groaned and thrust forward. A sharp pain took away the pulses of pleasure, and she stiffened, widened eyes going to his.

"I'm sorry," he crooned.

She tried to shift away, the invasion uncomfortable, tears gathering in the corners of her eyes. When she'd touched him before, she'd known there would be no room for him, and here he'd gone and proved it to her.

Toran leaned down slowly, his body still embedded in hers, and kissed the tears at the corners of her eyes. "I didna want to hurt ye. It will ease soon, I promise, and then I'll make ye see stars again. I swear it."

Jenny nodded, though she wasn't certain she should believe him. The sting of his entrance made her entire middle feel awkward and achy. He kissed her then, gently at first and then more insistently, his tongue sliding into her mouth to dance with hers. Soon she forgot about the pain, only wanting to kiss him more.

He stroked her breasts, teasing her nipples, and then he slid a hand between their joined bodies to stroke over that nub of flesh that had come to life when he'd touched it with his tongue. To her surprise and delight, pleasure jolted her again. The ache of him taking her maidenhead was completely gone, and she was instead filled with a heady need for movement. She shifted her hips beneath him, moaning at how good it felt, and so she repeated the motion.

"Are ye all right?" he murmured against her ear, biting the lobe gently and then kissing his way down her neck to her breast.

"Aye. Quite."

"Good." He flicked his tongue over her nipple, his hands on her hips, holding her in place as he slowly withdrew and then entered her once more.

Jenny moaned, her hands stroking over Toran's chest, his hips, until she reached around boldly to grip his buttocks and tug him closer. Moments ago, she'd not have thought making love could feel so good, but Toran was more than proving her wrong.

With a slow and measured pace, he withdrew and thrust, his pelvis rocking against hers, his mouth on hers, or her neck or her breasts. He never stayed anywhere too long, and she could barely think because of it. Her body sang with pleasure, erupting in climax once, then twice. He picked up his pace, owning every bit of her body as he drove deep inside her. And Jenny let him, wanted him, reveled in his body plunging into hers and the pleasure coursing through her limbs.

He let out a roar, his trembling arms braced on either side of her, every muscle tightening, and then he withdrew, warm slickness pooling on her belly rather than inside. She knew that look, that sound, that feeling. He'd taken his pleasure, as surely as she'd given it.

Jenny cupped his face as he stared down at her. "That was incredible," she murmured. "Thank ye."

"Och, lass, I have only ye to thank." He leaned over the side of the bed, took up his shirt, and tore off a sleeve, using it to wipe away the pool of seed on her belly and the wetness between her thighs. When she asked why he didn't spend inside her, he explained that to do so would bring about a child, and now was not the time. "All clean," he murmured. "For now."

She giggled. "I look forward to ye making a mess of me again."

Jenny woke with a start, having fallen briefly back to sleep after the most incredible experience of her life. Voices outside the chamber caught her attention. Several guards spoke in hushed tones about a regiment of dragoons led by a traitorous Scot headed east of Falkirk.

Hamish. In her gut she knew it had to be him.

The dying man had not been speaking in riddles. She'd just refused to believe him.

She had to leave. Now. Her gaze fell to Toran. She felt no regrets for having shared a bed with him. Would he expect marriage now? She stiffened at the thought. While marriage was something she'd rejected in concept before meeting Toran, being with him had softened the hard lines she'd drawn about such a commitment.

This war with the English was far from over—as evidenced by what she'd just heard. And after yesterday's victory she needed to stay the course, not be worried about marriage and children.

Which meant she couldn't continue to share his bed. Despite the words she'd said about anticipating the next time they made love, she chalked that up to the emotions running rampant inside her. The pleasure of lovemaking had blocked out the rational side of her brain. The knowledge of what she had to do saddened her, made her heart feel heavy.

And if Hamish was truly riding on her castle, as her gut bid her believe, she had to go. Surely the prince would understand. She wasn't abandoning the cause. She would return. Hazy gray light filtered through the small window of the chamber, and judging by the chill and the wet scent in the air, she was certain a storm was brewing. If they didn't get moving soon, she and her men could be stuck in Falkirk, farther behind her brother, farther away from protecting her people.

There was no way she was going to leave her mother to fight alone. Hamish had not appeared before her on the field of battle; there was no telling what he had been doing while the rest of them were at war, except for the burning dread in her gut—he was heading back to Cnàmhan Broch. He was going to reclaim the castle. She was certain. Her brother was resourceful, and she was fairly certain that by now he would have gotten wind of her plans, of her alliance with the Jacobites, and likely also her having laid claim to the lairdship.

She looked at Toran, sleeping peacefully, his dark lashes laid flat against his strong golden cheeks. She'd always thought him striking, but up close he was beautiful, as if sculpted from marble, the stuff of which ballads were sung and works of art created. Enough to take a woman's breath away. To have stolen hers.

Regret filled her as she slipped from their little cocoon of pleasure and warmth. She dressed quickly, wincing at the ache between her thighs. While the rest of the rebellion would be meeting up with the prince to celebrate, she needed to gather a few dozen of her men to take them back to her castle to defend it. The prince would understand. And she'd send a missive with Toran to Dirk, giving them both the choice to remain with the prince and await her return or head back to Cnàmhan Broch.

"Where are ye going?" Toran's voice was soft and groggy and made her want to turn around and crawl back into bed with him. To ask him to touch her the way he had during the night.

Jenny stilled at the door, her hand on the knob, her back to him. "I need to round up a few dozen men. I plan to return to Inverness. I was going to ask ye to take a message to Dirk for me."

The cot behind her creaked as he sat up, but still she didn't turn around.

"Ye're going home? And ye were going to leave me here?"

She shook her head. She needed to hold it together for another hour, and then she'd be well on her way. "I need ye to find Dirk. Tell him I've gone to Cnàmhan Broch. I need to protect my people from Hamish before a storm traps me here. He's already got a head start. Tell Dirk he is to fight in my stead beside the prince until I return. Then if ye wish, ye can join me upon the road. I will come back when my brother has been dealt with."

The roads were likely already covered with ice from yesterday's freezing storm. Another bout would lock them here.

"Jenny." His voice was soft, and the cot creaked again, the floor thumping as he stood.

She wrenched open the door, not wanting to be trapped as she certainly would be if she didn't force herself over the threshold.

"Why are ye running?"

"My brother. His own man said he was going to reclaim what I stole. Just this morning I heard troops discussing a regiment of dragoons heading east. It is Hamish, I feel it in my bones."

"Nay, lass, ye misunderstand me. Why are ye running from *me*?"

She hadn't misunderstood though. "I canna let what happened between us cloud my judgment or stall me from my duties."

"Do ye regret what happened between us?"

Such a direct question, she wasn't certain how to handle it. She did turn then, thinking he at least deserved that much. Meeting his gaze, she said, "I regret nothing. But neither can I lay aside the vows I made to my people."

"I'm not asking ye to."

"Good. Then ye'll understand and support my need to return to Inverness."

Confusion flashed over his features, bewilderment he didn't try to hide from her. "I did no' bed ye last night for the fun of it, Jenny."

That was what she was afraid of.

"That's no' to say I didna have a hell of a lot of fun," he added.

"Dinna say any more, Fraser."

Hurt twisted his features at her formal use of his name. She'd wounded him. And she'd have to live with that. One man's pain versus the pain of hundreds if she didn't get back to Inverness.

"I'm sorry," she said. "I wish it didna have to be this

way. I wish we were no' at war and that our prince was even now sitting upon the throne. But he is no'. And with our victory yesterday, we canna afford to hesitate, even for a minute. I canna allow my brother to torment my people."

Toran frowned, but he didn't disagree with her. She could practically read his thoughts, and she found it incredibly disturbing how well she now knew him—and how very much disappointing him hurt her heart.

He cleared his throat, and she had the feeling he was working to clear himself from her. "I will deliver your message to Dirk."

"Thank ye, Toran."

He stalked forward, and though her mind bid her to retreat, her feet did not move an inch. Toran reached her, filling her space. He clasped her face in his hands, his eyes locked on hers.

"I know ye want me to keep my mouth shut, to follow orders like a good soldier, but damn it, Jenny! I canna let ye leave without telling ye how I feel. I love ye, lass. And because of that, I'll do as ye've asked. But know this—I'll no' be far behind because I can see in your eyes ye feel the same way."

Jenny opened her mouth to protest, but no words would come out. Instead she wrapped her arms around his waist and tucked herself against him. At last her throat seemed to loosen enough for her to demand huskily, "Kiss me goodbye."

"Only because I plan to kiss ye hello soon." And then his lips were on hers, making her body sing. Making her want to drag him back to the cot and strip them both down to their skin.

He loved her. *Loved* her! And he was right… She loved him too, though she was too much of a coward in that moment to admit it. She felt as though if she let the words slip out, she wouldn't leave this chamber—wouldn't leave Dunipace. She'd follow him anywhere, and that would be the very worst thing to do right now.

Jenny pushed away, albeit gently. "My duty is to clan and country first above all else, Toran, and I thank ye for honoring that."

He nodded, stroked her cheek, and then took a few steps backward, every inch that separated them a painful stab to her chest. She could barely look at him, fearing the tears that threatened.

"I will follow wherever ye lead, Jenny Mackintosh."

Jenny turned and fled the room before the rest of her resolve evaporated.

Twenty-Four

"She went home?" Dirk looked astounded to hear that Jenny had left for Inverness without telling him.

"Aye. She had a sense that her brother was headed there to take back his holding since she has been otherwise engaged."

"Damn." Dirk looked toward the exit of the tent, and the shift in his stance showed his eagerness to follow, the same urgency that Toran also felt. "Why did she send ye here to deliver the message like ye were nothing more than a...messenger?"

"I believe because she knew ye'd trust me." He left off the part where he was also sure it was because she wanted to put some distance between them. That he'd made love to her all night and that he'd had to bury his shirt in among the anonymous stacks for the laundresses to hide the evidence after using most of it to clean the both of them up. "I dinna intend to stay here, Dirk. I need to be honest with ye about that. I'm going after her."

"Good, I was going to suggest just that. One of us has to stay and explain things, else the prince will wonder why a large number of soldiers have just up and disappeared. And one of us has to go to her. She canna face Hamish on her own. The bastard will try to crush her, and she will fight with every last breath in her body to see that he doesna win."

"Aye, I agree. She'll be glad to know that one of us is

staying here with the prince. I think 'twas a difficult decision for her."

"She's got heart, she does. Blasted brother of hers is a traitor to all of us." Dirk scrubbed a hand over his face. "Take good care of her."

"I will, I vow it. I will die before she does, I can promise ye that."

"And wait to exchange vows until I get home, will ye?"

Toran grinned. "I'm no' certain she'll have me, though I'll try my damnedest."

Dirk rolled his eyes. "She'll have ye. The two of ye are the most stubborn people I've ever known. Perfect for each other."

"I thank ye for the support, truly. I admire ye, and I know ye care for her greatly."

"She is like a sister to me."

"I know she feels that ye're a brother to her."

Dirk clapped him on the back. "I'll no' welcome ye to the family just yet, dinna want to curse it. But 'tis something I look forward to."

"The same for me, man." Toran gripped Dirk by the arm. "I'm honored to have gained your trust."

"Aye, but it is Jenny's trust that matters most."

"I will spend the rest of my life making sure I never do anything to break it." *Mo chreach*, would he ever. He'd rather skewer himself on a pike than break her heart.

"Good, else ye'll have me to contend with."

Not wanting to waste any more time than he already had, Toran left the camp to find Archie. His cousin sat among several men, all with minor injuries.

"I'm headed back to Inverness."

"What?" Archie wrinkled his brow.

"The lass may have an impending battle on her hands at Cnàmhan Broch."

Archie stood. "I'll go with ye."

"Ye dinna have to. Stay here with Dirk, fight for our prince."

"I canna let ye go off on your own." Archie passed him an incredulous look.

"I'll not be alone. I'll catch up to the lass and her men upon the road."

Archie looked ready to argue more, but Toran pressed a hand to his shoulder. "All will be well, Cousin. I'll see ye when the English have been vanquished or the prince relieves ye for a bit of respite."

His cousin pulled him into his arms, hugging him for perhaps the first time ever in their lives.

"Ye're a good man," Archie said. "Thank ye for saving my life."

"I'd do it again in a heartbeat."

"I hope to never have to return the favor, as I want ye to live a long and healthy life. But if it ever comes to it, then I'll repay it gladly."

"Ye already did, when ye didna give me away to the dragoons at the garrison and again when ye didna toss me through the door to Boyd at the croft."

Archie smirked. "I suppose ye're right, we are even."

"Spill some more *Sassenach* blood for me," Toran said. "I fear the Scots blood I'm about to let."

Archie nodded sorrowfully. "The poor lass."

Toran clasped his cousin to him one more time and then took off at a brisk pace, hoping to catch Jenny before too long.

But catching up to her seemed an easier feat in the mind than in the actual making. Toran spent much of the day avoiding the dragoons who seemed to be out in droves, more vigilant after the loss at Falkirk than any other time thus far.

Ballocks, but he hoped that didn't mean that the reason he'd not found Jenny yet was because she'd already been captured or, worse, killed.

———

If she never saw another red coat, or anything scarlet in nature, Jenny would consider herself a lucky woman. She and her men had been forced to split into three groups to keep the bastards off their tail, but even that wasn't enough. She spent the tense ride worrying nonstop about whether one of their other parties had been caught.

And that was nothing on her thoughts of Toran. Her skin still burned where he'd touched her, kissed her, and she'd just left him there assuming that she'd see him again. What if she didn't? What if he decided to stay with Dirk? What if staying with Dirk got him killed?

Her chest tightened at the thought, and bile burned the back of her throat. Part of her wished she'd have stayed. The other part knew she could not leave her mother alone, that she could not allow her brother to reclaim Mackintosh lands.

Damn ye, Hamish!

Of course, that was when the first part of her doubts questioned her instinct. What if Hamish hadn't been at the battle at Falkirk for different reasons entirely? What if he was in London? There was a possibility. But her gut refused to believe it. Instinct bid her to know deep down that her brother was marching on Cnàmhan Broch.

Hamish was a coward. He'd not want to face her head-on. She knew that. He was the sort who would have lain in wait and pounced on their holding the moment she was gone. Saints, but she prayed she wasn't too late.

"All clear," Jenny said, when the last of the dragoons they'd been hiding from had not shown their faces for at least a quarter of an hour.

She led her men back onto the road, but at a slower pace so as to hear better. The sun was starting to set, and soon they'd be riding in the dark. They needed to stop and hide for the night.

The sound of an approaching rider had them all scrambling off the road, hearts pounding, as they worked to silence their horses.

Bloody hell!

She kept her eye on the road in the waning light, waiting for the dragoon to pass, but no flash of red assaulted her eyes. Instead, the man wore a plaid, frock coat, and kilt. And she'd know that hard frame anywhere. *Toran.*

Jenny leapt out into the middle of the road, her pistol drawn.

"Dinna move," she said, repeating what she'd said

to him the very first time they met. "Else I put a bullet through your heart."

Even in the waning light, she could see recognition dawn on Toran's face along with his slow grin. "What's to say I willna put a bullet in yours first?"

Jenny tossed her head, smiled at him, her eyes full of teasing. "Ye're outnumbered, sir. Let's say ye did pull your weapon afore I took my shot, 'twould be wasted, for there'd be five more cutting through ye before ye were able to see the result." They could be set upon by dragoons at any moment, true, but this moment of connection was important.

Toran worked to hide his grin, ice-blue eyes boring into hers and making her body sing with the need to leap upon him. "Then I'll keep my weapon where it is and trust ye no' to end my life."

Jenny took several steps forward. "Glad to have ye back with us. Ye nearly scared us to death, soldier. Why are ye alone?" She peered around his horse, making out the shadows around them as trees, boulders, and .

"By choice, Mistress J. The rest of the men are with Dirk."

Jenny nodded, meeting his gaze once more, afraid to ask the question but needing to know the answer. "How many did we lose in battle?"

"Two. Robert Finley and Daniel Mackintosh."

A lance of grief hit her heart, and she bowed her head for a moment of silence. "They fought for their prince."

"Aye, and for ye. They died heroes."

Jenny swallowed around the lump in her throat. "Wounded?"

"A few dozen. Some more seriously than others."

Jenny nodded and again forced her tongue to form words. "And Dirk?"

"He is well. A few scrapes, took a bayonet to the shoulder, but he's been sewn up and is walking around, prepared to lead the men in your stead."

"Did he…" She bit her lip, eyes lowering before she could bring them back up again. She was asking this part more for him than for Dirk. "Did he understand why?"

"Aye," Toran said softly. "He is with ye all the way."

That was a relief. She itched to reach for him, to have him pull her up onto his horse and melt against him. To feel safe in his arms. But all of that was a fantasy, when reality was that they were on contested land in the middle of a war with an enemy known for its brutality.

"We need to make camp for the night. Have ye seen many dragoons?" she asked, ignoring the exhaustion and weariness that seeped into her bones.

"Too many."

It was not the answer she wanted but the one she'd expected. "'Haps we ought to ride on, then. We have already split into three groups to avoid any attention three dozen of us might gain."

"Smart. The bastards are looking for any reason to put their shot into us. We should try to get a few more leagues in, just to be safe."

"Aye." Jenny remounted her horse, and they rode side by side, the dozen men behind her quiet and on high alert.

The pelting icy rain started again, making the roadways slick and dangerous for the horses and skewing their senses, forcing them all to find shelter among the trees. The only good thing about it was that it would force the dragoons to stop their patrols too.

Wrapped in plaids, they crowded together, unable to make a fire which would signal their presence. They kept warm with whisky, plaids, and huddled body heat. The horses did much the same, covered in wool blankets to keep them warm. Jenny managed a few hours of sleep, jolting awake every half hour or so with the image of Hamish rushing at her and thrusting his blade into her chest.

Just before dawn they all gave up on trying to sleep and left their makeshift camp, bodies aching. They rode slowly throughout the day, shivering and cramped, until they came to a village near Perth that Jenny knew to be Jacobite sympathizers. They were able to house their horses in several barns that night, getting them warmed up, brushed down, and fattened with sweet oats. The men were also able to sleep out of the weather on piles of straw, with warm bread and stew from the crofter's wife. Jenny prayed the rest of her men were faring well.

In the morning, they were off again. The icy rain had ceased, and they were able to pick up their pace, but snow had begun to fall in thick clumps by the time they reached the Cairngorm mountains, slowing them down once more. Her limbs were mostly numb from cold, and she'd long since lost any sense of appetite.

Once more they found a crofter who was willing to take them in for the night. When they woke the next morning, a thick snow blanketed the earth, but at least they'd had a chance to thaw their bones. They wrapped their horses' forelegs in woolen strips for warmth and protection from the snow and then picked their way slowly along the thick snow-covered road.

Jenny had lost track of the hours and days, and the men were so exhausted none of them spoke. She'd had barely a moment to think about how grateful she was that Toran had come to join her. And every time she looked at him, she remembered their moments in Dunipace Castle. Heard his whispered words of love, saw the affection in his eyes, felt his kisses on her lips. How she longed to fall into his arms again. How she wanted to go back to that tiny room and the small cot made smaller by the bulk of his body.

That night they slept in an abandoned croft, with only half a roof and half the house filled with snow. Jenny leaned against him, accepting some of his body heat.

"Are ye all right?" he whispered, barely loud enough for her to hear. None of the men around them stirred, and she was grateful for his discretion.

"I will be when we get back to Cnàmhan Broch."

"Ye're freezing."

There was no use denying it. No matter how much she clenched her jaw, her teeth still chattered. He took her hands in his, warming fingers that felt numb. Then he slowly tugged off her boots, pulled off her hose, and did the same to her toes. The heat of his touch sent stabs of pain through her frozen digits, but she closed her eyes and forced herself not to wince. She needed this, else she might lose a few toes and fingers.

"Sip." He held a flask to her lips, and she drank greedily, the warmth of the liquor swirling in her belly and helping her to forget just how cold she was. Toran continued to massage her frozen fingers and toes until prickles of feeling came back and then finally warmth.

Toran put her hose back on, replaced her boots, and then pulled her onto his lap, tucking her beneath his own plaid. She closed her eyes in a wash of grateful warmth.

"Thank ye," she murmured, pressing a kiss to his chin.

"Ye need not thank me for taking care of ye, lass. I vow to do it for the rest of our lives."

Toran pressed his lips to hers in a gentle kiss and then tucked her head beneath his chin against his chest. Jenny burrowed closer, wrapped in a safe cocoon of warmth.

"Even if ye deny ye want me to," he added.

Jenny smiled, snuggling into his warmth. "I'd have it no other way."

She jolted awake in the middle of the night, instantly on alert, her heart pounding. Footsteps sounded outside.

When she tried to move, Toran held her tight. "Dinna move," he whispered in her ear.

The rest of the men had woken as well, the whites of their eyes shining in the moonlight that reflected off the snow in the croft.

The footsteps were light and stuttered, edging closer and closer to the door.

Toran slowly shifted her from his lap, and they both pulled out their pistols, her men doing the same. If they were about to be ambushed, they would face it head-on.

One by one, they slowly and silently rose to their feet.

The door and shutters on the window were closed to keep out the cold, though the caved-in roof blocked their view outside.

Toran tapped Jenny and pointed to himself and then at the door, indicating that he was going to open it and confront whoever was on the other side. She shook her head vigorously and mouthed, "Nay." There could be hundreds of King George's men out there!

He nodded again, and she again denied him. Opening that door, if there were enemies outside, was just asking for an attack.

"The horses," he whispered back. "They will know we're in here."

Jenny had forgotten about the horses. *Mo chreach*, but they would have to fight.

She pointed to herself, then the door, and then the rear window and Toran. If they were going to do this, then they were going to repeat the rout they'd done before—her distracting the enemy and him running.

Toran tried to argue, but she simply turned from him and walked toward the door, his fingertips brushing against her arm.

Her hand on the handle, she turned back to see him glowering. They stood for a moment, a complete argument in a stare only. Toran stalked forward and stood right behind her. "I'm not leaving ye," he murmured.

Jenny gave in to that. There was no use in arguing with him, and she could use his strength at her back. With the rest of her men in position and ready to fight, she slowly opened the door and peered outside—only to find four frightened deer staring back at her, heads turned her way, bodies as still as marble statues, eyes as wide as the moon itself.

"Deer," she murmured, a rush of relief flooding her, and gave a short laugh. "We were ready to go to battle with a herd of doe."

The men laughed, and so did she, the tension leaving their bodies. She started to close the door, certain she'd not be sleeping tonight, when one of the animals let out a piercing cry. The doe fell to the ground, an arrow through her neck. The remaining deer took off in terror, and Jenny felt the chilling thread of fear scaling her spine, vertebra by vertebra.

Whoever had just felled the deer could have just as easily felled her.

Toran yanked her back inside and stepped in front of her, pistol raised, as he scanned the woods.

Another of her men heaved open the window to stare outside, his musket poised on his shoulder.

There was a whirring noise in the air, and then flaming arrows blanketed the sky, some landing on the roof of the croft, others falling through the gaping holes to lodge inside.

"Get to your horses," Jenny ordered.

The men scrambled to do as she bid, holding their targes over their heads as they ran toward the stable to get their mounts. She was glad now she'd told them to keep their horses ready to go should they come under attack. She only wished she'd also thought about keeping the mounts inside the croft for easier access.

Jenny ran with her men, keeping her head low, her targe raised up in protection.

A volley of arrows hit the ground around them, one of them piercing the calf of a Mackintosh soldier. He cried out but didn't stop running, batting out the flames with his hands and breaking off the shaft before leaping onto his horse.

They rode away as swiftly as they could in the snow. For a breathless hour she veered this way and that, trying to avoid a pursuing enemy who would surely be able to follow their tracks in the snow. Finally, Jenny called a halt. There was no one behind them. No pursuer, and she wondered if there might never have been—if those who'd shot at them never intended to follow.

Who would attack and then not pursue?

One name came to her mind. One person who would want to toy with her—*Hamish*. If it were the English, they'd have come after the rebels, rushed them when they gathered their horses. They would have done more damage—and with bullets. If it were outlaws, they would have given chase, if only to rob them.

Jenny burned with rage. Had Hamish really fallen so low?

A small part of her had hoped that when she was finally able to confront him, she could convince him to come back to the Jacobite cause. That she could remind him of their father's and grandfather's legacy, prove to him that this had all been a big mistake. Maybe Hamish was confused, lured by the treasure trove of coin he had been promised, the titles, the land. It was greed that spurred him on, not allegiance to the pretender on the throne.

"They dinna follow," Toran mused.

"Nay. But dinna doubt they are behind us." Jenny gritted her teeth. "I'm certain 'twas my brother."

The men grumbled, their irritation with Hamish already at a high level after his constant drain on their provisions.

"He wants Cnàmhan Broch back. A stronghold in the Highlands for his English puppet masters."

Toran cursed under his breath. "We're not far now."

"Aye. If we ride through the day, we can make it by midnight."

"The horses will be exhausted."

She nodded. "'Haps when we reach MacPherson lands, they'll allow us to trade them out."

After tending to the warrior with the wounded leg, they continued on, changing out the horses at a MacPherson croft and updating them about the battle at Falkirk.

When at last Jenny and her men arrived at Cnàmhan Broch, Lady Mackintosh, Isla, and Camdyn greeted them with massive embraces. Mac gave her an update on all that had happened while she was away, which was thankfully void of any conflict.

Jenny ordered the men who'd arrived with her to get some warm food, ale, and rest and had those on guard duty lock up the gates tight and double their forces, telling them to look out for any signs of her brother or his impending arrival.

Inside the castle, Jenny's mother ordered her a hot meal from the pottage that still boiled in an iron kettle in the kitchen from their own dinner. Toran had gone out to sit with the men, and she wished he was inside with her now.

"Ye need a bath."

"Aye, a hot one," Jenny said, feeling the grime that was caked to her skin and the chill in her bones that just wouldn't go away. She remembered Toran's whispered words the night they'd made love, saying she needed a hot bath, and the wicked side of her wished he would climb into the tub with her now that she had the chance for one.

Between bites, Jenny filled her mother in on the events of the battle and her intentions for the next few days.

"Eat the rest of your supper and I'll have a bath drawn up for ye."

After scraping the last of the pottage from her bowl with the remaining hunk of her bread, Jenny climbed the stairs with heavy legs to her chamber, achingly aware of her exhaustion, grateful for the castle's staff, and reflecting on how damn lucky she was to be home when she could have died so many times over. To have escaped unscathed save for a few minor scrapes was a miracle.

In her chamber a steaming bath awaited her, strewn with dried rose petals and herbs. A fire had been built up high in the hearth, and already her room was feeling toasty.

"I've laid out a clean night rail and some thick woolen

hose to keep ye warm," her mother said. "Do ye want me to wash your hair?"

Jenny smiled and tossed herself into her mother's arms. "I love ye, Mama. And I know I must stink to the very depths of the netherworld, so thank ye for being so kind."

"There is no other way for a mother to be, sweet lass." Lady Mackintosh stroked her hair.

"I'm fine. Ye've done enough. Go and rest yourself."

"Are ye sure?" Reluctance filled her mother's features.

"Aye. I'm home and safe, and I can see from the circles under your eyes that ye're in need of a good rest."

"I'd stay awake for another month if ye wished it. I'm so glad ye're all right."

Jenny cracked a smile. "I'd never ask ye to do that, Mama. I'm just glad to be alive and that we beat Hamish here. I'd never be able to forgive myself if something had happened to ye."

"Likewise, my love. And Toran?" Her mother's brows raised in hopeful question.

"He stayed by me, even when I pushed him away."

A wistful smile crept onto Lady Mackintosh's lips. "He's a good man."

"Aye, Mama, he is." She bit the inside of her cheek, feeling the scars from where she'd torn her mouth apart during Toran's beating. "I'm fairly certain I'm in love with him."

Lady Mackintosh's mouth fell open in surprise, and she touched Jenny's cheek before her surprise melted into a smile. "'Tis a wonderful feeling, is it not?"

There was no censure from her mother, no pressure to fall into the duties of a wife and mother. She was allowed to simply bask in the glow of loving and being loved in return.

"Ye'd best get in that tub before all the heat is gone from it."

Jenny tore off her grimy clothes and sank into the glorious water. She laid her head back against the rim of the tub and closed her eyes, allowing the heat to thaw her bones. With the cloth laid over the side of the tub and a ball of scented soap, she scrubbed away the grime of battle and travel.

After bathing, she dressed and sat before the hearth to brush and dry her hair. The servants took away the tub, leaving her with a jug of wine and a plate of sweet biscuits. She nibbled on the treat and sipped at the wine, feeling warm and safe but still full of worry.

A soft scratch came at the door, and her entire body lurched with anticipation. Was it Toran? Was it a warning that her brother had been spotted? Something worse?

"Come in," she called anxiously, setting down her wine glass and leaving her biscuit half-eaten on the plate.

He entered the room slowly, scanning the chamber before closing the door and leaning against it.

"Toran," she said softly. "What's happened?"

"I wanted to be certain ye were all right."

Her heart melted a little at his concern. "As well as I can be, given the circumstances." She indicated the plate of sweet biscuits and wine. "Care for dessert?"

"Thank ye." He came forward and sat on the chair

opposite her, taking a bite of a biscuit. "Dear God, how did we survive on the road without these?"

Jenny laughed. "'Haps we ought to take a barrel next time, aye?"

"Without a doubt."

She nudged her wine glass toward him, and he sipped, watching her over the rim.

His gaze was full of heated promise, and Jenny found herself rising from her chair to close the few feet of space between them. She'd ached to be in his arms since leaving their haven at Dunipace. Toran set down the glass and pulled her onto his lap, his mouth crashing against hers as she wrapped her arms around his neck. Her fingers dove into his wild, thick hair, her body pressing against his muscular form. She shifted so that her legs were on either side of his hips, wanting to be closer to him, the apex of her thighs crushed to the part of him that was quickly growing firm with want.

"I canna wait for the war to be over," she murmured against his mouth. "I need ye. Now."

"Aye, lass, I want ye."

His hands on her thighs shifted her night rail up around her hips as she lifted his kilt up and stroked her hand along his turgid length. His firm grip closed over her hand, and together they guided his arousal with eager intent into the wet heat of her. Toran thrust up inside her, filling her, rocking her with the pleasure of his invasion.

"Toran," she groaned, her head falling back as he leaned forward and pressed his lips to her breasts.

His fingers curled into the ribbons that tied her night

rail closed, and he slowly unthreaded them, capturing her mouth with his again. The frenzied rocking of their bodies slowed, and her body pulsed around him with desperate need.

Velvet hot lips roved over her breasts until the fire of his tongue branded her nipples. Her fingers threaded in his hair, pushed and tugged all at once, uncertain if she wanted more or relief from the pleasure.

"Och, Jenny, ye feel so good," Toran groaned against her flesh. "I missed ye."

"Every second out of your arms has been a torment." She couldn't stay still, needed to move. She rocked back and forth, eager for more of the sensations the movement brought as his shaft slid in and out of her body. His fingers dug into her hips, willing her to stop, but Jenny couldn't. She needed more.

Her hands anchored against his shoulders, her toes on the floorboards, she took control, rising up and down, rocking back and forth, finding a rhythm that left her moaning and panting with pleasure. She moved faster and faster, and Toran's forehead fell to her chest, his groans a mirror to her own.

A hot bath, a warm meal, the safety of her keep's walls, all were needs that had to be met—but this, their bodies together, the pleasure, this was a need only Toran could satisfy for her.

She nuzzled her way to his lips as they rocked, kissing him as frantically as she moved her hips. Those first bursts of pleasure rocketed her to the ultimate pinnacle of rapture.

Toran groaned against her lips, thrusting harder before he freed himself from her and let himself go, spending against the flat of his belly.

Jenny collapsed against him, her ear pressed to his heavily beating heart. "I love ye," she whispered, curling against him. The words came naturally to her, not hidden or full of fear but the truth and an admission that needed airing.

Toran held her tighter. "Ye have no idea how verra much I love ye, lass."

Toran couldn't believe she'd said the words. More so, he couldn't believe the incredible lurching in his chest at hearing them spoken.

She loved him. She'd come to him, made love to him. He tugged one of the linen napkins from where her snack had been set on the table and used it to wipe his seed from her skin.

"I want ye to be mine," he murmured against her lips as he made a feast of her sweet mouth. "I want to be yours."

"I already am," she whispered back.

And he knew she meant it, but still, he wanted her for more than just kissing, more than just making love.

"When this war is over, say ye'll be my wife," he said. "Marry me." It wasn't a demand but a request.

She was quiet for a long moment, her eyes cast down, long fringed shadows on her cheeks from her lashes.

Toran pressed a finger to her chin and gently tilted her face up. "I dinna intend to take anything from ye, lass, only give ye all of myself. Raise a family, if ye're willing. I just know that I love ye and want to spend the rest of my life seeing ye smile, fighting battles beside ye, making love to ye."

"I want that too," she whispered.

"Ye need not give up your vows or your place as laird. Allow me to stand beside ye."

She bit her lip. Something was still holding her back, and he'd be lying if he said it didn't hurt to think that she might not trust him enough.

"Ye dinna have to answer just yet." He kissed her gently on the lips, hoping to forestall her denial. "But we canna keep this up, else I'll think ye've been taking advantage."

She giggled. "I, take advantage of ye?" There was mischief in her eyes. "Take me to bed so I can do it again."

Toran growled low in his throat and reached forward to nip gently at her lip. "I am thoroughly debauched."

He stood, lifting her with him and carrying her to bed. She laughed, head tossed back, the most beautiful sight he'd ever beheld.

Twenty-Five

JENNY BOLTED AWAKE THE FOLLOWING MORNING—
except it was most certainly morning no longer. The sun
beamed through the window of her chamber onto her
bed, blinding in its winter vibrancy.

The spot beside her where Toran had finally slept was
empty, and when she pressed her hand to the mattress, it
was warmed only from the sun.

Tossing back the covers, she wriggled her sore body
over the edge of the bed and stood on shaky legs. As
though her maid had been waiting for just that moment,
the slightest sound of her arising, there came a soft tap at
the door and a call of "My laird?"

Laird? Jenny whipped her head toward the door, staring at the wood as though it would answer her question.

She had claimed her brother's title and her people had
agreed, but then she'd ridden out to battle, and her men
had called her Mistress J as they always had. It was clear,
at least, that the staff honored her title.

"Come in," Jenny called.

Sarah opened the door, a beaming smile on her face.
"I'm sorry I missed ye last night, but Lady Mackintosh
insisted she would aid ye."

"Dinna fash, Sarah. 'Tis good to see ye."

Sarah's eyes went to the bed, and Jenny's followed to
the two dented pillows, the covers flung back from opposite sides. It was obvious that two bodies had slept there.

Fortunately, her maid was discreet and said nothing as she quickly refilled the water basin and just as swiftly made up the bed. Without missing a step, she headed to the wardrobe, flinging open the doors and sifting through Jenny's gowns.

Sarah asked, "What's proper for a lady laird, I wonder?"

"I suspect the same things that are proper for a lady," Jenny mused as she cleaned herself up with the water in the basin. It was cold, refreshing. After a night of making love, she was no longer chilled to the bone, but she was still incredibly exhausted.

"What about this?" Sarah pulled a somber-looking day dress from the wardrobe. "Seems serious, does it no'?"

"Aye, verra."

Jenny allowed the woman to dress her and answered all of her questions about the battle, especially those of her beau, wee Alaric—who was not wee at all but a strapping Highlander who seemed ages above his own.

Outside the bedchamber came Dom's distinctive low bark accompanied by a bop against the door as he tried to headbutt his way through.

"Somebody's missed ye an awful lot," Sarah quipped.

"Aye. I'd best see to him and the rest of the clan." Jenny needed to pass on her condolences to the families of the men who'd died and assure them that Dirk would bring home their swords, though their bodies would have been buried on the battlefield.

Dressed and with her hound beside her, Jenny hurried

below stairs, only to find that everyone had gathered in the great hall to await her.

Fiona's familiar face was one among the crowd. Jenny greeted her friend warmly, though inside she was a jumble of nerves. "What are ye doing here? I thought ye'd stay with the prince. 'Twas dangerous for ye to travel in such foul weather. Has Annie come too?"

"Nay, she remained behind to aid with the wounded. She's gained quite a reputation. In fact, the prince even requested her assistance for a sleeping draught and another when he was feeling an ague coming on."

"That's fantastic." Jenny beamed, full of pride for her dear friends who were fulfilling their passions in aiding the prince.

"Aye. And speaking of the prince, I've a message for ye, from himself."

"Oh?" Jenny's belly flopped somewhere down near her knees. Her feet felt numb, and she wiggled her toes to regain feeling.

"Aye, Laird Mackintosh." Fiona winked. "The prince is headed north into the Highlands and plans to stay a night or two at Cnàmhan Broch."

Jenny's mouth fell open at the news. "Dinna jest with me, old friend." Though the prince had promised to do so on two occasions, she didn't expect him to go through with it.

"I dinna jest at all. His entourage will have left Bannockburn just shortly after myself. General Hawley's men are holding strong at Edinburgh, and so the prince wishes to winter in the north to gain more confidence among his troops."

"We are to host the prince." Jenny was breathless with excitement. "We have much to do."

"Aye. And is there no' some news ye wish me to bring to your allies, Laird Mackintosh? It'd be my honor to share."

"Aye. Tell those who were no' at Falkirk that the prince was victorious and rides north. They need to be prepared to bring their support should their regent grace them with his presence."

———

For two weeks, the Highlands were quiet. The dragoons seemed to have disappeared, except for some who Toran knew were still occupying the garrison. Thankfully, fewer than there used to be. They were still holding prisoners, and men did ride out looking for trouble. But none of them came close to Cnàmhan Broch.

Was it because the castle, according to the English, belonged to Hamish Mackintosh? Or was it because the dragoons were concentrating on the prince's route north? They might be trying, but Toran was certain they couldn't touch him. Not with the thousands of followers in his retinue. Most of the English troops were still near Edinburgh after the recent rout, and the weather had prevented most from crossing into the Highlands.

Toran worked hard by day with Mac and the rest of the men, fortifying the castle and grounds, clearing snow, and any other way he could assist with the preparations. The majority of their men still rode with the prince.

When there had been no further attacks, Jenny had sent the soldiers who'd returned with her home to tend to their families for a few days. She could call them back if danger presented itself, but some of them were a half-day's ride away.

The days were filled with work and growing excitement about the prince's coming visit, and in the evening, Toran and Jenny challenged each other to different games—chess or games of boules with the furniture pushed aside. Some nights, if she stared at him a little too long, he snuck up to her chamber.

Toran had just reached the top of the wall to relieve Mac of his watch that morning when movement on the horizon caught his eye. A lot of moving horses? He gritted his teeth, praying his eyes were deceiving him.

"Either the prince is come, or we're about to be sieged," he grumbled.

Mac passed him the looking glass with a grin. "Take a look."

Toran extended the glass and peered through, catching sight of the prince's standard. He grinned widely. "The prince will be here within the hour," he said, handing back the glass. Toran took the stairs two at a time, racing across the courtyard to the castle. Jenny was likely in the kitchens tasting the dishes her staff had been hard at work preparing. A meal fit for a prince.

She was exactly where he thought she might be, scraping a sweet-looking sauce from a bowl with her finger and sucking the remnant into her mouth with a sigh of pleasure. "'Tis perfect."

Her eyes fell on him, widening as she took in his wild eyes and windswept hair.

"The prince?" she asked.

"Aye. We spied his standard on the horizon." Toran dipped his finger into the bowl, following her lead. The flavor was decadent.

"Oh, dear me. Oh…" She touched her hair, smoothed her skirts. "I have to change. I need to look like a laird."

"I think ye look perfect the way ye are," he said.

"Ye're verra sweet, Toran, but one does not greet their rightful monarch covered in flour and sugar." She danced around the kitchen and then out the door, rushing across the great hall with Toran in tow.

"Might I remind ye that ye greeted the prince before in trews and frock coat?"

"Quite right," she murmured, stopping short. "So ye think I should dress in trews? Is that what he'll expect of me?"

Toran let his gaze rake slowly over her luscious body, imagining each curve delicately peeled free of clothes. "I think any way ye dress the prince will be impressed with ye, lass. Ye're beautiful, strong, intelligent—"

"Och, dinna flatter me now!" She rushed from the great hall, calling out for her maid to help her prepare.

Toran stared after her, only slightly bemused.

Isla and Lady Mackintosh peered out from an alcove where they'd been sitting and sewing. "Is the prince coming?" his sister asked, excitement coloring her cheeks.

"Aye. Do ye wish to change as well?"

"Of course, ye dullard, the prince is so verra bonnie! I'll need to freshen up."

"Ye're not to offer yourself in marriage," Toran teased after her retreating figure, ignoring her insult.

Lady Mackintosh smiled over at him. "Ye're a different man than when ye first arrived, sir, and I hope ye dinna take offense to that."

"None at all." And he spoke the truth, for she was right.

Jenny had changed him—for the better. Made him realize who he was and where he wanted to be. She had snapped him from a bitter stupor of revenge so he could see clearly what his true values and beliefs were.

Toran went back up the wall to watch the progress of the prince's retinue, only to be startled by new movement on the horizon—from the opposite side. A single rider, approaching the castle at a speed that had warning bells going off in his head.

"Camdyn, with me."

They descended the stairs, and Toran called for their horses to be readied quickly and for Mac to be roused to take up his position on the wall. As they mounted and approached the gate, Jenny called out from behind. Her hair had been freshly wound into a modest coil, and golden-white tendrils fell loosely around her temples. She wore a plaid gown in Mackintosh colors, and a filigreed wildcat brooch pinned a modest shawl in place to cover her breasts. At her hip was pinned a white rosette cockade.

"Where are ye going, Frasers?" There was an edge to

her tone—worry and distrust. It cut deep into his heart. Had he not yet proven himself loyal?

Toran swallowed away the bitter question and faced her.

"There is a single rider approaching rapidly from the east. We aim to intercept him and see what he is about afore he gets close enough to the prince. We shall return, my laird, ye have our word."

She nodded, relief visible in her features before being replaced by worry. "Is it one of our scouts?"

He took some measure of comfort in her easy acceptance of his explanation. Perhaps it was not distrust that had her questioning him after all.

"Could be. I'm going to find out," he answered.

She wrinkled her brow with concern. "Take more men."

"Camdyn and I will be fine against one."

"What if 'tis an ambush?"

"The prince's army is minutes away. They'd be stupid to ambush us."

A slight grin crossed her face. "But, Fraser, they fight against the rightful heir to the throne. I think 'tis a given that they are lacking in intelligence."

"Good point. We shall return shortly with answers."

Jenny waved them off, and Toran didn't waste another minute in racing out of the gate.

Jenny watched Toran and his brother ride out, feeling more than a twinge of guilt at the doubt she'd showed him moments ago. But seeing him on horseback, prepared to ride out without saying anything to her—the sight had her instantly wondering if he was going to disappear on her forever.

It was unfair of her to think that way. He'd more than proven his loyalty to her, in both deed and word.

Was that remaining crumb of doubt the reason why she hadn't agreed to marry him? What message was she sending by repeatedly allowing him into her bed, even telling him that she loved him, if she wasn't willing to make the ultimate commitment? To forever bind herself to him and to prove with her own words and deeds that she valued him, trusted him, wanted to spend her life with him?

But there wasn't time to ruminate on those feelings or to run after him because seconds later the sound of a horn rent the air, announcing the prince's arrival.

Jenny's belly did a little flip. There was no need to round up her people to come and stand with her in the courtyard, as they'd all heard the horns and rushed to the courtyard, forming a line in order to greet the royal prince. The gates were opened wide as Prince Charles Stuart, Regent of Britain, crossed through the gates. Dirk and a dozen other warriors rode in behind him. The remainder of the army had stayed southward in case the English followed their path so they could cut them off.

"Welcome to Cnàmhan Broch, Your Highness," Jenny said with a low curtsy.

Prince Charles smiled down at her. He wore fancy garb similar to what she'd seen him in at Bannockburn

House, albeit a bit dirtier from his travels. "We are pleased to be here accepting your hospitality as laird of Mackintosh."

Jenny could have fainted at the acknowledgment, but she somehow managed to stay upright as she inclined her head. "We've prepared the best chamber for ye, if ye wish to rest after your journey." Hamish had taken their father's chamber for his own upon the older man's death, and when he left, neither her mother nor Jenny had felt right entering it. But the prince's presence would wash away any trace of traitorous shadow that her brother had left behind.

"I would." The prince dismounted in all his finery and passed the reins of his horse off to a waiting stable hand. "But first, I wish to impart to you our thanks for all you did at Falkirk." He glanced around at the other warriors standing there. "Your laird is very brave."

Jenny's face felt like the heat of a thousand suns burning her. Oh, to be so admired by the prince in front of her people!

"My daughter is a loyal Jacobite," her mother said, approaching. "Your Highness, I am Lady Mackintosh."

The prince approached her mother, took her hand in his, and brushed his lips over her knuckles. "I can see where your daughter gains her beauty."

Jenny was fairly certain she'd never seen her mother blush so much in her life. In fact, Lady Mackintosh was actually fluttering her lashes. Her mother smiled coyly. "Och, thank ye, Your Highness. Might I be so bold as to say I now understand why they call ye bonnie?"

The prince let out a laugh and clasped her mother's hand in both of his. When they finished their laugh, he said, "I understand your husband served my father in the '15."

"Aye, he did."

"My condolences on your loss. I have only ever heard praise of his name, and the two of you have raised a wonderful daughter."

There was no mention of her brother, and Jenny was glad the prince chose to save her mother the embarrassment of mentioning her traitorous son. The fact that the prince was here at all, that he trusted Jenny to fight with him, to protect him, was an immense honor considering the trouble her brother had caused.

The pounding of horses' hooves signaled Toran and Camdyn's return, their horses rushing through the gate.

The prince's guard quickly surrounded Toran, pulling out their weapons and making the very clear point that they were ready to execute anyone on sight.

"Your Highness," Toran said. "I apologize for my hasty arrival. I did no' mean to cause ye worry. But I come with grave news."

"What is it?" Jenny asked, feeling the glee of the prince's arrival evaporating.

"Your brother, my laird. He rides with an English and Scots army of several hundred men to take back the castle and take the prince. Boyd is with him—and so is Simon."

Jenny felt sick inside but had no time to reflect. She had to think fast. Had to protect the prince. They had perhaps only forty in total, for the prince's retinue was small in number.

They'd be annihilated, she knew they would, because her brother would show no mercy. There was no time to gather their allies. Only time to act or run—perhaps not even enough time for that. At least they had the benefit of the castle walls to protect them, but not for long if her brother's men dragged cannons.

Jenny glanced at Dirk, who was frowning fiercely. He would want her to run, for them all to retreat. But the road was more dangerous, especially if her brother's army was not the only one advancing. Then she looked at Toran, his blue gaze watching her steadily, calmly, as if he trusted her completely to solve this problem.

That moment of panic she'd had before had left her completely. In that moment, she knew she trusted him with all her heart.

"I have an idea," she said. "And I'm going to need your help."

Twenty-Six

JENNY RAN DOWN THE ROAD, HER ARMS LOADED WITH muskets and pistols as she set them up at points well hidden from any riders. As she sprinted back toward the castle for more, Toran ran past with an armload. Her feet ached from exertion, but there was no way she could stop.

Their plan was to set up multiple weapons along the road, caches manned by single fighters. They would post a warrior at each and begin using them as her brother's army started its approach. One Jacobite soldier would be turned into ten or twenty or more if he could shoot fast enough without the worries of reloading. The rout would be tricky, and there was every chance it would fail. That her brother wouldn't believe they were an army of thousands.

But they had to try.

The prince was safely tucked into the castle with her mother and one guard, the last line of defense should he need it. She prayed this worked, or else she would be responsible for Charles Stuart's capture. Not that she'd be alive to try to rectify her mistakes.

On her last run down the road, arms heavily laden with muskets and shot, Jenny nearly tripped when she saw the horizon darken with an advancing line.

"To your stations!" she bellowed. At her warning one of the men blew the horn, and hopefully sent a chill of fear running down the spines of her brother's men.

Saints, but she wanted to see him cower for once! What she wouldn't give to smack his haughty smirks off his face.

She started to run back down the road when Toran gripped her arm, stopping her. His face was fierce with worry.

"I'll be fine," she said, uneasiness making her insides twist.

"I know ye will, lass." His voice was soft, and the expression he gave her—so loving, so full of worry—was not one a soldier gave to his commanding officer before battle but instead the look of a man to the woman he loved.

"Ye'll be fine," she said with a teasing smile, trying to lighten the mood. She squeezed his hand, wished they had time to do more than embrace before they needed to run.

"Aye, love."

"I'll see ye when it's done." As much as she wanted to stay with him, to fight beside him as they had at Falkirk, this plan would only work if they were far apart, running from firearm to firearm. One Jacobite becoming twenty or more. She'd have to shoot two weapons at a time, drop them, and lift two more as fast as humanly possible.

The gates closed behind her and the couple dozen men she had with her. The group scattered for their positions before Hamish's scouts were close enough to see their movements. The guards upon the wall—two— blew their horns again, long and loud and ominous. Enough that her brother's army would hear the bellowing cry and know their approach had been spotted. The men on the wall pointed their crossbows toward the advancing army, and Jenny took off running.

Hidden in their places, each of them knew what they had to do. Jenny's heart was pounding, palms slick, and she couldn't stop biting the inside of her cheek. Time was slowly ticking by in what felt like hours.

Would it work?

The ground beneath her feet started to rumble. They were close.

Shots started to ring out, still some distance down the road. The first of her hidden men. Shot after shot cracked the air, followed by shouts in varying voices, men calling for the advance of their allied troops—troops that did not exist. Horns and pipes blew, drums beating. It sounded, for all intents and purposes, as though they were in the middle of a vast melee.

And then it was her turn. She fired one pistol after another, dropping them once empty and firing more. Deepening her voice, she called out orders for advancement.

Some shots hit their marks, and her brother's troops turned in circles trying to find the hidden army that was slowly diminishing their numbers. Boyd bellowed for his men to stay put, to fight—and Simon, the scoundrel, rode off in the opposite direction.

And then she saw *him*, Hamish, sitting tall upon his horse as his men fell at his feet. He had a pistol in one hand and his sword in the other as he turned this way and that, trying to locate her or her army. She lifted her musket, settling the butt against her shoulder, and blew out a long breath as she took aim. His heart was within her sights, and for a fleeting moment, she thought he was looking right at her.

There were his emerald eyes to match her own, above a frown that could cut through stone. His hair was pulled back in a queue, and a ridiculous powdered wig sat atop his head. She couldn't believe he'd stooped to wearing such a thing. It didn't suit him, and yet it did.

Anger burned inside her as she watched him, the brother who'd betrayed her family and clan. Hamish, who'd gone against his own country and rightful heir to the throne. He sat there, his advance halted, confused. She touched her finger to the trigger, knowing that all it would take was the tiniest bit of pressure and she could end his life, end this battle.

Still, she hesitated.

Ending his life would not end the war. She lowered her aim to his knee. If she shot him in the leg, he wouldn't die, but he would hopefully retreat.

Just as she was about to pull the trigger, he fired into the air and shouted, "Retreat! Retreat!"

His call was echoed by Boyd.

Jenny's mouth fell open, her finger relaxed, but then she firmed up again and took aim at a new target. She pulled the trigger, her shot ringing out louder than any others, and the bullet meant for his heart hit the ground beside his horse's hoof. The horse whinnied, rising up on his rear legs. Her brother dropped his pistol as he grappled for the reins in an effort to stay seated.

"Attack!" Jenny bellowed, continuing with the ruse, and fired from six more of her pistols, all toward the hooves of her brother's horse.

When her brother was finally able to gain control of his mount, he sent it galloping at full speed down the road, the men in his unit racing after him either by horse or on foot. She and her men continued to shout and fire their weapons until the last of her brother's men disappeared from sight. And still they waited, in hopes the men wouldn't return when they realized the nature of the ruse.

She'd ordered her men to wait an hour for Hamish's return, with weapons fully loaded. He'd not arrived with the full force of his army, after all, perhaps only a hundred. But her brother did not return. Jenny stared out at the road, at the dropped weapons and other accouterments, the blood of the wounded staining the ground. The few attackers who had been felled had been carried off by her brother's men. At least they'd had the decency to care for their own wounded and dead.

Jenny emerged from her hiding place in the trees and picked up the pistol her brother had dropped, running her hand over the snow-chilled iron. The hilt was carved with the Mackintosh wildcat symbol and beneath it, *JM*. Their father's weapon. How dare her brother use their father's weapon against the very people it had been made to protect? Fitting, then, that he should drop it and she should pick it up.

Jenny tucked the pistol into her frock coat and then started to gather some of her guns and carry them back to the castle, passing wagons that had been hitched to retrieve the weapons they'd distributed as well as the discarded items from her brother's routed force. The rush of battle still coursed through her veins, giving her energy to make several more trips to retrieve weapons before she felt exhaustion setting in.

Dirk approached her, dragging a man by the scruff of his neck. "I brought ye a present, Mistress, though I think 'tis more a gift Toran will enjoy."

Simon.

Toran came from around a wagon he'd been loading and stared in disbelief. Then a slow grin filled his face. "And I've got just the plan for ye, dear Cousin."

Simon muttered curses that fell on deaf ears until Dirk hit him over the head to silence him.

When they returned to the castle at last, the prince was waiting in the courtyard, a beaming smile on his face. Dirk took Simon off to the cell he'd made a home out of before, and Jenny curtsied to the prince with Toran beside her.

"You, Lady Jenny Mackintosh, are a hero. You saved my life this day, and that is a feat I will not forget," the prince said.

She smiled, remembering her silly conversation with Annie and Fiona, naming themselves Prince Charlie's Angels. Perhaps there was some truth to that nickname after all.

"I have merely done my duty, Your Highness. And it is no' over yet. They will return when they realize it was nothing more than deception."

"They may, but not before I have gone and not before the rest of Scotland has heard that your brother's army was beaten by a few dozen men."

Jenny felt a little light-headed and swayed on her feet, feeling the strength of Toran's hand on her back to hold her steady. They'd done it. They were alive, and her brother was gone. Boyd had returned to the garrison. How much longer would she be able to keep her seat? She'd already fought against her enemies twice now and been lucky to come out of battle barely scathed.

She bowed her head, overcome with emotion and uncertain what to say. "I am honored to have served," she said simply, for she was. She couldn't think of any other way to have supported her prince than by fighting for him.

Still, her heart was heavy. She'd hoped, though only faintly, that she might be able to bring her brother around, to make peace with him. Yet the look in his eyes when she'd thought he might be staring right at her had been one of hatred.

Hamish was firmly on the side of their enemies, a King George supporter to his very marrow, and there would be no changing that. Not if she had a hundred years to try to convince him.

Toran felt Jenny tremble slightly beneath his hand, though from all outward appearances, she was standing strong. When drinks were passed around and cheers sent up for their success, she barely sipped. The kitchen served a great feast, which she barely ate.

"Your Highness, if ye'll excuse me, I'm going to relieve the men on the wall." She stood abruptly from the table and curtsied to the prince, who was thoroughly engaged in a conversation with Lady Mackintosh.

Her mother started to protest, but Jenny waved her away, and the prince regained her mother's attention when he said something flattering about Jenny's dedication to the cause.

Toran slipped from the room, following Jenny outside. She'd already disappeared up the steps to the wall, two guards coming down.

"Anyone else up there?" Toran asked.

"Just the laird, she told us to get something to eat."

"Rest up too, lads. I'll take watch with her."

The men nodded and headed toward the castle doors. Toran took the stairs two at a time. When he reached the top, he found Jenny standing, hands braced against the crenellations and staring out toward the night sky, which was bright with thousands of tiny golden stars.

"When I was little, I used to stand up here and try to count the stars," she said, not even turning around.

He loved that she could sense him nearby, just like he could sense her.

"Did ye ever finish?" He stepped beside her, sliding a hand over her spine, gently massaging the knots of tension he found there.

Jenny glanced up at him, a wry smile on her face. "Nay. But there were a few times I was certain I was close."

He tucked his arm around her waist and pulled her to him. Jenny laid her head against his chest and then turned into his embrace, wrapping her arms around his middle, her cheek pressed to his heart.

"Ye did well today, and I know ye've heard it from everyone else, but I needed to tell ye myself. Ye're strong as hell, Laird Mackintosh. Dinna ever let anyone tell ye otherwise."

"I didna feel strong when I had my musket pointed at my brother."

"That had to have been hard." He couldn't imagine pointing his pistol at Camdyn, let alone having to consider pulling the trigger.

"I could have killed him." Jenny's voice sounded small.

Toran hugged her closer. "But ye didna."

"I couldna do it."

"Ye didna need to."

"He'll return."

"Aye." There was no doubt about that, and this time he would bring the full force of his army.

"What if he returns and takes the castle?"

"We'll no' let that happen. The prince has already recalled some of his men north to protect him. If Hamish wishes to capture Prince Charlie, he'll have a harder time of it than he realizes. And knowing that your castle is going to be vulnerable, I'm certain his Highness will allow ye more men to guard it." Even as he said it, Toran wondered if that was true.

The prince was charming and kind, but he had a greater goal in mind. Would he consider Jenny and her clan to be a minor casualty on his way to the throne? Toran hoped not. The lass had worked her arse off for the prince. If he were to betray her, how could he expect she'd keep her allegiance to him?

"Aye. I sent missives to my men, recalling them to Cnàmhan Broch."

"That is a good idea. Until your brother is dealt with, at least."

"Is it foolish that I had hopes of reconciling? That I had hopes of changing his mind?"

"Nay, no' at all. He is your brother, your blood. Ye may have differences of allegiance, but that doesna take away the bond of kinship. 'Tis only natural that ye'd want him to be on the right side of things."

She looked up at him, her chin resting on the center of his chest, and unable to help himself, he dipped down to kiss her. Her mouth was warm and inviting, and she tasted a little of the wine she'd sipped at supper along with an array of alluring spices.

"I love ye, Jenny. I want to spend the rest of my life with ye. Whether it's to be running along the road with my arms full of pistols or standing here and staring up at the stars, I canna imagine a moment of my world without ye in it. I ask ye again, will ye do me the honor of having me for a husband?"

She studied him for a long time before she spoke. Enough time went by that she must be figuring out a way to deny him. And to think that when they'd first met, he'd been determined to think of her as his enemy. What a fool he'd been. He wouldn't be surprised if she said no, but he wouldn't stop asking. He wouldn't stop fighting for her, if he had to do it until the very last breath left his body.

"I am yours, Jenny," he murmured, "whether ye want me or nay. Do with me as ye please. Love me, marry me, put me in the barn, or send me on my way, but know that every day for the rest of my life, I am yours."

Her face transformed then, her eyes crinkling. "Sending ye away is not an option, Fraser, for when I'm not with ye, I feel that a piece of myself is missing. I canna live in a world without ye. And yet I dinna know how to be all the things I must at once. A laird, a warrior, a wife, a mother." She shook her head, bit her lip, and the fan of her lashes closed off her eyes from his view.

"Ye dinna have to be everything, ye know this. But if ye want to try, I'll be right there with ye, aiding ye in every way ye want."

"I want it all, Toran. Is that selfish of me?" She blinked, eyes wide and imploring.

"No' at all. I want it too. Warrior, leader, husband, father…lover. Ye're the most determined person I've ever met. If anyone can do it, 'tis ye, and I swear, ye dinna have to do it alone."

Jenny lifted up on her tiptoes and pressed her lips to his. She slid her arms over his shoulders and threaded her fingers in his hair, tightening her hold on him, kissing him hard and deep. There was so much emotion in that kiss, so much flooding of relief, and yet at the same time, it was frantic. Their tongues slid over one another, caressing, tasting. It felt like meshing, as though in this kiss they were declaring to one another that they were on the same team—that pleasure and happiness would be the end result.

Toran turned them slightly, pressing her rear against the stones and pressing the hardness of his arousal against the apex of her thighs.

"Just one kiss, just one touch of your lips on mine and my body reacts. I want ye," he growled, sliding his lips over to her ear where he bit down gently on the lobe. "I need ye."

"Aye," she crooned, lifting her leg around his hip to give him better access to her heat.

But she was in trews and he was in his kilt, and they were standing atop the wall, on watch in case of a night-time ambush.

"We canna," he said, disappointment thick in his tone.

"We can," she crooned back, her hands sliding down the muscles of his chest, one circling around back to grip his arse and the other in the front to stroke his hardened cock.

Toran groaned, wanting nothing more than to lift her up and pound into her, to hear their flesh slapping against the stone and her whimpers of pleasure against his ear.

"I need ye, Toran, and I'll go crazy if I dinna have ye. I want ye for life. I want ye to be my husband."

Those words alone were enough to send him into a whirlwind. She'd said aye.

He had two options now—make love to her right here where anyone could find them and where they might miss the signs of an oncoming army or carry her into the castle and demand some of the men take their spots.

As if they'd been listening to his thoughts, Camdyn and Dirk's voices broke him and Jenny apart only seconds before the two men appeared. Toran shifted his sporran in front of his tented kilt, trying to hide the evidence of his arousal, even though in the dark it was unlikely they would be able to see.

"We thought we'd take over," Dirk said with a wink.

"Aye, my laird, if ye dinna mind, I was hoping to have my first watch." Camdyn had the nerve to wink at his brother too.

The bloody mongrels had been spying! But he didn't care, let them spy on two people in love. Toran grabbed Jenny's hand, muttered his thanks, and whisked her down the stairs.

They walked briskly across the courtyard, murmuring good evening to those they passed until they reached the inside of the castle. No one stopped them on the run up the stairs to her bedchamber, thank the saints, because Toran wasn't above tossing someone down the steep incline.

Jenny led him at a run down the corridor to her room and thrust it open, shoving him against the wall inside before crushing her body and mouth to his.

Tugging at her frock coat, he still managed to shut the door and flick the key in the lock. They stripped each other in desperate, frantic movements, tossing clothes to the floor and stumbling toward the bed, their mouths claiming one another over and over. Toran tumbled them to the bed, Jenny's legs coming up around his hips at the same time he entered her.

They cried out together in pleasure at the heated

contact, both too far gone with desire and need to be quiet or to go slowly. He pumped into her. A hand on her breast, massaging, the other beneath her rear, lifting her higher so he could drive deeper.

Their coupling might have been hurried, desperate, but no less pleasurable for all that. Jenny raked her nails down his back, arching her spine as she broke apart beneath him, her slick channel tightening in rapid flutters around his cock and pushing him over the edge.

"Dinna withdraw from me," Jenny demanded.

Toran obeyed her command, shuddering into her.

They collapsed onto the bed, both still breathing hard. Toran rolled to the side, tugging her with him, where he tucked her perfectly against him. This was a dream, exactly where he wanted to be for all the days of his life. How the hell had he gotten so lucky?

"I'm happy, Toran."

"Me too, *mo chridhe*, me too."

His heart.

———

They were married the following morning with Prince Charles and much of her Jacobite army present. Despite the cold and snow, great bonfires were lit from one end of the Mackintosh lands to the other.

Fiona and Annie arrived just before the nuptials began, hugging her tightly and squealing about her being the first of them to wed and what luck to have wed a man such as Toran Fraser.

In the week following her wedding, Jenny felt like her face would crack from how much she'd been smiling. Her body was sore from making love morning, noon, and night. But the ache was good, and she'd be just fine if it never went away. The prince took his men—and several of hers—northward to try to rally more support among the Highlanders, and so far, her brother had yet to return to Cnàmhan Broch. That seemed inevitable, however. The man would not allow her to win. And if he wasn't chasing after the prince, she could expect him at her doorstep any day now.

Twenty-Seven

One Week Later...

TORAN SAT ON THE SAME RISE HE'D BEEN ON A FEW months before, looking down at the curling smoke of Dùnaidh Castle. He'd not heard from his uncle since he'd left his castle with Isla and Camdyn in tow.

But he couldn't wait any longer. It was time to confront his uncle about the lies he'd told and the treachery.

Behind him were Dirk, Mac, Archie, and a shackled Simon. The old Fox wasn't the only one who could barter a life.

They descended the hill and waited outside the gate while the men ran to find his uncle, for he refused to go inside and be set upon.

"Bring out the old man, bring his guards, I dinna care, but we're no' coming in."

The Fox appeared a quarter hour later, one man by his side on horseback. They rode through the gate and met Toran on his terms.

"Let's no' beat around the bush, lad. What do ye want in exchange for my son?"

That was surprising. Toran had honestly assumed his uncle would tell him to take Simon to hell with him. But he managed not to show his surprise. "I know ye've secretly aligned with Boyd, which means ye've got information that might be useful to me."

"I know nothing." His uncle's voice was thick with mucus, and he coughed on the last note.

"Ye lie. Let's talk about my mother."

Not even a flash of guilt crossed the man's face. He remained completely unaffected. "What about her?"

"Ye lied to me about her death."

The Fox waved his hand in the air as if there was a fly buzzing about his head. "She had it coming. And ye served your purpose well."

Toran tightened his hands on the reins, imagining he was wringing his uncle's neck. It took every ounce of willpower he had not to launch himself over the horse and run the bastard through. But to do so would incite more war and create more enemies that Toran and Jenny weren't ready to handle. His death would have to wait until the next battle. "My mother was a good woman. A brave rebel. And ye had her killed."

The first show of emotion crossed over the Fox's face—a flare of anger. "She was a traitor. And traitors die a traitor's death." The emotion was so lacking in his voice he could have been talking about the porridge he had that morning.

That cut like a dagger to Toran's heart. Anything more his uncle had to say about Moire, Toran didn't want to hear it, and besides he knew he couldn't trust it. "Then I'll look forward to your execution when this war is over." Toran shifted his horse beside Simon's, grabbed the back of his cousin's neck, and gave him an uncomfortable squeeze. "And on second thought, I think we'll take wee Simon back with us."

Toran nodded to his men, and they started to turn, tugging Simon's mount with them, when his uncle stopped him.

"Wait." There was panic in his tone. "I'll give ye what ye want, but ye've got to give me Simon first."

Toran laughed. "Not bloody going to happen. Do ye take me for so much a fool?"

His uncle narrowed his eyes, and an uncomfortable beat passed between them in which Simon whined, "Da, please."

"Ye're a grown man, for Christ's sake," the old Fox growled. "Act like it."

Toran shook his head. "He's a grown man who's become accustomed to a cell. We've wasted enough time here. Clearly he's not worth anything to ye."

"All right," his uncle said reluctantly. "Hamish Mackintosh has orchestrated an attack on the prince, with the help of Boyd. It will take place just north of Inverness."

"When?"

"One week. Now give me my son."

"And ye'll send full warning we know of the attack?"

"What do ye think?"

Toran said nothing but tossed Simon from his horse without regret. The wastrel was lucky to be alive. He landed with a thud before his father's mount. Not wanting to waste another minute on either of them, Toran clucked to his horse and headed back to Cnàmhan Broch.

Missives needed to be sent post haste northward to warn the prince of an imminent attack before it was too late.

———

Just eight days later, while Jenny and Toran were playing a game of chess, one of the guards rushed into the great hall to report that a large party was headed for the castle.

Jenny stopped, her pawn midair and her eyes wide on Toran.

He nodded at her, just a slight dip of his chin, but it was confident. "I'll be right beside ye," he said.

Jenny placed her pawn back in its black square. "We'll finish our game when we've settled matters with my brother."

"Aye, love, we will."

Together they stood in the courtyard outside the castle and belted on their weapons, the broadsword on her back with the *JM* engraved on the hilt and the pistol she'd taken from her brother tucked into the waistband of her trews. Men were filling the ramparts, crossbows armed, and in the courtyard her soldiers had gathered, their weapons ready to hand.

Her mother was encouraging the other women and children to join her inside the castle, and Jenny gave in to her desire to see them safely tucked inside as well.

"Go now, listen to Lady Mackintosh."

Jenny hurried up to the wall to look down the road, hazy now with the setting sun. In the distance she could hear the beat of drums carrying on the wind, the sound more jubilant than ominous, and it gave her pause.

How dare her brother be so happy to come and annihilate his kin?

Toran handed her the looking glass, and she extended it, holding it to her eye to peer through. The strangest thing... In the waning light, it looked almost like the prince's standard being carried at the front of the line.

The prince...

Jenny cocked her head, trying to comprehend what was happening. The warnings from Toran's uncle had all been about her brother. She glanced at Toran, who looked just as confused.

"Is it a trick?" she asked.

"I dinna know." Toran's jaw hardened as he gazed at the approaching riders.

Jenny slipped her hand into his grasp and squeezed. "I hope Fiona was able to deliver our messages in time."

The muscle in his jaw clenched. "Aye. But I'd not put it past my uncle, that wily bastard, to be behind some falsehood. He was so willing to toss his entire bloodline over the garrison walls in order to save his own sorry arse." Toran faced her. "I hope ye know that I'll no' betray ye as my own blood has."

Despite the men surrounding them on the wall, Jenny took her husband's face between her hands, lifted on her toes, and pressed her mouth to his. For half a beat he was stiff against her, but then he softened, sliding his lips over hers.

"I love ye, Toran Fraser, my husband, and I trust ye. Know this."

Toran's blue gaze searched hers, finding what he

needed, and he kissed her solidly once more. "I know it, my love, and I return your trust wholeheartedly."

"Whether this is an ambush, a trick, or some other such wretched plan done up by my brother or your uncle, I will stand beside ye proudly."

"'Tis I who stand proudly beside ye, lass," he whispered.

"We willna be beaten."

"Nay, never."

"Ride with me." She studied his face, taking in the look of pure adoration and admiration when he locked his gaze on her.

"Anywhere ye ask."

Down in the bailey, their horses were already saddled and waiting. Jenny and Toran mounted, followed by dozens more of their men.

"We will stop the visitors in their tracks and see what it is they want. And if it is the prince, we shall return joyously and host our rightful sovereign for supper. Until then, ride hard, fight harder, return victorious, or die a glorious death."

The men sent up a volley of cheers that echoed against the ancient stones of the castle and walls.

"We ride," she bellowed and urged her horse into a gallop through the gates with Toran and Dirk by her side.

They flew over the moors, horns blaring, making the air sing with noise. They gained the attention of the approaching riders who halted their advance and waved the Stuart flag rather frantically in the air.

Jenny signaled her men to slow, for the closer they

drew, the more she realized that it was in fact their prince at the head of the army.

Prince Charles himself waved at her, a smile of greeting on his lips. "Ah, Laird of Mackintosh, you must have seen our approach. I hope I can beg another night of your hospitality. But this time I have come bearing a gift I think you'll be very pleased to receive."

The prince swept his arm back, and his men parted to show her brother, tethered behind a horse, his proud gaze focused on her face, his teeth bared in a snarl.

Hamish.

Jenny's mouth fell open in shock. How could it be? She didn't know quite what to say. She blinked, trying to see if she was mistaken, perhaps even dreaming. For it had never once crossed her mind that her brother would be captured by Bonnie Prince Charlie. The other way around, aye, but this? Never in a million years.

"Hamish," she breathed, her body stiffening all over. "Alas, it has come to this."

"We caught him just north of here, skulking about," Prince Charles said. "Perhaps he hoped to abduct me away from the might of the Mackintosh army. However, he was foolish to believe I'd let him take me." The prince winked at her, and Jenny flushed.

"Aye, verra foolish." When Jenny spoke, she kept her gaze directly on her brother. His chin went up a notch, defiant. "What is your plan with him?" she asked the prince.

"I'm glad you should ask, for I had hoped to parole this prisoner into your care."

Jenny dismounted from her horse, approaching her brother with the same caution a child might approach a wild boar. Nerves flooded her limbs, making her gait bounce just slightly, her toes feeling a wee bit numb.

When she reached him, she stared up at his towering form, the rigidity in his posture, and wondered just what she was to do with her brother as her prisoner. Words were hard to form. Everything she wanted to say sounded stupid or contrite.

Jenny worked to make use of her dry tongue. She was laird now, her brother in chains. For more than two years she'd been tormented by the way he had turned traitor, fearing him as the nighttime demon that might come and attack her. She had nothing left to fear, for the demon had been brought to heel before her.

"Your servant, Captain." The sarcasm of her chosen words and his title in the English king's army was not lost on her brother.

"Nay, but I am *your* servant, *Colonel Jenny*, your prisoner." There was a sneer in his tone and on his lips, and she had the distinct impression he wanted to strike her.

Colonel Jenny. Och, but that had a nice ring to it. "Aye, that ye are." It was on the tip of her tongue to tell him he should have stayed true to his Mackintosh heritage, but to do so in front of everyone was unnecessary. And she wondered briefly, had her brother fallen prey to lies and badly seeded information? Did he have regrets about switching sides?

With her brother imprisoned at Cnàmhan Broch, the dragoons would be certain to come looking for him. But that was a battle Jenny would relish. After their recent victories, she felt certain they could win any fight that came their way, especially now that she had Toran on her side.

Though it was hard to do, Jenny managed to tear her eyes from her brother's gaze to regard Bonnie Prince Charlie once more. She didn't smile, but she did nod in his direction.

"Thank ye," she said. With her brother imprisoned, she would not have to worry about meeting him on a field of battle. She'd no longer have to worry about pressing her pistol to his heart and pulling the trigger.

And she'd make damn certain he didn't make any attempts to escape that would warrant her doing such a thing. If it came down to it, as laird of the Mackintosh lands and with the prince having delivered him directly to her custody, she would also be in charge of deciding any punishments he warranted.

She walked back over to her horse, brushing her hand discreetly on Toran's calf before she mounted. They rode back to the castle, the future king's army in tow.

That night, lying in bed, curled against her husband's side, Jenny thought back to the moment they'd first met. How their eyes had locked and they'd challenged one another. How his sheer beauty alone had stunned her. How very dangerous he'd felt—and was.

She stroked a hand over his chest, the fine hairs tickling her palm, and she realized not for the first time how content she felt in his arms. How settled.

His hand came up to brush over hers, tickling her knuckles.

"Before I met ye," she started and stopped.

He brought her hand to his lips, brushing a kiss over her fingertips.

"Before ye met me, the world felt ominous and empty," he said very dramatically, and Jenny giggled.

"Something like that, aye. And English."

A low rumble of a laugh sounded in his chest, mingling with the strong beat of his heart. "And now?"

"Now I feel almost like I can do anything." She smiled into his skin, pressing a kiss to his ribs.

"Ye can."

"I have ye to thank."

"Och, lass, ye dinna have naught but yourself to thank. 'Tis I who am grateful to ye for making me see the light. If not for ye, I'd be dead or in London, which both seem about the same kind of hell right now."

She curled closer, pressed her ear to his chest right where she could hear his heart beating, steady, strong.

"And to think," he mused. "I considered letting ye put that bullet into my heart." His chest rumbled again with his laughter. "Would ye have done it?"

"Aye, I would, and I'd have regretted it immensely."

"Why is that?"

"I would never have found another man like ye. Ye're a special breed of Highlander, Fraser. For ye have retained your manhood and have a wife who is laird."

"I take a fair amount of ribbing for it, to be sure."

Jenny maneuvered herself over him, straddling his hips and pressing her hands to his chest as she stared down at him. "Who is ribbing ye? I'll put them in the stocks for three days and then see who is laughing at who."

Toran grinned up at her, skimming his palms over her hips to her buttocks and giving a good squeeze. "Och, I'd no' tell ye that, lass, else I wanted to be made an example of among the men."

"An example?" She stared down at him, incredulous, and then shook her head. For years she'd walked her way through the men's world, learning to think and act like them. "Never mind, I know what ye're getting at. They would see ye as weak, and we canna have that."

"Exactly."

She reached between them, sliding her palm along the thickening member that jutted from his body and rested between her thighs.

"They know nothing about ye, Husband, if they think ye weak." She lifted slightly on her knees and placed his arousal at her entrance before bearing down. Her head fell back as he filled her, stretching her in that delicious way.

"I am weak when it comes to ye," he groaned, pumping his hips upward. "So weak."

Jenny rocked her hips in time with his thrusts, stroking her hands over the corded bunching of his muscles. "Ye're strong, Fraser. And I demand ye show me just how strong. Right now."

Toran sat up, his hands on her rear as he swung his legs over the side of the bed. He stood, with her still wrapped around him.

"Like this?"

"Aye." He made her feel as light as a feather, beautiful and desired as he stood on his thick, muscled legs and pumped into her.

Jenny clung to him as he carried her toward the table, sat her down on it, and then dropped to his knees, momentarily leaving her body. His tongue replaced his shaft just as quickly, and she was drowning in pleasure once more. She cried out as delicious sensations whipped through her with each stroke of his wicked tongue. Just when she thought she'd die from the pleasure of it, he lifted her once more and plunged deep inside of her. He twisted them around to fall onto the bed, pumping with purpose. Back on the mattress, her legs high around his hips and her hands threaded in his hair, she let her wild husband take ownership of her body the way she'd never thought to allow another being, until she was shattering with rapture and his name was the only word on her lips.

"Toran, Toran, Toran."

He growled low in his throat as he pumped faster. He too was calling out her name, marked in deep guttural moans with each thrust of his hips against hers. He filled her, utterly, in body, heart, and soul.

"I love ye, ye wee rebel," he murmured against her ear, pressing hot kisses to her skin and stroking her flesh as she tried to regain her breath.

"Ye're my everything." And she meant it. For the one thing she'd not known before was that love was a greater reason to fight—for freedom, for right—than anger could ever be.

If you loved Eliza Knight's fierce Highland warriors, you won't want to miss the SCOTS AND SWORDS series from *USA Today* bestselling author KATHRYN LE VEQUE! Keep reading for an exclusive excerpt from Book 1:

HIGHLAND GLADIATOR

Available August 2020 from Sourcebooks Casablanca!

Chapter One

The village of Brechin, Scottish Highlands
Year of Our Lord 1484

HE'D SEEN HER BEFORE.

Lor knew that the moment he looked up from the business he was conducting with his grandfather's friend. In the midst of a busy marketplace on a glorious spring day, he caught sight of a woman he recognized, which wasn't unusual in itself, but with *this* woman, it was.

Lor and the old man with the missing eye had been going over the purchase Lor was making of slag material for his grandfather's blacksmith stall when he glanced up and saw her. In truth, he saw her only from the back; it was the hair that had his attention. In the sunlight, the red curls glistened like molten fire.

Everything about her caught his eye. She was dressed in a long tunic and braies from what he could see, unusual for a lass, but she'd marched down the road with her basket of skins in her arms in a cadence that seemed much more like a man's than a woman's.

Purposeful.

Confident.

He'd seen that walk once before.

"Lor?"

The old man next to him was trying to get his attention, but Lor couldn't take his eyes from the woman as she walked down the dusty avenue. She was weaving in and out among the villagers on this busy market day, and Lor didn't want to lose sight of her.

He put up a hand to the old man.

"Wait a moment," he said. "I'll return."

He didn't wait for a reply. Quickly, he headed out into the street while the old blacksmith watched him with some frustration.

"Where are ye going, lad?" he called after him. "If ye dunna come back, I'll rob ye blind. I'll tell yer grandfather that it's yer fault he was cheated out of a good price for his iron!"

The old man meant it as a jest, hoping Lor would return, but the young blacksmith simply waved him off as if he didn't believe him, which he didn't. His grandfather,

Nikolaus, and old Albe had been doing business since before Lor was born. He didn't much believe anything the old liars said.

At the moment, he was on the hunt.

The red curls were up ahead, and he followed them like a cat tracking a mouse. There was something about the woman that he remembered from long ago, and as he politely stepped aside to let a woman and her children pass by, it began to occur to him just where he'd seen that hair.

Gleann Deamhain.

The Vale of Demons.

It was difficult to say why an incident from eight years ago suddenly stood out for him. It had been a fleeting moment as far as moments in time went. But it had stayed with him: the young lass who had practically saved him from a band of bloodthirsty cutthroats. Never mind that they were only children; Lor remembered being as afraid of them as if they'd been the mightiest army of men.

Gòrach, they'd called him.

He'd been stupid once, but he wasn't going to be stupid again.

This time, he was going to be careful.

Lor continued to follow the lass. She finally came to a stop at a merchant who dealt in hides. As he hid back in the crowd, watching, Lor could see the lass holding up the fine pelts she'd brought, negotiating a price with an old man who seemed to be smiling at her too much. At one point, he reached out and pinched her cheek.

She slapped him.

Lor laughed softly.

But the slap had turned the merchant against her and he waved her away, unwilling to buy her pelts now that she'd rejected his affection. Frustrated and unhappy, the girl backed away from the store with her basket of pelts before finally turning away and slipping into an alleyway between the stalls.

Lor followed.

There were some residences behind the main merchant avenue and several big plots of land where the villagers cultivated their gardens. It smelled of animals and compost back here. Beyond the gardens was a grove of trees, a big one, with paths leading into it because more villagers lived back beyond the trees.

Suspecting that was where she was heading, Lor made his move.

As the woman entered the trees, Lor came up behind her with great stealth and snatched her basket away.

"Where are ye going, *gòrach*?" he said.

The woman gasped in outrage and perhaps even a little fear. As Lor stood there, his eyes glimmering with mirth, the woman turned on him and balled her fists.

"Give me back my pelts," she snarled.

Lor couldn't help the smile on his lips now. It was indeed the lass from the Vale of Demons. She'd grown from a skinny, freckled girl into a lush and beautiful woman. She was *quite* beautiful, actually. He found himself staring at her pale skin and rosebud mouth, but that was the last thing he remembered before a fist came flying at his face.

Down he went.

The woman reached down and yanked the basket of pelts from his hands as Lor shook off the stars. He put his hand to his nose, noting a small bit of blood as she turned and continued her trek.

He lumbered to his feet.

"Wait," he said. "I wasna trying tae rob ye. Don't ye remember me?"

She came to a halt, turning to him warily. She looked him up and down. "Should I?"

He felt embarrassed that she didn't recognize him as he'd recognized her. "It has been several years," he said. "I was just a lad when we first met in the Vale of Morning. Ye called me *gòrach* and tried tae steal my birds' eggs. Ye know...*gòrach*? Do ye remember now?"

She stared at him a moment before her eyes widened. "*Gòrach*," she repeated slowly. "Birds' eggs, ye say?"

"Aye. Ye tried tae take them from me but we made an agreement instead."

Her mouth popped open as the memory came clear. "Ye promised tae bring me more!"

He nodded, grinning as he realized that she did, indeed, remember him. "I did."

"Ye never brought them back."

"But I dinna say *when* I'd bring ye the eggs. There's still time."

He'd caught her on a technicality. She eyed him with an appraising expression as she retraced her steps in his direction.

"'Tis true," she said reluctantly. "So just when did ye intend tae?"

His smile broadened. "Soon," he said. "But I've been very busy."

"Doing what? Accosting women and stealing their baskets?"

He laughed softly, flashing big, white teeth. "Ye accosted me once," he said. "I was returning the favor."

It was clear that she was trying very hard not to smile; he was rather witty and charming. "*Gòrach*," she repeated softly when she came to within a foot of him, studying the man who'd grown from the boy she'd once remembered. "So it is yerself. Ye've grown up."

"So have ye."

"But not so much that ye dinna recognize me."

He clasped his hands behind his back. "Yer hair," he said. "I recognized yer hair. I saw it once in the vale, and when I saw ye again in town, I knew it right away."

"Red hair is nothing in the Highlands."

"But yours looks like molten metal."

Her brow furrowed as she pulled up a strand, looking at it. "It does?"

He nodded. "I see such things every day."

"Ye do?"

"Aye."

"Why?"

"Because I'm a blacksmith. 'Tis my trade."

"I thought it was stealing birds' eggs."

His grin was back. "Nay," he said. "'Twas an interest and nothing more."

"Does yer grandfather still have his birdhouse?"

"Aye."

"I still want mine."

He lifted his broad shoulders. "Mayhap ye'll have one someday," he said. Then he gestured to the basket in her arms. "I saw ye come in tae town with the pelts. Yer far from the Vale of Morning today."

She nodded, looking down at the lovely gray pelts. "I came tae sell them," she said. "I come as often as I can, as often as the traps will allow."

He reached into the basket, picking up one of the very nice pelts. "Ye've skinned them well," he said, putting it back. But his interest in the pelts was simply a cover for his interest in her. His gaze returned to her face. "Do ye remember my name?"

"Lor."

His teeth flashed, flattered she should recall it so quickly. "I dunna know yers."

"Isabail."

"Isabail," he repeated softly, rolling it over his tongue as if it were a fine wine. "A lovely name for a lovely lass. But I know ye're not from the Vale of Morning."

"Nay."

"Where are ye from?"

She hesitated. "Ye told me ye're from Careston," she said. "Why are ye here in Brechin?"

Lor wasn't oblivious to the fact that she was changing the subject to avoid giving him an answer. Since he'd stopped traveling through the Vale of Morning, he hadn't thought of the demons that trolled the vale in many a year. He remembered being told that the demons were part of Clan Ruthven, or even Clan Keith.

It occurred to him that in telling Isabail his name and village, she knew where he was from and that meant she knew his loyalties. Clearly, she didn't want him to know the same of her. He suspected the stories of the origins of the demons were perhaps more truth than rumor.

He couldn't think of any other reason why she wouldn't be forthcoming.

But it didn't matter. He had no sense of hatred toward clans that weren't allied with Clan Lindsay; his loyalty was to his family and friends, no matter their clan. That had never been a big factor to him. But he knew that the world at large felt differently.

Perhaps the lass felt differently, too.

"I'm in Brechin because I'm doing business with a friend of my grandfather's," he said finally, having the courtesy not to demand an answer to his question. "I also trained with the man for some years. In fact, I lived in Brechin for a numbers of years, but I dunna recall ever seeing ye come tae town with yer pelts."

She looked down at her pelts as if considering her answer. "There are other villages where I can get a fine price."

"Is that where ye're going now?"

She nodded. "The merchant here… I dinna want tae agree tae his price. I'll go elsewhere."

Lor knew what she meant by not paying the man's price because he'd seen it. What had happened had been unfair, and Lor wasn't a man who tolerated injustice. He never had been. Reaching out, he took the basket from her as she tried to snatch it back.

"Wait here," he told her, holding the basket away as she grabbed at it. "I'll get yer price for ye. What did ye want?"

She was confused, and a little miffed that he'd taken her pelts again, but she at least considered his question.

"A shilling a pelt," she said. "I'll take nothing less. *Where* are ye going?"

With a sly smile, he reached out and took one of her grabbing hands.

"Come with me."

Isabail did. She let him hold her hand as he took her back toward the village before leaving her in the small alley next to the merchant who had pinched her on the cheek. As she peered around the corner of the stall, she watched as Lor presented the basket of pelts to the merchant, who was busy eating something and getting bread and sauce all over his tunic.

When he looked at the pelts with some interest, Lor pushed the man's hands back so they wouldn't dirty the skins. He held them up for the man to show them the fine quality. But the merchant wasn't stupid; he'd seen the pelts, and the basket, before. He knew they belonged to the pushy lass from the hills. When he finally shook his head at Lor, denying him the sale, Lor reached out and grabbed the man by the collar of his expensive robes. As Isabail watched with increasing astonishment, Lor muttered a few select words to the merchant, and the man's expression went from defiant to fearful in one motion.

His head nodded.

Lor gave him the pelts, and the man counted out the shillings.

Astonished, Isabail ducked back into the alleyway as Lor returned to her, holding out a big hand that contained several silver coins.

"Here ye are," he said, putting the coins into her open palm and handing her the empty basket. "He was happy tae buy them."

Isabail's mouth was hanging open in surprise. She counted the coins; there were twelve. Twelve shillings, twelve pelts. Her gaze returned to Lor.

"I dunna know what tae say," she finally said. "When I saw the man, he refused tae buy them."

The ever-present smile was back on Lor's lips. "Sometimes a man just needs a bit of prodding, 'tis all. And a strong suggestion of what will happen if he doesna agree with ye."

Isabail looked back to the money in her hand before finally closing a fist around it. Her gaze returned to Lor.

"Ye told me once that ye weren't a warrior," she said.

She was referring back to the first time they met. Lor remembered that conversation, too, mostly because it was something that had confused him over the years. She'd told him that, being a Highlander, he needed to learn to fight as if it was part of his identity. Truth be told, that was something he'd always wrestled with, thanks to her.

"I'm not," he said, with perhaps a little less humor, given the subject. "I dinna fight the man tae sell yer pelts."

She shook her head. "That's not what I meant," she said. "I suppose…I suppose I meant that ye have a presence about ye, Lor Careston. I saw it those years ago when we met, and I saw it again just now. Ye have a way about ye that is...strong. If ye were a warrior, ye'd be a fine one."

He laughed softly as he shook his head. "I've no need tae be a warrior," he said. "I can get along fine as I am. I sold yer pelts, did I not?"

She nodded. "Ye did," she said. "And I thank ye for it."

The smile faded from his face as he looked at her, his eyes glimmering with something suggesting warmth. That pretty lass from the vale had his interest now as she had back then. It was an attraction that, although unnutured in years, was surprisingly strong. The childhood spark he'd felt those years ago had never died.

The spark was beginning to blaze.

"When will ye come back to Brechin?" he asked quietly. "Will ye come soon?"

From the expression on her face, Isabail seemed to understand his inference. "I canna say," she said honestly. "I only come when I have pelts tae sell."

"Do ye travel through the Vale of Morning tae come here?"

She shrugged. "Sometimes," she said. "Sometimes I take the road."

"Road from where? Where do ye live?"

They'd gotten onto the forbidden subject again, and she averted her gaze. "In the hills," she said, which wasn't a lie. "Ye canna go there."

"Why not?"

"Because my da willna like it."

Now, she was introducing a protective father so Lor backed off. But he was clever about it.

"But if I have birds' eggs tae bring ye, where will I find ye?" he asked.

She looked at him. "The vale," she said almost gently. "If ye go tae the vale, I'll find ye."

"Ye willna throw rocks at me again, will ye?"

It was her turn to grin now, a lovely smile that Lor found enchanting. "I willna," she said. "I willna let anyone else throw them, either."

"If I go tae the vale tomorrow, will I find ye there?"

It was an invitation and her eyes twinkled as she looked at him, a faint flush mottled her cheeks. "Will ye bring the eggs?"

With a smile flickering on his lips, he lifted one of her dirty hands to his lips, kissing the knuckles gently. He watched the flush in her cheeks deepen.

"I'll bring them."

"Then I'll be there."

Winking at her, Lor dropped her hand and turned away, heading back into town to finish his business with old Albe. He wasn't going to finish anything until he had Isabail's pledge that she would see him again, but now he had it.

He could go about his business.

When Albe wanted to know why Lor was smiling so much, he smiled more but wouldn't answer.

Acknowledgments

Behind the creation of every book an author pens is the vast support network of those cheering her forward. I could not have brought this book, or any book, to life without a number of amazing people. First and foremost, endless gratitude to my family—I love you all dearly and literally couldn't do this without your love of sandwiches and "foraging for dinner." Thank you to my agent, Kevan Lyon, for believing in me. Many thanks to the team at Sourcebooks for their excitement about the series and continued support. And last but never least, *merci beaucoup* to the most incredible writer friends a gal could have who helped me plot, read pages, offered advice, traveled with me for research, and handed me glasses of wine. Listed in no particular order: Andrea Snider, Brenna Ash, Madeline Martin, Lori Ann Bailey, Christi Barth, and my #ScarletSisters. Dreams happen when we believe in ourselves and persist no matter what.

About the Author

Eliza Knight is an award-winning and *USA Today* bestselling author of more than fifty sizzling historical romances. Under the name E. Knight, she's known for riveting tales that cross landscapes around the world. Her love of history began as a young girl when she traipsed the halls of Versailles and ran through the fields in Southern France. While not reading, writing, or researching for her latest book, she chases after her three children. In her spare time (if there is such a thing...) she likes daydreaming, wine tasting, traveling, hiking, staring at the stars, watching movies, shopping, and visiting with family and friends. She lives atop a small mountain with her own knight in shining armor, three princesses, and two very naughty newfies.

Visit Eliza at elizaknight.com or her historical blog History Undressed: historyundressed.com.